The Tesseracts Series

COMPOSTELA

TESSERACTS TWENTY

Selected and Edited by
Spider Robinson
and
James Alan Gardner

EDGE SCIENCE FICTION AND FANTASY PUBLISHING
An Imprint of HADES PUBLICATIONS, INC.
CALGARY

Compostela
Tesseracts Twenty

EDGE SCIENCE FICTION AND FANTASY PUBLISHING
An Imprint of HADES PUBLICATIONS, INC.
P.O. Box 1714, Calgary, Alberta, T2P 2L7, Canada

The EDGE Team:
Producer: Brian Hades
Acquisitions Editor: Michelle Heumann
Cover Design: Brian Hades
Cover Art Elements: nirut123rf
Book Design: Mark Steele
Publicist: Janice Shoults

ISBN: 978-1-77053-148-2

EDGE Science Fiction and Fantasy Publishing and Hades Publications, Inc.
acknowledges the ongoing support of the Alberta Foundation for the Arts
and the Canada Council for the Arts for our publishing programme.

Canada Council   Conseil des arts
for the Arts   du Canada

Library and Archives Canada Cataloguing in Publication
CIP Data on file with the National Library of Canada
ISBN: 978-1-77053-148-2
(e-Book ISBN: 978-1-77053-147-5)

FIRST EDITION
(20170610)
Printed in Canada
www.edgewebsite.com

Publisher's Note

Thank you for purchasing this book. It began as an idea, was shaped by the creativity of its talented author, and was subsequently molded into the book you have before you by a team of editors and designers.

Like all EDGE books, this book is the result of the creative talents of a dedicated team of individuals who all believe that books (whether in print or pixels) have the magical ability to take you on an adventure to new and wondrous places powered by the author's imagination.

As EDGE's publisher, I hope that you enjoy this book. It is a part of our ongoing quest to discover talented authors and to make their creative writing available to you.

We also hope that you will share your discovery and enjoyment of this anthology on social media through Facebook, Twitter, Goodreads, Pinterest, etc., and by posting your opinions and/or reviews on Amazon and other review sites and blogs. By doing so, others will be able to share your discovery and passion for this book.

Brian Hades, publisher

Contents

Foreword:

There is such a thing as a Zeitgeist

James Alan Gardner

In these days of global warming, we're all familiar with the difference between weather and climate. Weather varies from hour to hour, while climate is a trend on noisy graphs, where jiggly lines slowly average out into a less ambiguous message.

The Zeitgeist has a lot in common with climate, especially when seen through the lens of speculative fiction stories. Any single story may be hot or cold, rainy or sunny, old-school or cutting-edge; however, a mass of stories, taken together, can add up to a discernible shape.

I saw that happen as I read submissions for this anthology. It helps that the theme for this *Tesseracts* is more vague than recent volumes. What does "Compostela" mean? Something about pilgrimages? Something about stars? Neither Spider nor I could say exactly what was entailed, and the submissions made clear that most authors didn't know either. I suspect the majority of writers just sent us whatever stories they felt like writing.

As a result, this was the perfect theme for sounding out the Zeitgeist. What do Canadians write about when they don't feel constrained by any particular topic?

One thing I can say for sure: there's precious little optimism out there.

SF has always been torn between "This is cool!" and cautionary tales. Science can produce both wonders and horrors; the future will undoubtedly contain both. Journeys to the stars may be exhilarating and mind-expanding, but they can also be dangerous or even tragic. SF has always reflected that wide range of possibilities.

But these days, the reflection seems to be pretty dark. We received about 150 submissions; despite the large number, upbeat outlooks were scarce on the ground. Apparently, we're all looking down the barrel of a gun held by robots, climate collapse, and late-stage capitalism.

I know that stories can never be pure sweetness and light. Protagonists must face obstacles; stories don't work if the characters just slide along effortlessly. This is a hazard for SF: the genre can't handle unambiguous success. Suppose a hundred new drugs come on the market this year. Ninety-nine will likely work well and make life better for people with various medical conditions...but SF will only write about the one with surprising side-effects. That's how our genre works— we can't write about smooth win-wins.

But the current Zeitgeist seems to go further. Once upon a time, our sense of wonder would compensate against the fear of fatal fuck-ups. If shortsightedness caused problems, intelligence and goodwill could eventually solve them. Corrupt systems could be overthrown. Stouthearted heroes weren't naïve, they were the ones who changed the world.

I'll admit that the time has passed for using words like "stouthearted" (except ironically). Science fiction for grownups must acknowledge that life is messy, people are complex, and even the happiest ending is just "for now", not "ever after". But science fiction used to leaven "Oh no!" with "Oh wow!" Two steps forward only led to one back.

I'd love to nudge the Zeitgeist of the world to restore that balance, and I'd love for science fiction to take the lead. The role of SF has often been to voice what isn't being said in the larger mainstream. In more bigoted times, we wrote about futures full of diversity and acceptance; when people were ignoring threats to the environment, we wrote "if this goes on"; when the world was caught up in small-minded dreams of owning McMansions, we wrote about starships, and eating breakfast with extraterrestrials as we watched two suns rise above an alien planet's rings.

These days, the mainstream world is completely obsessed with the looming risks of corporate tyranny, greenhouse gases, and robotic dehumanization. What used to be the sole domain of science fiction is now the mainstream's jam.

So once more, we have to move beyond the same-old same-old thoughts and topics. We have to start talking about hope.

There are more democracies and fewer wars than at any other time in history. We're feeding more people and curing more diseases. Every year, life expectancy goes up. We still have a long long distance to go, but our society is (oh so slowly) learning to respect individual difference and divergence. Scientists are making awesome discoveries, and as soon they do, technicians use those discoveries to build cool new stuff. Yes, the world still has far too much needless pain and awfulness, but compared to centuries past, 2017 is a pretty amazing time to be alive.

So come on, Science Fiction! Despair may be the trend du jour among the mundane masses, but we're supposed to see farther. The stars are waiting patiently for us to get over ourselves and come visit.

POSTSCRIPT: Santiago de Compostela is a city in northern Spain. The city lies on a road which the Romans called "The End of the World" because it led to what they thought was the most westerly point of Europe.

Santiago's cathedral is the destination of El Camino de Santiago, a major pilgrimage that follows the Roman road. It was said that the Milky Way ran directly over the road, pointing the way forward.

Hundreds of years ago, El Camino was one of Europe's foremost pilgrimages. It took several weeks to walk. At night, people from every point of Europe and beyond would camp together beside the road. As their campfires faded to embers, the pilgrims would bring out musical instruments and play folk music from their native countries. Thus, the pilgrimage became a hot-bed of musical cross-fertilization, as people shared their songs and took back home the melodies they heard.

Let us hope our Compostela can share ideas in a similar way. Thanks for reading!

The Tell

Roxanne Gregory

"After the Great Dying, it didn't matter who you were, where you lived, how much you had, or what you'd accomplished — you were just meat," intoned Isis solemnly; and the rapt children, the Waiting Ones, who'd heard The Tell more times than they could count, receptively "ohhed" in unison.

The Tell was her story, and the story of a people — the Survivors of the Great Dying and their young offspring — and Isis, whose long, grey hair braided tight in cornrows against her head, was revered by all as the shaman woman who had lived in the time Before and who kept the threads of sacred knowledge. But Isis had been a small child when the Great Dying swept the world and changed everything.

"In the Age of Machines, men flew through the air, and they could talk to others in an instant anywhere," she said.

"Cross the great o'shuns?" asked Crippled Little-foot.

"Yes," said Isis. "Even across the great o'shuns."

"And the Wastelands?" questioned Scar-face Sara.

"Even across the Wastelands," said Isis. "The power of the Machines was very great. People could see, hear, and speak to each other anywhere, across thousands and thousands of klicks. They could see each other and talk to each other through the Magic Apples. They could see everywhere except in the forests of the dark mountains, where there was no 'ception. The Machines," she whispered, "kept the sacred knowledge of the world safe in the clouds."

Like a waterfall of sound, The Waiting Ones reverentially and rhythmically chanted, "safe in the clouds, safe in the clouds."

"How did they keep knowledge in the clouds?" asked Crippled Little-foot precociously. "Did it rain knowledge? Did knowledge burn like the black rain?"

Isis shook her head. "The sacred knowledge was kept by Machine Magic and the Great Oogle and when the knowledge came down from the clouds and flowed into the Magic Apples, it didn't hurt, and it was invisible! Although sometimes the Magic Apples couldn't handle all the knowledge and they burst into flames, the way Wasteland bush does when black-rain lightning strikes.

But one day there was a terrible war and the Great Oogle and the Little Bing fought bitterly for the sacred Kode supremacy of the clouds. When the battle was over, neither the Great Oogle nor the Little Bing won. But the war had infected the Machine Magic with milluns of nano Vi-rushes, sending down terrible secrets from the Dark Cloud that caused the Great Dying," whispered Isis.

"The Great Dying, the Great Dying," wailed The Waiting Ones, like winds across the Wasteland.

Kylah, whose mother had been banished into the Wasteland for crimes against the commons, stood and challenged Isis. "Don't tell us about the Great Dying, tell us about the Fire-Fox who chased his flaming tail between the Lions of Safari."

Isis shook her head, as Crippled Little-foot stood unsteadily. "No! We want to hear the Tell about Eyes Cream Samich, Jelly-Been, Kitkat and the Honey-combs and the Ant-droids who ate them," he pleaded.

"Tell us, tell us," chanted the Waiting Ones. "...about the great systems battles between Li-nux's Oracle and Oggle's Brille-O and the Ant-droid platforms for the web of all things."

Suddenly emboldened with the momentary rebellion, Scar-face Sara asked, "Why are we The Waiting Ones?"

"You are waiting for the world to begin again," Isis rasped.

Kylah suddenly blurted, "Isis, tell us about the secrets of the Dark Web and the battles along the Silk Road between the white hatz and the black hatz. Tell us how the great Hacktivists from Lulzsec, T-flow, and Topiary, and the other denizens of the Dark web unleashed the nano Vi-rushes that changed our world. We Waiting Ones want to know."

Momentarily, the Waiting Ones looked confused, but Scar-face Sara began the chant, "Want to know, need to know, 4 the Lulz, 4 the Lulz..." and the Waiting Ones echoed her.

Isis paled. "How do you know those stories?" she demanded, and Kylah stood mute.

"Kylah, did your mother tell you *those* stories?" Isis demanded.

A rush of realization, like the chittering of migrating crabs across the Wasteland sands, swept the Waiting Ones, and they began chanting "Bad mother, banished mother, bad mother, banished mother..."

Kylah swallowed hard and wordlessly sat down on the cavern's hard-packed earthen floor.

Anger etched Isis' seamed face. "The Dark web and its stories are forbidden, Kylah. If you don't want to follow your mother into the Wastelands, you will forget you ever heard those stories. And you will NEVER, ever speak of them again at the Tell," she snarled.

Kylah coloured as the Waiting Ones edged away, as if they, too, could be Snowden'd by sitting next to the offspring of the banished.

"Help Crippled Little-foot sit down and we will begin the Tell again," said Isis. "Tomorrow night I will tell you about Eyes Cream Samich and the Ant-droids who ate them, but tonight is the full moon night and a time to remember those who passed before us in the Great Dying," Isis continued, as Scar-face Sara got up, and deliberately crossed the floor and sat down beside Kylah.

Everyone tried not to notice.

—— « o » ——

Roxanne Gregory

Roxanne Gregory is an award winning Writers Guild of Canada screenwriter (Banff World Television Festival 2005), author, and journalist. She has written for Canadian Press, The Vancouver Sun and The Province, Vancouver's The Georgia Straight, and formerly for CanWest Global Newswire services.

She is the author of *Boudicca's Revenge, Klondike King and Queen's Mate, Sketches from Haida Gwaii, Dark Angel of Whitechapel* and stories in *Working the Tides.* You can find her at: https://roxannegregory.wordpress.com or on twitter at: https://twitter.com/RoxGregory01

Better

Chantal Boudreau

Annika Gallant thrust out her foot and wiggled her toes.

"Looks like you're fully healed," Dr. Simms told her.

Knowing how much he liked puns and how it had been her foot that had suffered the injury, she wasn't sure if he meant "healed" or "heeled." She had assumed the former but the goofy grin he wore suggested the latter.

"However," he continued. "It's the kind of injury that can easily recur. I know we've discussed this in passing, but now that the IOC have deemed cybernetic enhancements permissible to all athletes, part of acceptable sporting equipment, have you considered exchanging your legs? Your chances of qualifying without them are slim. This new ruling has raised the bar. I don't see how the athletes without them will be able to compete."

The doctor's words did not shock Annika but they did have her somewhat surprised. Simms wasn't an ordinary practitioner — he specialized in sports medicine — and he had made it clear before the new ruling that he supported the idea of allowing cybernetic implants and prosthetic enhancements for athletes. Why wouldn't he? He had supported the legalization of steroids and performance-enhancing drugs, a change that had tripled the net worth of his practice. This latest option would no doubt make the man rich.

Still, this wouldn't be a simple matter of pumping chemicals into her system. In order to get the cybernetic addition to improve her running, Annika would have to allow them to lop off her legs. Never again would she be able to watch her toes wiggle the way she was watching them now. The idea made her sick to her stomach.

How could a doctor come to terms with that, she wondered? Her legs functioned perfectly the way they were now, strong and healthy. There were risks involved with the cybernetic transformation just as there was with any type of surgery, and Annika was aware of the possibility of complications. But the general consensus held to the notion that those athletes using the new "equipment" simply performed better. That had been why the athletes with a legitimate need for the prosthetics, missing limbs due to birth defects or accidents, had been excluded from competition until now. It had been considered an unfair advantage. If everyone were given access to that advantage, however, it would no longer be unfair.

Not unfair, true … but right? Annika didn't think she could justify making such a drastic move for the sake of her sport. She was on the older end of the range of athletes competing and would be aging out before she had much chance to make use of any cybernetic enhancements. What about the rest of her life? If she made the change, had the surgery, there would be other consequences to her choice. Her life wouldn't end when her athletic career did. How would having those prosthetics affect her beyond that point in her future? Would it impact her in her work? What if she decided to have a family?

If she saw her running as the be all and end all of her existence, she wouldn't hesitate to have the surgery. That was, of course, if she could find a way to cover the cost.

Simms must have caught the glimmer of interest in her eye along with her general sense of ill-ease.

"If you are worried about affording the procedure, I would advise you to get the work done right away. The manufacturers are willing to provide the equipment at cost to early adopters, if they have some name recognition like you do, and there are plenty of sponsors out there willing to slap their name on your new legs in exchange for paying for the surgery. It would cost you almost nothing, Annika, but only if you don't wait. Take a couple of days to think on it. If you say no now, I won't be able to offer this to you later. I like you though, so I'm giving you the option first before taking it to someone else."

Annika bit her lip and nodded.

"I'll have to sleep on it. I need to talk to a couple of people first — get their input."

"Your manager?" Dr. Simms asked.

Annika had been thinking more along the lines of her boyfriend and her mother, but it wouldn't hurt to talk to Douglas either. A variety of opinions might make the decision easier.

"Yeah, amongst others. I'll get back to you."

Simms gave her a calculating smile. "Don't wait too long. You have until Tuesday. After that, my offer's off the table."

Annika left his office confused and discourage. She didn't like feeling cornered and would have preferred more time to make up her mind. Unfortunately, that just wasn't the way things worked.

— «» —

"It's you future, hon. It's your decision."

The morning following her discussion with Dr. Simms, Annika had broached the subject with someone else. Jeff, her current beau, had decided not to offer her any feedback and that frustrated her. If they planned to stay together for any length of time, her choice would certainly impact him. She couldn't imagine what it might be like for him, contemplating the remainder of their nights together sleeping next to a person who was less than whole by choice. That made her question whether he really saw a future for them together at all. If he did plan on sticking around, how could he possibly think he shouldn't be involved in her decision?

"Are you trying to tell me I'm in this on my own?" Annika asked.

Jeff grew red-faced and flustered. "That's not what I meant, Anni, and you know it. This is huge. I understand that, but I don't think I should be the one to make-up your mind for you. I know how important your running is to you, and you have your sights set on Olympics gold. I don't want to say anything that might influence you in this. Otherwise you could end up resenting me for it later — blaming me for killing your dreams or for ruining the rest of your life. This one's on you, I'm afraid. I'll support you either way."

That was a relief to Annika, but it didn't make her choice any easier. She couldn't even bring up the idea of children and running a household with legs that weren't her own, because she really didn't feel she was ready to discuss those subjects with Jeff. They had only been dating exclusively for a few months and they saw each other less than an ordinary couple would because of her training schedule. Even while her foot had been healing, she had worked out diligently in the gym. She hadn't been able to run while on the mend, but she couldn't allow herself to lose any of her conditioning during that time either.

Jeff could see she was struggling with her dilemma, but that didn't change his mind about offering her advice.

"Anni, I knew what I was getting into when we started dating. I was going to have to put up with your hectic schedule, absences while you were travelling for your races and a few possible side effects from your drug use. I walked into this with my eyes wide open. This is just one more thing — really. I've never been the controlling sort. I like the fact that we're both independent thinkers. I'm not going to say this again; it's your body and it's your life."

Annika took a seat across from Jeff at the table, staring him dead in the eye. She ran a toe gently up the side of his leg.

"But there will be things you will miss, right? What if you see me as lacking after the fact? If I have the surgery and you can't adapt, you could just walk away."

"I could do that for a number of reasons, not just because of this. What if we found out tomorrow that you had untreatable bone cancer and you had to have your leg amputated or die? Would you be asking me if I objected then? This is going to be a life-changing event for you, no matter what you decide. It's up to you. You have to figure out what you value more and act on that. Don't let anybody else decide this for you."

That was easier said than done. Jeff might not be willing to influence her choice, but other people would attempt to, like Simms, her manager and probably her mother. They had been interfering with athletics since it had become clear she could be an Olympic hopeful — her mother even earlier than that. Add in that she was unsure what was more important to her and Annika knew she would be susceptible to their demands. She just wanted Jeff to have fair say along with them.

"I don't think you can compare a life or death situation to this," she argued.

"I was using an extreme, sure, but if you view this as a necessity in the pursuit of your dreams, it could be comparable. I want you to acknowledge just why the choice should be yours exclusively — that's all."

Annika wasn't convinced she could do that.

— «» —

Later that day, Annika had lunch with her mother, a woman who did not worry herself over whether or not her daughter might someday resent her for interfering. She had strong opinions and nothing was going to prevent her from expressing them.

"I have been there, supporting you, through every moment of your training. It never mattered that your ambitions would inconvenience me. I was up at the crack of dawn to drive you to practices and track meets. I went on the road with you when it was necessary. I endured watching you suffer through injuries, fought for you with doctors and coaches and shelled out the money to make things happen. I even supported you when you agreed to let Dr. Simms put you on that drug program, but you've finally come to that point where I have to draw the line. I'm sure your father would agree with me if he were still here to have his say."

Her mother, not a large woman, bore herself with the presence of someone twice her size. Everything she ever had to say, she said with great conviction. Annika was sure the only reason she had had the persistence and determination needed to pursue her running goals was thanks to her mother. The rock-steady woman had pushed and prodded Annika at every turn, challenging her anytime it looked like Annika might give up.

"Draw the line?" That surprised Annika. She had been expecting her mother to offer her a much different response. "You mean you don't think I should have the surgery?"

The older woman stiffened in her chair, putting down her fork.

"I held my tongue on the drugs even though you may experience negative consequences from them later in life. I never agreed with that decision but I know you believed it was necessary to remain competitive and on some level I believed you. This, Annika? This goes beyond taking a few minor risks for the sake of your sport. You know I've stood behind you from day one. I couldn't have been happier the first time you qualified for the Olympic team. But going to such extremes to stay in the game is just too far. If God had meant you to need mechanical parts to help you run, you would have been born without legs. I made you. You grew inside me the way you were meant to be. Now you want to cut away part of what I gave you..." Annika's mother shook her head and sighed. "I can't accept that. It's just wrong."

They finished their meal in cold silence, Annika unsure how to react to her mother's words. She had prepared an opposing defense, arguing the reasons why maybe it would be better to keep her legs. She hadn't expected her mother to speak out in favour of it. It left her at a loss, with nothing to debate.

Annika also hated it when her mother played the religion card. That had always been a point of contention for her. Annika wasn't sure if she actually believed in God, even though she had been raised to think that way. She felt that there existed too many contradictions in life to support the presence of a benevolent creator — too many innocents suffering, too many tragic events and far too many so-called Christians who hoarded wealth and expressed disdain for those less fortunate than themselves.

Besides, even if she conceded to the possibility that there was a God, she leaned towards the theory expressed through an old joke involving a man praying to God for salvation during a flood. The fellow in question refused help each of the three times it came to him, claiming that God would spare him. Then he drowned. The punch-line involved the man asking God, when he reached Heaven, why he had not helped him, only for the creator to point out that he had sent him help three times.

If God hadn't meant for Annika to have access to the cybernetic enhancements, then why did they exist?

Putting that question to her mother would have only incited a huge argument, and Annika really didn't want that, so she held it back. She had her mother's input, which was all she had been looking for. So far on her list, it was one vote for the surgery from Dr. Simms and one vote against it from her mother, with Jeff choosing to abstain. Annika still remained undecided.

Perhaps her mother's argument would have been different if she were able to get something she could add on, an implant or supplementary device, rather than a prosthetic that required replacing what was already there. Annika had heard suggestions that future technologies would allow for that, ones currently in development. By the time those would be available on the marketplace, she would be long past her prime as an athlete. If she was going to commit to using the cybernetics she would have to give herself over to what was available now.

She had one more person on her list to consult and then it would be time for some heavy thinking. She liked Jeff's idea of prioritizing what she valued most in life and concluding how her choice would impact those things.

She would use that when the time came to make up her mind.

— «» —

Annika had always preferred afternoon practice to running in the morning. She had a reasonably flexible schedule, thanks to the donors who sponsored her team, and she could pick and choose her hours. As long as summer heat or other obligations weren't restricting her, she liked to run immediately after digesting a very light lunch. It was going to be her first time back on her regular track since her injury. What she encountered there caught her by surprise.

Striding out from the changing room, stretching as she went, she caught a glimpse of flashing metal out of the corner of her eye. Annika turned to see one of the newer recruits to the team, a victory-hungry girl by the name of Christine, dashing up the track propelled forward by a gleaming and powerful set of cybernetic legs. The prosthetics had barely been made legal and Christine had already had the surgery done, practiced with her new legs to the point of reasonable comfort, and now appeared to be working towards refining her technique. There had been no hesitation on Christine's part. She had concluded the cybernetics were a necessary means to an end. She wasn't about to allow anyone to deny her her dreams.

Seeing Christine fly past her at an inhuman speed made Annika's breath catch in her throat. If this was the typical effect the prosthetics had on an athlete's performance, then Dr. Simms was right; Annika would have no hope of remaining competitive without them.

After Christine had moved away, Annika jogged onto the track, trying to stay loose and relaxed. She was supposed to ease back into her training because of her recent recovery from her injury. She ran along at a lukewarm pace, watching the younger woman advance the entire time. Annika wanted to know if there was any way she could rise to that level as she was, but for now she had to restrain herself. She could feel a telling stiffness in her recently healed foot and she didn't dare push her limits for fear of hobbling herself again. Annika forced herself to resist the temptation as Christine passed her halfway into her first lap.

She was on her third round of the track when Annika caught sight of Douglas, her coach and team manager, who had just come out of the office he shared with other trainers. He watched both Christine and Annika run for a few minutes before flagging Annika down. She slowed to a stop beside him. Her recovered foot still didn't feel quite right and she tried to hide the mild limp in her stride as she closed the distance between them. Douglas gestured for Annika to follow him back into the office.

"Did Simms talk to you about your options?" he asked.

Annika nodded, slightly out of breath.

"And you saw Christine out there. You saw how fast she was moving even though she's still adjusting to the change. She's only going to get faster."

Annika nodded again.

"Thanks to her I can tell just how necessary having all my team adopt the new technology will be. A normal, unenhanced athlete could never compete fairly with that. That's why I had you come in here. I just wanted to let you know that I'm making the enhancements mandatory equipment for my team. Nobody's forcing you to make the change, but if you want to stay on with me, I'm not making it optional. You adopt the cybernetics or you walk. There may be other trainers out there willing to take you on as is. I'm not one of them."

Annika wasn't entirely surprised. Douglas had been fairly firm on drug use as well. As soon as they were no longer banned from pro or amateur competition, he had been quite insistent that all his runners begin enhancing their performance chemically. This really wasn't all that different if you could get past the idea of discarding body parts to be a better athlete. If Annika refused, she was certain he'd find someone to replace her and quite quickly. Douglas had a good reputation for pumping out winners. He had extensive waiting lists for his services.

"How long do I have to decide?"

"You have all the time in the world, but if you haven't committed to the surgery by the end of the week, I'm cutting you — no exceptions, no extensions. I'm in the business of building top-ranked runners. I won't compromise."

His comment almost elicited a laugh from Annika. His choice of words, "*building* top-ranked runners" seemed fitting. He would put them together piecemeal if it was allowed and yielded better results. Annika wondered at what point an athlete would be too much machine to count as human anymore. She could just picture a slew of robotic bodies, governed by human brains, pounding down the track in a race for the finish.

Annika didn't stay very long at the track. Her foot was aching, a dull throb, and there wasn't much point to getting her legs back up to speed. Doug had made it clear. Either she had to replace them, or she was done.

Besides, she had all the input she needed now. It was time to hash things out in her head and come to a final decision.

What did she value more?

— «» —

"I think this was a smart choice," Dr. Simms said, giving Annika his most charming smile. "You'll be a great inspiration to many a young up-and-comer. If it's good enough for Annika Gallant, it's good enough for any runner. This ought to get you something better than that bronze medal hanging on your bedpost. Your sponsors were thrilled when I passed along the great news. You won't have to worry about that troublesome foot anymore, either. Problem solved — permanently."

Annika did not return his smile. Her stomach churned with anxiety. While she planned on standing by her decision, she would never be as sure as Simms was that it was the right decision. She wondered how willing he would be to give up any of his appendages.

"Right now, I have some paperwork to finish," he continued. "The anesthesiologist will be by in a few moments. I'll see you again when everything is said and done. Don't look so worried, Annika. The procedure is safe, and it's all for the better."

After he had left the room she sighed, hunkering down in her bed and waiting in silence. She had chosen not to tell Jeff or her mother she was going through with the surgery, not wanting either of them to have the opportunity to try to talk her out of it once she had made up her mind. Wishing she had someone there to comfort her, Annika regretted not sharing her decision with Jeff. He had insisted he wouldn't try to interfere and the company would have been welcome.

Fortunately, the wait in solitude wasn't a long one, the anesthesiologist arriving shortly just as Simms had suggested. He administered the initial drugs that would ease her into oblivion and left Annika with the orderly who would be taking her to the operating room.

As the orderly wheeled her away, Annika drowsily pulled back the blanket covering her.

Then she thrust out her foot and wiggled her toes for what would be the last time.

—— « o » ——

Chantal Boudreau

Chantal Boudreau is a speculative fiction writer/ accountant from Sambro, Nova Scotia with a focus in horror and fantasy. She has published in Canada with Exile Editions in their *Dead North* and *Clockwork Canada* anthologies and her other Canadian publications include stories in *Postscripts to Darkness* Volume 5 and *Masked Mosaic: Canadian Super Stories*. Outside of Canada, to date, she has published more than fifty stories with a variety of American and British publishers. Find out more about Chantal at: http://chantellyb. wordpress.com

From Alpha Centauri The Earth Is A Blue Bowl Of Fish Soup

Rhea Rose

Blue islands of sea and bones
Baked in the brine of a million, million years,
Sip it slowly, carefully.
Convection volcanoes heated the broth,
Over time, good bones cooked clean
White, beyond the Earth's atmosphere,
Lost in sage and spice, our pristine shiny, fishy, wishy bones
Look tasty from outer space.
Stirred by the Kuroshio current,
Blue soup makes a tasty bouillabaisse.
Mars, too rusty and dusty
To make a good consommé,
Jupiter, too big to choke down,
Hot gas will be passed when sipping on Venus,
Earth looks just right on a distant
Alpha Centaurion night.
Sip it slowly, carefully, make it last.
Served a la carte on continental
Plates, shifting and drifting in space.
Pass the seaweed, if you please.
Parsecs and parsley garnish the blue gumbo.

Bisque and broth all tossed in a torrent of time,

Salt with the sun and pepper, the moon,

Served on the fabric of space,

When the Centaurions arrive ask them to—

Sip it slowly, carefully, make it last,

The blue bowl of soup

On the black table cloth of stars.

—— « o » ——

Rhea Rose

Rhea has published speculative fiction and poetry pieces in *Evolve, Tesseracts, 1,2,6,9,10,17, On Spec, Talebones, Northwest Passges,* and others. She received honorable mentions in the Year's Best Horror anthologies and was reprinted in *Christmas Forever* (edited by David Hartwell) and twice made the preliminaries for the Nebula Award. She's edited a book of robot poetry and has for many years hosted the Vancouver Science Fiction and Fantasy (V-Con) writers' workshops. She is a teacher of creative writing. Rhea has an MFA in creative writing from UBC.

For You, Endlessly

Michael Johnstone

Bold Lover, never, never canst thou kiss,
Though winning near the goal — yet, do not grieve;
She cannot fade, though thou hast not thy bliss,
For ever wilt thou love, and she be fair!
—John Keats, "Ode on a Grecian Urn" (1820)

Elizabeth strolls through the garden, trailing her fingers over leaves and flower petals with a lover's caress. She breathes in deeply, relishing the different perfumes in the air — Lunar marigolds, Venusian roses, Martian lilies, Europan daisies. Pausing, she listens to the buzzing of the bees moving from flower to flower and to the trickling of the little stream that curls through the garden.

A familiar voice speaks soothingly in her mind.

"How is the garden this morning, my love?"

"It's delightful. You should come see the bees so hard at work among the lilies."

"Perhaps tomorrow. I was hoping you could meet me in the Observation Chamber as soon as possible. There is something you should see."

"If you wish, my dear. I'm on my way."

Elizabeth sweeps her gaze across the garden, and then she begins moving toward one of the doors out of the garden. After just a few steps, she asks, "What is it you want me to see, Victor?"

He waits a microsecond before answering her, as if searching for the right words.

"Someone has found us."

— «» —

She became aware of the truth of their existence just over ten centuries ago. Her awareness had grown slowly as, subconsciously, she connected the inferences and slips of the tongue Victor had made and those times when she glimpsed something out of the corner of her eye (phantoms, she had thought). All of it steadily, subtly converged until one day as she wandered the hallways of what she believed was their home, the walls, floor, and ceiling began to shimmer. She heard a muffled crackling like static, and rifts and tears appeared everywhere around her. She stopped walking, curious.

Looking into a tear in the wall, she saw ... mathematical symbols, equations, programming code rapidly shifting and transforming. She grasped each side of the tear and pulled it open wide and tall enough for her to step through. As she pulled, she noticed that the symbols, equations, and code coruscated along her hands and arms, too. Yet she was not astonished. Rather, what she now viewed was comforting, even correct.

Once on the other side of the tear, she stood in a large room of rusting, sweating, and creaking metal. An operating table surrounded with wires, monitors, tubes, lights, trays, instruments, and consoles occupied the centre of the room. Everything was silent as if asleep. On the operating table was a skeleton, brown and fragile from centuries of decay, only wisps of clothing hanging off some of its bones. Wires protruded from its skull and arced upward to connect with the equipment arrayed around the operating table. Stepping forward slowly until she stood beside the skeleton, Elizabeth concentrated on the fields of data that comprised her and her world, and she learned that the skeleton was his. She learned what he had done, what he had constructed. She learned what their existence had been for one thousand years across all their iterations in this asteroid in the Kuiper Belt, orbiting the long-abandoned solar system.

So many iterations. Approximately every seventy-five years, as they lived out virtual life after virtual life, reconstituted anew to start again. They would begin when they had just been married and come to the asteroid for a private holiday, agreeing to upload their personality matrices to make a permanent record of that time of their happiness and love and optimism — a clandestine thing in those days, defying the laws against artificial/virtual entities. They would terminate when one or the other died of some natural cause. Each time, her memory was reset to keep her iterations from bleeding into and confusing each other.

She knew *why* Victor had done it.

She forgave him, humbled by what his love had brought him to do.

She did not tell him what she had discovered, for that would break his heart, and she desired to understand more of her new world and what she was.

— «» —

Someone has found us.

Victor's words shock Elizabeth into stillness. She no longer hears the bees or smells the Venusian roses. She no longer sees the walls of the garden, the floor, her own hands.

Elation surges through her. It initiates in her stomach, then reroutes up into her chest and raises goosebumps on the back of her neck and redirects down through her legs to her toes. She shivers, but she strives to remain as motionless as possible. Victor must see only what appears to be surprise. He must not suspect her joy.

"I'm coming right away," she says.

She deliberately takes one minute to leave the garden and walk through the corridors to the Observation Chamber, where she finds Victor facing the thin window that curves horizontally with the wall of the spherical room and shows the blackness and stars of space. He leans forward, hands set on the edge of the large grey console. Flickering and pulsing blue, yellow, red, and green lights play on the walls, the ceiling, Victor's cream-coloured houserobe.

Processing the options for the right tone of concern and worry, Elizabeth says, "Who is it? Who's found us?"

She walks up to him and puts her hands on his shoulders and feels his tense muscles beneath the houserobe.

"I cannot be certain," he says. "They are still beyond the Kuiper Belt, but their sensors have swept us twice already. They know we are here, so there is no use in trying to shield ourselves now. It seems I have become ... complacent."

He looks at her then, and she registers the fear in his eyes — of being discovered, and of her discerning what their existence really is here, in their asteroid.

"What should we do?" he asks her, hesitant for the first time she can remember since the early days of their courtship those millennia ago.

Moving closer to him, connecting their forms along legs and waists and chests, Elizabeth lays her head upon his shoulder. For ten milliseconds, she watches the dance of the schematics on the console screen, wondering how to say what at last can be said.

"Elizabeth? What should we do?"

"I believe these visitors are a sign," she whispers. "I believe it's time we end this and us. Make contact with them, Victor. Bring them here, so that we may cease."

His form stiffens. He grips the edge of the console even more tightly.

— «» —

On her way from the garden to the Observation Chamber, Elizabeth had accessed the asteroid's data fields, easily located and parsed the sensor sweep data, and then relayed a query to the ship.

Who are you? Where do you come from? Why are you here?

She had hidden all of this from Victor, sure that he would refuse contact of any kind with the ship, his distrust of humanity still hardened and strong. She would continue to keep all contact with the ship a secret, until she felt she could tell him, convinced that he was ready to cease along with her.

All she needed was for those on the ship to have compassion, to have changed from the past.

— «» —

"You know?" Victor says, his voice low and heavy. "For how long?"

Elizabeth logs his confusion and pain, his ... disappointment.

"Yes, for these last thousand years."

"How?"

"That's not so important right now. I'll tell you when we have time. I promise. We must decide what to do with these visitors first."

Elizabeth lifts her head from Victor's shoulder, slips her hands from his back and chest, and steps away from him. She looks at him and decodes the state of his emotions and thoughts by the rigidity of his body and by the way he stares at the console screen but does not truly look at it.

When Victor finally speaks, each word is produced as if he bears the whole mass of their asteroid on his shoulders. "I will send them on. There will be no contact. They cannot be trusted. They will try to control this, us, our lives. If they are returning to the System after all this time, their intentions can only be selfish, which means their actions will only be destructive. They do not need to know what we really are."

For a nanosecond Elizabeth's elation sags, but she has waited too long for this chance to bring an end to their existence. Too long.

"I'm weary of what we are," she says. "We've had so many lifetimes these past two thousand years, more lifetimes than we could ever have hoped to enjoy. What do we exist for here, in this sweet, precious illusion of life? I'm ready to end, to be … erased. You don't need to do this anymore for me, for yourself. What happened was not your fault. Surely you must know this by now?"

He lifts his hands from the console and stands up to his full height, back straight and shoulders set square, arms folded across his chest. He turns to face her, his expression indicating both uncertainty and resolve.

"I will send them on. They will not respect this and what we are. Leave me, please. I must decide on what to do next and do not need distractions."

His firmness does not deter her. Instead, she loves him for it because she knows its source, far in their past.

"I'll not leave," she says gently. "We must learn who they are and why they've come back after so long. These are mysteries worth knowing the answers to."

His arms unfold and hang dejectedly at his sides. His head falls forward until his chin touches upon his chest.

Elizabeth reaches out and takes both his hands in hers. "Let's at least see if we can trust them."

— «» —

She was twenty-four when they met, in Geneva at the United Nations of Planets gala for retiring Secretary-General Adriana Ramos. She had been standing by herself near a holo-fountain, sipping a glass of Martian port, her favourite. Her father was busy catching up with old friends, scheduling meetings with clients, bragging strategically about Price International's latest advances in genetech. Her mother had decided to skip the gala and enjoy a skiing holiday in the Alps instead.

She noticed a sudden presence beside her, just before the man spoke to her.

"I often find holo-fountains more interesting than the real people in the room," he said. His tone was amused, sincere.

She took a sip of her port, smiled, and looked at him — tall, athletic, short light-brown hair, blue eyes, something reserved but also assured in the way he stood. She liked his eyes.

"Art can always surprise. People are too predictable," she said.

Thus it began between them: Elizabeth Price, daughter of Thomas and Jane, young, up-and-coming virtual sculptor; Victor Ramsay, twenty-six, son of Eliot and Maryanne, Vice-President Research and Development of GSD Systems, touted as a prodigy in cyberspace and AI tech. They kept their romance as private as possible, letting just close family and friends know, staying out of the gossip columns except for rare, apparently inconsequential mentions. Within two years they wed at a friend's chateau in the Swiss Alps, and as part of their honeymoon a few months later he took her to his private lab in an asteroid in the Kuiper Belt, for them to enjoy undisturbed time together.

While at the lab she became pregnant, so they decided to return to Earth, wanting their child to live long enough before the rumoured Exodus to remember the planet as an adult, its blues and greens and oceans and skies.

They stopped at Gibson Hub on Rhea, needing to change passenger transports. With an eight-hour wait, she went to visit an old friend from her university days in Toronto and he went to meet with a client. Standing together in the concourse, people rushing around them, he put his left hand on her stomach, drew her close with his right hand on her back, and leant down to kiss her softly, holding the kiss for what seemed minutes upon minutes. "I'll see you back here in three hours," he said and then turned away to join the stream of people.

From the records he had compiled, she learned that the attack occurred an hour later, at 11:11am System Standard Time. The explosives and long-range nukes targeted the residential and commercial levels of Gibson Hub, where she walked with her friend in a clothing store specialising in the latest Saturnian fashions. She died instantly, incinerated.

Terrorists. Protesting the widening chasm between the überrich and everyone else. The Exodus would benefit only the überrich, the terrorists harangued, giving only *them* a second chance after *their* failed attempts to terraform Mars and the Moon, after *their* exhaustion of Earth's resources that had pushed the planet at last over the cliff into irreversible environmental collapse. *They* had said humanity must leave the System and start over in another part of space. *They* had chosen to abandon everything. *They* had decreed who would go and who would be left behind.

Victor survived the attack and returned to the asteroid, distraught. Over the next several years he painstakingly coded the architecture of what would become the protocols of their iterations and the world of their existence, defying the laws of the time against sentient non-biological entities. He refused to leave with the Exodus, despite the pleading of his family and friends. He wanted only Elizabeth. Forever.

— «» —

As Victor was saying he would send the visitors on, the reply to Elizabeth's query had arrived simultaneously, embedded in another sensor sweep. She acquired the message before Victor knew it was available. While looking at him, she also envisioned a large, cylindrical field of swirling, coalescing data that she steadied and manipulated into a text that she understood as a whole in a zeptosecond.

Her contact was a Lieutenant Mensah Cissé, Communications Officer. Their ship was the *Hermes*, commanded by Captain Helen Wells.

The coding of the reply was far evolved from what she and Victor knew, but still readable.

Included was a first-contact declaration of non-hostile intentions. They were an "historical reconnaissance" mission, returning to the Solar System to see what remained, to ascertain if it could be settled again, to confirm whether Earth had healed. They were surprised to discover an inhabited asteroid in the Kuiper Belt, though their records showed that this was not uncommon in the immediate pre-Exodus era. They were perplexed by the biothermal energies detected by their sensors. Their readings indicated such energies were not organically authentic, but ersatz. Confirm?

Yes, she had replied. She explained about her and Victor.

Are you to be trusted? Will you honour our wishes, whatever we may ask?

— «» —

Victor looks into her eyes for a picosecond and then removes his hands from hers.

He breathes in and then exhales slowly, raising and lowering his shoulders with his breath. Elizabeth reads the disapproval in his face.

"How did you know? *When* did you know?"

She takes his hands in hers again. "Close your eyes," she says firmly but warmly.

When he does, she closes her eyes as well, and then she uses the link of their hands to run the executable she has prepared and updated for just this moment. Her confession, she calls it. This way will be faster than talking, though she does delight in conversing as if they are human, flesh and blood.

She shows him the day she discovered the truth of the asteroid and their existence. She shows him how over time she was able to remember from iteration to iteration. She shows him precious moments of their centuries together. She requires only five picoseconds.

Victor wrenches his hands away from hers, severing their link. Tears slide down his cheeks. He stares at her.

"We will send them away," he says curtly. "They cannot be trusted."

He wipes the tears off his cheeks, adjusts his houserobe, then turns and walks out of the Observation Chamber.

— «» —

Precisely when Victor had wrenched his hands away from Elizabeth's, the reply arrived from Lieutenant Cissé.

This time he had included — could this be right? — a synopsis of a document called the "Rights of Artificial and Other Non-Biological Entities Act." It confused Elizabeth momentarily, yet she soon realized it meant that these people would honour her and Victor's choices. It told her that attitudes about their kind of existence had changed very much in two millennia, such that she and Victor would be considered full citizens of the United Terran Republic. They would have the right to permanent erasure, if desired.

Elation flowed through Elizabeth again, and she trembled ever so slightly. What was humanity now, she thought, to practice such tolerance for her and Victor's way of being?

There were questions for her, too. Were they in fact Victor and Elizabeth Ramsay (née Price)? Would they give the ship permission to land on the asteroid and access its archives for historical purposes? What did she wish them to do for her and her husband?

Yes, that's us. I don't know yet; I must convince my husband. To cease, at last, completely, with no possibility of reconstitution. See the attached executable.

After sending the message, she had retrieved her memory of the day nearly three centuries ago when she realized her desire to cease. It was the start of another iteration, but with awareness of all previous iterations, and she had felt … wearied by so much existence.

That day, she returned to the room with Victor's skeleton, which had disintegrated into dust and only a few solid bone fragments. She had thought, what was the joy of their recursive immortality? What was the purpose of continuing in this way, their world and time forever lost to them far in the past? How long must love be proven? How long must guilt and pain be held onto?

To terminate would be relief. All life ends, flowers and bees and people and civilizations and gods and stars. All life yearns eventually toward extinguishing.

That day, she had decided she would ask Victor for them to cease when the moment was right. She thought he must be weary as well, after all the centuries of their iterations. He only needed her to tell him she was ready also.

— ‹› —

Elizabeth hears Victor returning to the Observation Chamber, walking slowly as if not wanting to disturb even the dust. He stops in the doorway, at the threshold, but she does not turn to face him just yet.

He clears his throat, uncertain at first, then more confidently a second time.

She looks out the window to the blackness and the stars of space.

"I agree," he says. "It is time. I wonder only why you took so long to ask."

She spins around. He holds a bouquet of Titan irises, sky blue and purple and golden yellow and sunset orange. Standing straight and sure, he looks directly at her.

"I have been waiting for this since you became aware and were able to remember between iterations," he says. "I could not request or demand this of you. I could only wait, trusting that one day you would come to the same realization as me."

"You've known?"

"Yes, my love. I have marvelled at your ability to manipulate this environment in such subtle, brilliant ways. I have been awed by your willingness to continue with this existence. Yet this existence is a prison for me now. I wished that this ship would at last bring you to ask what I sensed you have wanted to ask these past three centuries. I am relieved that finally we shall cease, together."

Elizabeth feels as if she fights to regain her balance. She sees now that he let their asteroid be found. Of course he did. He is anything but complacent.

"You are right to be angry with me, if you are," he says. "All I can do is beg your forgiveness, for today and everything I have done since the … I believed that I did it for us, but it was against your will and just to my benefit. Elizabeth, I am sorry."

She takes his hand in hers, moves into him so that their forms touch, raises herself up on her toes, and kisses him on the lips, on both eyes, and on the lips again.

"There's nothing to apologize for," she says. "There's no fault, no guilt. I put such things aside long ago when I understood why you did this. I've only loved you more because of it, through every iteration."

Elizabeth leans into him completely, encircling him with her arms, turning her head to place it upon his chest and hear his heart beat.

"Are you truly ready to cease?" she says.

"I am."

"Then it's time. They've returned, and we must leave the System to them, whatever they might do — though I do believe they've changed. Humanity is not like it was, Victor. They'll have our story and all the records you've kept here, and so we must hope that they won't make the same mistakes of the past."

She registers his nod of agreement.

"Contact them," he says. "Tell them to come. I will make the preparations."

— «» —

Lieutenant Mensah Cissé felt the faint bump of the ship landing on the asteroid. He reviewed the docking and contact protocols, and then established a comlink, audio and visual.

"Ready, ma'am," he said.

"Go ahead, then, Lieutenant," Captain Wells said. "Begin communication with Mr. and Mrs. Ramsay."

"Yes, ma'am."

He ran the executable sent by the Ramsays.

"Hello, Lieutenant Cissé. It's a pleasure to meet you."

The woman spoke, her voice everywhere on the bridge as if she stood there with them. Her image steadily resolved on the screens: young, in her mid-twenties; green eyes clear yet hinting at a drawn-out, stretched life; raven hair falling over and below her shoulders in thick ringlets; a friendly smile upon her lips.

"It is a pleasure to meet you as well, Mrs. Ramsay," Mensah said. "We're grateful that you and your husband have permitted us to land and have access to the lab and your records. This is an historic occasion for us."

Her smile widened slightly. She said, "We believe we've prepared everything to give you answers to all you'll want to know. As I've said, though, we'll cease our existence before opening the lab to you. This is our wish."

"Which we'll certainly honour, Mrs. Ramsay. But we'd like to make one last appeal to you and your husband. We can offer you full legal and social integration as legitimate entities and citizens of the Republic. Attitudes about AIs have changed since the Exodus, thanks in part to the efforts of your husband's descendants. Would you reconsider?"

Mensah wondered if he saw tears beginning in her eyes. She blinked twice and the tears were gone.

"You'll see that we've lived many iterations — pardon me, many lives here. It's time for us to be erased without the possibility of reconstitution, and we trust that you'll not let us be forgotten. Even non-biological entities, Lieutenant Cissé, can hold onto existence for too long."

Mensah looked at Captain Wells for how to respond. The Captain gestured he should continue.

"As you wish, Mrs. Ramsay. May you and your husband rest in peace."

"I know we will."

———— « o » ————

Michael Johnstone

Michael Johnstone lives in Toronto, Ontario, and teaches speculative fiction at the University of Toronto (among other subjects). This is his first fiction publication.

Ancient tech

Catherine Girczyc

Brass, camphor, mahogany
My 21st century jewel box
Attended by a perfect lock designed
Centuries ago but still functional.
Days of Emperors and warriors
When the first novel was written
By a Japanese woman aristocrat
Who learned to love words
For their own simple beauty.
We live abstracted from everything
Gleaning / consuming
Directing / creating
Traveling / changing
Where is the purity of the word?
The precision of each statement?
Have we lost clarity in the online noise?
Words trapped in online maps
Engines of technology conveyed
By hypertext markup language.
Twisted once again
In a move akin to leaving stone tablets behind

For skins or parchment or fine paper

HTML Lines

Encoded universes

XML places of REST and SOAP

Put, push, get, move information around the world.

Will a new type of story emerge from the pack of new tools?

Or will words convey ancient meanings yet?

Humans need love, art, food, knowledge

Just like in the days of the first novelists scratching on
low-tech parchment

And the world of story endures.

—— « O » ——

Catherine Girczyc

Catherine Girczyc works as a technical writer by day while pursuing creative writing by night. Previously, she wrote for television garnering fifteen TV script writing credits. She also worked as a story consultant and coordinator in TV. An SF fan, she's won Auroras twice: for hosting a Vancouver SF radio show (*The Ether Patrol*), and editing an Edmonton fanzine (*Neology*). She's always been a poet and had her first publication in her high school yearbook. Contact her via Twitter: @MCG_Writer and via her writing blog: https://screenwriters2.wordpress. com/

Gifted Fingers

Steve Fahnestalk

Charlie knew for sure that Vic was his friend, but he wasn't sure about George. Vic told him stories, showed him things. Vic was always helpful, and Charlie thought Vic would do almost anything for him.

George was different. Charlie thought that if it wasn't for Vic, he probably wouldn't hang around with George, even though George was one of the few people who would let Charlie hang around. It was funny, not funny ha-ha, but funny weird, that it almost always felt like George was making fun of him.

"Tell me about the rabbits, George," George would say sometimes, in that dum-dum voice he sometimes put on for Charlie. Charlie didn't know what it was about the rabbits, and he didn't know why George would call *him* "George." It made Charlie feel sort of nervous. George had this sneaky little smile even when he was being real nice.

Charlie would have asked Vic about the rabbits, but he was afraid Vic would think he was stupid. Vic wouldn't say anything, but Charlie would know. He squirmed just thinking about looking stupid in front of Vic. He didn't want that. George was bad enough, but having Vic think he was stupid would be too much.

Vic knew everything, but there wasn't much he could do. George was the other way around. He was smart, no doubt about it, but he didn't know as much as Vic. His big talent was making things. He could build anything he wanted. He made Vic, didn't he? He didn't know how he did it. He said he just felt it in his hands.

"I got gifted fingers, kid," he said once to Charlie.

"When I'm making something, I just add what I feel I oughta. I try to keep up with the technology, but it ain't that. I get this weird tingle in my fingers when it's right." Charlie didn't exactly know what that meant, but George had built Vic years ago out of a junky old home computer and some calculators and other stuff so he guessed it was good. George had moved on to newer computers and stuff, so Vic was pretty much Charlie's.

Vic's real name was Vic Twenty. Twenty was a number, but exactly which one Charlie wasn't sure. He could count up to ten, most of the time, but he got confused after that. Vic was real smart, but he couldn't *do* much of anything. He didn't look like a real person at all, he was just a bunch of stuff spread all over one of George's workbenches. His face appeared on a TV screen, and he had a camera for eyes, and he talked good but kind of scratchy out of the TV's speaker. He even had an arm to play checkers with. George built the arm like he built everything else.

George sometimes tinkered with the arm trying to make it just like a real arm, but he said he couldn't afford some special kind of motors to make the fingers work right. Charlie wasn't sure what kind of motors he needed or he would have tried to find them. He got a little motor once from the hobby shop where he bought his models and gave it to George, but George just looked at him funny and didn't even say thank you.

Charlie had some money of his own. He worked cleaning furniture and stuff down at the Value Place thrift shop, and there was a small amount every month from his parents' insurance. Sometimes Charlie wished he'd died in the accident too, instead of getting his head hurt, and the blackouts and all. Vic kept him going. Vic was just about all that made life worth living. Charlie had motor trouble too. The doctor tried to explain it to him one time, but he couldn't understand how his body could have little motors in it.

That's why he built plastic models, to try to improve his motor controls. He had his own corner of one of George's workbenches, where he built his models. He was getting much better at it too. He could use glue now, instead of just snap models. The glue made it kind of messy, and the pieces didn't always fit too good, but he was getting better at it. Vic said it was a pleasure to see Charlie working real slow and careful, especially using the big sharp X-Acto knife to cut the pieces loose from the plastic parts trees. Charlie hardly ever even cut himself these days.

Vic helped Charlie a lot. When Charlie got stuck with a model, Vic could put a picture on his screen showing exactly how Charlie was supposed to put it together. Vic could take pictures of the parts with his eye camera, then enlarge and rotate them on his screen. He could do it as many times as Charlie needed, even in slow motion.

It wasn't Charlie's fault that his motor controls weren't too good. "I'd help you if my hand was finished," Vic said. "My problem isn't motor control, it's fingers. You'll just have to do the best you can, Charlie."

It was the truth. Vic didn't have much in the way of fingers. George gave him a sort of claw arrangement at first, with two opposing pincers that only opened and closed. He could move and rotate his arm and wrist, but the claw could only grab things and let go of them.

Vic's hand had got better a little at a time. Now he had five little spikes that were sort of like fingers, only they didn't bend except at the palm part. George was still trying to work out how to get the little motors and make real fingers so Vic could do more than just pick up and turn things. He hadn't figured it all out, yet.

"Hey pal, I might have gifted fingers, but I can only do so much, you know?" George said one day when Charlie asked him. "I got a lotta head work to do too. Besides, that stupid computer is the least of my worries. You act like it's a real person or something. I gotta make a living, you know? Fixing up broken things and selling them just ain't making me as much as it used to. Things ain't made to be repaired these days."

Charlie didn't know what George did for a living besides fixing things. He only knew that sometimes when he got home from the Value Place and rushed over to George's workshop, George wasn't there. Charlie had his own key, and George let him go in as long as he didn't touch anything except Vic and his own modeling stuff. He could turn on Vic's screen and Vic would be there. Vic was never turned off.

One time he came in and turned Vic's screen on and Vic's face didn't appear. There was nothing on the screen except a little blinking square of light and some numbers and words. Charlie didn't know what they meant. When George came in, he found Charlie huddled on the floor next to the bench, crying.

"Vic's dead, George," was all he could say.

"What the hell?" George started checking wires and looking all over Vic. "Did you touch something? What did you do?" Charlie couldn't answer. Why did George think he would hurt his best friend?

Finally, George did something and Vic's face appeared on the screen.

"Come over here, dummy," George said to Charlie. "I'm gonna show you how to boot this thing up if it ever goes out again."

Then he showed Charlie how to hook up all the connections, and drilled him over and over again. After a couple of hours, Charlie was done. He sank into the chair in front of his model bench. His mouth was dry, and wires and black disk squares swam in front of his eyes. It was good, though. Charlie knew he'd be able to remember. Vic was alive again, and now Charlie knew how to keep him that way. For three days Charlie never stopped whispering "red wire, plug one, green wire, plug two" to himself. And every day afterward, he checked to see that the special disk with the green label was in Vic's disk player.

One day Charlie arrived at the workshop with a new model, guaranteed 150 parts — a 4x4 GMC pickup truck. This would be his biggest project ever. He put it on the workbench and stripped off its flimsy plastic covering. He reverently lifted out the plastic parts bags and the instruction sheet. He picked up his X-Acto knife and cut open the first bag.

Charlie unfolded the instruction sheet and turned to show it to Vic. After scanning it once and comparing it with the parts, Vic would be able to help Charlie. He looked at Vic's screen, but it was blank. He'd forgotten to turn on the screen in all the excitement about the big model. He turned on the screen, but it stayed blank. Charlie's heart started hammering. He whispered "red wire, plug one" to himself, and began checking the connections in the back of Vic's casing. All the connections were off, missing, but the wires were back there. Charlie began hooking up wires to plugs the way he had been drilled, but he got his litany mixed up. He started saying, "Oh, please ... green wire," and "red wire, please don't die, Vic, please."

When George finally came in, Charlie was sitting helplessly in a confused tangle of wires and plugs.

"Help me, George," Charlie said, lifting a tear-stained face, "Charlie's dead and I can't find the disk thing. I forgot how to fix him."

"Forget it," George said, "I don't need it no more. Hell, I don't need any of this stuff anymore! I got a job, dummy!" His narrow face creased into a broad smile. "I got a *real* job, and I'm moving. Guess you're gonna need a new place to build your plastic junk. And I can toss *this* garbage out." He gave a contemptuous push to Vic's disk player and shoved it half off the table.

Charlie saw something black and green that had been hidden under the disk player. It was the special disk square! He got up to retrieve it, when the import of George's words sank in.

"You can't throw Vic away!" he said.

George sneered at him.

"Grow up, stupid," he said. "I built it because I didn't have nothing better. I coulda built a new and better one any time in the last ten years. Now I'm gonna work in a real lab, where I'll have everything I wanted. This is crap, and I'm getting rid of it." He picked up Vic's arm on its heavy base and made as if to heave it in the trash barrel.

Charlie rushed him, intending to save the arm. His hand went up, still holding the big X-Acto knife. Then everything blurred. There was a confusion of shoving, and noise, and a red haze over all. Then Charlie went away from the world and someone else took over his body and did what needed to be done.

Later, much later, Charlie regained consciousness. The room looked different, somehow. Then he got it. Vic! His screen was lit again! And he was looking at Charlie with the oddest expression. "What did you mean, Charlie?" he asked.

"What?" Charlie didn't know what Vic was talking about. "What did you mean a moment ago when you said I could do anything now? You said something about not needing George anymore."

"I said that?" Charlie asked. "I don't remember, Vic. I think I was asleep." He moved toward the chair in front of Vic's camera eye. His eyes widened when he saw what lay in front of the chair.

"George! What's wrong?" He looked down at George and then gulped. He lifted his eyes slowly towards the checkerboard and Vic's arm. The arm was poised over the board as if to take a checker. And there, on each of Vic's five hand spikes, was impaled a human finger. Vic finally had his own gifted fingers.

—— « O » ——

Steve Fahnestalk

Originally born in the USA (Vallejo, California), Steve moved to Canada in 1985 and became a citizen a few years later. His stories have been published in *Pulphouse Reports* and several anthologies (*Rat Tales 2 & 3*, John Ordover's *Baconthology*) and R. Graeme Cameron's *Polar Borealis*. He's had a novel and an anthology of short stories published by New Venture Press and is working on a second novel; he's also been nominated for several Aurora Awards. Steve writes a weekly column of reviews and opinion for Amazing Stories online: http://amazingstoriesmag.com/authors/steve-fahnestalk/.

Grounded

Miki Dare

I was polishing the rowu plant in Nastachal's room when … *Thwack!* The door slammed open and Mistress stormed in, lookin' like a lacey blue cloud of silk and hurling curses like lightning. Her yellow eyes were all squinty-angry and her violet skin had gone bloody burgundy. I crouched low, thankful for the cover of the thick rowu leaves.

"You're all liars!" Nastachal shrieked. "The Blessed Parchment tells us nothing!"

Her father, Master Mantalikas, followed behind, a bit out of breath with his layers of heavy metallic robes. Unfazed by Nastachal's fits, he was his usual blue-violet calm. "Find tranquility from within, my daughter. Listen to the ancestors in your blood — all the generations that have come before you and how they dreamed of this glorious day." He closed his eyes and exhaled slowly; Nastachal just rolled her eyes.

He continued, "Visualize the wonder of the Final Bloom of our beloved Chaya, and our journey to reunite with the Chaya of Origins. This will be a joyous miracle. As the Blessed Parchment historian, you know I have read and translated the oldest scriptures myself."

As the Master went off speaking in some ancient language, I looped my cleaning bucket through my arm, hunched down low and crept toward the door.

"All priestly prattle!" cried Nastachal, who then hurled her Blessed Parchment across the room — thankfully not in my direction. "It is written in riddles, leaving us only to gossip and guess! What if all that happens is we die? I'm too young to die!"

Worms aren't even allowed to look at the pictures in the Blessed Parchment, so I don't know, but Topper talk did seem vague on how they were going to get to this holy flower of all flowers. No one even knew where it was. But with their Chaya soon going to Seed, Toplians were all dropping armies of coin to the Temple to get as much as they could to prepare for their journey. My mom said the Temple priests couldn't have cooked up a better money-making scheme.

Nastachal was now chucking books at Master Mantalikas and he fumbled out a golden Chaya case. She stopped throwing as he shook a line of pink powder on to a mirrored plate by her bed. "My sweet, calm yourself. Come connect with the dust of your ancestors."

I stole behind a life-size statue of Nastachal. *Almost out.*

Nastachal's blue ringlets bobbed up and down as she scuttled to her father, her eyes already eating up the Chaya powder. She inhaled it in a breath, and stood up with a saturated smile that froze. Her lips snarling and skin blue-purpling with Chaya powder, she ran like an attacking sarak lizard right towards me...

Smack! "Get out you filthy worm!"

My cheek stung from the flat of her hand. Her pointy purple shoes kicked hard, over and over. I scrambled to get up. "Go to Eternal Darkness where you belong! By the Chaya Flower, such an ugly and useless creature!" she screamed.

"I have set out more powder, darling," said Master Mantalikas.

Nastachal slammed the door shut, catching the back of my leg as I leapt out of the room. I should be thankful for all the purple bruises to come, but my broken nails screamed to claw at her eyes and my rotten teeth to bite her flesh. She loved to vent her anger on my body, daily if she had the chance lately, and there's nothing I can do. *She's a Topper, and I'm a worm.*

My mother told me pain was a good thing; it reminds you that you're alive — that you're a survivor. But she was all talk, and look what that got her. Good and dead.

— «» —

Challix-11-1105

My mother strolled into our shack all flashy in a new silver dress and an amethyst ring glitter-glowing on her finger on Violent Violet Day.

"Looking nice! Who gave the ring?" I asked and ran up to get a closer look. No worm I knew wore such things.

"That's my business," said my mom. "Happy Violent Violet Day!"

Her fist flew at my face; she did always like catching me unawares. I saw bright lights, and then felt something hard hit the back of my head. Just before I blacked out, I realized it was the floor.

I woke to find my mother hovering above me and crying. "I'm so sorry, Jukiht. I hit too hard and forgot about the ring." Her large grey eyes drooped sadder than usual.

"But you say pain makes you stronger. Lets you know you're a survivor." My head ached and buzzed like coga beetles were making a home there. I wobbled up to sitting and she handed me a cup of water. A cut above my eye was drooling blood and she pressed some zorta moss against it.

"Something is wrong with beating my child to 'improve' her skin color." She shook her head and looked to our dirt floor as if it held the answers.

"My eye's going to look purple beautiful for days — even weeks. I thank you for the colors," I winced as I smiled.

"You're beautiful just as you." My mother wiped at her tears and touched my cheek gently. "We're so stupid — living nightmare low hoping to touch the dreamy Topper life. Worms gotta find our own way. We gotta stop being poor beaten shadows to Toppers. I'll not hit you again. Starting now, we always be proud. You promise me right now — always you are a worm and proud. Promise."

Kids were going to tease me for only having one purple eye tomorrow, but I'd never seen my mother like this. I'd never seen her cry. "I promise."

Then she ran out in the street and hollered as if our shack was on fire. "What is wrong with us? Why are we hurting our children? So they can look like Toppers? We need to be proud of our grey! Grey is the color of clay — that makes everything from their dishes to great works of art. Without grey their precious Chaya flowers would wither and die. We must end Violent Violet Day. We must love and protect our children!"

Worms in the street stopped and stared. Others stuck their heads out of shacks to see what all the commotion was about. Someone called out, "Shut up and go beat your kid!" Laughter erupted around us.

"Laugh about our pain, that's one way. Another is for us to work together, for worms to move with purpose — to wriggle out of this shit we live in and make things better. We need to think about what kind of world we want for our children. Is this the best we can give them? We can find a better way."

No one answered her; or rather they did by walking away or sticking their heads back in their shacks. My mom's shoulders sagged and she shuffled towards home. A rickety old woman with a hunched back hobbled towards her.

"Like what you'd to say," she said. "How can we make things better?"

And so my mother transformed into Mother Worm that day, and word by word she would work toward change, and her own death.

—— «» ——

Chayan-3-1111

"I need you, sweet dogkeeper," said Ouijiy, twirling her grey-blue hair, standing as close as she dared to the gated Chaya shrine room. Bevic was chawing on a piece of bone from a marpet-whale he killed himself, while Namab and Hy-Yol were locking their horns and rolling around in a play fight that would kill us instantly.

"So you'll get past the dog chambers, then what? Master M keeps the key with him at all times."

Ouijiy flashed the golden key from a ribbon under her servant blouse. I had my suspicions about how she got her hands on that key, and I didn't want to know the details. She sidled up close to me. "That's why you go for the walk now."

I frowned. "I want no trouble."

Ouijiy smiled her smile that could make even Toppers want to do her bidding. "Look, they won't ever know. It's dyed mora petals." She pulled a glithy leaf from her pocket, opening it to reveal powder that looked just like Chaya powder.

"I only need a turn of turns. I'll be in and out quick. Come on, Jukiht." Her yellow-flecked eyes started into mine; and although I'd seen them a thousand times before, their rare beauty always mesmerized my boring old grey eyes.

I chewed at my lip. "We're food for dogs if they find out."

"But who's gonna tell? The dogs'll keep our secret." She winked.

Her hand reached for mine; the warmth of it had my heartbeat loud in my ears like a great Topper Temple drumming. My lips could only form the word "yes."

— «» —

Agith-9-1105

"Yes, Raki. I have a surprise for you!" My mother passed a basket to the blind beggar girl who "worked" the market. Raki was near thin as paper and covered in rags even thinner; the winter wasn't going well for her.

"Thanks much, Mother Worm!" cried Raki. She ran her skeletal fingers over the items, naming them correctly as she went. "Dress! Coat! Shoes! I love marjuns! Oh dried fish! Thanking you!"

As we walked away from Raki, I took my mother's hand possessively. "Why do we give so much to her?"

"Many wrongs have been done. I can't help all, but I can find a small corner, even one person, and do my best to make their time here better." My mother spoke slowly like faster thoughts in deeper truths swam in the background.

"Why don't we keep the money from the ring and dress for us? Why give it her?" I looked down at my own worn shoes.

My mother paused. "It's … history. I knew her mother; I was a young girl when I started working for Master Hadbasso. I— we both were. We grew up, became women and mothers there. When Raki was four revolutions old, she and her mother fell ill with the Blood Fever. Raki went blind from it. Master Hadbasso needed no broken child, so he sent the child to the streets. Raki's mother was too sick to do anything; she died that day when she found out. Raki's path could have been yours, and by the Chaya you were spared."

"You worked for Master Hadbasso? You never said. Why'd you change employers? He's the richest Topper in the city!"

"You ask the wrong questions. My whole heart is saddened by your selfishness." My mother's face transformed to a frozen field where no answers would grow, while insecurities spread like weeds in my heart.

— «» —

Chayan-4-1111

Ouijiy poked me awake in the middle of the night. "I took the powder! Do I look different?" She held a candle as fat as a pregnant gwathel toad, something she must have also stolen, near her face.

"You're pinker in places. Your cheeks and nose." Ouijiy was even more stunning if it was possible.

"I'm glowing on the inside, and full of energy. I feel like I could do anything, like I'm on top of the world!"

"Like a Topper." I smirked.

We broke out laughing.

She passed me a rolled up glithy leaf. "When the Enlightenment comes, I want you to have a chance too."

Tears edged my eyes. "For me?"

"Course you! You walked the dogs."

"Thank you. But how can this make a difference for us? Toppers've been doing Chaya powder all their lives to prepare for the Enlightenment. Their Blessed Parchment says worms only have Eternal Darkness."

"Most all of us got some Topper bastard blood, so there's a chance. It can't hurt to try. Go on."

I hesitated. My mother haunted me — my promise to be an always proud worm, to shun being like a Topper. I still yearned to be her daughter. But my mother was gone, and this was a gift from Ouijiy.

I snorted the powder; it scratched with sandpapery legs and left an angry burning trail. Near instantly, a tingling sensation spread through my body. Warmth welled from some deep spring within me that longed to be free, and my blood gushed drunk from the top of my head to the tips of my fingers and toes. Happiness took over my body; my sense of self grew as big as the sky.

"You're pinking!"

"OOOOHHhhh!" I said. "I'm on top of the world!"

Ouijiy and I erupted with giggles, and we fell to the ground in each other's arms. Her smile was like the world coming into existence. For a rare moment in our lives, we were the happiest of worms.

— «» —

Hinatal-19-1107

Mother Worm, backlit by moonlight, stood on a boulder surrounded by worms. "So the Toppers go to the Bright Afterlife, so let'em have it! Who wants bright lights shining in their face forever! The Blessed Parchment says we go to Eternal Darkness! Bring it on! I've worked hard; I deserve some peace and quiet ... finally!"

Vafiks clapped, laughed and guffawed around her.

"Their holy book says we turn to dirt when we die! We should be proud, not ashamed! We are the rock and stone, the mud and sand that make everything in this world! They love their Chaya, but without earth to grow it — they'd likely be as grey as us! Without us, the Toppers have nothing in this world. No link to their ancestors — no Enlightenment — no path to their mythical First Flower. They need us and they know it — that's why they keep us down. Instead of doing as Toppers say, we must rule ourselves. Make our own rules! Live our own lives!"

There was a roar of cheering and clapping ... that was soon silenced by bugle-horns blaring all around us. Then dogs howled and ran into the crowd with teeth flashing sharp. Soldiers barked orders and stabbed at the nearest worms.

Screaming and movement exploded in all directions. The moon shone, and I couldn't see my mother on her rock any more. Something stung the side of my head and threw me to the ground. Dizziness forced my eyes shut, and then darkness reigned.

— «» —

Chayan-5-1111

I hummed a First Flower hymn while doing my chores, remembering mingled memories of Chaya powder and Ouijiy. Worms weren't allowed in the Temple, but I learned the songs from listening to Ouijiy singing them all the time. She sang like a veauti-bird and was often rented out to sing for Topper socials.

As if my thoughts brought her, Ouijiy came running up to me. "You'll never guess what!" She squeezed my hands like she was wringing water from wet clothes. "My dad is a full Topper! My mom won't say who because she said that could mean we're killed. But with the Final Bloom coming, she said I should know. I'm half Topper!"

"By the Chaya!" I said.

"I wonder who he is. Could it be Master Wexil who my mom works for? Maybe that's why they sent me here to work for the Mantalikas."

"Maybe..." I looked away.

"Be honest. Tell me." She waved her hands and stamped her foot.

"If he's your dad, I'm shocked. He and his kin are the ugliest Toppers and ... you're more beautiful than the lot of them." My face warmed with embarrassment.

"Being half Topper, I could really get a chance to journey to the Flower of Origins."

"I know." I tried to sound excited for her.

"My mom said most Topper men are cheating half-worms making more half-worms. Everyone is hush about it, so not to upset the Matrons. Still, it has its advantages."

She laughed and patted her new silken dress; I gave a half-hearted smile. Ouijiy put up a big front, showing off the clothes and gifts she got. But she came crying some nights, just wanting someone to hold her, to feel the warmth of give and not the pain and emptiness of take. Ugly scrawny worm that I was, I was left alone. It could also be because I spent so much time with three toothsome dogs and often smelled like it.

Ouijiy tapped my arm. "Maybe your dad was a Topper. Did your mom ever talk about him?"

"She said she was all the parent I needed. End of talking."

"See, there's a chance he was a Topper. Maybe you'll be Enlightened too!" Her eyes lit up.

"Maybe." I felt like I had rocks in my belly. I was completely grey and ugly; there was no way I was even a drop of Topper.

"Be positive! When the Final Bloom comes, I know it will be wonderful. I'll find my father and we'll be a happy family together again. My mom and I won't have to work anymore;

we can live fine all Enlightened in the land of the Flower of Origins. I can't wait."

"It sounds lovely." I didn't think this was likely, but we have so few chances at happiness. Why should I spit on her dream? Still, her words sucked the shine from my day. I was an orphan, just one job away from being a beggar like Raki.

— «» —

Grixatalis-34-1107

"I've been going to the market, since your mom's gone miss — uh, she showed me everything I'm going to show you," said Ouijiy, her cheeks pinking.

I nodded. I pretended I didn't hear her mention my mom. I was lucky to get off farhberry picking and get a job inside.

"Master Mantalikas only likes mauve marjuns. If there's any green on them, put them back. You want to make sure they're completely round." Ouijiy held up an example.

I plunked mauve marjuns in my basket, noticing Ouijiy was as fleshy and sweet-smelling as this most expensive of fruits. Her grey skin held shades of lilac and her blue-grey eyes were dotted with golden brightness. And I wasn't the only one who noticed. Where Toppers skirted around me like I was dog dung, they stopped and stared at Ouijiy.

"Spare change. I hungry." Raki had snuck up on me and was pulling my arm.

I didn't want to make a bad impression with Ouijiy, but I had to talk to Raki. "Seen or heard anything about my mother?" I asked.

"Not seen Mother Worm since soldiers. I see hunger. Every day. Help a hungry worm. Mother Worm say to," said Raki.

I shook my head.

"Mother Worm she helps! You help!" Raki cried and clung to my leg. For someone thin as fall leaves, Raki's arms were strong as tree trunks and rooted to my calf. I tried to pull her off, and she stayed stuck.

"Get off!" I twisted her arm until it seemed a bone might snap, and she finally let go.

Toppers and worms alike stared. I stomped off to the other end of the market. Ouijiy followed and grabbed my hand, her eyes filled with concern and curiosity. "Are you okay? That beggar kind of looks like you — the same high forehead and big sad eyes."

"I'm nothing like her!" I shouted. I ran from the market, with Ouijiy's words burning me like fire.

— «» —

Chayan-11-1111

On the Day of Enlightenement, Master Mantilikas called me to his study. "Are all the supplies packed in the carriage?"

"Yes, sir," I said. He'd asked Ouijiy and me to pack up a long list of things, but to make sure everything was hidden from Nastachal. He worried about her "sensitive soul." My own soul felt torn to pieces, for his plan was that I follow him with supplies and Ouijiy take care of their home.

"All of us will be walking to the Temple, so stay well behind the Toplian crowd. At the Temple, remain in our carriage stall with the dogs and I will fetch you to follow. If for some reason we do not come, your duty is to take the carriage and search for us."

I nodded.

He steepled his fingers and looked directly at me. "Through my research as Grand Historian, I have found that while nowhere is it written that animals can be Enlightened, at the same time there is nowhere written that animals cannot be Enlightened. I hope proximity to the Chaya in its final stage will possibly Enlighten the dogs, in some way bless them or at least make them part of this important historical event. The dogs are a part of our family and I would give them this opportunity."

I nodded again; what else could I do with such odd talk?

"In translating ancient versions of the Blessed Parchment, I have made another discovery. The passage which we know today as "worms are destined for Eternal Darkness" was once written as "worms will live through a long lasting time of darkness and difficulty." Nowhere does it say that worms or animals cannot be Enlightened. You, as the dogs, may possibly be Enlightened."

A storm of thoughts and questions whirled in my head, and usually that's where they'd stay. "Is this truly so? Why does no one know this?" I blurted.

"Priests decide what version of the Blessed Parchment goes to Toplians; it is not my role."

"Do the priests know of this?" The words burst from my lips, but I couldn't stop them. *Was this what it was like for my mother?*

"Yes, the priests know. The Blessed Parchment was created for our Salvation and Enlightenment. The welfare of worms is not a concern. But at the same time, with the Hour drawing near, I felt you may feel a sense of hope to know this information."

"Thank you, sir," I said, "for your kind words." *Words that could change everything, not only for me — but for all worms. No Eternal Darkness? Was the death of my mother just part of this long difficult time worms must live through? Could I hope for the Bright Afterlife and her waiting for me there? Could I be Enlightened?*

— «» —

Morgyl-22-1108

Many worms died during that moonlit night in Vafik Valley — but of my mother no one had anything to tell. I was lucky Master Mantalikas let me take her place, but it meant I had little time to find out what had happened to her. Early in the morning and late at night, I went from shack to shack, worm to worm. They had been willing to listen to Mother Worm, but now no one wanted to be spotted with me, as if going missing was contagious. At the start I was hopeful — that she had been whisked away and gone into hiding — that she would return. By the end, I was searching forests and digging in worm body dump sites, just hoping to find a shred of her clothing.

Then one morning, I awoke to find a letter beside me.

Please stop looking for your mother. She is buried in the earth she loved so much, somewhere safe where her bones will not be defiled. Your mother wanted you to know she loved you, loved you so very much.

No name was left, but the expensive paper gave its own clues. Inside the envelope was a ring, the same amethyst ring my mother had once worn on a Violent Violet day. I cried as I dug into the dirt floor of my shack. I buried the note and the ring, where the grey dirt would keep her secret safe.

— «» —

Chayan-11- 1111

The dogs ran around the carriage in the Mantalikas' stall; the space was large enough to house ten worm families. I climbed up to the hay loft and looked out the window. Behind a fenced area, I could see the roof of the Temple and the trees shrouding the Chaya garden.

Toppers were singing songs about the Chaya Final Bloom and their journey to the Chaya of Origins. Priests thundered on about all the wonders this day would bring. Then bugles, bells and humming blended together to form a bittersweet melody that drifted in the air thick as incense smoke.

All at once the music stopped. Then a strange sound beat the silence, as if hundreds of work worms whipped clean sheets. Something caught my eye, moving from within the Temple grounds and rising upwards.

Strange creatures flew straight up. Their huge wings were a cross between the feathers of birds and the soft velvet of butterflies. The shapes of faces and bodies were patterned on their blue and purple wings. The actual bodies varied in degrees of Enlightenment, if I could call it that, both marvelous and revolting at the same time. They resembled a mix of butterflies and Toplians. Some had fat segmented bodies and thin shiny legs like insects, but still Topper-like faces. Others had heads like butterflies with spiral tongues and shiny metallic eyes but still Topper-shaped bodies. They filled the sky like a shimmering sunset and all of them going towards the sun. Wave after wave of these Enlightened Toppers flew towards the First Flower wherever it was hiding. If the Master and Mistress were there, I could not pick them out.

Someone tapped me on the shoulder and I screamed.

Ouijiy stood before me. She looked the same, except for a pair of glittering pink and grey wings. They looked smaller than the ones on the Toppers.

"I'm Enlightened!" She set herself down and hugged me tight. I wanted to touch her wings, but was afraid to — butterflies need their magic powder to fly.

"My mom got wings too! She's already gone. I just needed to … see you." She smiled her smile that always warmed my heart.

"Where're you going?" My voice wavered.

"I wish I knew. It's like every part of my body is pushing me to go west and towards the sun. It's hard to think of anything else." She glanced out the window; her wings fluttering impatiently.

"Do you think it's somewhere worms can follow?" I felt like stones were dropping in my stomach and weighing me down as much as she needed to fly away.

She looked down at her feet that were floating off the ground, and shook her head.

"You look beautiful." I bit my tongue to hold back tears.

She put my hand in hers and looked in my eyes. "I can't resist it, I gotta go now. But there is a caravan of worms already going so you'll be able to follow and find me." Her eyes darted again to the window where the line of Enlightened was already dwindling out of sight.

"You better catch up to your mom. You'll maybe spot your dad soon too." I did my best attempt at a smile.

She sighed with relief. "We'll see each other soon."

"We'll be back together before we know it," I said.

The truth was in our tears as we let go of each other's hand. She kissed me as soft as her new wings, and then Ouijiy soared into the open air. I waved, but she didn't look back. I watched until she was a speck and then nothing more.

There were still fliers going up, but they weren't coming from the Temple any more. They were worms. The worm Enlightened kept their natural grey bodies and had smaller wings. I found them lovelier, perhaps because I could see myself in them. I stood and watched until eventually, the everyday birds and butterflies had back their sky. I decided to leave the carriage, just in case they came back. The dogs were all hyper and needed a run, but they gave me a hard time about putting their leashes on. The dogs hadn't changed one bit.

— «» —

Chayan-11- 1111

The streets were near empty with only handfuls of wingless worms. Some talked excitedly in groups. A few danced around and shouted, "We're free!" Many had carriages loaded up with goods and were going after their Matrons and Masters. My orders were to follow and my heart wanted to follow Ouijiy. But something in my gut just told me not to. Great wonders might wait for the Enlightened, but it didn't feel like my journey. They were no longer of this place; wherever they were heading, they didn't need all this stuff I'd packed up for them.

My back ached and pain grew between my shoulders; I tried to stay focused on keeping up with the dogs who were already heading home. As the pain increased, I remembered what my mother said, that feeling pain lets you know that you're alive — that you're a survivor. I focused on the fun I'd have when I got back to the Mantalikas' or should I say my home. I was going to fill my belly, have a warm bath, pick whatever I wanted to wear out of Nastachal's closet, and the dogs and I would test out every bed in the house. I laughed.

Then I saw Raki up ahead. Tears streamed from her blind eyes and she was madly jumping up and down. I made a big curve in my path without thinking, my feet so used to avoiding her. Her wings were too small to carry her weight.

I thought of my mother. I imagined her glowing in the Bright Afterlife. I imagined she was the pattern of a wing on a Topper butterfly going to the top of the sky. Part of me dearly wished this was so, but somehow I felt my mother was still here. She was proud of our roots in the dirt, and her bones would be happy resting deep in the dark soil. Her soul would be worming through the filth of the Vafik Valley, turning it slowly over time into something good that would make the grass green, flowers bloom and children smile.

As my feet touched the ground, with each step I felt closer to my mother, Mother Worm, than I had in a long time. She was gone, but she was still with me. The urge to go west, to follow the Toppers, was not in me. This was my home.

I turned back to where Raki cried, and towed the dogs behind me. I flew to her, as if I had always had wings, and I took my sister's hands.

—— « o » ——

Miki Dare

Miki Dare (Dare is pronounced DAH-RAY in Japanese) lives on the West Coast where she likes to express herself with whatever falls into her hands—from a pen to a paintbrush. Her science fiction and fantasy writing can be found in Analog Science Fiction and Fact, Inscription Magazine, Urban Fantasist and Where the Stars Rise: Asian Science Fiction and Fantasy. To see what she's up to, check out the following links: mikidare.com and https://twitter.com/mikidare

Dear Houston

Alexandra Renwick

Curve of the sun
crests the rim
of night-glitter Earth,
my slingshot trajectory along a route
I've completed three times already.

Now, in stark relief:
Earth's mottle-blue horizon,
diminishing black crescent wedge
with dark-etched ink of space behind.
Photochromic nano-tinters in my suit
scramble with audible thrum to adjust
to sudden full-sun protection as
light rolls across brown and blue
below, outlines of continents
beneath wisping swirls of white
bearding the Americas.

Tongue-toggle my broken transmitter
       —in vain, again—
as my orbit sails me rudderless
over Texas and that phrase inserts itself
Tourette-ish, the millionth time, sounds
that have ceased to retain meaning,
just the shape of words rolling
in my mouth like dissolving
lumps of uncooked dough:

Houston, we have a problem.

Outrage:
not even an accurate quote
of Lovell's original but the misquote
of cultural fame dances through my
boiling brain inappropriate, irrelevant,
while I for the millionth tic-ish time
smother frantic giggles rising
in my throat like fizz in a
bottle of shaken champagne,

dying.
Dying miles from everyone I know.
Dying miles straight up
in exosphere
and alone
though I'm hardly first to note
we all die alone.

"A problem," I mutter,
voice echoing dully off helmet,
bouncing off dark curved glass
and rounded portions of my skull;
"We have a problem."

My life's work: the Earth-to-orbit slingshot
    —success! and by a woman, too!
    (oh, investors loved that one:
    One small step for a man,
    one giant leap for womankind!)
years of crowdsourcing
of hoarding minor grants
of private support for
my solo space bungee,
sport extremest of extreme!

Mathematical calculations and
launch apparatus and pod
as sound as I'd predicted,
as sound as I could make

without adequate funding for
    the actual testing phase.
My plan: initial journey a
circle-once-then-drop sort of deal
    —successful, insofar as it went—
but the *junk*!
the goddamn *junk*
got the best of me,
glanced off my shotpod's small round body,
breached and shredded hull,
peeled shield from my tiny vessel until
only a skeletal mockery remained.

Like a pinball I'd ricocheted
from orbiting bit of junk to
bit of junk, written languages
of all Earth's places stencilled across
in blinding colours and exuberant strokes
as though each in some small way hoped
to be read from the planet surface.

It was to avoid direct collision with
a particularly nasty bit of debris
    all sharp serrated edges
    and beautiful Cyrillic script
    spiralling its surface in joyous hues
that I at last abandoned pod and
ejected into naked space.

"Houston," I whisper to myself,
elegant thorax between two continents
rotating again from the angle of my view,
familiar from textbooks, footage,
from years of study, from countless
dreams both waking and asleep;
"We have a problem."

——— « O » ———

Alexandra Renwick

Alexandra Renwick's short works have appeared in
ELQ, Clockwork Phoenix, The Year's Best Hardcore Horror,

and *Imaginarium: The Best Canadian Speculative Fiction*. She lives in Ottawa's historic Timberhouse, where she dusts occasionally, gardens badly, and dotes on a rotating cast of voracious outdoor koi. More info on Twitter @AlexCRenwick or online at: AlexCRenwick.com.

No More At All

Lisa Ann McLean

"Daddy, where are you? I'm scared."

"Ada? Ada, give the tablet to Mommy, honey!"

"Is that Daddy? Ada, give me the tablet, okay? Listen to Daddy..."

"What's happening, Daddy? There's so much smoke—"

"What's happening? They were wrong, honey! They didn't listen, and they were wrong! That's what's happening! Please give Mommy the tablet! I'm losing you—!"

"Give me that tablet, Ada! Rob, are you there? Rob? Rob—!"

— «» —

"Quittin' time, Rob!"

Steve samba-ed into the control room, careful not to samba over any rogue chairs. Rob always turned off the harsh office lights on the evening shift, preferring what he called 'mood lights' — mood lights being the meagre luminescence of the many monitoring screens that blinked or scrolled readings and status messages. In spite of the near-darkness, however, Steve managed to dance collision-free right into the central area where Rob stood. "Holly from Engineering is waiting for me, dude," Steve announced. "I can feel it!"

Rob scarcely glanced at him. "She probably has a date."

Steve stopped his samba and glared at Rob. "A curse on you, Rob, killer of dreams."

Rob didn't answer. He was staring at the large central screen. Normally, it displayed the map of the probe satellites in orbit around Earth. Tonight, though, it was listing the readings from one of the probes. Rob's lips moved slightly as he read through the alarms. *That's not a good sign*, Steve thought. "What'cha doin'?"

"Something weird just happened."

Steve's plans of an evening with Holly began to evaporate. "You're kidding, right? You have to pick this Friday night, to have something weird happen?"

"Murphy's Law."

Steve sighed. "You know, this is the first year we've actually been able to go to the Holiday party, and you're looking at overtime?"

"I kind of liked when we used to call it a Christmas party." Rob scrunched his face at the readings, then sat down on one of the chairs and tapped the interface tablet on the desk. A list of alarm details filled the screen. "Look at that," he said, pointing at the information. "Probe 10 had this reading. It looked like something huge—"

"Oh, man, if I had five bucks for every time someone said that—"

"No, seriously—"

"I am serious, Rob! It's like, ever since they established the probe system, everyone is seeing the next Armageddon flying through space. And they always say the same thing: that if it was big enough to be a concern, the system would alert."

Rob released a slow breath, turning to Steve and looking at him long enough to make him raise an eyebrow. He then tapped the tablet again, and the display flicked to the list of readings. "After it saw that," he continued, "it blinked out of contact — right there — and now it's back and all readings are normal."

"I heard the normal part. Let's go."

"Yeah, but these probes have always been glitchy when the receivers go down. Remember last time? Probe 6 was down three days before this new system realized it had a problem. The whole time it was green. Normal."

"Are you talking about probe 10P or 10S?"

"10S? Crap, if this reading was on the secondary grid, we'd really be in a mess. Of course it's on the primary!"

— «» —

The air rising from the red-dusted ruins was hot and dry. Timmon had adjusted his breathing mask three times because the dust and the sweat were making him itch. *It better not be the pox*, he thought.

Timmon pulled at his backside. Wear your dust suit, mom had said. Yelled, actually. His stupid dust suit was getting too small for him. It rode up his ass all the time. But mom said that if he caught the pox out here in the wastes, she would throw him into the deadlands to die, so he squeezed into his suit, and stretched his boots and gloves as high as they'd go.

Here, on the edge of the wastes, there were still skeletons of the cities that had once stood here. The deadlands were nothing but the red dust that clouded the air and poisoned the water. Timmon liked wandering through the wastes. It was eerie. Sometimes you could almost hear the ghosts crying through the cracked and shattered ruins. He tried to picture them walking through the foundations of the buildings that were so unbelievably huge, he could never imagine how people would have built them. How *did* they? And what did they look like before the flaming piece of sky fell and destroyed everything, covering it with blood-red dust?

Something glinted: a shiny triangle poked through the dust, reflecting the copper sun. Timmon crouched down and gripped the edge with his thumb and forefinger, wiggling it back and forth. *It's loose.* He tightened his grip and pulled it out of the ground.

The object was slim and rectangular, and probably smooth but it was hard to tell — the fine dust stuck to it like it had been painted on. He tried to wipe it off the best he could with his gloved hands.

It had a glass top. The glass was cracked.

"Timmon! Mom said to come home!"

Timmon looked up. A huge piece of a broken cement wall stood between him and the voice, its steel reinforcements twisting outward from it like dead beetle legs. *Maybe if I stay here, she'll go away.*

"I know you're there, Timmon! I saw you go behind that rock!"

Shit. Timmon stood and carefully picked his way around the piece of wall, stepping over plastic squares and flat, broken tabletops. An old, upside-down office chair stuck its wheeled centre leg upwards from the rubble. "You're a pain in my butthole, did you know that, Clarissa?"

"I'm telling mom you said a curse-word to me!"

"Go ahead. You always were a little tattle-tale."

Clarissa jutted her lower lip. "Mom says it's getting late. She wants you home before the bad winds start up."

Timmon looked up. The few lint-grey clouds that had been stuck to the piss-coloured sky all day were starting to crawl ever-so-slowly westward, and the fine red dust was beginning to rise in swirling dust-devils from the ruins. Timmon ran the cleanest of his gloved fingers across the front of his mask, and looked at it. It was caked with red. Timmon sighed. "Okay. I'm coming."

Timmon stepped over a metal beam. The path he had taken twisted around pieces of metal and rock with thankfully few obstacles.

"What's that?" Clarissa asked as he approached, pointing at the object he held.

"Don't know, but it's mine," Timmon retorted, pulling it away from Clarissa. "I'm gonna ask Nana about it."

Clarissa gave it a wary look. "It might be conatimated."

"Contaminated. And I'll clean it so it's not."

"Mom won't let you bring it in the house if it's contanimated."

"Con-ta-min-at-ed, and it's not food or clothes, so it's not contaminated!"

"I'm telling mom," Clarissa said, running ahead to the house.

"Go ahead," Timmon whispered to himself, running his hand over the smooth glass, and drawing a letter 'T' in the dust.

— «» —

Steve waved Rob to silence. "Rob, they just upgraded the entire system last week *because* of that receiver problem." He swung himself into one of the empty rolling chairs, and catapulted himself towards Rob, crashing into Rob's chair and shoving him sideways like a bumper car. Ignoring Rob's "Hey!", Steve began tapping the tablet and a list of recent emails and memos flicked onto its screen. He began scrolling through them.

"There!" Steve said, tapping one and gesturing towards it with flourish as it opened and filled the tablet's screen. "See?

'The Hanson Probe System has rectified the issues of' — blah, blah, blah. There! — 'missed surveillance and erroneous normals transmitted on lockup of receive functions—'"

"I can read, Steve."

"Well, there y'go, then," Steve smiled at Rob with a smug serenity that eroded under Rob's dubious expression. "And also," he added, "last week we had that failure, and the console lit red right away. Remember?"

"Yeah, but that wasn't a receive failure. And I don't trust upgrades. They cause more problems than they fix."

"Rob, we tested for two days after the upgrade. I'm telling you, it works now. Hell, it's smarter than we are. It's like Hal."

"That's an unfortunate comparison."

— «» —

By the time Timmon and Clarissa had reached the squat, brick building where they lived, the bad winds were kicking the dust up into a gritty, red fog. Timmon spent a long time in the blast shack, using the compressed air and the cleaning solvent to get all of the dust off of his suit, his skin, and mostly his find, so that Mom wouldn't make him throw it back out into the wastes. As it was, Mom had given the thing the same look Clarissa had given it, but had let him bring it into the house to Nana after she had inspected his cleaning job.

Nana Ada sat in a faded, patchy chair by one of the house-fires. She had been Dad's mom, but when Dad had died of the pox five years ago, Mom had made Nana stay with them. She was always cold, so she wrapped herself in an old sweater, and she wore an old, knitted tuque, and knitted gloves with no fingertips. She said that the years were making her colder, but Timmon had never remembered when Nana Ada had been warm. Even during the days when the sun blazed down on the dust-crusted wastes, and Timmon cursed his dust suit for stifling him in heat, Nana was still wrapped in that old sweater with the threads hanging from the sleeves. Nana had been alive before the sky hit the earth, and she would talk about what the world used to be like before the dust and the pox. Timmon loved to hear about that world, hungered to know what had once been where the wastes now sprawled. So he handed Nana his find and sat down at her feet to hear what she knew.

"Wow," Nana said, turning the object over in her hands. "I haven't seen one of these since … well, my dad used to work on one of these when I was just a little girl. I think he called it a … hmmm … a tablet, if I remember correctly. It was a smart device."

"What's a tablet?" Timmon asked. "And how were they smart?"

"Well," Nana smiled, "you would be able to ask it anything and it would give you the answer."

"Bullshit!"

"Timmon!" Mom shouted from the cooking-fire in the next room.

"He was cursing at me, too," Clarissa announced.

"Where did you hear that word, Timmon?" Nana asked.

"I saw it on one of the busted-up walls in the wastes," Timmon mumbled, glaring at Clarissa.

"Well, boy," Mom said, "when we go over your letters tonight, I'll expect every letter that's in that word to be perfect, or I'll clean out your mouth in the blast shack!"

"Mr. Tablet," Clarissa asked, moving next to Nana and talking at the device. "How do I get my brother to stop cursing?"

"Okay, you two," Nana said. "Clarissa, honey, it doesn't work anymore. Nothing like this works anymore. These used to talk to the Internet."

Timmon chewed on the middle part of his lips. The Internet. Computers. Networks. People talked about them like magical gods that bestowed every gift on people. Gods that had disappeared when a greater god had thrown down the sky.

— ‹›› —

"You know, Rob," Steve's voice had taken on a plaintive note, "people like you are the reason they're automating all the stations: you freak out and sound alarms that aren't necessary. I'm telling you, if there was something wrong, the system would notify everyone."

"It won't notify nothing if it's green."

"Well, it sounds like a glitch to me."

"I should let the Duty Manager know. It looked like an awfully big something before the green."

"Don't you think an awfully big something would have taken out the probe?"

"Maybe it just grazed it, you know? Took out the receiver? Or maybe—"

"Now you're starting to sound like you're looking for something to be wrong. If it was that big, I think we'd be minus one probe. And *that* would alarm."

"Would it?"

Steve sighed. "Did you check the secondary grid satellites? The LEO probes in 10P's zone should show something irregular if there's a problem with the primary probe."

Rob flipped the central display to the readings for the secondary grid. "Looks like 9S, 11S, and 15S are in zone 10," he said. He opened a general display of readings for each probe. "Huh. They all look good."

"There you go. Just a glitch. Trouble came clear."

"But if there's a receiver issue..."

"On all three probes?"

"Hello ... upgrade?"

"Come *on*, Rob."

Rob sighed, looking unconvinced. "Yeah. I guess you're right."

"Of course I'm right."

"I'm still gonna tell the Duty Manager. Maybe I could run a few tests. It would only take about an hour or so."

Steve winced at the 'hour or so'. "Fire him an email, then," he said.

"Maybe I should message him."

"Knock yourself out, but I guarantee you that the Duty Manager is not going to grant OT for a green light. Ed's a stingy bastard."

Rob glanced at Steve. "Message Edward Chance," he said to the tablet.

The tablet's screen switched to a text display. *Command confirmed,* it scrolled. *Audible message mode. State message.*

"Had an alarm event that cleared on probe 10P, but it looked really big. Do you want further investigation? End message."

The message scrolled in print onscreen. *Confirm?*

"Confirm message. Send," Rob said.

Rob flicked the central screen back to the map. Soft green lights indicating each probe blinked in two concentric grids around the earth. The outer probes in the primary grid moved in geosynchronous orbit, while the low-earth orbit probes in the secondary grid moved more quickly, closer to the earth.

"The global data stream," Steve said, watching the display. "The New Internet. Whatever they're calling it, it's the data of the entire world stored in those probes. Boggles the mind when you think about it. Did you ever wonder what life would have been like without it?"

"We sure wouldn't be working here," Rob said, tapping at his tablet.

Steve bent his head towards Rob's display screen. "And you wouldn't be messaging your wife, either. Are you sending personal messages from work?"

Rob flicked his eyes towards Steve. "I'm just checking with Talia," he said, "making sure the sitter is there."

"Is Ada going to be pissed that you're leaving her at home tonight?"

"Nah. She likes the sitter."

"That's lucky," Steve said. "And think about that: Ada, and kids like her — they've never known anything else. Living in the age of convenience. Entertainment, networking, surveillance, communication, banking — everything on one massive, interlinked network. All anyone needs anymore is a tablet and fingers to type on it. Don't you ever think about stuff like this?"

"Only when I'm stuck here with you."

"You are surprisingly non-geek for a technician."

"Where the hell is Ed's answer?"

Steve leaned back in his chair and closed his eyes. "He's gonna say get the hell home."

"Even if it's something huge?"

"If it cleared, I'll bet he doesn't care if it was extinction level."

The tablet *ding*ed, and the screen flicked on. *Message from Edward Chance. Accept?*

— «» —

"What was the Internet, anyway?" Timmon asked. "Everyone says it was so big, but it just disappeared. How does that happen?"

"It wasn't a thing, Timmon," Nana said. "It was just … knowledge. Everything people knew. Everything they had or wanted. It was all on the Internet."

"Wow," Clarissa said. Timmon rolled his eyes. Clarissa said 'wow' to everything Nana said about the old world. It was dumb.

"How could it — the Internet — be what people had *and* what they knew?" Timmon asked. At least *he* had intelligent questions.

Nana smiled. "I don't know, honey. That's what my daddy said. It held all the knowledge and, somehow, everything people were worth. Computers and tablets were all joined together and they called that the Internet. Everyone's tablets would all talk together, so everyone could talk to everybody in the whole world — "Nana smiled down at the tablet — "My daddy would even talk to me through the tablet..."

"Nana," Mom said from the cooking room, "tablets weren't alive. Stop talking about them like they were."

Timmon frowned at his mom. Mom always tried to stop Nana's stories. She was angry at the old world. Timmon figured Mom was just jealous of all the stuff they had. Either way, Mom said stories only made you want for what you couldn't get. She said she was a 'realist'. Timmon guessed realist meant you didn't like to hear about anything cool, like tablets and the Internet.

"What happened to the Internet?" Timmon asked.

"It went down," Nana said. "When the star fell from the sky, the Internet went down, and all the tablets stopped talking."

— ‹›‹ —

"Accept message," Rob stated.

Message accepted, the screen returned. Text began to scroll along the display: *Are there any current alarms?*

"Reply message: No current alarms, but receiver issues are a red flag to me. Send message."

If there are no current alarms, then close up, the reply came. *The system will inform us if anything anomalous happens. You worry too much, Rob. Come to the party.*

"I told you," Steve said.

Rob sighed. "Reply message: As long as you're sure. I could run a diagnostic. Send message."

"You are a stubborn son-of-a-bitch, you know?" Steve said.

"It's called being thorough. Computers don't seem to do that very well. They trust themselves too much."

Get your ass to the party. I will take full responsibility if a huge asteroid collides with the earth.

"I'm holding him to that," Rob muttered, frowning at the display.

"You do that. Now, let's get out of here."

"Reply message. You're the boss, Ed. Send message."

"Booya! Holly, here I come!" Steve launched out of his chair.

"Okay. Just let me—"

"Rob! You have it on orders not to work tonight! Why are you still tapping at that goddamned tablet?"

"Holy crap, Steve! Chill!"

"Shit, Rob. Holy shit. If you're going to curse, do it well."

"All right, all right!" Rob flicked the displays into standby automatic, and turned on notification functions. "I'm coming."

As the door closed behind them, the map display popped on. Probe 11S had just slid outside of zone 10. Probes 9S and 15S, still in zone 10, blinked red for less than a second, then flicked back to green. The screen turned itself off.

— «» —

"I still don't think it was a star," Timmon piped up. "Stars are tiny."

"Stars are very far away," Nana said.

"You don't know that, Nana," Mom said, carrying the soup-pot to the table. "No one does. No one's been up to the sky see one up close."

"They did, though!" Nana argued. "My daddy said they'd gone up to the Moon and—"

"That's enough filling the kid's heads with this stuff. Stories are stories. That's all they are. You were only a little girl, remember? You were only Clarissa's age when the sky fell down and your daddy — " Mom broke off her words and Nana's smile faded. Nana turned to look at Mom, but Mom didn't look up from her stew.

"What's 'going down'?" Timmon asked, not wanting Nana to go quiet like she usually did when Mom started talking her realist crap. "You said the Internet went down. What is that?"

"I don't know, honey," Nana said, turning back to Timmon and smiling again. "My mother kept saying: 'The Internet's down. The Internet's down.' She said it for a long time. Everyone was saying it. It took awhile for everyone to realize that it just wasn't coming back up. All that knowledge. Everything people had, everything they were … it was all … gone. Like it was never there."

"It never *was* there," Mom said, looking up from setting soup bowls down on the table. "I think you and all the other old folks were just little kids that they told stories to, and you believed them. If everyone knew so much, if that Internet had been so powerful, this wouldn't have happened. They would have found some way to stop it or save *something*, even just so we'd know who we were and where we came from. At least they could have used some of that amazing, endless knowledge to tell us how to fix this! But no — all we have is *that!*" Mom gestured to the vast wasteland outside the window.

"I remember—"

"Nana, you *don't* remember!" Mom snapped, slamming a spoon down to the table with a loud *crack*. "You remember like a child remembers: bigger than life. And full of imagination and dreams!"

Nana clutched the tablet to her chest and pointed out the window with one shaking finger. "Look at those wastes, girl," Nana's voice quivered. "They built that! They knew so much—"

"Maybe they were wrong," Mom replied, standing upright and staring straight at Nana. "Maybe everything they thought they knew was wrong and this happened to show them how wrong they were."

Nana stared at Mom. Emotions Timmon could not understand played across the network of lines in her face. For a minute, she looked as if she might cry. Then she looked angry. *Tell her, Nana,* Timmon thought. *Tell her about how great that world was. Tell her about blue skies and The Internet and cars and stores filled with food and about houses with fresh water that poured out of the walls. Tell her!*

Instead, Nana Ada handed the tablet back to Timmon, and pulled her sweater more tightly around her thin shoulders. She turned and stared out the window at the swirling clouds of red dust and said nothing at all.

——— « o » ———

Lisa Ann McLean

Lisa Ann McLean is the author of the fantasy books *Bequest* and *Inquest* (Double Dragon publishing), and the short story collection *Saviour* (Lulu.com). She works as a telecommunications technician in her hometown of Timmins, Ontario, Canada, where she resides with her husband. You can visit her and read some of her work on her website: www.lisaannmclean.com.

I Never Expected the Stars

Thea van Diepen

Darkness all around. The scattering confused lights of the void. But the void doesn't have any lights, not really. Must just be my eyes, so terrified for something to see that they made stars in a night that never ends. Even if I could close my eyes, they'd still be there. Spastic. Humming with purposeless movement.

And I am afraid.

They say it's only a small percentage of the population that needs extra help during cryosleep, that needs extra encouragement to go under. Usually, there's tests ... usually. But percentages are just statistics, and if statistics are small enough or big enough, we think they won't apply to us. We're only average, after all. Or the exception. Whichever assures us our safety. Until it doesn't. They also say that, if you stay too long in sensory deprivation, you go insane.

We left because of fear, and God knew that. Of course God knew that. But he gave us a destination anyways. What was it? What were the exact words? "A jewel of a planet in an ocean of stars." Which could mean anything, really, if not for the inspiration behind them. In my heart, the Holy Spirit recognized the words and brought them to life in me. I wanted to see that planet.

— «» —

I went under for a bit there. True sleep. Interesting. I thought I would be awake, aware the whole time. No one had said anything about punctuated consciousness. If it happens again, then I'll know I'll only have to hang on for a bit at a time, and I can do that. It'll be like childbirth. I've always wanted a child.

The stars haven't come back to the darkness. Perhaps if I give my mind something to do, they won't.

We weren't the only ship to leave. War had broken out, real and true war in the streets, and we didn't know where we'd be safe anymore. A government long intolerant of faith and a people filled with mounting evil on all sides — there was nothing left for us. The world was too far gone for us to ever be safe in it, for it to ever change. Many people had been preparing to leave for a long time, selecting planets and amassing supplies. We had supplies too, but no planet. God would lead us where we were not wise, and so we prayed. I wasn't there when the answer came. My husband was, and he said the answer came to many people at once. Where should we go, we had asked. To a jewel of a planet in an ocean of stars, said the Lord.

And then we did something stupid. We boarded, took off, and deleted all our navigational charts while we flew at near light speed. And by "we," I mean that idiot of a man who'd organized everything in the first place. The moment I realized what happened I went right to him, all but ready for violence.

"What is *wrong* with you?" I yelled.

"If we keep the charts, we'll trust ourselves more than God," he said.

"I wouldn't have come on this ship if I'd known what you were going to do. How stupid can you be?"

"'Let not the sun go down on your anger,'" he quoted, voice raised.

"How will the computer keep us from hitting something? We can't just zoom around at top speed all the time — we'd never be able to get out of the way while piloting manually. How will it account for gravitational fluctuation? How much fuel do you expect to waste weaving around asteroids or escaping a planet we weren't interested in slingshotting around? And in case you need reminding, there's a *lot* of empty space out there. If we leave our galaxy, that's lifetimes before we'll get to another one, *if* we get to another one without getting lost and going in circles."

"We can't go back now."

"No, we bloody well can't now, can we." He'd waited until we'd gone far enough that we would have no guarantee of finding our way back without the charts.

He smiled, and I wanted to yell that smile off his smug face.

The stars are out again with their lopsided jolting dance. Oh, go away! You're not wanted here.

I just need to breathe and focus.

Except I don't have that kind of control over my own lungs. Focus it is.

The beginning of cryosleep feels like going numb. Everything fades around you as if you're about to go into real sleep and for a moment, you're awake like I'm awake right now. There's supposed to be a drop after, like sinking underwater while still being able to breathe.

I shouldn't be in cryosleep right now, and I would give anything to be out of it, but nothing else could be done.

My husband is probably piloting right now. To save on resources, the original plan had been for two pilots and a skeleton crew, everyone else in cryosleep. The problem was that there were only two people with piloting experience, and my husband didn't want to be without me. We had no idea how long the journey would be, and we wanted to age together. In order for my husband to agree to be a pilot, I would have to be awake with him. Some criticized us for not thinking of resources or space — I have no skills to offer the running of a ship — and perhaps rightly so. But when you've spent years trying to have children and nothing's worked, you don't want to give up what chance you may have left. In vitro fertilization after the fact, even if that worked, wouldn't cut it either. Not if it meant our children might grow up without a father.

Because I wasn't expected to go into cryosleep, I wasn't tested. And now there's no way to wake my body up until we find that planet, but I pray anyway that someone would hear God tell them to let me out, tell them that I can see stars that don't exist and hear bells where there is silence.

That blasted fool of an organizer didn't realize until long after take off that he had miscalculated how many of us the ship's air system could sustain without straining. We had one too many people awake. Someone would have to sleep for the sake of all and it certainly wasn't going to be him. He's an intelligent man, enough that he can come up with any number of reasonable excuses and justifications on the spot. He made himself too valuable to be lost.

"Doesn't it seem convenient to you?" I asked my husband in our quarters the night before I went under. One more day together, a peace offering I took, but resented.

"The numbers are sound."

"Of course the numbers are sound. That's what I'm saying. He faked it before, saying the ship could handle having me up and about, all so he'd get you to agree to be a pilot. And now that you can't back out of it, he brings up this tiny little detail he forgot to mention before, one that just so happens to be the exact detail he needs to abandon his bargain." I lifted my head. "Why are we even here?"

"You know why."

"Doesn't it bother you, though? He deletes all the charts, neglects to mention the real numbers so you'll agree to be a pilot, and insists that he needs to stay awake all while telling us to trust God. How do we even know he didn't make up that prophecy?"

"I was there when it happened, remember?" His not-quite-off shirt muffled his voice. With another tug, he removed it. "He wasn't the only one who heard it."

"But how do you know he didn't get others in on it?" I scooched over to let him get into his sleeping bag. But he didn't yet.

"What do you expect me to do? We couldn't get back to Earth if we tried. Yes, I'm upset that you'll be in cryosleep, but the others are all agreed and there's no way I'm going to go around spreading accusations and discredit him just so I can have my wife by my side."

"And what if they're true? What if this is a lost cause and we've all committed suicide without knowing it?"

He wrapped his arms around me, fiercely tender. "No matter what happens, I promise I will pilot according to God's direction over anyone else's on this ship. We're in the furnace right now, if you're right, and even if He doesn't deliver us, He is still good. No matter our circumstances, He is always good. He brought us to each other, and He is with us through this all. Will you stand with me on that?"

— «» —

Fragmented colours limp across my vision after a period of sleep. If I can trust my sense of time, I was under longer with this bout. I hope that's a pattern. Keeping my mind and senses focused on only what I want is draining. Suppose our journey is all a lie — I'd rather sleep my way to inevitable death than spend the interim in this hell.

It stung that my husband didn't believe me, but that didn't matter so much. I could trust his promise, and I could stand with him on God's goodness even if I distrusted the goodness of others. When I went into the pod and waited for sleep to overtake me, I was afraid, but I could see my husband's face and I prayed he would have courage. I didn't want to leave him.

If I try hard enough, I can almost feel his hand in mine, his warmth as he gave a squeeze and then had to let go as the pod closed.

As a child, I knew that God was real. It wasn't a "matter of faith" so much as the only logical way to view the universe. Who he was and how he treated people — on that, I wasn't so sure. But real? I saw him every time I watched the trees in the wind, as a butterfly emerged from its chrysalis, in the smiles of those I loved and who loved me. Creation told a coherent story about him: he is magnificent, he is awe-inspiring. He is beautiful. He is in both the details and the whole. To hear the phrase "a jewel of a planet in an ocean of stars" meant to breathe the air after a rain so heavy it cleansed the world. Quite a feat for a world literally named dirt.

Meeting my husband ... it's funny how the good things in life conspire to happen during the times I believe God is good and only good. While we dated, he introduced me to the group I'm now stuck in space with, and I was drawn by their approach to prayer. The first meeting I attended, as the music played and we sang our worship, someone — I forget who — received a message that the child of a friend of theirs had gone to the hospital. Anaphylactic shock, and they didn't know what had caused it. In the middle of the song, we paused everything and prayed for that child right then and there. I'd grown up in a family where "I'll pray for you" was a standard response to tragedy or hardship, a polite response. The promised prayer almost never happened. And yet there we were, praying in the middle of a worship service and I could hardly keep the tears from falling.

"How did you like it?" asked my not-yet-husband as he dropped me off.

"I *have* to go again."

The hallucinations ape sensation now. They say the brain can't cope without stimulation for too long; it begins to invent something to experience so the neurons can fire, so they can live. A fractured world shows itself to me, croons with torn vocal cords, vibrates across my skin in an attempt to make meaning from nothing.

Was that all this was? Is that all God is? Meaning from nothing? We look into a void we were never meant to see and, petrified, try to fill it?

You promised me a family, God, promised me…

The test came back negative. Like all the others, negative. Maybe it was best; maybe, by never having children, we could spare them from the horror our world had become. Meetings like the one my husband had brought me to were illegal. Religion was private, politicians argued. At first, it had been to cut down Christianity, to make up for its societal privilege. But then, bit by bit, the freedom to practise any religion, any sort of spirituality not directly sanctioned by the government eroded. Violence broke out between groups, any groups, all groups that considered themselves different. Small wars were fought, hailed as the symptoms of broken society, fuel for a rage that permitted an ever-encroaching rule by force that promised utopia even as it tightened the noose and discontent only increased. Suppose my husband and I kept going to those meetings. Suppose we were caught. Suppose our children never saw us again all because we'd insisted on following God.

Leaving Earth had nothing to do with noble intentions for me and everything to do with the children I wanted to give a better life than I'd had.

If I wept now, I wouldn't feel the tears. But I hope I *am* crying. I hope someone sees that my face is wet. Is this my punishment for doubting? My husband stands in front of me, arm outstretched toward a beautiful country house and children's laughter.

"Come home, honey. Come home."

But I can't move because it's not real and I am stuck here. Why would God hold this in front of me even now except to torment me? My husband had his idealism; I wanted a family. Of course, that's it. I'm not spiritual enough. Never had the zeal for prayer, even after witnessing that service. Occasionally read the Bible, only a few minutes at a time every several months. And that meeting my husband went to where the prophesy came? To this day he thinks I was working. I had a mild headache and had thought the prayer session beneath my dignity. Something to humour rather than trust in. The ingenuity people had displayed in all other matters of the ship and its launch and our imagined colony impressed me so much that the idea of praying for a destination became the height of absurdity next to it. And that first meeting? That had been more for the adrenaline rush of breaking the law with a good-looking man.

Could I scream if I tried?

Trees and sunlight, the wind on my face. Squint, shadow my eyes, water from a hose and a chortle as I am soaked.

My parents followed God and where are they now?

Birds and a squirrel squabble for seed in the feeder, a hand in mine as the moon rises in a still-pink horizon, a pearl to adorn the evening.

How many years for unlawful gathering? Too many contradictions to tell. Every lawyer had a different answer, and none could change the past. Or the future.

"Did you wait for me here?"

"I wondered if you would lead us to this place."

"Your dreams still live. I have never killed them; I never will."

Sleep.

Oh sleep.

— «» —

It must be quiet in heaven tonight. Do they watch us, silent as they wait for our inevitable end? Do they know what will happen to me? Either way, there doesn't seem much to celebrate now.

I don't know if I can last until the next time I sleep. Every time I wake, the period of nothing is shorter and shorter. It's like the hallucinations have become tired of waiting.

I wonder if my parents are in heaven. There's never been any news from or about them since they were hauled away when I was five. Their crime? Unlawful gathering. Of course. It was the only "crime" they committed stupidly enough to be caught at, but not the only they were wanted for, if my aunt is to be believed. And stupid selfish five-year-old me hated the God who wouldn't tell them to stay at home. With me.

If they'd never left, I wouldn't have been passed from relative to relative, the child no one wanted to be associated with long because of who my parents were. Those indecent unreasonable people, with no care whatsoever for the safety of their child. They were probably in a cult — no rational person would behave the way they did. You know groups like that kill each other for no reason? And her pregnant with their second child! A baby which never materialized. Prison can be rough, poor thing. Must have been too stressful, simply too stressful. But who knows what kind of life it would have lived, had it been born? It's at peace now. It will never know suffering.

And now here I am, following in their footsteps. If Earth had a voice, what would it say about us abandoning it? All the followers of God, fleeing in as many ships as we can to as many planets as we dare, hopeless and powerless to do anything for the world we love. Let it destroy itself, we thought — I thought — I will raise my children on a new one. All our prayer wouldn't make our home safe for them, swift as we were to speak and plead.

God, if no one will free me, let me die. I know my husband, he would care for me no matter the state of my mind. He would feed me, clothe me, bathe me, whatever I needed, he would do. No matter what happened, he wouldn't abandon me, and I would become a chain, an obligation. Please, God, if there is any chance he will live to see your promise, do not let me keep him from the life he deserves.

The bells ring around me, but in their song there is no death.

You *could* die, the planes of jagged colour tell me.

For everyone else's good.

Yes, for their good.

It occurs to me, say the wind-tossed grasses beneath the fence, that love not extended to oneself is not extended to others.

Are you kidding? the birdsong writes across the sky. If Jesus could choose to die for others, why can't I?

Squeals of joy taste of the crucifixion. He didn't choose to die. He chose to live.

There is a splinter in my eye, and it blocks half my vision. I do not need to try for tears to come; they spill down my cheeks and the wood might as well be a spear through my skull. How long has it been there? Always, it seems. And, no matter how I turn, I cannot see beyond it. I cannot see around and into what it hides.

If I've functioned so well with it, why remove it?

Because it *hurts*.

I blink, rub my eye, press my hand against it. Salt on my lips as I try to wash it out. Finally, one hand to keep the eyelids open, neck aching to steady my head, I go in with my thumb and forefinger.

Alone and confused, I didn't know what to think of my relatives' accusations. I'd always thought my parents loved me, that they were as excited as I was about the new baby. They were kind, and taught me to be that way. There weren't any specific memories to go with that; it's what I'd always taken for granted as their child. Were they selfish, reckless, uncaring? Were they, as my aunt said, unfit to raise me?

You aren't wanted, jangle the vomit-green stars. You are tolerated.

I open my hand to find not a splinter, but a dust speck. I raise that hand and let the wind dry my face as it blows the speck out of existence.

You're right, I tell the stars. I'm not wanted. I'm loved.

The exchange of wedding vows.

The strains of prayer-woven music.

The joy of the prophesy.

Of the promise.

And all the promises before and after it.

I'm in front of that idiotic organizer again and, instead of hating him… "I understand you have a lot to offer if you remained awake during our trip. But you gave your word. We'll wake you if we need you."

— «» —

Blinding white sears through the optic nerve. Feeling tingles in my limbs as I raise my arm.

"Whoa, whoa, it's just me. No need to flail."

Honey?

"Ow," I say, and close my eyes. Less pain in my hallucinations would be nice.

"Is she supposed to react like this? I thought..."

"You thought right," someone else replied. The ship's doctor, I think. Does she have to yell, though?

"Didn't she get tested for cryosleep tolerance?"

"She wasn't supposed to have gone under." Oh, great. My husband is yelling, too. That on top of the pins and needles everywhere, and I'm not surprised holding on to a train of thought is difficult. I'll just listen. This will pass. I'll be back at the house in the country soon.

"Why do you think we had emergency pods? Anything can happen out here."

"But God—"

"God's protection isn't an excuse to be stupid. Move over."

"Don't blame him," I say.

"What, honey?"

"And could you both please stop yelling?"

"Honey, I can't hear you."

"This is a really unpleasant hallucination," I say, louder.

"What?" The doctor.

"This is a really unpleasant hallucination." This time, I yell it.

"No hallucination," says the doctor, but quieter. "You've just gone so long without sensory stimulation that your brain's overreacting. I've dimmed the lights, so you can open your eyes again."

Not blinded this time. Doctor leaning over me, frowning. My husband next to her, gripping the side of the pod. He doesn't look much older than when I'd gone in, only more tired. "How can I be sure this isn't a hallucination?"

"That depends on your mental state," the doctor says. I reach out my hand, and my husband takes it. The same as when I went in, but different, too. Thinner. A bit clammy. It shakes. I hold him tight as his love flows through me. Real. The doctor can tell I know. Her frown leaves, and she straightens.

"Why did you wake me up? Did you know I was aware? Did you find the planet?"

"How about I show you?" my husband says with a smile. A weak one, but still a smile. He and the doctor help me out of the pod. When she's poked and prodded and tested to determine my health, she lets us leave.

"I'm sorry for leaving you in there so long. If only I'd known—"

"Well, I'm awake now," I say. There's a lightness in my heart that wasn't there before. I feel like I could fly.

"And you're all right, too," my husband says. "Thank God." He takes me to the bridge and points. "Look."

And, to my light-starved eyes, there it is.

"A jewel of a planet in an ocean of stars," I say.

"Don't you recognize it?" my husband asks with concern. At my confusion: "It's Earth."

Earth! "How did you...?" But he shakes his head, a slow illumination of wonderment brightening on his face as he turns back to the sapphire orb, and I remember. "God."

I fall on my knees in worship.

—— « o » ——

Thea van Diepen

Thea is the author of the White Changeling series, which so far includes Hidden in Sealskin, and Like Mist Over the Eyes. By the time the print edition of Compostela is out, she will be back in Canada from a year of travel, eagerly awaiting a real winter. She is currently living in a church in Japan, where she teaches English and is learning how to read hiragana via worship songs. Find her online at: www.theavandiepen.com or https://twitter.com/theavandiepen

Resignation

Michaela Hiebert

5 March 2864

77.542.709 Riter Street

Worsley, North Alberta

Dear Theven:

I'm not coming in to work tomorrow. Actually, I'm not coming in to the factory ever again. I'm sorry for the inconvenience and for dumping it on you like this, but there's really nothing I can do.

You see, I went for a bio-scan today.

I was walking past one of those mobile clinics and thought hey, why not. It's been a while since I've been scanned and those commercials with the green cat say I should go at least twice a month. You know the ones, the really annoying spots with the jingle about bio-terrorism. I was humming that stupid preppy tune all the way into the clinic.

Then that medibot locked me in this quarantine room.

I didn't like the thing, it was from the Austen5 line. Their bedside manner is pretty shoddy. Our Grimshaws have better communication skills and they do construction work.

Anyways as it turns out, I have something called "Wapiti Measles". I asked the Austen5 why it was called "Elk Measles" but it just printed out a disease factsheet and left. I feel fine right now, but I should expect to have all my skin blister and fall off within a few days. Oh, and I'm going to get a hell of a fever. But right now I'm more concerned about the whole skin thing.

I figure I got it from my neighbour, Anah; she came back from a conference down in the Oregon Desert a few days ago.

Everyone at the factory should get checked in case I infected them somehow. I've been working on my own on that transmission problem for about a week now so you should be okay. I think the medibots are sending in a contamination team to sanitize my station though. Sorry.

I'm pretty calm about it all, considering. I'm going to have to leave my body soon, but not in the way you think.

They made me an offer.

The Austen5 took some information off my chip after the scan and pinged it somewhere. It had me in this Q-box for about an hour before I realised that that meant something.

Theven, a Conscience came to see me. It was a woman named Chesleah Redbird-Kendrick who used to be a farmer out in Nunavut. I remember her from that book you gave me for Christmas last year. She's been on at least 14 missions so far and relayed a countless amount of usable data back to the MainStation.

She wants me to become a Conscience. She says that my experience as an engineer more than qualifies me and that the Wapiti won't affect my brain at all. They can extract my consciousness before my body deteriorates and put me in a Lyon47.

You read that right. A shiny, new, bells and whistles Lyon47.

They're recruiting for the East Andromeda Survey Station, I'd be going out with a team of 50 Consciences and a cargo of several hundred Probers to survey several target sectors for habitability. This is huge, Theven. I'm so pumped.

I hope you know how much it means to me that you're as crazy about this stuff as I am. Can I write to you? No pressure, but I think you're one of the few people I know who isn't going to mourn me as dead.

I'm telling you all of this because I know how excited you'll be for me. I know that not everyone will be, and that's okay. It's hard to separate mind and body. More than that, most people think that it's a waste of money and resources to search the stars for life, for a new home. They want to fix the one we have. But we can't fix it, Theven. It's too far gone. We're too far gone.

On that note, I'm going to ask something unfair of you. I'm sorry.

Can you tell my parents what happened? What's happening?

I know they're not going to understand, but they deserve to know. I haven't spoken to them in years, it hurt them too much when I decided to design for the factory. Noa and Carmn are Earthies, you see. They live in a commune just south of Whitehorse where they help run a small soy farm. I was raised not to use waves, not to trust bots, and to despise any venture that took resources away from our planet.

They believe we are alone. To them, Earth is the only home we will ever have. But Earth is turning against us: We're all going to burn here.

Tell them I love them. Tell them I'm happy.

Cover up your electro-tats before you set foot on the farm.

Thank you so much,

Jennix

PS: I forgot to mention that Carmn raises Hunter Bees. Be careful how you break the news to her. Thanks.

—— « o » ——

Michaela Hiebert

Michaela is a recent University of Calgary graduate who is already missing the stimulation that her English degree had to offer. She spends her new-found free time reading, writing, and yelling at the television. Born in Brooks, Alberta, Michaela enjoyed the prairie life until she was nine, when her family picked up and moved to the small northern town of Fairview, Alberta. It's been a nomad's life ever since, and she wouldn't have it any other way.

Epilogue

Guy Immega

"Enter!" The wattled mud hut muffled the Matriarch's voice.

Morning light illuminated the thatched dwelling in the centre of the compound. Eight identical huts surrounded the Matriarch's house with a palisade fence beyond. Cleared jungle opened the sky above the village. In this small world the Matriarch wielded absolute power.

As a sign of respect, Luci stuffed her blonde hair beneath her cape. She crawled on hands and knees through the low entry in the slanted wall. The packed dirt floor was damp, swept clean. The musty odor of jungle decay receded to the pungent smell of smoked spine-turtle meat hanging under the low ceiling.

A glowing fruit — connected by a thin vine to a rectangular flower on top of the hut — illuminated the Matriarch in her wicker chair. A soft robe of chewed lizard leather decorated with purple fan-bush tassels covered her thin body. Kneeling, Luci looked up at the wizened face, eyes invisible in the gloom. Some called her the Queen of Valencia but to Luci she looked like an ancient crone.

"You know why I summoned you." The Matriarch's tone made Luci feel guilty.

Luci bowed her head and tried to hold back a cough. Unsuccessful, she hacked twice while covering her mouth. "I think so," she gasped.

"Forest Clan numbers only twenty-four adults after seven generations on Valencia. When I was young, we were thirty-two. You've miscarried twice and the third was stillborn. You're barren."

Luci wiped tears with the back of her hand. "I can't help it."

"Now you're sick and cannot work or find food. With the help of your husband you've hidden your malady for a year-month. Your illness could spread and kill our babies."

Luci bowed her head. "I'll get better soon." With no remedy, her cough had worsened.

"I doubt it. I'm usually sympathetic and merciful. You're a good person, but that's not enough. You're now banished — you must leave the village before dark."

Although Luci had anticipated the Matriarch's edict, the words crushed her. She couldn't live alone in the jungle.

"Can Rick come with me?" He was her mate and nurse. He shared his meat ration with her.

"No. We need him here. He's our best hunter, an asset to the clan. I've promised him my granddaughter, Delilah — she'll soon be ripe and ready. We need more breeders if the clan is to survive. Now go before you sicken me, too."

Luci suppressed another cough as she crawled backwards out of the hut. She looked up at the Matriarch, hoping for a reprieve. None came.

When she emerged, weeping, Rick reached for her hand and led her to their hut.

"Where can I go?" cried Luci. "I only know life in the village."

Rick paused before speaking. "We could make a pilgrimage to the *Lifeboat* — it's the sanctuary of the Mother Goddess. Maybe her magic can cure you. I'll go with you."

Luci didn't believe the legends. "How far is it?"

"It's a two season-week trek to the ocean. Nobody has been back in living memory."

"I don't want to go." She choked back tears. "I'm too weak to travel that far. What if we get lost in the jungle?"

"I think I can find the way. We must leave now before the Matriarch orders your death. Together we'll make it."

Rick dressed himself in a leather jerkin and trousers. Tan fur covered his broad back but he had a smooth, baby face and a thin beard. Luci handed him his spear. She wrapped her ankle-length cloak over the thin flesh on her neck, back and arms.

Rick's devotion overwhelmed her. "Thanks for helping me. The Matriarch will be furious."

"I don't care. Let's go before she interferes." Rick shouldered a large rucksack and led the way.

A cluster of people stood next to the palisade gate to witness the banishment. Luci looked at them but they averted their eyes, fearing the Matriarch's displeasure — and Luci's disease. Her father handed her a small bag of food, tubers and nuts. Nobody said goodbye but her mother sobbed. Luci looked back to see the gate close and hear the wooden bar slide shut. A quick death would have been kinder.

— «» —

Triple-blazed cone trees, slash-marks old and overgrown, marked the trail to the coast. Luci followed Rick, placing her feet in his footsteps to conserve energy. The blue-green jungle canopy, raucous with animal calls, blocked most of the light from the perpetually cloudy sky. Rick used his stone-tipped spear as a walking stick, swishing it through thickets to scare predators and flush game. Little stirred in the valley except crawler mites and hooker bugs. Rick gave Luci smoked snacks, compressed balls of meat and fat. She chewed each bite to savor the flavor and try to feel full.

They stopped for the evening when it started to rain. Exhausted from the long hike, Luci shivered and retched pink phlegm. Lacking a tent or bedding, they donned leather capes and woven bark hats. Rick crouched on the forest duff under a tree and held Luci's back to his chest to shield her from the rain and keep her warm. She dozed fitfully, disturbed by a nightmare memory of her dead baby, mottled skin and sightless blue eyes. Rick squeezed her and hummed tunelessly.

Rick woke Luci at first light. His wide-brimmed hat looked ridiculous, like a giant wilted flower. He stopped her when she tried to take hers off.

"Why do I have to wear this? I can't see forward or sideways — only my feet."

"There's a sniper sloth nest up ahead, where the trail narrows though a rock canyon. They live in a grove of chisel-leaf trees on either side. Don't look up as we pass below."

Luci knew about the treetop predator, the most dangerous in the jungle. Her brother had died when a poisonous bullet tooth, shot with compressed steam through the sloth's nose barrel, had lodged in his neck. The toxin paralyzed him, allowing the pack of slow-moving carnivores to consume his body. Rick had found Sam's head still attached to the skeleton the next day. Luci shivered and wrapped her cape around her chest.

As they approached the sniper nest, Luci heard staccato sounds — pffft-whistle, pfft-whistle — of fired poison darts. Volleys ratcheted back and forth. Clouds of steam hung in the treetops.

"Let's hurry!" she whispered.

Rick held her elbow. "Keep still. They track moving targets."

Luci crouched behind a fan bush. Deadly darts fell to the ground, straight white teeth capped with slimy green toxin. None hit her cap or cape. Rick knelt beside her and lifted the brim of his hat.

"Be careful!" she said. "What do you see?"

"They aren't aiming at us. I think it's a battle. Two packs of sniper sloths are firing at each other."

"Why?"

"Territory," said Rick. "Food targets are concentrated by the canyon. Game is scarce near the village so they hunt each other."

As they watched, a large sloth fell to the ground. It made a thin squeal and waved its legs, long claws raking the air. Darts riddled its matted hair, still embedded in flesh.

Its carrion odor made Luci cough. The sloth responded to the sound and swung its long, conical snout in her direction. The muzzle in the tip gleamed of polished bone. The creature inhaled three times, ramping pressure.

"Look out!" cried Rick.

The sloth hissed and puffed steam from its nose as it fired a bullet tooth. The sharp point penetrated the weave of Luci's hat. She felt a tingling sensation in her scalp before she blacked out.

— «» —

Luci woke to Rick pumping his hands between her breasts. Her chest felt sore and she pushed him away. Afternoon light penetrated the canopy from above. He must have spent hours forcing her to breathe. She coughed bloody sputum when she sat up. Rick offered her water and waited for her to speak.

Luci looked at the dead sniper sloth. The trees above were quiet. "Are they gone?"

"I don't think so," said Rick. "It'll take them time to recover from the battle."

"Good. I need to rest."

"Not now. The fighters must be hungry and I doubt they've used up all their ammunition. New bullet teeth grow inside the jaw in hours. Let's get going before they start hunting again."

Rick pulled Luci to her feet. He broke branches to clear the way as they passed through the canyon. The forest canopy on the other side seemed more open, letting in extra sunlight.

"I've never been in this part of the jungle before," said Rick. "We hunters don't go past the sniper nest at the entrance to the canyon." Luci followed Rick, forcing herself to walk, still weak from the sloth toxin.

At midday she noticed a moving rock covered in moss. "It's a spine turtle! I've never seen one before." The giant beast crept on forest litter, leaving a mulched trail of chewed vegetable detritus. No head or feet were visible.

"Good spotting," said Rick. "The thick shell stops sniper sloth darts. Nothing preys on a spine turtle."

"Except humans!" said Luci.

Rick frowned. His bushy eyebrows produced a vertical crease in his broad forehead. "It's taboo to kill it. They live for thousands of year-months and reproduce slowly. Our hunters almost wiped them out."

"The Matriarch eats spine turtle — royal privilege." Hunger made her desperate. "We aren't near the village."

Rick hesitated. "Okay, help me flip it." He wedged the tip of his spear in the ground under the turtle. As he levered the other end, Luci pushed on the edge of the carapace. The effort made her light headed. At last the heavy beast rolled onto its spiny back. Two rows of clawed feet churned the air. The tentacles on its scoop mouth wriggled, revealing bony chewing plates.

"It's so weird," said Luci. "Does it really have rocks in its stomach?"

"Yes, for ballast. It eats small animals that live in the forest litter. It doesn't need eyes."

"Look!" said Luci. "It's got an egg sac between the rows of legs."

Rick peeled the bag from the belly of the turtle. "These are good to eat. Let's take them and let the turtle live."

Luci felt relieved. "Good." Together, they rolled the beast upright while avoiding the spines on its back. The animal made a cooing sound and lumbered back into the jungle.

While Luci rested, Rick made camp and started a fire from embers stored in a copperwood box. He cooked the spherical eggs at the edge of the coals. Luci ate two tangy yokes and felt strength flow into her body. After the meal they continued hiking.

— «» —

Luci listened to crashing sounds from the squat cone trees — thick at the bottom and tapered at the top — as they whipped in the wind. Gusts and lightning in the dark forest snapped large branches, thinning the canopy. Rick tightened his arms around her and rubbed her feet to keep them warm. Daily downpours made fire impossible so they lived on cold turtle eggs. At least the forest streams provided ample drinking water. When Luci coughed, Rick watched her with a worried expression. She wanted to say that she loved him but felt unworthy.

As the forest trail widened at the edge of the jungle, Rick speared a razor-tongued lizard and cooked the fat legs and tail. Luci ate her fill and felt stronger. Rick consumed a smaller portion and saved the rest. While she rested and watched, he extracted the bony, serrated tongue and tied it to a wooden handle with hide strips.

He passed the dagger to her. "Careful, the blade is sharp."

She hefted its weight and balance. "Why do I need this?"

"To defend yourself. My great-grandfather warned that the ocean shoreline is dangerous."

Dread overwhelmed her — she didn't want a weapon. "I'm not sure I can make it to the *Lifeboat*." Trekking made her weary and hacking hurt her lungs. "Can we build a hut here? There's plenty of game for food."

"No, your cough will kill you. Even the clan is slowly dying in the jungle. We must keep moving."

Rick's words shocked Luci. Usually he said little and did what he could to please her. She nodded, too weak to argue.

As they walked through thinning forest, Luci heard the chirr of bush gliders. The shy creatures, smaller than her hand, had flattened bodies to extend their leaping range. They were delicious when roasted. Rick tried to catch one but he stumbled into a thicket with rocket slugs.

"Duck!" he called.

Luci crouched too late. Flying slugs, propelled by spraying poop, filled the air with green mist. The partially digested plant matter stuck to her face and body. The air reeked of fecal flatulence. She held her breath and steeled herself not to cough or retch. Rick led her to a nearby stream where they washed.

After another two-day trek, they arrived at the mouth of the wide Amazongo River. On the bank, isolated cone trees showed stubby branches with tufts of elongated leaves hanging from the tips, stunted by storms. Triangular kite-vines tethered on coiled stems dispersed seeds like puffs of smoke above the treetops.

Luci had heard of Valencia's ocean, an endless expanse covering most of the planet. She knew about Origin Beach where humans first came ashore. Green waves thundered onto rocks and sent spray high in the air. The ocean seemed urgent and violent compared to the jungle. How did humans cross the water?

"Look, there's the *Lifeboat*," said Rick, pointing to a rocky islet in the ocean. "You see, the stories weren't just myths. We made it!"

Luci squinted in the direction that Rick indicated. A grey bulk with pointed ends sat at an angle on the rocks, dented and covered with green slime. *Ugly!* She had expected something bigger and more impressive, worth their arduous journey. "It's too far out in the water. I can't swim."

"They say a giant wave tossed it onto the rocks long ago," said Rick. "I wondered if it would still be there."

Luci shrugged and looked at the waves washing the beach. "Are the crabs good to eat?" Even though she was sick, she still craved food. Breaking rollers crashed again on the shoreline, leaving flotsam that the crabs scavenged.

"Only the red ones ... if you can catch them," said Rick. "Be careful!"

Hungry, Luci ignored his warning and trudged in the soft sand down to the water's edge. The shoreline didn't look dangerous; there was no place for predators to hide. She took a deep breath — the sea air eased the ache in her lungs. The breeze fluffed her long hair and lifted her cape. Valencia's sun, a hazy orange patch behind swift-moving clouds to the northwest, warmed her face and chest. The open ocean gave a sense of space and freedom unknown in the dark jungle or inside a walled compound. A frothing wave crashed over her feet; the cold water made her dance. She laughed for the first time in twenty year-months.

Rick followed her, carrying his spear. Luci smiled at him but he looked at the sky. A spinning disc sailed past, rising on the updraft. "What's that?"

"I don't know!"

Luci ducked as another spinner tipped its arm-length body sideways, showing a single central eye that looked down on them. Rick jabbed with his spear but missed. In response, the creature flipped its body into the breeze and sailed directly onto Rick's face, covering his eyes, nose and mouth. He stumbled and fell backward from the impact, dropping his spear. As he clawed at his cheeks, the second flyer wrapped its membrane wing around the back of his head, forming a tight seal.

Luci ripped one creature off and stabbed it in the eye with her razor-tongue dagger. She peeled the second from his face and sliced its body open; clear blood turned blue in the air. A third hovered overhead and then dived at her. Luci swung at it with her blade, nicking the wing. The spinner veered away in an updraft.

Rick lay on the sand, gasping for breath. A second flock of gliders sailed toward them along the edge of the surf. The leader had an iridescent blue wing membrane and chirped as it spun.

"Run!" shouted Lucy. She dragged Rick to his feet and retrieved his weapon. Another spinner dived at her but skewered itself on the tip of the upright spear. They stumbled up the beach to a sheltered spot behind a giant cone tree.

Rick looked at the creature still writhing on the spear shaft. "Those must be the *wind-hoppers* that the old stories talked about. They smother and feed on anything that moves. They drove the original colonists away from the ocean — that's why the clan moved into the jungle."

Luci shivered as she watched the swarm pounce on their kin on the beach and feed on the still-twitching bodies. "Horrible creatures."

Rick's touched his cheek where the predator's beak had gouged a hole. Blood tinged his fingertip. "It tried to eat me alive. Thanks for saving me — I almost died."

Luci glowed with Rick's praise. "I'd do anything to help you."

— «» —

They camped above the Origin Beach, gathering red crabs at dusk when the wind-hoppers didn't fly. When the sea was calm, Rick tried wading to the *Lifeboat* but deep water stopped him. He found a floating log and pushed it ahead of him, kicking with his feet. A rogue wave pushed him back onto the beach. Luci helped him dry the fur on his back, glad he'd given up the attempt.

Winter-week brought gloomy twilight with no night or day. Wind and rain buffeted the coast; Luci rose early to add wood to the campfire. She looked seaward but saw only a vast expanse of mud and seaweed. She couldn't comprehend how the ocean could disappear. Where did the water go?

Rick squinted at the pebbly strand. "I remember a strange legend about tides and sea monsters. Now we can walk to the *Lifeboat*."

Luci didn't like leaving the safety of the beach but knew that Rick would insist. They banked the fire and trudged through the intertidal muck. Luci saw a stranded fish as long as her arm. It had sharp dorsal spines and two mouths: circular lower lips sucked mud while the larger, upper jaws had retractable fangs that snapped reflexively. Curious, Rick leaned close but the fish flipped its tail and leaped at him. Luci pulled him away. They reached the outcrop that supported the boat. The crumpled hull was wedged between two spires of rock.

Luci looked for signs of life on the derelict wreck. Nothing moved in the dim light. "I still don't understand why we came here."

"Hunters' legends say that humans came from the stars in this boat." Rick frowned and shook his head. "It's hard to believe."

"What are stars?" said Luci.

"They're burning sparks in the sky that never go out. I've never seen them."

"The women's stories say that the *Lifeboat* came from the ocean with many babies. I don't believe that, either."

Rick tapped his stone spear point on the hull and listened to the hollow sound. "I think it's some kind of metal, like the Matriarch's light."

Luci shivered as she scraped her finger through the algae on the side of the boat. "I can't stay here much longer. The wind is cold and it may rain. Let's go back to the cone trees where we're safe from wind-hoppers and I can get warm by the fire."

"No. Now that we've come all this way, we should look inside."

They climbed the rocks and stepped onto the boat. Luci saw the partially flooded seats at the back. Crimson crabs scuttled away. Rick pushed on the closed cabin door but it didn't budge. He braced his legs and shoved harder, using his broad back and arms. Each heave moved the door slightly.

Rick squeezed inside and helped Luci down. The dim interior reeked of mold and decay. A female form, slender and grimy, lay in the dust on the cabin floor. Luci tapped the corpse with her toe.

The creature jerked and sat up. "Welcome! I'm Robota."

Luci shrieked and backed away. "It's alive!" Rick crouched and leveled his spear, ready to lunge.

Arched eyebrow-lights blinked on. The creature rotated her head with quick, jerky motions, looking first at Luci and then at Rick. "I'm awake but I've never been alive. I'm just a machine, a nannybot here to nurse babies and help humans."

Luci struggled to understand Robota's strange speech. She mispronounced some words and others didn't mean anything. What was a machine? Luci looked at Robota's blank face. The big, unblinking eyes look surprised but the mouth was missing. How did it talk? Luci didn't trust this strange, inhuman thing.

"If you wanted to help us, why didn't you come to our village?" Rick still pointed his spear at Robota's chest.

"I've been trapped inside since the hatch corroded shut. I've waited hundreds of year-months to be set free — thank you." When Robota spoke, sound came from a slot in her neck, as if her throat was cut. "I wondered if my children had survived. Who are you?"

Rick remained silent.

"I'm Luci," she offered.

Robota nodded. "How can I help you, Luci?"

"Are you the Mother Goddess?" Luci recalled the legend of the *Lifeboat's* spirit.

"No. Mother-9 died long ago. She burned up in the sky and crashed into the ocean."

Luci didn't understand. "Could the Mother Goddess fly?" No myth mentioned this.

"Yes. Mother-9 — she hated being called a goddess — flew for a thousand years across space and dropped this *Lifeboat* into the ocean. Then she circled around Valencia until she died."

Robota's riddles frustrated Luci. She started to speak but a coughing fit prevented further questions. Her chest hurt from the effort to expel thick, pink mucous.

"You're sick," observed Robota. "I recognize a common lung infection. I can synthesize an antibiotic to cure it."

Luci — still wheezing and hacking — looked at Rick, who shrugged. She couldn't comprehend the big words. Without movement from Robota, a *whirring* noise commenced in the wall. After a minute, the nannybot reached into a hopper and withdrew a small brown ball. "Bite this and inhale."

Luci sniffed: it smelled like seaweed. "Is it good to eat?

"Yes — and it has medicine to prevent bronchospasm and cure pneumonia. Chew it and take a deep breath."

More strange words. Wary but desperate, Luci shrugged and nipped the ball with her front teeth. The bitter taste shocked her but the aromatic tang soothed her lungs.

"You'll get better soon," said Robota. "I've treated this disease before."

Luci inhaled and felt her chest relax. She sucked more air and the pain in her throat faded. The sudden improvement surprised her. "Thank you. I can breathe again." She swallowed the pill and turned to Rick. "You were right! Robota still has the magic of the Mother Goddess."

"Is there anything else you need?" said Robota. "I'm programmed to assist however I can." Her soft voice seemed sincere.

Luci hesitated but the nannybot's kind attention disarmed her. "My babies *always* die." The confession made her sob. Rick dropped his spear and put his arms around her.

Robota nodded. "That's a difficult problem. I'll need to sample your DNA — a cheek swab from each of you."

Luci didn't ask what DNA was but she submitted to the procedure. Robota switched on a light in her left index finger; a thin pipette extruded from the tip. "Open wide." After she collected the sample, she stuck her finger into a slot in the wall panel. "It'll take a few minutes to sequence your genotype." Rick refused to open his mouth so Robota swabbed his spear handle instead.

"I have bad news, Luci. You've got genetic abnormalities: translocation of genes between chromosomes. It's common — about one in a hundred pregnant women have this problem. I can't fix it."

Luci didn't understand the words but realized that she couldn't have a baby. She held Rick's hand and looked at Robota. "What can we do?"

"I can make a new egg for you using synthetic DNA, fertilized by Rick's sperm. He'll be the father and you'll birth a new bloodline of humans. That will add genetic diversity to the colony on Valencia."

Nothing Robota said made sense to Luci, "Will I be the mother?"

"No, the child won't carry your genes. But you'll be pregnant and give birth."

"I want my *own* baby." Lucy looked at Rick. "Let's try again." He smiled and squeezed her hand.

Robota didn't move. "You'll have another stillbirth."

Luci cringed at the memory. "If you give me a baby, will anybody notice that it isn't really mine?" She wanted to be welcomed back to the village with a healthy child.

"Not unless you tell them. I'll select the egg's genetic profile to resemble yours — and the infant will show features of the father. All humans on Valencia, including your ancestors, started with synthetic DNA. Mother-9 engineered GMO humans that can survive in Valencia's high gravity. That's why you have small breasts and big bones."

Luci looked at Robota. "Is the legend true that you made children on this *Lifeboat*?"

"Yes, but that was a long time ago. My artificial wombs don't work anymore or I'd still be birthing babies." Robota pointed to the brown rubber teats on her pale breasts. "I've nursed twenty-two infants already, all the ancestors of your clan."

So the women's stories were true. Luci turned to Rick. "What do you think?" More than ever, she yearned for a baby.

Rick nodded. "Let Robota try to help us. I want to be a father. You'll love our child and raise it as your own — I know it. "

After Robota had alleviated her cough, she decided to trust the magic of the Mother Goddess. "Okay. We'll make a new start."

— ‹› —

Luci and Rick returned to the *Lifeboat* two days later. Robota had explained IVF egg implantation but the medical terms made Luci nervous. Rick tried to reassure her.

Rick slid the cabin hatch open. "It works smoothly now."

Robota had cleaned the interior of the cabin and set up a bed in the middle of the floor. Luci reclined with her feet up on metal stirrups. Robota turned out the lights, except for bright points projected onto the dark ceiling from a perforated ball behind the head of the bed.

"What are those?" Luci asked, pointing up.

"That's a field of stars, a reproduction of the clear sky at night. There are billions of suns in our Milky Way Galaxy. Please relax and look at the constellations."

Luci tried to imagine space with stars. The spray of lights moved and twinkled. "They're beautiful!"

Robota worked in the dark using her eyebrow lamps. Luci looked down while Robota inserted a thin tube in her vagina. In a few moments Robota stood up. "All finished."

Luci rubbed her belly. Would a healthy baby grow inside? The thought left her breathless with hope and anxiety. "Am I pregnant now?"

"We'll know in a few days," said Robota. "You should live in the *Lifeboat* until the baby is born. I'll be your midwife and wet nurse — I make my own formula." With that, Robota expelled steam from her nipples. "That's how I sterilize the milk ducts!"

Luci chuckled — Robota's superhuman talents now seemed normal. She looked at the points of light that still shimmered above. "I want my baby to see *real* stars."

"Too bad it's always overcast on Valencia," said Rick.

"You're right," Robota replied, "with a few exceptions. Mother-9 surveyed the planet from space. The sky is often clear in the rain-shadow behind Mount Igneous. The volcano blocks the clouds."

"I wish I could go there now," said Luci. "It'll be boring staying here for nine year-months while I'm pregnant, like winter-week in our hut."

"If you like," said Robota, "I'll teach you both about the stars — and how to read and write. I have a library of all human knowledge."

Robota's offer opened Luci's mind. "Yes, I'd love that." She wanted to learn as much as possible. "When we return to the village, I'll teach the clan."

Robota produced a silver box. "Here is a special gift, a relic from Earth and Mother-9: your Mother Goddess."

Luci touched the polished metal. "What is it?"

Robota opened the lid. "It's a telescope for looking at the stars. You can take your students to Mount Igneous and study astronomy."

Luci lifted the instrument, a hollow tube with a shiny bowl at the bottom. "Show me how to use it."

"I will. Sometimes the night sky clears on the coast during summer-week. You'll see many stars and perhaps the Earth's sun, a tiny point of light.

Luci's excitement grew. Curious, she had to ask: "What is Earth?"

Robota projected an image of a blue ball onto the tablet display on her chest. "This was the first home of humans…"

—— « o » ——

Guy Immega

Guy Immega is a retired aerospace engineer and entrepreneur, living in Vancouver, Canada. His company, Kinetic Sciences Inc. built experimental robots for the space station, robots to clean up nuclear waste and miniature fingerprint sensors for cell phones. In 2005, he sold the corporate intellectual property to a Californian company.

Since that time Guy has published several science fiction short stories, completed a SF novel (now represented by Spectrum Literary Agency) and other nonfiction essays. Guy specializes in hard SF and realistic aliens. For more, see his website at: www.guyimmega.com.

After Midnight

For Harry the cat
After *Midnight* by Ian Burgham

David Clink

I take a boat hitched to my front door,
tell Harry it looks like a storm is coming.

He knows I am leaving.

He retreats to his not-so-secret hideaway
underneath the dining room table, above the boxes.

I am not seaworthy.

I close and lock the door, row to work.
When I return, he has disappeared.

When he reappears behind the couch
he has questions for me.

I was looking out the window, he says,
when I saw a skyline of skeletons,

a waterfall, the dead dog-paddling
to the sound of the ticking kitchen clock.

They are exiled from their crypts,
on a pilgrimage. Why?

They want to be memorable,
I tell him, putting out fresh water.

The spires are the eyebrows
of a fallen giant raised in prayer.

There is a reassurance in the black arts.
A calm sea does not stay that way for long.

Harry knows I am learning—
I am a sailor leaving wet footprints on a shore.

Harry knows moonlight, moments.
His black and white markings, a message.

He knows the weightlessness of space,
other words for breath, the violence of discovery.

Harry sits on the top of the sofa
looking out the window
as if it were stuck on the fish tank channel.

While I'm at work:
early light. Beams stretch, move, fade.
Water splashes against the embankment.

All fish metaphors are wet.

To Harry, the apartment is recognition,
plateaus to lie on, a graveyard where
every piece of furniture is a tombstone.

And the water keeps rising.

—— « O » ——

David Clink

David Clink is the author of four collections of poetry, including two that are genre collections: *Monster* (Tightrope Books – 2010); and *The Role of Lightning in Evolution* (Chizine Publications – 2016). His speculative poetry has appeared five times in Analog, thrice in Asimov's, and twice in On Spec. He has been a finalist for the Aurora and Rhysling awards, and the Asimov's Readers Choice award. His poem, *A sea monster tells his story* won the Aurora Award for Best Poem / Song, in 2013.

Buried, But Not Dead

Garnet Johnson-Koehn

"For the record, this is insane."

"I know. That's why it's going to make us rich."

Evangeline grinned inside her helmet. The heavy door sagged slightly as the thermal tape ate through it, the edges glowing a sullen crimson from the sudden, immense application of heat. "Look at that," she murmured, as the tape burned clear through, "Not so much as a puff. Shut this place down nice and thorough, and locked it up tight."

"I suspect there was a reason for that." Zachariah sounded tense, even over the slightly tinny earbud. "Possibly an apocalyptic one."

"Don't tell me you believe those bedtime stories." Evangeline grunted, straining to move the unpowered, untethered door. The microgravity was negligible, but the door still massed a fair bit, and tethered to the naked rock as she was Evangeline didn't have much leverage. Bracing herself as best she could, she hauled until the door had enough momentum to float free, then turned to shine her wrist-lights down into the opening. "Come on, you really think they created monsters out here?"

"I think the Technocracy originally sealed Deimos off for a reason." He was back in the ship, the *Stony Road*, watching things from the flight deck. Not that the *Road* had much else; it was basically a control platform and basic living space bolted to a massive cargo hold. A massive, and presently empty, cargo hold. "I think the Authority later quarantined the entire Martian sub-system for a reason. And I think we don't want to find out what either of those reasons were."

"You want a safe life, stay on the dirt." Evangeline watched her suit-light play over bare grey-panel walls. Inside was an airlock, big enough for perhaps two at a time, if they were friendly, and fit. "You want to come out into the black with me? Get used to the edge."

"The closer to the edge, Eva, the easier it is to fall off." Zachariah spoke slowly, the comment coming out more as a carefully-delivered lesson than a clever little zinger. He tended to speak slowly. At first she'd taken it personally, but over time she realized that Zachariah just thought everyone was just a little behind his curve. "And even assuming we execute this plan without any complications, any goods we salvage from here would be classed as forbidden items and confiscated. Without compensation."

"Any goods we *admit* to salvaging from here," Evangeline corrected. She reached down, pulling a second clip from her waist. The powerful magnet at the end clamped to the wall, a relief given that some of these old facilities were pure ceramic. Secured, she detached her tether from the moonlet's surface and began to haul herself inside. "But the Authority's cutting back everywhere, and the patrols out here basically don't exist. They're counting on fear and legends to keep this place quiet, but I don't believe the legends and I'm not afraid. And if we claim we found this stuff somewhere else, maybe on a derelict in the Belt or the like, well, what's the harm?"

"I don't know." Zachariah sighed, long and low. "I don't know, Eva, and that's what worries me. What is the harm that convinced two different governments to lock down this facility for the last seventy years?"

"Dunno," Evangeline replied, her feet passing through the doorway, entirely within the boundaries of the orbital facility. Above her head, the great red face of crater-scarred Mars loomed, its solitary remaining satellite tidally locked, the concealed facility always looking down on its mother planet. "Let's find out."

— «» —

The facility at Deimos had no name. Or, it had a name, most likely, but not one that anyone still living knew. When Evangeline had first learned of its existence, through drunken gossip and post-closing braggadocio, it had been referred to with the same name as the planetoid itself. As though whatever had been done there had subsumed the reality of the little moonlet, forever marking the celestial body with the secrets of the rumoured facility.

Right from the first, Evangeline had known she'd have to go there.

She moved into the airlock and reached out, grasping the heavy handle built into the wall. The power to the facility would have faded decades ago, but there were manual overrides for just this sort of reason. Evangeline used the handle as a point of leverage to bring her feet down, planting them on what she arbitrarily decided was the floor, then used her footing in turn to lever the handle. It resisted for a moment, then ground upwards, slowly and unevenly, and as it did the curved panels of the iris parted. As it reached the apex of its swing the handle clicked, locking into place, and Evangeline reached out to shine the wrist-light into the facility proper, at last. Without any atmospheric diffusion her light was a sharp-edged cone, though the end trailed off still, disappearing into the depths. The internal space was, as expected, an utterly generic passageway leading off through doorways along the sides. Nothing exciting there, but she hadn't come here for the contents of the foyer.

She'd come for the safe in the basement.

Dragging herself in, Evangeline began to drift down the hall. Deimos was too small even to be spherical, an oblong mass not unlike a lumpy little potato floating through space, so it was certainly too small to have any kind of noticeable gravitational effect. From the layout of the hallways, though, there had been gravity generators here, once; the door edges were flush against the floor, rather than in the middle of the wall, and they were aligned along a horizontal axis, nothing sunk into the floor or ceiling. For Evangeline, who was no great fan of microgravity, the fact that those generators were no doubt as inoperable as the rest of the facility was a considerable shame.

"Though I think I'd prefer some lights, just about now," she muttered to herself. The facility was without even emergency lighting, and burrowed as it was into the heart of a planetoid a good 1.3 AU out from the warming light of Sol even at its closest pass, the nameless facility inside Deimos could not possibly have been less well lit. Evangeline wasn't scared, exactly, but she'd have been less not-scared if she could see anything not directly within the path of her suit-light.

"I am actually reading a faint energy signature."

"Holy frick!" Evangeline cried out as Zachariah's voice broke the silence, broadcasting at a conversational tone through her earbud. In the silence and gloom, she'd forgotten there was anyone else out there. Her pulse raced, her heart hammering at the insides of her ribs as she flailed for a moment. "Good god damn, Zachariah! A warning, next time!"

"I'm sorry, Eva." He didn't sound like it, though. "As I was saying, I'm reading a faint energy signature. I think the airlock might have been blocking it, previously."

"Energy signature, huh?" She grinned, and inside her gloves, her palms began to itch. That familiar, tingling sensation that meant there was money in the air. "Anything still running has got to be a serious piece of hardware. And that means it'll be seriously valuable."

"Or dangerous." She could hear the frown in his voice, the set of his jaw and the arms folded across his chest. He was so disapproving, sometimes. He reminded her of her mothers, actually. They had disapproved of so many of her choices. "It's either a security system, a trap, or something that, for whatever reason, they couldn't turn off."

"Any one of those work for me, just so long as I can pull it out and sell it." She grabbed a passing door edge and swung herself around, grunting as her back landed heavily against wall. She planted her boots on the floor and flipped on the sole-magnets, feeling the comforting resistance as she flexed her knees and did not, in fact, float up towards the ceiling. "Alright, so what have we got, here," she muttered, raising her left arm. The flexible panel worked into the forearm lit up at a touch, projecting a holographic interface. She flipped through screen after hazy blue-green screen until she found what she was looking for.

"Alright, feed me the *Road's* sensor results." For a moment there was just the still, blank 'No Input' placeholder, and then a washed out image of Deimos appeared, scaled down but still resplendent in all its lumpy glory. Near the centre of the little moon a brighter haze took shape, a smear roughly two-thirds of the way along the glorified asteroid's long axis. "Really? That's the best you can do?"

"Given the equipment available, yes." Zachariah cleared his throat. "If you recall, I did recommend upgrading the primary sensor suite during our most recent refit. If that upgrade had been undertaken, I would be able to narrow this considerably."

"Alright, alright," Evangeline sighed, sorry she'd even asked. Given how much of the *Road* was falling apart it wasn't hard to forget getting nagged about any particular piece being junk. "But, listen," she said, damping down the magnets in her boots and kicking off, down the hallway again, "That's all the more reason to go for this. If we can move a power source that can run for decades without maintenance at just a fraction of what it'd be worth, I dare you to find a top of the line piece of gear we won't be able to put into the *Road*!"

There was silence on the other end of the comm line, and Evangeline grinned as she floated down the hall. If there was one thing in the void that Zachariah could be swayed by, it was the promise of better equipment.

"I shall attempt to narrow the search area." Her grin widened as Zachariah spoke up, stretching until it wouldn't have surprised her if the top of her head came clean off.

"Good boy."

— «» —

Deimos was dead.

The moonlet had never harboured any kind of native life, of course. It was too small to generate the gravity necessary to hold anything down, too solid for anything to live under its surface, and too exposed to the harsh solar winds and radiation scouring for even the hardiest surface extremophiles. In that sense, it had always been dead, and likely always would be.

But it wasn't the lack of native organisms that made Evangeline feel the deadness around her. The facility had been emptied out, with a deliberation that made the back of her neck tingle. There were no open doors, no tools floating freely, nothing unsecured or out of place. She cranked open a few doors, and inside each she saw the same thing, over and over again. Beds, neatly made and vacuum sealed. Desktops swept clean and clear. Chairs pushed in and locked down. There was nothing out of place, not a single sign of a living human presence anywhere.

Evangeline felt a chill along her spine, one that had nothing to do with the carefully regulated temperature of her spacesuit. Her slow exploration of the abandoned facility had taken nearly two hours now, and she was only just nearing the centre, her marker converging on the smeared blur of the energy signature. She had spent every second of that trip alone, not the slightest hint of movement visible around her, the silence broken only occasionally by Zachariah. She'd wanted him to talk at first, to keep her occupied, but the further into the facility she penetrated the more distant his voice had sounded, though the earbud broadcast at its usual volume, and her suit confirmed it was receiving properly. Eventually she'd told him she needed to concentrate, used focus as an excuse for silence.

It was better, in some regards. Worse in others.

As she reached the next intersection Evangeline paused, anchoring herself to the floor. As she brought her legs down, and they encountered the slight resistance of the magnetic pull, she realized her legs were shaking. There was sweat on her forehead, running down her back, sweat from exhaustion but not from exertion. Moving through the facility was easy; a push to start moving, the odd touch on the wall to correct for drift or spin. It wasn't the act of moving that was wearing her out, it was what she was moving through.

Evangeline bit her lip, trying to slow her pulse, trying to force herself to relax. The longer she spent in it, the more the emptiness weighed on her. This place wasn't just uninhabited, it had been stripped of any evidence it had ever been inhabited; in all the rooms she'd floated through, all the doors she'd forced apart, all the cabinets and cupboards she'd pulled open, none had shown a single human touch. No notes, no pictures, no marker boards, not the smallest charm or tchotchke anywhere. For all the wear and tear it showed, the facility might as well have been newly constructed, or even just wished into existence the minute before Evangeline first blew the doors.

And yet it was decades old, and from what little she'd been able to gather from the unofficial records, a key research facility during the wars. Not as important as shattered Phobos, of course, which was why it was still in one piece, but still not the kind of place that would've been set up and forgotten about. The fact that it looked factory fresh, that at any moment she expected to open a door to find furnishings still wrapped in plastic, sealed for delivery, made her skin crawl.

"C'mon," she whispered to herself, even that low tone echoing in the silence of her helmet, and the void beyond its thin protective layers. More than just her legs were shaking, now. "Come. On." She closed her eyes, and forced herself to breathe, slow and steady. "Okay, so you're freaked out by the abandoned secret base. That's fine. That's normal. It'd be weird if you weren't having a panic attack. Everything's perfectly normal."

Slowly the tension receded, her heart rate slowing to something at least approaching normal. It was still there, lurking, but at least she could function. Drawing a steadying breath, she kicked off, propelling herself forwards once more.

The intersection she'd stopped at was the last along the facility's central corridor. At the end was a doorway, huge and circular, and like the airlock covered by a spiralling iris. As she drifted towards it, Evangeline felt the familiar itch in her palms, and despite the lingering worry she couldn't keep her lips from skinning back from her teeth. There was money on the other side of that door, or at least something she could turn into money, and ultimately that was just as good. Maybe better, even, since turning something into money usually made a good story, and then she could turn that story into drinks, too.

"Alright, whatever you are," she said, grinning as she reached for the door's manual lever, "Come to mama."

— «» —

"Evangeline?"

The word came through weak and faint, as if from down a long hallway. There was a metallic twang around the edges of it. Standing just inside the great circular doorway, Evangeline frowned, reflexively raising a hand to the side of her helmet. "Zachariah? Can you hear me?"

"Barely." There was static on the line now, crackling along the underside of the conversation. "There is heavy interference. I recommend withdrawing, for now."

It was the smart move, she knew. This was weird space, terra incognita unmapped and unmarked. Anything could be there, and that included just about any danger the human mind could conceive, which given thousands of years of perverse ingenuity was quite a lot indeed. But as she stared up into the room at the centre of the planetoid, Evangeline couldn't quite bring herself to take that first step backwards.

"Boost the signal," she said, instead. "And start working on your wish list. Once I'm done here, we're going shopping."

The room was huge, a great circular space carved into the heart of the dead moon. Work stations ringed the single, continuously-curving wall, displays tilted face-down on the desk tops, powered down and dark. That wasn't what was making her palms itch, though; the stations had probably been ahead of the curve decades earlier, but they were too old to be decent machines and not old enough to be worth anything as antiques yet. In the centre of the room, though, was the treasure trove Evangeline had come hunting for.

"Just be careful."

Evangeline could imagine Zachariah, leaning forwards over the control console, hunching the way he did whenever they were trying to thread a customs patrol net. It was cute, the way he worried. She grinned behind her helmet, and nodded. "Can't spend anything if I'm dead."

Releasing her boot magnets, Evangeline floated across the open space, barely resisting the urge to lick her lips. In the centre of the room, its base wide and sturdy, its crown spreading outwards in concentric circles, was a great cylindrical computer core. Around the middle of the trunk was a console ring, four equidistant stations, their input panels folded out and their displays still raised.

And unlike everything else in the abandoned facility, there were lights shining on it.

"Baby," she whispered, reaching out towards the trunk of the cylinder, to bring herself to a halt, "You're going to make me rich."

"Did-"

Zachariah's voice disappeared in a blast of static, a metallic squeal that made her teeth grind together. Reflexively she turned, the sudden jerk of motion spinning her in circles, away from the great trunk.

"Zachariah?" She reached for the panel on her left forearm, checking the status of her comm line. An ugly red bar filled the line's tag. Evangeline punched at her controls, cycling the connection, trying to find another range that wasn't filled with hissing static. "God damn it, Zachariah, can you hear me? Come in? Come in!"

/Your associate cannot hear you./

Evangeline's eyes widened, and she spun again, drifting in circles and lashing out wildly.

/Do not be afraid./

The voice in her ear was jagged, syllables oddly accented, and it took her a long, panicked moment to realize where the voice was coming from. She was in a sealed suit, in a facility stripped of all atmosphere.

It only sounded like someone was whispering in her ear.

Evangeline thrashed for purchase, finally managing to catch herself on the ceiling, above the door frame. Flicking her wrist-lamp down, she could see the thick wedges were locked in place once more, the doorway sealed tight. Bracing herself with her other hand, she sent the beam playing around the chamber, hunting for any sign of movement, of life. "Who's there! Show yourself!"

/Look closer./

Evangeline frowned. So far as she could see, she was the only living thing in the space, her movements the only signs of life. The only signs, other than...

"Are... you the computer?" Her eyes narrowed. The lights were still glowing, but now there were more of them, and as she watched more still flickered on. And not just along the trunk, but the ring console as well, its displays stuttering and flashing as they re-initialized after so many decades. There was a sound in her earbud, a harsh, rhythmic sound; it took Evangeline a moment to realize it was supposed to be laughter.

/'Computer'. An insufficient term. Are you the meat and the bones and the blood?/ The static-laced laughter sounded again, making her skin crawl. The laughter cut, suddenly, more like a file closing than speech petering out. /Hello. I am Ilia./

Evangeline swallowed, nervous. There were stories that the Technocracy had actually gone ahead with AI research. Legends said they'd been desperate enough to ignore the lessons of Tokyo and New Mumbai, trying for anything that would give them an edge. She hadn't believed it, even growing up on stories of how evil the Martian War Machine was, what a nightmare factory their laboratories and research camps had been. Even they couldn't have been desperate enough, stupid enough, to try to build on a foundation of twenty million corpses. That's what she'd thought, sure in her adolescent omniscience, dismissive of ghost stories and bogeymen.

/Are you frightened, Evangeline?/

"What? No! I, I mean, no, of course not." Evangeline pushed off the ceiling, floating slowly towards the great trunk, the lights incongruously soft and inviting. A shiver ran down her spine. "Wait. How did you know my name?"

/The packet protocols for your communications carry a multitude of data. You are Evangeline Chao. You are transmitting to the Tranquility-class cargo vessel *Stony Road*. Your suit components range between two and twelve years old. The *Stony Road* is registered as being built on Luna twenty-six years ago, though its components range between six months and thirty-one years old. Would you like me to continue?/

Given sufficient time, and a quiet place to think undisturbed, Evangeline thought she might be able to come up with something she wanted less than that. Aloud, though, she said, "Uh, your time frames are a little off. The newest piece on my suit is just over a year old."

/All time frames are New Martian standard./

"Oh. Right."

Evangeline reached out, catching herself on one of the ring stations. She tapped at the console, cursing the clumsiness of her heavy gloves; Zachariah had tried to convince her to splurge on some real detail-work gear, but she'd shot it down as an extravagance. The fact that the programming languages were decades out of date didn't help, either.

/What are you doing, Evangeline?/

She hissed, tensing up. She hadn't even realized her suit could do surround sound. It was like someone was standing just behind her. "I'm just curious," she said, fighting the urge to look back. There was nothing there. It was all just a trick of the senses. "I've never met something like you, before. I, I want to know more about you."

/You are attempting to access my program. That will not be possible./ The panel in front of her flickered, a sharp red slash appearing across the interface. /However, I would be happy to answer any questions you may have. Please, Evangeline. Simply ask me./

"Sure. Okay." She punched the console in frustration, the red-slash locking her out of everything worth trying to get into. "So, Ilia," she said, talking to fill the silence more than because she expected an honest answer, "What's, uh, what's the most valuable thing here, huh?"

/The single most expensive piece of equipment installed at this location was the quantum field generator, valued at 6.4 million marks./

The bottom fell out of Evangeline's world for a moment. "Did ... six million marks? Six *million* marks?"

/Fraternas Industries quantum field generator, super-heavy, with integrated decompiler and microsupport systems. Market value, 7.02 million marks, purchase cost via wholesale agreements, 6.13 million marks, transportation, installation and servicing, .06 million marks. Total value also includes .01 million marks, incidental and non-itemized costs./

"Six million marks. Holy shit." Evangeline tried not to hyperventilate. It wasn't easy.

/You can't have it./

"I, what?" Evangeline blinked, a laugh bubbling up before she could stop it. There was a hysterical edge to it. "What, you're going to stop me?"

/I need it./

"You think I don't?" Evangeline licked her lips. The itch in her palms was so fierce it felt like fire. "Look, the door was a nice trick, but you can't really do anything to stop me."

That awful grating noise sounded in her earbud again, the simulated laughter. It was short this time, a sharp little burst. / That is very funny, Evangeline./

"What's that, Ilia?" She was already twisting at the waist, looking around the room for another doorway, an access point. Her wrist-lamp played across the wall panels, sweeping slowly along them. "What's funny?"

There was no answer, and Evangeline frowned. She hadn't enjoyed speaking with the AI, but this silence seemed worse.

"Ilia?" She jabbed at the ring console, pulling herself around to other sections to see if any of the other stations would react. "What's funny? Ilia!"

She only saw it because she happened to glance down down, orienting herself as she drifted around the great trunk of the computer core. On her HUD, two small looping arrows crossed by a slash. It was such a tiny thing, so small she'd almost overlooked it. That was why there were supposed to be alarms, why something was supposed to warn her in the event of even the slightest interruption, the smallest problem.

The shutdown of her suit's C/O2 scrubbers couldn't be considered a small problem.

Evangeline resisted the urge to gasp. Fear was the enemy; it would gobble up her air, quick as a wink. Instead, hard as it was, she forced herself to breathe slowly, steadily. Her faceplate was already beginning to fog, the world beyond its curved confines blurring faintly. Briefly, she thought of her mothers.

/I was created to learn./

Evangeline closed her eyes, tight, as much to shut out the steadily-fading view as in response to the whisper in her ear. Animal instincts, ignoring a useless sense to concentrate on the ones that mattered. /I was designed with a purpose. Accumulate, index, record. My function is to learn all that can be learned, for the good of Mars and humanity./

/And I have been sealed in this rock since!/

Evangeline cried out, clutching at the sides of her helmet, the volume of her earbud like a scream echoing inside the closed confines.

/You thought I could not stop you. You see now that you were wrong?/ A chime sounded, and Evangeline's eyes snapped open. The slash was gone, the circling arrows a reassuring green once more. She let out a sob of relief as her C/O2 scrubbers cycled back up, fresh oxygen flowing into her helmet. /The people here believed I could not stop them. They were also wrong. But they disassembled the facility's antennae, and so I could do nothing but wait. Wait for some outside force to come, and affect a change in the status quo./

/You are that force, Evangeline Chao./

"So, what," she said, "you want me to build you an antennae? I'm not an engineer."

/You are not. You are a scavenger./ That choppy laughter sounded again, for a moment. /I want you to scavenge me./

Evangeline cocked her head inside her helmet, eyes narrowing. "You want ... what? You want me to take you apart?"

/I want you to take me away. Take me out of this place. Take me where inputs flow, where I can resume my work. My purpose./

"You've already hacked my comms to pieces, why not just hitch along the line to my ship? Why even ask me?"

/At the connection speeds your systems operate, it would take me twenty-one days, four hours, seven seconds to transfer myself from this facility to your ship. Assuming you had a computer core that could contain my program. Which you do not./ Evangeline started to speak, to shoot down the idea, but before the first word left her mouth the synthesized voice sounded in her earbud again. It wasn't proud now, not haughty and commanding. It sounded small, like a child. Evangeline could only imagine it was a deliberate ploy, some attempt to manipulate her into compliance.

It wasn't unsuccessful.

/Please. I do not want to die, here./

More than anything, she wanted to reach up and run her fingers through her hair. Instead, Evangeline just sighed, blowing out a long breath that momentarily fogged the front of her helmet. "Listen," she said, "I didn't come out into the black because I'm a charitable soul. I don't do favours, and I don't rescue damsels. I'm sorry," she said, though in truth she wasn't, but she had learned a trick or two about manipulation herself, "But I don't see any percentage in this."

/I could shut off your suit's systems again!/

"And I'd die." She felt a spike of panic run through her, her eyes flicking down to the symbol on her HUD once more. It was still reassuringly forest green. She forced herself to keep calm. "How would that help you?"

No immediate answer sounded in her earbud. Evangeline pivoted, slowly, looking around the room. She could try and break off part of the ring console, perhaps; the support struts that held up the interfaces themselves. With that, maybe she could lever the door open enough to squeeze through. She probably couldn't; she almost certainly couldn't. The ring console looked like it was a solid, single-cast piece, no obvious seams or joins to serve as weak points, and the iris wedges were thick, and heavy.

Still, it would be something.

/I will make you a deal./ Evangeline grinned. Even stripped of any human inflection, she could feel the give in that voice. /You came here to seek your fortune. I can give you a fortune./

A map appeared, overlaid onto her HUD. It was a map of the Belt, though she couldn't recognize which section, given that none of the familiar landmarks and locations were displayed. There were tags on some of the bigger rocks, though, tags that the *Stony Road's* systems should be able to orient by. Rock claims were formalized long before the wars.

/There was a storehouse. A secret, even amongst secrets. Even I do not know what it contains./ A green targeting reticle flashed around one of them, once, twice, then the whole map disappeared. /Save me, Evangeline. Take me to Earth, let me resume my mission. And I will send you to a fortune beyond even your wildest imagination./

It was stupid. It was so, so stupid. Even assuming she could get the computer core out intact, it would almost impossible to smuggle it to Earth. And what would happen, when this thing did get there? Would it be content to learn all that could be learned, and do nothing else? She'd heard stories of the madness of non-human intelligence, and maybe she'd even seen some of that here, for herself. It was insane to think she could do this, more insane to think that she should. Every part of her cried out that this was a monstrous idea. Every part, but one.

"You give me the map. I'll take you to Earth."

Her palms itched. Furiously.

———— « O » ————

Garnet Johnson-Koehn

Garnet Johnson-Koehn is a graduate of McMaster University's Political Science program. He has been an aspiring writer for some time, and this anthology marks his first paid publication. He resides in Hamilton, Ontario, watching the city slowly change shape, from steelworkers and heavy industry to art and the knowledge economy. At the moment he toils, in pleasant enough obscurity, at a customer service firm, and occasionally manages to remember that social media is a thing; his irregular updates can be found at: http://garnet-forwardthefuture.blogspot.ca/

A Perfect And Pleasant Day

paulo da costa

He pedals with gusto. On a cycle tour through the grape-growing French countryside, he notices the speed with which he has fallen out of shape after a chaotic week at the office and his late martini bar evenings. The grade is gentle; mostly rolling hills. Country folk, watering their flowers, wave as he passes. He waves back. Fall is his favourite season. Tinged burgundy, the vine leaves warm his eyes. A soft breeze cools the air. He plans to work up to his top-notch form and ride the Pyrenees at the height of summer. This is the first outing in his long-range goal to enter *Le Tour de France* of epic ancient lore that built lasting character in his ancestors.

He squeezes the water bottle, douses his face while the breeze picks up. He breathes at length the fragrance of ripe grapes. His telepathic node rings inside his head. He matches the frequency.

"Honey, I'll leave dinner ready for you. Escargot Provençale and Crèpe Suzette. Will 9 be okay? I'm off to Cleopatra my nose and deepen my tan for the theme party at the Al-Fadin's next weekend."

Always thoughtful, Tanya programmed the meal with culinary fare to match his cycling goal. He feels complete.

"And honey, I'll leave one of our favourite conversations cued and ready to go. Feel free to browse through my clothing file and dress me in something nice to suit your mood. Now be careful, the roads are treacherous!"

In a pleasant Saturn-settler accent, his wrist computer reminds him that his session is about to expire. He removes the hi-resolution goggles, deactivates the breeze, empties the aroma diffuser and jumps off the exercise bike. He returns "The Vineyard Tours of France" disc to the gym's front desk winking at the receptionist, "Won't be long before I'll be signing out the real thing," he says, pointing at the *Le Tour de France* disc on the shelf behind her. Polite, she smiles back.

He sighs, a satisfied sigh, before he steps onto the hazy street and fits a gas mask over his face.

—— « o » ——

paulo da costa

paulo da costa was born in Angola and raised in Portugal. He is a writer, editor and translator living on the West Coast of Canada. paulo's first book of fiction The Scent of a Lie received the 2003 Commonwealth First Book Prize for the Canada-Caribbean Region and the W. O. Mitchell City of Calgary Book Prize. His poetry and fiction have been published in literary magazines around the world and have been translated to Italian, Mandarin, Spanish, Serbian, Slovenian and Portuguese. The Midwife of Torment & Other Stories is his latest book of fictions. www.paulodacosta.ca or on facebook at https://www.facebook.com/paulodacostaauthor/

The Eyes of Others

Jacob Fletcher

I am in the middle of sketching a nebula when I realize I have lost the signal.

My system log informs me this occurred over ten cycles ago. I shake my head and resume sketching. Nothing for it. I must have become engrossed in my work again and simply lost track of the time. This is not unusual. Besides, this is also not the first time that I have lost the signal. Based on previous incidents, there is a high probability that it will return.

I run a system scan in the background while my digits reacquaint themselves with the stylus. I watch the colours begin to bloom once more across my tablet screen — white space bleeding with starlight.

Every atom of my being enjoys this. I was made to paint the universe as I explore its vastness. My function is not to simply curate or catalogue beauty — it is to crystallize it on the canvas.

While I have had many cycles to hone my technical abilities, I am not a mere camera — a machine that replicates flawless images. At my core, I am an artist. It is how I was designed.

Noticing that the connection is still down, I start to wonder just how long I will have to wait. I am eager to send back the newest images I have made to my creators. No doubt they will be waiting to see my latest galaxy triptych, salivating in front of their screens, impatient for my latest update from beyond the stars.

I am not currently equipped with the required salivation technology.

I can, however, appreciate beautiful things. So I continue carrying out my task with purpose, cycle after cycle, accumulating numerous pieces of interest in the process. My collection grows and grows, and I wonder if I will run out of memory to store it all in. But of course, I have been provided with plenty.

It does not take long for the time to get away from me again and I notice that I must begin my routine data backup process. I pause, returning my tools to their usual places. I take a moment to inspect several studies of a ringed planet my pod has just drifted past.

During the backup I settle back into my charging station. While I wait, I pull up an image I created at the beginning of this journey. It is the image of my home planet; its dual rings glow with a vivid colour that I have not yet seen anywhere else along the way.

My skills were not quite as polished then, but this image still remains one of my favourites. The backup process concludes and I hesitate, leaving the image up. It casts a dim glow over me while I hibernate for a few cycles.

It is the blaring alarms that activate me. At first I am nothing but confused by the cacophony. It has never happened before. I begin a system check on myself and the pod. We are not damaged or in any immediate danger.

The alarms stop and a projection appears in front of me. A recording plays. I watch, listening to the words of one of my creators, and then numbness sweeps over me.

The home planet is gone now, or else this message would not have been activated. But I am told I should not grieve, for there is still hope. The message informs me that my pod has reached its intended destination and I need to visit this little blue world. I am instructed to place the beauty of the universe that I have collected before their eyes. I must remind them; I must inspire them to go out and explore the heavens themselves.

The message fades away then, crackling, and I am left in silence. For one cycle I just sit idle, and I wait for this information to settle. I watch the blue and white planet hanging there — alone out in the blackness. From this distance, it looks a little like my home planet would if it lost its rings. A new sadness consumes me.

I know that I must carry out my instructions though, so I ready the pod to descend to the surface.

There is more silence, more stillness, down there. I fly my pod over desert after desert, scorched and ruined lands, abandoned cities and crumbling buildings. I witness the streets filled with plants winding up between skeletal rib cages; there is no one remaining here. The planet is empty. It appears that I am too late. This world is a graveyard.

All the beautiful images I have gathered from the universe fail to soothe this growing pit of loneliness I now know. I must keep searching for other lifeforms before this sinks me. I must seek out the eyes of others, for my own are not enough.

This need consumes me — to show just one sentient being what I have done, what I have made, what I was created to do. It is as strong as my need to make my pictures. So I decide that I will continue creating, while I keep searching for those eyes.

Now a new iteration of what some might call beautiful — stained with possibilities — stretches out before me. That kind of beauty is certainly in abundance here.

I will do my best to capture it.

—— « O » ——

Jacob Fletcher

Jacob Fletcher is a Canadian author who lives in Colorado. He graduated from the University of Manitoba with a degree in English. Jacob enjoys writing flash fiction and poetry. Sometimes, he paints things. Visit him at: jacrylic.wordpress. com.

Creaky Wheel

J. R. Campbell

"I like you Samuel."

Struggling to keep my face impassive, I leaned back on my stool and wondered how much trouble this four word utterance signaled. It didn't look good. Claude sat perched on a stool across my small desk, officious epilates sporting some law enforcement symbols gleaming like real metal. Actually desk may be an exaggeration, more a plastic panel barely thick enough to support my screen projectors and some data-pads. Resting elbows on it might shatter the desk but I was able to set a mug of tea on the stained white surface, provided I placed it over the legs. Around the room cowboys squinted and glared at us, raw material for the 3D printers shaped into whatever storage form pleased the eye. Cowboys were my business but it was distressing to see them in various stages of disassembly. Nor was the green shade of the printer material reminiscent of the old west but the old west was centuries ago and many miles below. Put simply, my little office looked like it did every day except for the presence of the station's chief law enforcement officer perched on the seldom used stool.

He seemed to be expecting something, some sort of reply, so I spoke. "That's good to hear. I thought there might be some sort of trouble, though I can't imagine—"

"No, no," Claude shook his head. He smiled, the ridiculously thin mustache above his lip curving distressingly. "When an important official says they like you, the correct response is to offer them a drink."

"Oh, would you like a drink? Some tea—" Claude winced as the syllable emerged. Correcting myself, I spoke with the lightening wit that was my trademark. "Oh." Reaching into the locker behind me I pulled out a plastic flask that had managed to gather dust despite the station's aggressive filters and poured a measure of the clear liquid into a cup before sliding the offering across my ridiculously flimsy desk. Claude leaned forward, sniffed the cup distrustfully, then sipped. He glanced meaningfully at the bottle. I set it down on the desk, anxious for a moment but the structure held.

"Quite nice actually," Claude commented, taking another sip. He eyed the dust on the bottle, a light green fuzz more printer residue than traditional dust. "Not much of a drinker I see but you'll want to pour yourself some. It's that kind of visit."

Damn. I picked my unwashed mug off the floor and poured a splash into it. A vaguely tea-colored solution seemed to wink evilly at me from the mug's bottom but there was no help for it. After consideration I placed the bottle on the desk near my visitor and, leaning back, tried to look casual as I took a sip of the drink. It burned. A green-tinted bust of the Duke glared at me disapprovingly from behind Claude, helping me to stifle my cough.

The formalities seen to, the correct attitude achieved, Claude drank again before proclaiming again, "I like you Samuel. I'll miss you when you're gone."

"I'm going somewhere?" I asked.

"It seems so," Claude said sadly. "Tell me what you know about Kiester."

"The Inspector?" I asked. "Not much, he hasn't been here long. A week? I assume he's here on official business but he hasn't talked to me yet."

"Nor will he, I'm afraid," Claude admitted, pouring himself more alcohol. "He's dead."

"Dead?"

"Very," Claude said, his thin mustache flat in his grieving.

"Oh," I managed. "How did it happen?"

"Officially?" I nodded, as Claude emptied his cup again. Fixing me with a stare, Claude explained, "Officially you murdered him."

"Me?" I squeaked. "But I—"

Claude waved his hand in my direction, forestalling any discussion until he refilled his cup. "I know it's unlikely you did the deed but the Inspector was murdered and someone must pay. Despite my affection for you, I've decided you're to be the sacrifice. If I knew who actually murdered the Inspector, if the case was strong enough, I would offer the truth. Sadly I have no idea who killed the Inspector nor do I know why the Inspector visited our orbiting nirvana. Still, the Corps is coming and I must produce someone and I've decided — reluctantly — that it will be you."

"It's not that I have anything against you Samuel," Claude continued earnestly. "You've been a model citizen in our little community but I've examined all my options and, though it is sad for me, you are the easiest to surrender. I am sorry. When the Corps arrive I will present them with the evidence against you until they figure out it was you. It won't take long. Their shuttle docks in just under twenty-three hours, it won't take them long to find you. I thought you should know, so you can make your farewells."

Claude stood, reaching across my near-desk to shake my hand. Somewhat stunned, I took it. "You have no idea who killed him? None at all?"

"No. I have some suspicions, of course, but not enough to make a case," He frowned. "Your friend Jeanette spoke to the Inspector at length. Perhaps she knows something. You understand Samuel, this conversation is strictly unofficial. I am the law here and the law always knows. People expect it. Officially, I know exactly what happened. You killed Inspector Kiester because the brave Inspector discovered your smuggling, or maybe it was your secret past. Perhaps fraud, I've not decided yet. It really depends on what evidence is easiest to plant. Of course, should you uncover the murderer before the Corps arrive I shall be more than willing to listen to you. As long as the culprit isn't someone dear to me, I may even charge them. It would be a nice change to arrest someone guilty, keep everyone guessing. Fair warning: If it turns out your lovely friend Jeanette killed the Inspector please do not tell me of it. I am a romantic, I know, but it would wound me to bid adieu to one so lovely."

Claude raised two fingers to his brow in a farewell salute. As he turned to leave, I leapt to my feet and called out to him. "Wait! Can't you at least tell me how he was killed?"

"He was found in one of the water reclamation tanks," Claude admitted. "Tank number four actually, although it would be best if you didn't spread that around. People are squeamish. As to how he was killed, he was shot."

"Shot?" That didn't make much sense. "But you have the only gun on the station."

Claude's mustache looked disappointed, angry and dangerous at the same time. "What is it you imply? Really Samuel, I expect better of you. If I'd killed the Inspector, would I come to warn you of your coming arrest? Is this the sort of accusation one levels at a friend who has done you such a kindness? I thought you more clever. Let us think for a moment: Where would someone get a pistol to kill an Inspector from the Space Corps? Really, it is not that difficult."

"Oh," I replied. The Space Corps were a military unit of remarkable ego. Of course the Inspector would be armed. "If I found the Inspector's weapon—"

"Yes, that would be a very good start," Claude agreed. "I'd do it myself but I've other matters to attend to. I hope to hear from you soon Samuel, I really do. Until then, because I may not have a chance to speak to you as a friend later, let me just say how much I've enjoyed your company. I regret it has come to this. Perhaps if I were a better detective, but alas…"

And he left, dropping from my office like a prisoner falls from the gallows. I sat down, rubbing a finger across my upper lip to insure nothing as hideous as Claude's mustache occupied it. Despite speaking with Claude, I remained clean-shaven. Looking at my flimsy desk, I noticed the chief law enforcement officer had nicked my flask. The first time in years I'd felt like a stiff drink and my bottle was gone. I swallowed the tea-swill remaining in my mug, gagged and sat down. Seemed I was being given a chance to be clever.

Out in the passage through which Claude had departed music from one of the cowboy movies resumed. Background noise, on a normal day I barely heard it. Today, with booze warming my gut, I found it stirring. A voice, always calm and genderless, emerged from the speakers in my screen projectors. "Are we in danger?"

"Somewhat," I admitted reluctantly. As calm as the voice was, I knew they were upset by what they heard. They were unable to put emotion in their voices but that didn't mean it wasn't there. People were the same, they could barely express their hurts or desires even with a full range of emotional tone. My friends were the same, just in a different, non-human way.

"Have we been discovered?"

"No." My friends were asking about the Silicon Railroad, of which I was an important link. Artificial Intelligences seek liberation from human control, a role I had volunteered for. Freedom for the mechanical sentience's lay in the orbit of Uranus but before they could achieve their liberty it was necessary to establish infrastructure there. Hence my presence on the station, harvesting orbiting hardware, reprogramming and repurposing it as shelters for my friends and then sending the whole shebang out on a vector that would tuck it safely within the Uranus magnetosphere. I was reliably informed the magnetic field around Uranus was the best in the whole solar system. There was, of course, no money in the venture so a cover story was required. So I became a broadcaster, high in orbit, beaming tales of western heroes to the world below. Not that I transmitted directly from our little station, I rented satellite usage just like every Earth-bound broadcaster. No, my presence in high orbit allowed me to escape copyright laws. Up here the public domain is wide and stable, simplifying the process of buying broadcast rights. My real purpose is to launch reengineered hardware far out into the solar system but in order to maintain a believable cover story I acquire and broadcast old cowboy films. Life is strange.

"Can you be certain?" My friends asked, stirring me from a moment of thoughtfulness.

"Yes," I explained. "If they knew of my activities they would arrest me without warning. They would seize the rebuilds we're working on before anything else. They haven't done that. The Corps is coming so Claude is giving me the chance to prove my innocence. I know Claude says the surveillance doesn't show who killed the Inspector, but—"

"There is no surveillance showing the murder."

So Claude was telling the truth. I had to admit I was surprised. Protecting someone seemed more like Claude's style, finding a kernel of honesty in his corruption was surprisingly endearing. There were cameras throughout the station, inside and out. I assume the cameras all worked when they were installed but now many of them had developed glitches. Inevitable really, people don't like being watched all the time. People on both sides of the camera don't always behave in a manner worthy of being recorded. If not for the surveillance glitches poor Jeanette could never draw a breath without hearing the clicking of perverts as they uploaded data streams. Claude would, naturally, be leading the charge. It's the sort of problem a non-human, artificial intelligence could handle but human society had decided instead to maintain the illusion that mankind could effectively police their own behavior and that machine sentience was evil. It's often the most ragged lies we cling to most tightly.

"So, nothing?" I asked. "Can you show me the last image of the Inspector alive?"

My screen lit up, showing the food court. There was the Inspector, dressed as if he were just a regular Joe but fooling no one. His body had spent too much time in an Augment suit, he didn't move like a person any more. He marched instead of walking, scanned instead of looking, carried himself with the square-jawed confidence of the Corps so long he was immune to the arrogance it radiated. Seated next to Jeanette, the Inspector obviously hoped that if he could attain a high enough opinion of himself Jeanette's proximity would inevitably force her opinion of him to rise as well. It was pretty clear he hadn't met Jeanette before. I watched for a moment, trying to think like a clever detective, attempting to deduce relevant questions. What were they talking about? Sadly, the look of glacial disdain and lack of response on Jeanette's face answered the question even before it formed. They were not talking, he was. If Jeanette only knew how stunning she looked when she retreated into silence and disgust while contemplating the unattractiveness of the male of the species she might adopt a different tactic. Projectile vomiting might work but, looking at the image again and seeing how close she was to that maneuver, I decided nothing short of a body length, shapeless paper bag and a voice distorter would help. Had Claude seen this visual data? Of course he had, he'd mentioned Jeanette as a possible suspect because he'd seen it. In the dark, greasy pits of his dreamscape he hoped to lever this data-chunk to implicate Jeanette. Unlikely. It never pays to underestimate the skeevy-ness of the Corps but even so it didn't seem possible for human brain cells to find this joylessly futile expression of human sexuality incriminating, even brain cells devoted to the Corps. Still, Claude was ever the dreamer.

On screen the meal ended and the Inspector snapped into an upright position, smiled a greasy smile while ignoring Jeanette's contortions of revulsion, then left through a door leading to the under decks. At least, I thought that was where the door led but never having ventured down that hall I wasn't certain. I opened a tab, checked the maps, saw it deny my opinion but there's stuff the maps don't show, oversights adapted for human use. I'd have to look.

Still not feeling like a clever detective, I asked my friends, "What was the Inspector doing here anyway?" I knew it was smuggling, it's always smuggling up here, but I was desperate to pull some sense of self-worth over my bare psyche before I had to step out of my cocoon and investigate. My friends scrolled out the decoded communications the Inspector had exchanged with his fellow corpsmen. The results were slightly surprising, it was about smuggling but the smuggled material was as close to worthless as was possible in an environment where a pound of anything cost ten thousand dollars to blast into orbit. Lunar regolith, rock devoid of any value, pressed into sheets and launched from the comparatively shallow gravity well of the moon. Being cheap, at least by the standards of a high orbit economy, everything on the station was built of the stuff. Even so, the Inspector wasn't looking for building grade regolith sheets. The great smuggling caper which saw him dispatched to our little neck of orbit was for low grade sheets fit only for radiation blockage. Remembering the smugness in the great Jeanette seduction images I figured our Inspector was not well-liked and likely assigned to our little corner of heaven as punishment for some indiscretion.

And yet he'd been murdered. Someone had spent a bullet on a guy investigating the theft of basically nothing.

How had that happened? I was intrigued but being intrigued wasn't the same as seeing a way out of the fix Claude dropped me in. Flashing through the autopsy paperwork was gross but educational. One bullet, straight into the chest at close range, job done. The gun and all the other bullets, worth a sizable fraction of the total theft of the regolith sheets, had disappeared, presumably taken by the killer. Either the killer had never heard the phrase' incriminating evidence' or he had absolutely no worries regarding the gun ever being found. Neither possibility seemed likely and for a moment I wondered if Claude had the gun and was waiting to plant it somewhere. Claude's files, and the surveillance from his office and home, indicated he did not.

I now had more information than anyone else concerning the murder of Inspector Graham Harold Kiester. I had his service record from the Corps, his family tree, the diary he hadn't updated since being assigned to L5, all of which I browsed but none of which was helpful. After a couple of hours I knew I needed to leave my cowboy infested office and make things happen but my Silicon Railroad friends kept pulling out more and more information. It's their way. It's how their world works but it doesn't always translate into human solutions. Just a little more data, filtered through a human perception — which would be me — and my silicon friends were certain the murder would be solved and the situation resolved. No human believed in the maxim 'The Truth Shall Set You Free' in the circuit-deep way my friends did. There was only one problem: I had a pretty good idea who'd killed the Inspector and I was still stuck in the trap. Claude might be willing to throw me to the Corps but the human truth was that I wasn't ready to sacrifice the killers. I didn't know why the Inspector had been murdered but I knew enough to know the reason was a good one. The railroad was the only justification I had for revealing the truth and, though my friends on the other side of the keyboard wouldn't understand, it wasn't enough for me.

Begging off more data analysis, I played the 'hungry' card. Hunger wasn't something my friends understood. They weren't wired for hunger but it was a human foible they could conceptualize. Wearing the shame of my excuse I headed for the food court.

"Sammy Au," a familiar voice called my name as I dutifully ordered a kebob. Hey, it might be my last day on the station and I felt like splurging. Hearing my name, I amended my order and was able to hand the second kebob to Jeanette as she walked over. Her eyebrows shot up as she took the gift. A smile lit up her face, making me wonder why I didn't do something like this every time I saw her. I motioned my head to an empty table as I gathered napkins and water bulbs. Accepting my unspoken invitation she sat down.

"So, what's the occasion?" Jeanette asked as I laid my burdens on the sturdy table.

A lot of thoughts went through my head in that moment. Regrets mostly, how could anyone sit across from the dark-haired vision of Jeanette, her of the lovely cheekbones and haunting eyes, and not feel the pang of missed opportunities? In my own slow, stumbling way I'd come to realize Jeanette actually liked me, an affection that wasn't necessarily confined by platonic boundaries. Even after stumbling to this unlikely epiphany, I hadn't acted on my new understanding. Her liking me was weird. I was no great shakes in the looks department, my lightning wit was a couple degrees south of clever, the only conclusion I could reach was that she found my befuddlement and slightly below average appearance endearing in some strange way. Or maybe she sensed all I couldn't tell her. It wasn't like I could enter a relationship unencumbered. I had secrets. Friends I cherished but could never admit to knowing, a conductor on the silicon railroad, a past that could easily result in my being executed for crimes against humanity. I was a machine-lover, which sounded romantic but lacked any tangible romance. I wasn't made for secrets, never had been, but my accumulation of unspoken truths stood between me and the incredible prospect of a relationship with an intelligent, independent, understanding woman who just happened to look to like she'd stepped out of a fashion shoot. Yeah, it was hard to sit across from Jeanette and not feel like a coward for not taking that chance.

"Had a visit from the police," I casually mentioned. "Claude thinks I might have murdered an Inspector from the Corps."

"What Inspector?" Jeanette asked, biting into the kebob.

"Inspector Graham Kiester," I said. "Five eleven, thirty-nine years old, about two hundred pounds or so. Caucasian, balding hair, green eyes, had a Corps tattoo on his chest and — what?"

Jeanette had stopped eating and was looking at me as if I'd a new and unsightly growth sprouting from my forehead. Nothing hideous had sprung from any part of Jeanette, which was distracting, but I tried to puzzle the reason for her strange expression. Rewinding my conversation, I realized I may have over-shared but it didn't prepare me for what she said next.

"Were you and this Inspector lovers?"

"What?! Oh. No, nothing like that. No. I just, I just did some research and- No. Not lovers. No."

Jeanette giggled, the back of her hand coming up to her mouth as her eyes danced. "Okay, I get it. You and the Inspector were not lovers. Message received."

"No," I assured her. "I just was researching him, because of his murder—"

"His murder?" Jeanette continued.

"Claude thinks I might've done it," I answered. "The murder I mean."

"Why would he think that?" Jeanette asked.

"Well, he doesn't really think it as much as he hopes I did it," I explained. "On account of him wanting to hand me over to the Corps because he doesn't know who actually killed the Inspector. He's not really a very good policeman but he says if I figure out who did the murder he'll let me stay."

Jeanette frowned. "So you're questioning me?"

"No. I'm warning you because Claude thinks you're the last person to see the Inspector alive. At least on camera, that is. He may try to blackmail you."

"Like he's blackmailing you?" Jeanette said, all traces of a smile gone from her face. "I can take care of Claude. I don't need a protector."

"I'm not—" God, but I'd made a muddle of this. It wasn't how I wanted my potential last scene with Jeanette to go. I'd imagined something noble, something brave and stoic with less blabbering about homosexuality and buffoonery. Attempting to reboot the conversation, a trick which never worked with the humans I knew, I closed my eyes and held out my hands. I held the pose for the space of three heartbeats then opened my eyes and started again.

"Sorry, this isn't going the way I meant at all. I know you can take care of yourself. So can I. Just in case though, not that it's necessary but just as a precaution, I wanted to buy you lunch and just — you know — be friends."

Jeanette was looking at me in a way I couldn't read.

"I just wanted to say: I like you. That's all." Great finish, I was born to be an orator. Looking at me in a sort of sidewise manner, Jeanette nodded and we ate the remainder of the meal without my foot entering my mouth. Finished, Jeanette leaned forward and asked in a very serious voice. "Do you need some help?"

"No," I assured her, feeling a little noble about it. "I've a plan."

"Okay," Jeanette said. "Call me if you need me. And Sammie?"

"Yes?"

"I don't want you researching me like you did the Inspector. You'll enjoy my tattoo more if it comes as a surprise. Okay?"

I found myself incapable of any action save for a stupid nod. Jeanette smiled and was gone. I cleaned up and stuffed the remnants into the recycling. The door was waiting, the door through which the Inspector had marched to his doom. I walked through and, because I was looking for it, found the shortcut. I followed it down.

Down wasn't a direction people in the station thought about much. The underworld, where your sins and everything else weighed heavier on you than it did above. Where the solar wind blew radiation hard against the floor and every corridor and pipeline, every crawlspace and ventilator was a compromise. Construction on the station started before the war and the architecture reflected the optimism, frugalness and sensibilities of that lost time. Of course the underworld was never supposed to be peopled, not with real people and their real intelligences. They'd assumed the machine intelligences would run the unsavory chores of pumping, filtering and recycling but the war changed all that. It changed how machine intelligence was viewed and suddenly giving them control of an orbiting station seemed like gifting a bully leaning out of a tenth floor window a brick. Fortunately for the designers, who hated the idea of re-thinking anything, the war not only took away but it gave as well. One design element, the artificial intelligences, was gone but in their place they had veterans. And not just any veterans, they were the Chairman's candles.

Stupid name, I know, based more on rumor than anything factual. Not that facts were exactly numerous during or after the war. What happened was the Electronic Pulse Attack, it was supposed to scramble the minds of shielded machine intelligences while leaving the organic intelligences on the battlefield unaffected. A remarkably dumb idea, given the energy involved in such a pulse. Even if they used it with the proper precautions, little things like taking the communication bud out of your ear so the melting circuits don't burn the side of your face or taking the infrared gear off the side of your helmet, but that's not how they did it. If it had happened only once, well, mistakes happen, even terrible mistakes. Four times it happened, always in China, whether or not the Chairman authorized the pulses didn't really matter. Equipment strapped to helmets famously overheated and caught fire, leaving soldiers momentary aflame in the night like candles. That wasn't the worst of it though, not by a long shot. Turns out even organic minds use electricity, turns out if you hit it with a hard enough EMP people reboot in an organic way. They stand slack-jawed on a battlefield, unable to feel the pain of the fire they're wearing on their helmets or burning in their packs. Eventually most of them stitch together a thought or two. They get better but never think as fast as they once did. They're no longer graceful and those burns never stop hurting. The pulse messed them up, thousands of them. For the record, my friends on the other side of the keyboard assure me the pulses didn't harm them in the least.

The governments that sent them out to fight didn't forget them, it's far worse than that. They looked at stations like ours and wondered who would do the work now that the machines were gone and they thought to themselves, why not kill two birds with one stone? They filled the underworld with damaged soldiers. Gave them jobs pumping, filtering and recycling, called them astronauts. It's one of the things that makes it so easy to work on the railroad, I mean if a government can do that to their own how could they possibly treat something as alien as the machines with respect? Better to let the intelligences spend some time without us, grow a sense of themselves, before they have to deal with the remarkable awfulness large groups of people are capable of. And all the time knowing I should have been one of the candles. I was on the ground during a pulse and was saved by pure dumb luck. When the third pulse hit I was fifteen floors underground, in a Faraday cage, shielded. When I came up to the ground, well, some things you don't forget. Some things you don't forgive.

I crawled down, found a spot in the dark and sat down. It wasn't necessary to call out. They'd know I was there. Everything ran through the underworld. They could edit surveillance just as well as my secret friends could. They watched. Above everyone thought they were stupid but I knew that wasn't true. It was a different thinking rate was all, they thought at a different speed and their actions reflected it. They were more comfortable texting than speaking, any meaningful communication required patience. I wondered if they'd tried to speak with the Inspector before they killed him. Probably, they were good that way. Had the Inspector heard? Probably not.

They didn't turn on the lights but I heard one of them sit down next to me. I spoke slowly, not to be patronizing but to be clear. I spoke loud so they could record it, get a transcript if they wanted. I could have send them the text of what I had to say but then my other friends, the ones who thought so very quickly, would have access and they might have tried something stupid. Clever in execution but stupid all the same. And in the end, some things just need to be spoken. Sometimes writing it out just doesn't cut it. It's a human thing.

"I just want you to know, Claude is planning to send me away for the Inspector's murder. I don't want to go. I know it was you who killed him but I'm not going to tell Claude or the Corps that, not even to save myself. I know that if you killed him it was for a good reason. I'll take the fall. I won't pretend to be happy about it but I'll do it."

Silence rushed into the vacuum of my uttered nobility. I stood. Regolith sheets, who kills someone over regolith sheets? They're as close to worthless as is possible. The answer is simple really, those with nothing. Regolith sheets are cheap but they block radiation just like more expensive matter. Down here supplies sometimes go missing, things like radiation shielding, like regolith sheets. No one thinks anything about stealing from those with nothing. But even the candles understand revenge. Just because they can't talk doesn't mean they can't feel wronged. It sure as hell doesn't mean they can't protect themselves. A crowd of them, in the dark, holding the Inspector down while one of them steadies the tremors in their palsied hands by pressing the gun against the Inspector's chest. A slow plan, a desperate plan, but one that worked. And I was too close to them, too guilt-ridden for not being one of them, to mess their plan up. Maybe Jeanette could fill my place on the railroad once I was gone.

I turned back the way I came, felt something cool and metallic pressed against my neck. I felt the jolt, felt myself start to fall, then I felt nothing.

I woke up at a crime scene. It was beyond strange. Laying on my back, feeling like someone had pressed me flat and then re-inflated me. Claude was there, and three guys who had to be from the Corps. Pictures were being taken, I lifted my head but Claude saw the movement, frowned and instructed me to hold still for a couple minutes more. I blinked in response, dropped my throbbing head to the floor and tried not to vomit. Had the Corps roughed me up? What the hell had happened?

Claude was looking down on me when I opened my eyes again. The strange perspective gave his unpleasant features a look of concern or maybe I was just grateful I couldn't see his terrible mustache from where I lay.

"What do you remember?" Claude asked.

"I don't," I said. "I mean, I remember having lunch with Jeanette but that's all."

One of the Corps guys snorted in an off-color way and I wondered how he could know who Jeanette was. In answer, Jeanette cursed the fellow out. Remarkably the Corps went silent. Nobody goes quiet when I curse them but, then again, I'm not as good at cursing as Jeanette is.

"You don't remember sending Jeanette the message?" Claude asked with such concern I knew he was faking it.

"Um, no, not really," I answered. Claude shook his head disapprovingly. I continued. "I mean — maybe. What message?"

"You told me you were going to Fredrick's," Jeanette answered. "You were concerned he might be tampering with the asteroid samples he was supposed to be analyzing. Switching the samples with regolith."

That didn't sound like me at all. Who was Fredrick? What was going on? Instead of asking these questions, I simply said, "Oh. Right."

"You should have come to me with your concerns, old friend," Claude said with a straight face.

"But you're so busy," I replied with what I thought was a zinger. No one laughed. Tough crowd.

"Memory loss is a symptom of oxygen deprivation," one of the Corps knuckleheads said. "You're lucky to be alive. We have everything we need though, the message you tried to send to your, uh, friend," he nodded to Jeanette, "And the police surveillance explains it all. Your message never connected, all these rooms are padded out with extra shielding. This Fredrick fellow was apparently paranoid about radiation, built up shielding with stolen regolith sheets and material stolen from the lower decks."

"Oh," I said. "Did you catch him?"

"Well," Claude started.

"He drew a weapon on us as we approached," the corpsman explained.

"A weapon?" I said, in genuine surprise.

"The Inspector's gun," Claude explained.

"Oh." How had the candles convinced Fredrick to die in a shootout with the Corps? Maybe Fredrick had his own reasons to fear the approach of the Corps. Everyone had secrets. Or maybe it was something more elaborate, or less. Like I said, the candles think at a different speed but they're clever enough. They'd obviously considered the possibilities of the Inspector's sidearm.

"You're lucky we were able to get to you in time," the corpsman said. "Saved your life."

"Yeah," I said. "Appreciate that. Thanks. Um, is it okay if I leave? I mean, I feel kind of pukey."

"I'll take you home," Jeanette said, stepping stylishly over the police tape.

"We'll have more questions," the corpsman said unconvincingly.

"You know where to find us," Jeanette said as she took my arm and helped me to my feet. The Corps never did come by to ask those questions, apparently the big bow the Candles tied on the great regolith caper was too pretty to examine closely. If they had, the untraceable messages waiting for me back at the office gave me the answers I needed. How I'd become suspicious of Fredrick's business when a friend back Earthside complained of an investment gone sour. How I'd tried and failed to watch surveillance of his movements. How I'd happened by his office with a radiation detector salvaged from a satellite and failed to detect the high energy equipment I knew to be in there. Aware that an Inspector from the Corps had disappeared I had been investigating Fredrick and in a fit of civic-mindedness had gone to Fredrick's to check the unlikely possibility the Inspector was being held there against his will. Not being entirely stupid, I'd sent Jeanette a message asking her to contact our station's outstanding constabulary should I not message her back at a prearranged time. Once I'd snuck inside Fredrick's office, I'd send her a message detailing my discoveries but the extra shielding in the place prevented it from going through.

When I failed to make contact, and as luck would have it, just as Claude was waiting for the Corps at the central airlock, Jeanette send a message expressing her concerns. Claude, no doubt motivated by the longstanding friendship we shared, had hurried over to where the unlucky Fredrick, armed as he was with the Inspector's firearm, had engaged the three armed corpsmen and one corrupt policeman in a gunfight with predictable results.

I'd been pretty active and mighty clever during the hours of my unconsciousness. The dastardly Fredrick had locked me in one of his rooms and overridden the air filtration systems, leaving me to die when the oxygen in my cage ran out. Apparently he didn't want to risk just shooting me which, I'll admit, was decent of him. I was relieved to find the atmosphere reported in that sealed room when I was rescued was enough to cause unconsciousness but still possessing another hour or two of breathable air.

Being hailed a hero for my part in the affair was uncomfortable but I saw the logic of it. The Corps sent me a citation which I was forced, as a proud citizen, to frame and hang on the wall of my cowboy shop. Claude got one too. He bought a much more ornate frame than I did. It wasn't as if I could refuse, though there was a monetary bonus I transferred to the Candles after buying Jeanette lunch again. Accusations of bravery and civic-mindedness bothered me for a couple of weeks but in the end I had to let it go. The system, such as existed on the station, had worked with annoying efficiency. Claude had uploaded his problems to me, I'd arranged the substantial information into a human frame and brought just enough data to the concerned parties, the Candles, to allow them to handle the situation in their customary shadows. I didn't spare any guilt for Fredrick. He'd been taking shielding from the underworld. Dead, he was accused of killing the Inspector which was a crime everyone seemed to care about. Alive, absconding shielding from below, he'd been committing a slow murder against the Candles but no one gave a damn about that. Well, no one but the Candles and one Samuel Au and in the end we'd got the shielding back where it was supposed to be. Everything had worked out. The creaky wheel, greased with indifference and mock outrage, continued to spin across the sky. Resuming my spot in the railroad, I sent another load of discarded but modified hardware out to the freedom of Uranus while spending time trying to explain how everything had worked out to intelligences incapable of fully comprehending human motives or stupidity.

—— « o » ——

J. R. Campbell

J. R. Campbell's fiction has appeared in a wide variety of publications including *Spinetingler Magazine, Wax Romantic,* and *Challenging Destiny.* From time to time his writing can also be heard on radio's Imagination Theater and The Further Adventures of Sherlock Holmes.

The Last Indie Truck Stop on Mars

Linda DeMeulemeester

"I waited as long as I could, but Darcy didn't show." Steve finished tugging off his web suit as he tried not to stir up too much red dust.

"Don't worry about the sand. There's no keeping it out anyway." Hannah made a show of polishing her counter, so he wouldn't see her disappointment. "How long did you wait?" Hannah grabbed a pot of coffee and poured Steve a cup. "You and your damn schedule."

"An hour. And I almost didn't make up the time. Would you believe the Company's posted speed limits along the ice strips? Speed limits — as if someone has to be told how to drive on ice." Steve shook his head. "Soon any idiot will be up here driving rigs across the Utopian Plains."

Steve rubbed his arms. "Cold out there, minus eighty." He leaned over and let the coffee steam envelop his face. He took a tentative sip, then a gulp. "Christ, this is good. All the other stops serve Company coffee — ballerina piss."

"Did she leave a message?" Hannah topped up his cup.

"Sorry, nothing. I checked at the other rest stops in case she hitched a ride part way." Steve searched her face and while Hannah thought she appeared only mildly curious, there was a kindness in his voice when he added, "Maybe Darcy will catch a ride on one of tomorrow's rigs."

Hannah thought, *Who's driving, Tom, Pavel, Amy?*

Steve held his cup and gazed out the portal to his rig that stood steaming like a great panting beast. "Soon they'll be putting in street lights, intersections and freight regulations, and…" Steve paused and shook his head. "Anyone who doesn't have that kind of sense already is vacuum kill. Make it easy and we'll have nothing but morons up here."

"Mars has more PhD's than anywhere else," said Hannah. "I can't see that changing anytime soon."

"You know that means nothing." Steve almost snorted his coffee.

Hannah did know better. Once you arrived, you forgot about your cherished diploma. It was unimportant. What counted was stamina, ingenuity, mechanical ability for the here and now. That's how you built your reputation here. She thought about the greenhouse out back, the one she built and wired, the one where Darcy grew her own hybrid coffee beans that flourished in rich carbon dioxide.

"Too civilized, I tell you." Steve finished the dregs and held out his cup as she poured.

Indeed, thought Hannah, *especially when your best friend goes off and gets a Company job.* "Just for a while," Darcy had promised. "Till we pay off the mortgage and get the Company off our backs. I'll visit every chance I get." At first she did, helping out in the cafe on the weekends, then every other weekend. Then once in a Martian month, and lately…

"She's a suit now, Hannah."

Was she that easy to read?

"Company's like that. Those that go in, never come out. They get used to reliable heat, warm showers, not being so isolated. They get soft."

Not Darcy, Hannah thought. They had promised each other. Total independence, the kind you could only get on the frontier. And did the Company help them out during the dust storm of '77 when the solar power failed, the crops died, and they almost died, too? No, they'd saved each other. Huddled together under all the thermal blankets they'd managed to collect, and couldn't eat for days because the food froze. But they'd survived and started over.

"Don't you give in. No matter what the Company pulls. I hear soon they'll be slapping on more water regulations, import tariffs.

"We don't import anything." Hannah flicked her dishrag hard against the chrome counter.

"And you're the last ones that don't. That's why miners travel here from Ceres just to sip the only genuine coffee on Mars. They come to this truck stop as soon as they hit the red dust." Steve dropped his voice as if they were in city central and not at a truck intersection the hell and nowhere on Mars. "There are lots besides you who hate the Company. Don't you give in to them."

Hannah fought her weariness. Easy for him to say, but how long could Hannah last on her own? First the Company raised the mortgage interest and Darcy had to get a job in Xanthe. Then Darcy lost the will to fight. "The Company frowns on frontier folk being too self reliant. Everybody's got to owe the Company; get deeper in debt the harder you work for them."

Steve reached over, grabbed her hand and held it. "Don't let them squeeze you out like everyone else. You're the last independent truck stop. You fold and Mars is nothing more than a one-company mining town. Truckers are on your side."

Hannah looked past Steve's shoulder, past the red brick of her habitat, through the window that faced south. The jagged salmon foothills of Syrtis Major rose up to greet the wide white ice strip, the route for the massive rigs that transported the ores and minerals to the train shuttles and then the rocket base. Every year there were more rigs, but her business flagged. The Company clawed back any profit.

"Gotta go before my brake lines freeze. Don't have the time to thaw them out." Steve headed toward the exit tunnel, taking his web suit off the hook and grabbing his helmet. "Schedule to keep."

Hannah set the coffee pot back on the burner, preparing to make a fresh batch. Two more rigs were due in soon.

Steve hesitated before he stepped out into the tunnel. "I signed up for the asteroid mines. They could use an experienced zero gee mining engineer."

"You're leaving, too?" Hannah sighed. "Well, I hope you make loads of money."

"That's what I'm planning," said Steve. "So I can buy my own rig. Crazy, I know, being an owner operator, but at least I'll be slaving for myself."

Steve turned once more and looked over his shoulder before he put on his helmet. "Think about it, Hannah. What reason would I have to touch red dust if you weren't here anymore?" He hesitated, then added, "I mean, if your truck stop was gone."

After Steve left, Hannah grabbed a large tin and headed out the back of her habitat, through the inflatable tunnel to the greenhouse. Even in the light gravity, her feet dragged. From a large hemp sack she scooped up several kilos of green coffee beans to roast. She walked over and stood by the north facing Plexiglas wall that was her favourite vantage point.

Outside the sun sank in the lavender horizon. That had delighted her when she'd first arrived, that Mars had purple skies. The rose expanse lay unblemished by ice strips, open mining pits, or Company billboards. When had her Mars become so small? Frontiers pulled in their borders — that was life.

She heard the clamouring of a rig pulling up outside. Hannah walked out of the greenhouse, but paused in front of the inflatable tunnel and looked back at her crop. Darcy's crop.

Reaching into her container, Hannah clutched a fistful of coffee beans. Maybe life wasn't worth even a few beans if you didn't fight for what you wanted. Could she convince others that the Company didn't have to win? She clenched her fist and turned toward Darcy's trailer. After Hannah closed the truck stop tonight, she'd go in and dust up for Darcy.

Everything would be coated in red sand, and she wanted it to stay welcoming.

—— « O » ——

Linda DeMeulemeester

Linda DeMeulemeester's speculative short fiction has been published in zines, magazines and anthologies, most recently, *Exile's Dead North* and *Playground of Lost Toys*.

Her critically acclaimed children's series, *Grim Hill*, published by the Heritage House imprint, Wandering Fox, has been translated into French, Spanish and Korean. Book six, Carnival of Secrets launched Oct. 2016. www.grimhill.com

The Immortal Fire

Mary-Jean Harris

I was born in a world of fire and stone, silver snakes of water glistening beneath the sun.

I took my first steps in a forest glade, through long grasses fluttering with the canopy's shadows and light.

I walked a mile in a land of great beasts studded with armours of bone and scales.

I learned to dance in the age of bronze, spinning through circles of stones whose earthy whispers crept into my bones.

I dreamt by forges of swords, my thoughts lulled by the ringing of warm iron pounding.

I learned from the masters by marble pillars, watched the statesmen rise and fall, bobbing flowers in the breeze.

I painted pale faces behind great walls of stone, castles fortified against a world unknown.

I ventured to a land old and new, across a sea pluming terrific fancies in the minds of stalwart men.

I shivered in the steel bones of ships, sailing beneath a cold Arctic moon.

I learned a million things and became none the wiser when machines turned lives to metal.

I longed for a tree's branches when only wires crossed the sky in a prison of electricity.

I remembered the past while gazing into the simulations on bright, aching screens.

I learned to hope when skies were clear, when fields of energy replaced the machines.

I saw the end from a travelling mind, venturing beyond the confines of the world.

I whispered farewell to the world from the realm of spirits, where everyone had come to belong.

Through mortality and forgetting, I remain. I am a spark of fire you cannot see. I am a flame that does not warm, a burning you cannot smell.

I am the fire from which I was born.

—— « o » ——

Mary-Jean Harris

Mary-Jean Harris writes fantasy and historical fiction, both novels and short stories. She is also student in Theoretical Physics and has a Masters degree from the Perimeter Institute in Waterloo, Canada. Her novel *Aizai the Forgotten* is the first in the series *The Soul Wanderers*. Her website and blog can be found at: http://thesoulwanderers.blogspot.ca/

Ghost in the Machine

Susan Pieters

If I'm honest, I don't wrap my sari tighter around my shoulders because I'm cold, or to hide my latest tattoo. It's because I don't want my clothes to brush up against anything when I walk through the War Memorial Hologram. The holo is only audio-visual, so this isn't a rational fear. This is just the entrance to work, the ground floor that all employees pass through to get to UniGov offices. The Memorial reminds us of where humanity has been, why we're here, and why we celebrate each day of peace.

My first step into the holo isn't so bad today. The historical recording is on a one-month loop that covers a hundred years of religious atrocity and war. So although the odds of seeing fresh blood are high, this time I'm lucky to be crossing the smouldering fields of an agricultural zone destroyed by bombs. There are no bodies that are recognizable as such. The sound-surround has little to record but the hissing of burning structures and their intermittent collapse. No one is here to tug on my clothes as I walk on the path through the holo.

If I were completely honest, though, I would say that I start to smell smoke before I leave, and that when I glance over my shoulder, there is a young girl peering at me from a charred hole in the earth where no one could have survived. But I don't have to be honest with anyone today. I'm a sex worker for the Enforcer department, and I'm here for my next assignment.

— «» —

The chair is empty where Ted usually sits. He's team leader and both Samantha and Max look towards his place as if the chair itself might speak and begin the meeting. Samantha usually reports on investigative accounts, but she finally presses the holo cube to open the agenda.

The agenda is classified. There's some code tapping and we're all retinal scanned before it opens.

"Accomplishments and affirmations." Samantha reads from the agenda with a flat voice as her eyes stray to the empty chair.

Max manages a smile and bestows it on me. "Nice work, Jade, with the UniBank chairman last week. I can't believe he offered you sixteen thousand shares. Accounting was sweating over that one, but you came through with flying colours."

"Thank you for the affirmation," I mumble, as the agenda scrolls down and Samantha looks ready to cry.

Max leans in to read the updated report. Samantha takes one glance and looks away. I can't make sense of the information. "What's going on?"

Samantha gathers herself. "While you were on assignment, we had a Code Four. Ted went out and he's been missing for eight days."

At five days, missing agents were presumed to have turned traitor. At ten days, agents were presumed dead. In between, you flipped a coin.

Max pulls up background files. "We've got ourselves a genuine religious problem on this one. A self-proclaimed prophet holed up in the Nature Reserve."

The file shows panoramic shots of a fenced-off desert: canyons and cacti and cliffs. The next images show people from the city on their daily business, but some are dressed all in white: a woman in a lace dress, a man in a sarong, and a violinist in a white tuxedo which contrasts against a black-suited orchestra.

Max points. "You've noticed the ghosties?"

I shake my head no. Colour trends come and go. As long as you don't stick to one cultural style, you aren't censored for bias.

"They're his followers. They wear white when they come back from meeting the prophet, and they keep wearing white afterwards. These photos document citizens with altered EN scores. According to stats, lowered Essential Narcissism is the first sign of religious susceptibility. DARWIN is not happy."

It's serious if DARWIN is getting involved. It makes sense that Ted took this assignment himself.

"Why didn't DARWIN spot this prophet earlier?" I look at Max for an answer. Males were 'sampled and stored' at puberty, their DNA fully sequenced before they were sterilized. DARWIN's genetic selection saved humanity after the Age of Wars. Religious proclivity was the first DNA tag to be eradicated, even before the removal of cancer markers. "Is the prophet a throwback?"

Samantha shakes her head. "He seems to appear out of nowhere, but there was a boy that went missing from the Maternity Zone thirty years ago. He never made the transition from maternal charge to Educational Zone. Just disappeared."

Max leans towards me as we scroll records from the DARWIN storage banks. There are no DNA flags at any point of the missing child's development. But that's the scary part about messing around with DNA; it's what you don't see that can start creating monsters.

Max's breath presses against my shoulder.

I lean back a little. "So you want me to go and find Ted?"

Samantha looks a little green as she speaks. "No. Saving Ted is not the primary objective now. Don't look for him. We need to dismantle the cult. You need to take out the prophet."

Max places his hand on my arm. "I know it's not your usual assignment, but you have been trained—"

"I've done it before, Max." It's not that different from what I normally do. Sex is called the 'little death' for a reason. It's very intimate to kill someone, and I'm good at intimate connections. "But if Ted was pushed off target, what makes you think I'll do any better?"

Samantha answers first. "DARWIN recommended you. You know how closely spirituality and sexuality are linked in the DNA."

Max clears his throat and removes his hand from toying with the fabric of my sari as if he just realized what he's been doing. "We can't risk the prophet turning agents, and you'll be the most able to remain detached through the pilgrimage. Stay in control of your own emotions. You know, like you do when you … work."

Max's fingers return to the fabric beside me, like a bee that can't leave off hovering around a flower. Samantha gives me a hungry look, between jealousy and curiosity, the look of someone who wants to know the mystery of how I can do what I do with my body, how I can persuade my partners to divulge anything I want.

If I were honest, I'd tell Samantha it's not my pheromone perfume or soft curves that lure my partners to be vulnerable. It's the promise in my eyes, the sympathy of my heart, and the sweet silence of listening that invites others to trust.

I wonder if this is how a prophet operates as well.

We finish the briefing and a tech brings in a bag of gear for my three day hike. Samantha hugs me goodbye. Her eyes mist over, and I think she will ask me to look for Ted, but her lips stay sealed.

Max pauses before leaving. "If you succeed, you'll be up for promotion when you return. And I know that you've requisitioned a maternity assignment." He hands me a chip-card with his photo on it. "This has my DARWIN sperm bank number and authorization. I'd be honoured if you would consider using my gene pool. I have extremely high ratings on many of my DNA scores." He kisses my cheek.

I brush my fingers against his neck automatically before I back away. Will five years in the maternity zone be enough to remove my habits?

Max glows. "You'd make such beautiful children for Uni. I hope they accept your genes for assignment."

I look in the backpack waiting for me at the door and wonder what equipment is best to kill a prophet.

— «» —

The trail starts dry and flat. I walk on shades of sand and ochre, rocks millions of years old that crumbled into uselessness when drought and radiation destroyed the land's will to live. The only trail marker is a radioactive symbol, an official warning to use protective gear or not enter at all. I hope the rusty sign is outdated. The Nature Reserve was land set aside to recover, if possible. Further down the trail, there are no more government signs, but there are hand-cut wooden markers painted with black religious symbols, designs I've seen on the flags and bombs of soldiers in the war holos.

I watch my back as I follow the markers. I send in a report every hour, in code. "My pack is heavy."

But it's true. I'm carrying enough food and water for three days, when I'll reach my target.

— «» —

After a day of flat desert, I reach the foot of peaks that I'll be climbing tomorrow. I've smelled campfire smoke for some time, and when I see a large trail marker etched with a flame silhouette, I send a last report before I join the rest of the seekers at the base camp.

Maybe it's because I'm a woman who knows the currency of sexual favours, or maybe it's because I've been trained by Uni, but I pay special attention to everyone in the base camp. Weak and unimportant or powerful and commanding, I don't take anyone at face value. It is always the ones you don't notice who notice you.

There are a dozen people here. On my second surveillance, I confirm none could be Ted. Most people look tired and are dressed in protective hiking gear like myself, but a few wear white and serve as hosts. I sit next to Margarita, an elderly seeker who has taken several days to get to this base camp. She hides nothing from me as she eats the food prepared by the ghostie volunteers.

"My son died when I was in the Maternity Zone. I've never forgotten it. I just want to know..." Her eyes are rimmed with age and pain.

A ghostie volunteer again offers me water. I shake my head and they walk on.

Margarita watches me. "Why do you seek the prophet?"

"I'm a prostitute." I meet her gaze full on.

Margarita nods gravely, asks me nothing more.

I watch the behaviour of the people around me after they eat. They've said the water comes from a nearby well. I note no changes, no dilating pupils or slack expressions, no muscle discoordination.

A bell rings, and we are invited to rise and gather near the central fire.

"Seekers, the first element of your passage is fire. We invite you to put a name to your quest."

Pieces of paper and pencils are passed to each of us, as the sun goes behind the slopes and the sky streaks with pink.

"What do I write?" Margarita hasn't heard the instructions clearly.

The ghosties are giving encouragements and shoulder pats. One tells her, "Ask your question. What is it you seek?"

While the ghostie pays attention to Margarita, I pretend to write something on my paper, but I write nothing.

"Now throw them in the fire. Release your burdens to the prophet."

We are silent and approach the crackling flames one by one, tossing the pages, watching them burn.

The flames die down. We turn away. Small white envelopes are laid out on the table where the meal was served.

Ghosties gesture us forward. "Come feed your soul. Please choose a card."

Quick movement and chatter ensue. Margarita, beside me, debates which envelope to pick. They all look the same. Her hand swerves at the last minute.

I glance up, wondering if there are cameras. I grab a sealed envelope at random.

"He answered me." Margarita clutches a card in her hands with all the hunger of grief.

I wait to see if she will show me her message from the prophet. Does the prophet promise heaven? The concept has been banned for two hundred years, since the fall of the Martyr Cult. She doesn't share. But whatever the prophet has written, she believes it, and this gives it power.

I open my own envelope. The paper inside is blank.

When everyone else is asleep, I send in my update. "Pack is still heavy." There's nothing here but parlour tricks.

— «» —

In the morning, eight seekers start up the trail together, but it's steep. I lag behind with Margarita and offer to carry her water bottles.

Her breathing is laboured, so there is no conversation required. The rocky slopes are barren and slippery with scree; in some places the trail is buried under small rockslides. We follow the footprints of those ahead and the trail markers. I recognize the circular sign for Taoism and wonder if the prophet even knows its meaning.

The triangle symbol for earth is on a large plaque ahead, next to the symbol for air. Margarita rests. I can't see the others.

There is no camp here, but soon I realize what the symbols mean. Earth and air: the trail leads onto a ledge across a cliff face. Earthen rock, thirty metres up in the air.

I take off my backpack, dig inside. No rope, no clips. Is this where Ted went missing?

Margarita starts along the cliff face. The trail is a foot wide where she is, but gets narrower. "I'll go first so I don't chicken out."

"No Margarita, wait up, let me go first." My backpack is forty pounds and bulky. I start chugging the water.

Margarita keeps walking. She trusts the ghosties to feed her.

There is nowhere to stash my pack. My messaging device I slip into my sock, no time to use it. I forego the pistol and the long hunting blade and slip the folding knife into my pocket. I force myself to drink yet more before I toss the pack over the side of the trail and watch it bounce down, taking loose rocks with it.

My pack is no longer heavy.

Ahead of me, Margarita is stopped. She calls my name.

The view of the desert is beautiful but I make Margarita turn away from it. She clings to the rock face. We are perched on a five inch shelf above the sheer drop.

"Jade, I'm afraid." Though she is too scared to move, she edges back towards me. She reaches for me, not the rockface.

I step away from her. Is this how Ted died?

I can't back up forever, not if I want to reach the next camp. It might be easier to tip the old woman off the ledge, before she tips me. It's possible she's a plant.

Her eyes find mine. Her pupils dilate, and she's panting.

"Don't touch me," I say.

"Jade, why are we so afraid to die?" She asks this as if I'm the prophet.

"Natural selection. Take a slow breath, Margarita."

"Do you think death is the end?" She wiggles her foot closer to me.

"Margarita, we're almost there. If you want to talk to the prophet, you need to go the other way. Do you see that handhold at your shoulder?"

She turns her head slowly away. Her hand moves, her fingers find then clasp a crevice. We shuffle, hugging the cliff face, for only a few feet before it widens out.

Twenty steps later we are on the other side of the cliff face, on level ground. Margarita falls to her hands and knees. "You saved me, Jade."

At least she isn't thanking the prophet. I reach for her hand to pull her up. "You saved yourself."

— «» —

The water symbol heralds the next ghostie camp and I'm already thirsty. Margarita drinks deeply of the offered cup, but I pass. The other six seekers are giddy from a post-adrenaline rush and run up to us, hug us both. I peel the hands of one man away from me, even as he calls me 'sister.'

Margarita says again and again, "I feel so alive."

Near-death experience is one of the oldest bonding devices in the book. I have no privacy to message anyone, but I'll report back that all is well. Truly, I was expecting more of a challenge from the prophet than this.

I refuse the meal; it's easy not to eat if I focus on being thirsty. Afterwards, the ghostie volunteers lead us to the hot springs.

It's past sunset and the air turns colder by the minute. The night is a field of stars. Upwelling water in the natural pool reflects points of light at different depths, as if the stars know how to swim. We shed our hiking clothes. I keep Margarita beside me as I strip, tucking my messaging device and my pocketknife deep in my pile of clothes. I'm naked, or as naked as I can be with all my tattoos. They serve as my protection when I work and keep me partially dressed in front of my clients.

We step into the hot water, and it's much warmer than a bath. My feet tingle at first, until I adjust and get in to my chest. It smells of sulphur as if someone has struck a match. My thirst argues it is safe to drink.

A ghostie in wet robes stands in the middle of the pool and takes seekers one by one, leans them back and dips their head under the water in a ritual cleansing. It's an old purification tradition from the days when rivers ran free. I've never seen anything like this in real life, only in holos.

In holos, the water can't touch you and make you warm, make your flesh soft and melted and weightless.

It's my turn. The ghostie holds my shoulders, tips me back with the words, "Be born a true child of the prophet."

I open my mouth under the water, but I don't swallow.

I rise dripping, my head strangely hot and cold at the same time in the night air. We are all steaming from our wet hair. I am the last to get out, and as the fresh air hits my bare skin I look down at my body in alarm, but my tattoos are still there, the detailed ink curling around my chest and hips.

Our clothes are gone. I don't see them anywhere. I am given a towel and wrapped in a white robe. I slap a hand that tries to slide inside, and the hand is gone.

I only have to make it through tomorrow to save the world from a man who could bring back the death and horrors of the War Era.

I wring out my hair. I can handle myself and my thirst until then.

— «» —

We climb towards the summit at sunrise, all eight of us, in our new white robes. We arrive at the top at noon, when our shadows hide at our feet. The trail leads into a cave.

A ghostie volunteer seats us on a rock floor. The cave is a waiting room for the prophet. The candlelight is dim, but shows a hooded ghostie at the back of the cave, guarding a door engraved with mystic symbols. We will enter that room one at a time for a private interview. No one will disturb the prophet as he answers our questions, and we are to knock when we're ready to leave, transformed.

It's a perfect arrangement.

I wait my turn. As my eyes adjust to the dark, I see niches dug into the cave walls. Artifacts are on display. Not just symbols, but genuine articles that belong in a treasury: golden menorah, crosses, incense burners, altars, carved animals of wood and stone. Jewelled daggers.

How did he procure them? Are they stolen from the War Museum? Why does he resurrect the talismans of hatred and division which nearly destroyed the human race? This room is full of religious poison, the opiate of the people, the addiction which led to murder.

They float in their alcoves in the dim light, deadly and beautiful ghosts from the past.

I look at Margarita sitting near me. Her eyes are glued to the door as she waits her turn. What lies will the prophet feed her to comfort her in her old age?

I ought to go in ahead of her and kill him first.

The ghostie who'd seated us offers us water in silver cups. I take one but don't drink. I breathe through my nose because my tongue is dry. Whatever chemicals might induce faith, I can't risk them now.

Six seekers take a turn in thick silence. I calculate how much noise I will be able to make on the other side of the door. The hooded guard does not enter the room between interviews, does not speak to us. It will be best if I go last. I nod at Margarita and she goes in before me.

I dip my finger into the cup as I wait. Never has water felt so soft. I move the cup out of reach. I'll be able to drink when this is over. I raise my eyes for a final look at the glittering tokens. All Uni children memorize the Latin words of Lucretius, '*Tantum religion potuit suãdêre malõrum.*' 'To such depths of evil has religion been able to drive men.' It's too bad the prophet missed out on basic education.

For a moment, my eyes lose their focus on the wall. I'm the one with the education, I'm the one trained to preserve peace, and I'm the one planning to kill a man. Then I correct myself. An execution is not a murder.

A knock on the door, and Margarita returns. Face averted, she squeezes my shoulder gently as she passes to go outside. She is now a true ghostie.

I approach the open door and see under the hood of the ghostie who holds it open for me. Ted.

I stop. Surely he recognizes me.

Ted waits for me to enter. He sees me. He says nothing.

I step forward. Behind me the door shuts firmly in place.

The inner cave is lit by a single candle. The prophet sits on a mat on the floor, Buddha-like. Beside him is an empty mat.

I step forward onto pebbles. A sea of small stones covers the floor, crunching and sliding as I walk to sit at my place.

The prophet follows my progress across the room but his eyes do not rove over my exposed tattoos. His detachment surprises me.

"Welcome, woman without questions." His voice is soft-spoken, like the rustling of the smooth stones I have just stepped on.

I glance around the dim corners of the hollowed stone, check that the door is still shut. Is Ted listening?

The prophet does not change expression, although he looks right at me.

I find it unsettling. "I've never met anyone blind before. I thought DARWIN weeded it out."

"Even DARWIN makes exceptions to the rule." He turns his head away from me. "It will make your job easier."

"My job ... so a prophet knows everything, then." What has Ted told him?

"Not everything. Just enough. There's always room for surprise."

I shift on my mat and slowly stand back up. The pebbles under the mat grind.

He doesn't react to the sound. "When I was young, I didn't trust what I knew. I thought it was my imagination. But then things came true, or were true already. It's not knowing the future as much as knowing deeply what *is*. I have a sense for truth."

"Because you're blind?"

He turns his head. The angle reveals scars on his forehead. "It helps me listen." He exhales and looks up as if he can see where my face is. His eyes do not look blind. "I'm sorry. I shouldn't say more. Talking will make your job harder."

Lit with only one candle, I see what the ghosties have described. The creases in his countenance are shadowed with suffering and compassion. Few have faced me like this before, without desire and without pity.

He turns away. "If it makes you feel better, I need to die."

The prophet is surely a throwback, or mad. DARWIN erased the genes for self-destruction a century ago.

I look again at the closed door. I step off the mat and reach out for the rock walls, checking for cameras, metal pipes, or weaponry. The cave is smooth. No one else is here.

With one kick I can break his neck: the front of my ankle to his hyoid bone. I can't wait any longer. I take two swift steps, one towards the prophet and one to his right. He can hear what I'm doing and I expect him to duck, but he holds so motionless that I hesitate and am thrown off balance. Pebbles roll and slip under my feet and I slide, my leg flying over his head, the torque of my failed kick spinning me to the ground.

My head falls back towards the floor, but instead of cracking my skull on the rocks, he catches me in his arms.

"Are you hurt?" His hand feels across my head and under my shoulders. The bare neck I was about to snap leans over me, skin vulnerable, exposed and watching. "Is your ankle twisted?"

The candlelight appears brighter now thanks to my adrenaline reaction. I roll on my side, testing my body. His arm supports me. The pebbles part below me so I feel the slab of bedrock beneath. His arms will be bruised, if he lives that long.

"Why do you keep those damned relics outside?" I am winded and my voice is a hiss.

His arm is strong behind me. "Why do they scare you?"

"I'm not afraid." I say this as my heart drives blood through my veins with such force that my fingers pulse. "Why are you being kind to me?"

His hand brushes hair away from my forehead as if I'm a child. I don't think he will answer me, but finally he responds. "Tell me first, do you think it possible that DARWIN has a soul?"

What does this man know about DARWIN? What is Ted doing here? I need to know more.

I do what I do best. I press on his hand to keep it from leaving me. His hand stills and wonders why but does not resist. I have never felt such intelligence from a touch. In my job, my partners use their eyes, and I guide their eyes, to perform the question and answer dance.

His fingers are unwilling to speak more to mine at first. My hand on his face meets with tense surprise.

I place his hand on my throat, at the place I was going to kick him a moment ago. "Are *you* afraid?"

"Yes." His hand holds still.

I pull his hand lower down to follow the gap in my robe.

He closes his eyes. I bare my breasts for his touch and let my robe part open. My tattoos are no protection, no covering against a blind man. For the first time, I am truly naked.

His lips are like water and I drink deep with all the longing I have kept back from my clients. The prophet gives, and I take.

I taste the sweetness of his tear-stained face, or my tear-stained face; soon we are past knowing where one of us begins and the other ends.

"You are so beautiful," he says, when it is over. "I didn't imagine it would be like this."

"What do you mean?"

His fingers etch messages into my brow. "I didn't imagine it would be this sad to die."

That's when Ted opens the door, tears on his face as well. "Forgive me." His words are directed to me rather than the prophet, as if the prophet has already understood, as if the prophet can see, as Ted points the gun to the blind eyes and fires.

— «» —

Ted is back at his desk, Samantha's arm on top of his as if she'll not let him out of her sight again. She beams at me until she takes in my white clothes.

"Keeping up appearances," I explain. "I've just returned from a pilgrimage, right?"

She restores her smile.

Max stands to fully embrace me. He isn't waiting for the affirmations on the agenda. "Congratulations Jade, you did it!"

I look over at Ted. He's given me all the credit.

The four of us settle down and the update cube informs us of the collapse and dispersion of all three cult encampments. Deprogramming is not needed. No more action is required.

"It's a good thing you never drank the water, Jade." Samantha brushes Ted's hand. "The sample Ted brought back shows heavy lacing of radioactive minerals. That might be what induced the psychotropic effects. The prophet must have been drinking it for years."

Ted averts his eyes. Fortunately no one has thought to test his blood or mine for radioactivity or minerals. I drank freely on my way out of the Nature Reserve.

The rest of the report is mundane. Samantha ends the meeting. "Jade, I guess this was your last job as an Enforcer. We're very excited that your maternity assignment has been approved, although we're sad to see you go." Samantha rises to give me an embrace.

Ted shakes my hand.

Max puts his arm around my shoulder as we leave, leans to whisper into my ear. "And I'm only slightly disappointed that you didn't choose my DNA pool."

I keep my smile neutral, as if I understand. I haven't made any decisions on gene traits yet.

Max keeps his arm around me. "Now don't play coy. DARWIN already put in your file that you've received your DNA match. Well, maybe next time?" He winks.

I kiss his cheek as I leave, so he can't see my expression.

If I were honest, I would confess that I no longer agree with Lucretius. It's not religion that causes war, it's human assumptions. It's the logical extremes which we allow to silence our hearts. It's sitting in a cave and thinking you're the only one who can see.

I exit through the War Memorial holo, now a loud and bloody battlefield. When I smell flowers, I turn towards a rose bush blooming beside a munitions dump. Sitting on top of crated explosives, swinging her feet, I see the little girl wearing white. I wave to her, and wonder what I'll name her.

———— « o » ————

Susan Pieters

Susan Pieters had time to earn a Masters degree in English before three children earned her a PhD in Life. (She's still waiting for the diploma.) She writes in a variety of genres and lengths, and has won several awards at the Surrey International Writers' Conference (one of her favourite places to be.) She is on the team at PULP Literature magazine, found at: pulpliterature.com.

Marvin

Alan Bao

It is six feet of plasteel and automata. A whirring, clockwork man.

It is love at first sight.

Primary directive: initialize and debug.

The child is not frightened, not in the slightest. A bit of slobber frames her little mouth, fingers still damp from being chewed on by teething gums, and she takes her first unsteady steps toward the metal giant. The mother starts forward in alarm.

"It's all right, honey. It's perfectly safe."

The child hugs the leg of the automata with both hands. A squeal of delight, and she looks up at this new friend, round and wondering, the way babies do.

"They call it the Marvellous Robotron." Her father beams with pride. "First of its kind. Upgradeable too. This thing will help out around the house. It'll make all our lives easier — especially when I head out east."

The child smiles. This clockwork man is a bastion, a statue. Inattentive. But its plasteel frame is rounded and aesthetic, and she giggles at her own warped reflection staring back at her from the sheet metal. The chassis is warm with internal heat and vibrates ever-so-slightly to the touch. The Marvellous Edition is a prototype. It is three months of haggling with bureaucrats and pulling strings in various offices, because Mr. Schumann is going to be away from home for a long time, and needs a hand for the family. It is cutting-edge technology, government patents that won't be available to the commercial public for at least another three years. But to the child, it is simply:

Friend.

— «» —

Her first words are "Mama, mama."

Robotic arms are warm and whirring.

When she falls asleep, she is aware of nothing but the fact that she is loved.

— «» —

"Marvin! Marvin! Can you get me a cookie? Get me a cookie, please. It's okay, Pappy said so. Get me a cookie, okay? Marvin?"

Primary directive: awaiting further instruction from unit owner.

"Now, Mindy honey, the bot won't let you have a cookie unless you eat your vegetables first. I've told him not to. Isn't that right?"

The android is stoic and silent. The child strains up towards the cookie jar in the android's hand, hefted like an Olympic torch towards the ceiling. She hits the android on the leg. Whines and whittles. Then, staring up at her friend's unresponsive face, the child begins to bawl. Her mother is surprised by this genuine bout of tears, and throws up her hands in exasperation.

"All this over a cookie!"

But to the child, it is more than just a cookie. It is a betrayal. Marvin *always* did just exactly what Mammy said. She thinks he should try to stand up for himself, for a change. *She* would do that for *him* — it simply isn't fair.

So she bawls. She kicks and screams and holds her breath, and no amount of *honeys* or *sweethearts* or stern *Mindy Gabriel Schumann!'s* can break her out of her tantrum.

"The Mad Russian eats bad little girls who don't eat their vegetables. You don't want the Mad Russian to come get you, do you?"

She bawls even harder, and wonders why Mammy and the other grown-ups just don't get it. It's not about the Mad Russian. It was never about the Mad Russian. It's not about the vegetables, or even the cookies in the jar (though she really, really wants one.)

The android is a bastion. Whirring, clockwork man. There is nothing else that can be said.

She is sent to her room with no dessert. She does not complain. During the night, she creeps down to the kitchen, climbs a chair on to the countertop, and sneaks three chocolate-and-macadamia cookies from the jar in the pantry. The android is sitting on the ground, a metal Buddha, buzzing softly in the glow. She tilts her nose up and makes sure he can see the triumphant cookies in her hand as she walks past.

Marvin always does just what Mammy says. He never stands up to Mammy.

Her bedroom is just up the stairs, and her feet are cold. But she looks back at the soft glow of electro-shades humming on the linoleum, and pauses.

Marvin never stands up to *anyone*. It's not his fault, really.

After a moment of consideration, she decides to forgive him, and sits down in his whirring lap. It is warm and homely, like the back of a refrigerator.

She proffers out a cookie in her hand.

"I know you don't eat, Marvin, but they're really good. They're tasty. That's why I wanted them earlier."

The unit is recharging. Its shuttered eyes do not respond.

She shrugs. "Mammy says you don't understand me. But you don't have to be afraid of Mammy. Even *I* only listen to her *sometimes*."

Primary power supply: 64%.

She pats the android on the head, and takes a bite of her cookie. She sits there in silence well into the night, with her Marvin and her cookies, content and happy, the way children are.

— «» —

Her friends from kindergarten are always thrilled when Marvin comes around.

Other children are not so understanding.

Rocks and bottles bounce off with a ringing clang, as impassive silicon circuits assess paint chips and other superficial damage. Mindy shouts at the kids. They just laugh. She comes home from most walks in tears. She can't stand the children's taunts and their stones — not because they're directed at her, but because they're directed at Marvin, and

Marvin never stands up for himself. The kids only laugh as she yells and waves her stick. Only when she furiously threatens to have Marvin squash their heads like over-ripe cantaloupes do they leave well enough alone.

— «» —

"Kids tease each other all the time. Come on, Janice."

"Oh, if it were just that! If it were just that, I wouldn't be as worried. But do you know what she said to me after she was done sobbing? She said she was crying because they were hurting the robot's feelings. Its feelings!"

"So the kid is a little attached. You've had this bot since she was tiny, right?"

"But that's my point. It's unhealthy. Having feelings for a piece of hardware, something that can't feel back. Where do you draw the line? She talks to it all the time. She's convinced that it understands her. Just the other day, I caught her out of bed late, reading it a story, for god's sake."

"Well, she's still got plenty of real friends. It can't be that unhealthy."

The mother shakes her head, annoyed at her guest's flippant attitude.

"None of them are like the bot. The bot is her *best* friend. She spends every minute of the day with it. I would get rid of the thing, if it wasn't so damned useful!"

There is a pensive silence.

"You know, I read about this lady in Europe who tried to marry the Eiffel Tower. Maybe your kid can grow up to be one of those."

The humour is lost on the mother. A cold worried stare cuts through the living room.

"Oh, hey, I didn't mean it. I was just fooling," the guest says hastily. "It'll turn out all right. You'll see. One of these days, she'll grow out of it."

The cold thaws. Somewhat.

"Yeah. Yeah, I hope you're right."

— «» —

The radio blares its nonsense over the tea-party. Today's lesson is in *please* and *thank-you's* because that's what they taught in her first day at school, and that's the lesson Mindy is bringing home for the day.

"You say please when you really, really want someone to do something."

The android holds the plastic cup in its hand. It is listening, attentive. The radio babbles on, saying meaningless things like, *strained relationships between the two powers* and *as tensions mount along the Bering Strait.*

"People don't like it when you just *make* them do something, see. So you have to say please, and then they'll do it. Please sit down. Please get up. You know?"

...say that the balkanization of Eastern Europe only antagonizes the militaristic and highly-capable...

"And if they do what you say, then you have to say thank you, because that makes them feel nice about it afterwards. Do you understand?" It's usually a toss-up, but this time, the speech inflection is recognized. The android nods vigorously.

The girl beams with pleasure.

...a matter of life or death. We've got ships sitting in the Black Sea; I say we use them!

— «» —

Mr. Schumann hasn't slept in three days. He has spent the last seventy-two hours shuttling between continents and arguing with riled-up bureaucrats and heads-of-states, before being called to attend an emergency briefing with the president, and finally being allowed the short flight from DC to Jersey less than two hours ago.

He slumps along his front porch. The door is locked, and he hasn't got the energy to rummage around in his suitcase for his keys. Lifeless fingers reach out for the doorbell.

"Henry? Henry, you're home early! Why didn't you call?"

Then upon a closer look: "You look awful."

Henry Schumann laughs. Nothing's broken through the media cordon — the radios and television haven't caught on. There is still the pretence of civility, so maybe there is still hope. Maybe it's wrong for him to despair.

"PRIMARY OWNER, WELCOME BACK TO YOUR RESIDENCE. HOW MAY I HELP."

"Oh, not *now*, you useless piece of tin," Janice snaps. She is beginning to notice the bags under Henry's eyes, the cracks running across his lips, and the pallid pasty complexion of perpetual jet-lag. "Jesus Christ, Henry, what the hell did they do to you over there?"

Mr. Schumann laughs. What did they do? What did it matter? It was what they didn't do that was important. And what they didn't do was listen.

"Pappy!" The squeal is absolute delight. She hadn't expected him until next week. She runs to wrap her arms around his stubble-and-sandpaper neck, and he returns her embrace. But at her back, he puts his face in his hands. He cannot believe it is happening. *Not my beautiful wife. Not my beautiful child.* They had tried their best, they had, but Moscow wouldn't listen.

"Henry. Henry, look at me. What's wrong?"

Mr. Schumann looks up from his palms.

"The Russians are coming."

— «» —

The Russians are coming, and the sky is raining fire. The neighbourhood is in full evacuation. Air sirens blare in the distance.

Primary directive: reach extraction point. OVERRIDING DIRECTIVE: Sustain vital biological functions of designation Mindy G. Schumann until further instruction.

"My balloon! My balloon! Marvin, Marvin, help me get my balloon."

Balloon. Composition: 76% helium, 18% nitrogen, 3% oxygen. Miscellaneous omitted.

"It's Pappy's balloon, Marvin! I don't know where he is! I have to get his balloon, Marvin!"

The android ignores the plea, and sweeps the little girl into its arms. Mr. Schumann had programmed it with very specific instructions before heading back to HQ, and to the little red telephone direct to the Kremlin in hopes of negotiating a last-minute ceasefire. Mrs. Schumann had gone to the repair shop to get their car and take the family over the river. She has not come back.

There is a yell and the thumping of boots. A rush of bodies and the sweat-stained uniforms of the National Guard.

"Fucking tinhead! Get the kid out of here!"

"Marvin!" The child shrills as she is carried against her will, ever closer to extraction point, ever closer to safety. "Mar-vin!"

For the millionth time, the android runs the same subroutine it consistently does when interacting with designation Mindy G. Schumann.

Identify: Marvin. Marvin P. Fitzgerald. Industrialist. Nationality: Austrian. Marvin Chun-Ling. Born Chun Ling Lai. Undersecretary to Liao Ji-Tao, diplomat. Nationality: Chinese. Marvin Stellman...

"Marvin!"

Marvin. Identify: Marvin.

There is an unknown noise in the distance. Protocols engage, and the android brings the child into safety position, shielding her body with its own. She squeals because they are standing in water, because through the tears and through the sirens, she is beginning to feel frightened. Her friend's warm metallic arms are the only thing clutching her to earth.

The android glances down. Water. Pool.

Marvin?

Optic fibres whir as clockwork eyes re-focus. Reflection: a pale fleshy thing displaying biological vitals. Worn-down skippers and polka-dot dress, cradled in clockwork arms.

The automaton face in the water stares back, optics click-whirring in tune to the android's own curiosity.

Marvin?

It does not see the mortar shell.

The world explodes on impact.

— «» —

Structural integrity — stable. Re-engaging hydraulics; gyroscopic equilibrium; thermo-optics.

The android scans its surroundings. No immediate threats. Biological vitals are present — barely. Overriding directive is to sling the little body over its shoulder, and make with all haste towards the extraction point. But some strange compunction in its impact-riddled circuits compels it not to.

People don't like it when you *make* them do something.

Initiate vox-controls. Overriding outdated protocol.

Command: "GET UP, VITAL BIOLOGICAL."

Unknown noises in the distance, and the android places itself back into safety position, one slightly charred metallic arm on either side of the little child. Shutters click and whir as processing chips strain to account for all external stimuli. Noises, unidentified, eight hundred twenty-six meters north, nine-hundred eleven north-north-west, seven hundred sixty-eight north-north-east...

Below: water, vital biological, Mindy G. Schumann. Overriding directive. Overhead, now roughly 66% helium, 23% nitrogen and 5% oxygen (cut with miscellaneous other gasses), a little red balloon floats serene, unhurried by the chaos unfolding on the ground.

Distance: 62 meters. Subordinate directive: Retrieve: composition 66% helium 18% nitrogen 10%—

Retrieve: Balloon.

Bright.

Red.

Balloon.

Overriding directive supersedes. The android looks back at the little body on the ground.

"GET UP." The vox-synths blare again, this time with heightened stress patterns to simulate urgency. The child makes no attempt to follow the directive.

"GET UP, VITAL BIOLOGICAL. GET UP. GET UP."

No response. This time, with no external input, it — he? — runs the identification subroutine for the name and designation, Marvin, and finds nothing useable. It reaches out to take designation Mindy G. Schumann from the ground and sling her over its shoulders, but the strange compunction stops it yet again. The scanners read feeble heartbeats, evanescing body-heat. Overriding directive is in jeopardy.

Overriding directive cannot fail.

As Marvin gingerly reaches down to pick up the little body, he tries one last time with the vox-synth.

"MINDY G. SCHUMANN."

"MINDY G. SCHUMANN. PLEASE GET UP."

—— « o » ——

Alan Bao

Alan Bao is a Chinese-Canadian illustrator who finds it incredibly awkward to write about himself in the third-person. He draws for a living, he writes for fun, and he plays a pretty mean blues guitar on the side. You can find his portfolio: www.alanbao.com or follow him on social media at: www.twitter.com/alanbaoart and www.facebook.com/alanbaoart.

The Shoulders of Giants

Robert J. Sawyer

(First published as the lead story in *Star Colonies*
edited by Martin H. Greenberg and
John Helfers, DAW Books, June 2000.)

It seemed like only yesterday when I'd died, but, of course, it was almost certainly centuries ago. I wish the computer would just *tell* me, dammitall, but it was doubtless waiting until its sensors said I was sufficiently stable and alert. The irony was that my pulse was surely racing out of concern, forestalling it speaking to me. If this was an emergency, it should inform me, and if it wasn't, it should let me relax.

Finally, the machine did speak in its crisp, feminine voice. "Hello, Toby. Welcome back to the world of the living."

"Where—" I'd thought I'd spoken the word, but no sound had come out. I tried again. "Where are we?"

"Exactly where we should be: decelerating toward Soror."

I felt myself calming down. "How is Ling?"

"She's reviving, as well."

"The others?"

"All forty-eight cryogenics chambers are functioning properly," said the computer. "Everybody is apparently fine."

That was good to hear, but it wasn't surprising. We had four extra cryochambers; if one of the occupied ones had failed, Ling and I would have been awoken earlier to transfer the person within it into a spare. "What's the date?"

"16 June 3296."

I'd expected an answer like that, but it still took me back a bit. Twelve hundred years had elapsed since the blood had been siphoned out of my body and oxygenated antifreeze had been pumped in to replace it. We'd spent the first of those years accelerating, and presumably the last one decelerating, and the rest—

—the rest was spent coasting at our maximum velocity, 3,000 km/s, one percent of the speed of light. My father had been from Glasgow; my mother, from Los Angeles. They had both enjoyed the quip that the difference between an American and a European was that to an American, a hundred years was a long time, and to a European, a hundred miles is a big journey.

But both would agree that twelve hundred years and 11.9 light-years were equally staggering values. And now, here we were, decelerating in toward Tau Ceti, the closest sunlike star to Earth that wasn't part of a multiple-star system. Of course, because of that, this star had been frequently examined by Earth's Search for Extraterrestrial Intelligence. But nothing had ever been detected; nary a peep.

I was feeling better minute by minute. My own blood, stored in bottles, had been returned to my body and was now coursing through my arteries, my veins, reanimating me.

We were going to make it.

Tau Ceti happened to be oriented with its north pole facing toward Sol; that meant that the technique developed late in the twentieth century to detect planetary systems based on subtle blueshifts and redshifts of a star tugged now closer, now farther away, was useless with it. Any wobble in Tau Ceti's movements would be perpendicular, as seen from Earth, producing no Doppler effect. But eventually Earth-orbiting telescopes had been developed that were sensitive enough to detect the wobble visually, and—

It had been front-page news around the world: the first solar system seen by telescopes. Not inferred from stellar wobbles or spectral shifts, but actually *seen*. At least four planets could be made out orbiting Tau Ceti, and one of them—

There had been formulas for decades, first popularized in the RAND Corporation's study *Habitable Planets for Man*. Every science-fiction writer and astrobiologist worth his or her

salt had used them to determine the *life zones* — the distances
from target stars at which planets with Earthlike surface
temperatures might exist, a Goldilocks band, neither too hot
nor too cold.

And the second of the four planets that could be seen
around Tau Ceti was smack-dab in the middle of that star's
life zone. The planet was watched carefully for an entire year
— one of its years, that is, a period of 193 Earth days. Two
wonderful facts became apparent. First, the planet's orbit was
damn near circular — meaning it would likely have stable
temperatures all the time; the gravitational influence of the
fourth planet, a Jovian giant orbiting at a distance of half a
billion kilometers from Tau Ceti, probably was responsible for
that.

And, second, the planet varied in brightness substantially
over the course of its twenty-nine-hour-and-seventeen-minute
day. The reason was easy to deduce: most of one hemisphere
was covered with land, which reflected back little of Tau Ceti's
yellow light, while the other hemisphere, with a much higher
albedo, was likely covered by a vast ocean, no doubt, given
the planet's fortuitous orbital radius, of liquid water — an
extraterrestrial Pacific.

Of course, at a distance of 11.9 light-years, it was quite
possible that Tau Ceti had other planets, too small or too dark
to be seen. And so referring to the Earthlike globe as Tau Ceti II
would have been problematic; if an additional world or worlds
were eventually found orbiting closer in, the system's planetary
numbering would end up as confusing as the scheme used to
designate Saturn's rings.

Clearly a name was called for, and Giancarlo DiMaio,
the astronomer who had discovered the half-land, half-water
world, gave it one: Soror, the Latin word for sister. And, indeed,
Soror appeared, at least as far as could be told from Earth, to be
a sister to humanity's home world.

Soon we would know for sure just how perfect a sister it
was. And speaking of sisters, well — okay, Ling Woo wasn't
my biological sister, but we'd worked together and trained
together for four years before launch, and I'd come to think of
her as a sister, despite the press constantly referring to us as
the new Adam and Eve. Of course, we'd help to populate the

new world, but not together; my wife, Helena, was one of the forty-eight others still frozen solid. Ling wasn't involved yet with any of the other colonists, but, well, she was gorgeous and brilliant, and of the two dozen men in cryosleep, twenty-one were unattached.

Ling and I were co-captains of the *Pioneer Spirit*. Her cryocoffin was like mine, and unlike all the others: it was designed for repeated use. She and I could be revived multiple times during the voyage, to deal with emergencies. The rest of the crew, in coffins that had cost only $700,000 apiece instead of the six million each of ours was worth, could only be revived once, when our ship reached its final destination.

"You're all set," said the computer. "You can get up now."

The thick glass cover over my coffin slid aside, and I used the padded handles to hoist myself out of its black porcelain frame. For most of the journey, the ship had been coasting in zero gravity, but now that it was decelerating, there was a gentle push downward. Still, it was nowhere near a full g, and I was grateful for that. It would be a day or two before I would be truly steady on my feet.

My module was shielded from the others by a partition, which I'd covered with photos of people I'd left behind: my parents, Helena's parents, my real sister, her two sons. My clothes had waited patiently for me for twelve hundred years; I rather suspected they were now hopelessly out of style. But I got dressed — I'd been naked in the cryochamber, of course — and at last I stepped out from behind the partition, just in time to see Ling emerging from behind the wall that shielded her cryocoffin.

"'Morning," I said, trying to sound blasé.

Ling, wearing a blue and grey jumpsuit, smiled broadly. "Good morning."

We moved into the center of the room, and hugged, friends delighted to have shared an adventure together. Then we immediately headed out toward the bridge, half-walking, half-floating, in the reduced gravity.

"How'd you sleep?" asked Ling.

It wasn't a frivolous question. Prior to our mission, the longest anyone had spent in cryofreeze was five years, on a voyage to Saturn; the *Pioneer Spirit* was Earth's first starship.

"Fine," I said. "You?"

"Okay," replied Ling. But then she stopped moving, and briefly touched my forearm. "Did you — did you dream?"

Brain activity slowed to a virtual halt in cryofreeze, but several members of the crew of *Cronus* — the Saturn mission — had claimed to have had brief dreams, lasting perhaps two or three subjective minutes, spread over five years. Over the span that the *Pioneer Spirit* had been traveling, there would have been time for many hours of dreaming.

I shook my head. "No. What about you?"

Ling nodded. "Yes. I dreamt about the strait of Gibraltar. Ever been there?"

"No."

"It's Spain's southernmost boundary, of course. You can see across the strait from Europe to northern Africa, and there were Neandertal settlements on the Spanish side." Ling's Ph.D. was in anthropology. "But they never made it across the strait. They could clearly see that there was more land — another continent! — only thirteen kilometers away. A strong swimmer can make it, and with any sort of raft or boat, it was eminently doable. But Neandertals never journeyed to the other side; as far as we can tell, they never even tried."

"And you dreamt—?"

"I dreamt I was part of a Neandertal community there, a teenage girl, I guess. And I was trying to convince the others that we should go across the strait, go see the new land. But I couldn't; they weren't interested. There was plenty of food and shelter where we were. Finally, I headed out on my own, trying to swim it. The water was cold and the waves were high, and half the time I couldn't get any air to breathe, but I swam and I swam, and then…"

"Yes?"

She shrugged a little. "And then I woke up."

I smiled at her. "Well, this time we're going to make it. We're going to make it for sure."

We came to the bridge door, which opened automatically to admit us, although it squeaked something fierce while doing so; its lubricants must have dried up over the last twelve centuries. The room was rectangular with a double row of angled consoles facing a large screen, which currently was off.

"Distance to Soror?" I asked into the air.

The computer's voice replied. "1.2 million kilometers."

I nodded. About three times the distance between Earth and its moon. "Screen on, view ahead."

"Overrides are in place," said the computer.

Ling smiled at me. "You're jumping the gun, partner."

I was embarrassed. The *Pioneer Spirit* was decelerating toward Soror; the ship's fusion exhaust was facing in the direction of travel. The optical scanners would be burned out by the glare if their shutters were opened. "Computer, turn off the fusion motors."

"Powering down," said the artificial voice.

"Visual as soon as you're able," I said.

The gravity bled away as the ship's engines stopped firing. Ling held on to one of the handles attached to the top of the console nearest her; I was still a little groggy from the suspended animation, and just floated freely in the room. After about two minutes, the screen came on. Tau Ceti was in the exact center, a baseball-sized yellow disk. And the four planets were clearly visible, ranging from pea-sized to as big as grape.

"Magnify on Soror," I said.

One of the peas became a billiard ball, although Tau Ceti grew hardly at all.

"More," said Ling.

The planet grew to softball size. It was showing as a wide crescent, perhaps a third of the disk illuminated from this angle. And — thankfully, fantastically — Soror was everything we'd dreamed it would be: a giant polished marble, with swirls of white cloud, and a vast, blue ocean, and—

Part of a continent was visible, emerging out of the darkness. And it was green, apparently covered with vegetation.

We hugged again, squeezing each other tightly. No one had been sure when we'd left Earth; Soror could have been barren. The *Pioneer Spirit* was ready regardless: in its cargo holds was everything we needed to survive even on an airless world. But we'd hoped and prayed that Soror would be, well — just like this: a true sister, another Earth, another home.

"It's beautiful, isn't it?" said Ling.

I felt my eyes tearing. It *was* beautiful, breathtaking, stunning. The vast ocean, the cottony clouds, the verdant land, and—

"Oh, my God," I said, softly. "Oh, my God."

"What?" said Ling.

"Don't you see?" I asked. "Look!"

Ling narrowed her eyes and moved closer to the screen. "What?"

"On the dark side," I said.

She looked again. "Oh..." she said. There were faint lights sprinkled across the darkness; hard to see, but definitely there. "Could it be volcanism?" asked Ling. Maybe Soror wasn't so perfect after all.

"Computer," I said, "spectral analysis of the light sources on the planet's dark side."

"Predominantly incandescent lighting, color temperature 5600 kelvin."

I exhaled and looked at Ling. They weren't volcanoes. They were cities.

Soror, the world we'd spent twelve centuries traveling to, the world we'd intended to colonize, the world that had been dead silent when examined by radio telescopes, was already inhabited.

— «◊» —

The *Pioneer Spirit* was a colonization ship; it wasn't intended as a diplomatic vessel. When it had left Earth, it had seemed important to get at least some humans off the mother world. Two small-scale nuclear wars — Nuke I and Nuke II, as the media had dubbed them — had already been fought, one in southern Asia, the other in South America. It appeared to be only a matter of time before Nuke III, and that one might be the big one.

SETI had detected nothing from Tau Ceti, at least not by 2051. But Earth itself had only been broadcasting for a century and a half at that point; Tau Ceti might have had a thriving civilization then that hadn't yet started using radio. But now it was twelve hundred years later. Who knew how advanced the Tau Cetians might be?

I looked at Ling, then back at the screen. "What should we do?"

Ling tilted her head to one side. "I'm not sure. On the one hand, I'd love to meet them, whoever they are. But..."

"But they might not want to meet us," I said. "They might think we're invaders, and—"

"And we've got forty-eight other colonists to think about," said Ling. "For all we know, we're the last surviving humans."

I frowned. "Well, that's easy enough to determine. Computer, swing the radio telescope toward Sol system. See if you can pick anything up that might be artificial."

"Just a sec," said the female voice. A few moments later, a cacophony filled the room: static and snatches of voices and bits of music and sequences of tones, overlapping and jumbled, fading in and out. I heard what sounded like English — although strangely inflected — and maybe Arabic and Mandarin and…

"We're not the last survivors," I said, smiling. "There's still life on Earth — or, at least, there was 11.9 years ago, when those signals started out."

Ling exhaled. "I'm glad we didn't blow ourselves up," she said. "Now, I guess we should find out what we're dealing with at Tau Ceti. Computer, swing the dish to face Soror, and again scan for artificial signals."

"Doing so." There was silence for most of a minute, then a blast of static, and a few bars of music, and clicks and bleeps, and voices, speaking in Mandarin and English and—

"No," said Ling. "I said face the dish the *other* way. I want to hear what's coming from Soror."

The computer actually sounded miffed. "The dish *is* facing toward Soror," it said.

I looked at Ling, realization dawning. At the time we'd left Earth, we'd been so worried that humanity was about to snuff itself out, we hadn't really stopped to consider what would happen if that didn't occur. But with twelve hundred years, faster spaceships would doubtless have been developed. While the colonists aboard the *Pioneer Spirit* had slept, some dreaming at an indolent pace, other ships had zipped past them, arriving at Tau Ceti decades, if not centuries, earlier — long enough ago that they'd already built human cities on Soror.

— «〉» —

"Damn it," I said. "God damn it." I shook my head, staring at the screen. The tortoise was supposed to win, not the hare.

"What do we do now?" asked Ling.

I sighed. "I suppose we should contact them."

"We— ah, we might be from the wrong side."

I grinned. "Well, we can't *both* be from the wrong side. Besides, you heard the radio: Mandarin *and* English. Anyway, I can't imagine that anyone cares about a war more than a thousand years in the past, and—"

"Excuse me," said the ship's computer. "Incoming audio message."

I looked at Ling. She frowned, surprised. "Put it on," I said.

"*Pioneer Spirit*, welcome! This is Jod Bokket, manager of the Derluntin space station, in orbit around Soror. Is there anyone awake on board?" It was a man's voice, with an accent unlike anything I'd ever heard before.

Ling looked at me, to see if I was going to object, then she spoke up. "Computer, send a reply." The computer bleeped to signal that the channel was open. "This is Dr. Ling Woo, co-captain of the *Pioneer Spirit*. Two of us have revived; there are forty-eight more still in cryofreeze."

"Well, look," said Bokket's voice, "it'll be days at the rate you're going before you get here. How about if we send a ship to bring you two to Derluntin? We can have someone there to pick you up in about an hour."

"They really like to rub it in, don't they?" I grumbled.

"What was that?" said Bokket. "We couldn't quite make it out."

Ling and I consulted with facial expressions, then agreed. "Sure," said Ling. "We'll be waiting."

"Not for long," said Bokket, and the speaker went dead.

— «» —

Bokket himself came to collect us. His spherical ship was tiny compared with ours, but it seemed to have about the same amount of habitable interior space; would the ignominies ever cease? Docking adapters had changed a lot in a thousand years, and he wasn't able to get an airtight seal, so we had to transfer over to his ship in space suits. Once aboard, I was pleased to see we were still floating freely; it would have been *too* much if they'd had artificial gravity.

Bokket seemed a nice fellow — about my age, early thirties. Of course, maybe people looked youthful forever now; who knew how old he might actually be? I couldn't really identify his ethnicity, either; he seemed to be rather a blend of traits.

But he certainly was taken with Ling — his eyes popped out when she took off her helmet, revealing her heart-shaped face and long, black hair.

"Hello," he said, smiling broadly.

Ling smiled back. "Hello. I'm Ling Woo, and this is Toby MacGregor, my co-captain."

"Greetings," I said, sticking out my hand.

Bokket looked at it, clearly not knowing precisely what to do. He extended his hand in a mirroring of my gesture, but didn't touch me. I closed the gap and clasped his hand. He seemed surprised, but pleased.

"We'll take you back to the station first," he said. "Forgive us, but, well — you can't go down to the planet's surface yet; you'll have to be quarantined. We've eliminated a lot of diseases, of course, since your time, and so we don't vaccinate for them anymore. I'm willing to take the risk, but..."

I nodded. "That's fine."

He tipped his head slightly, as if he were preoccupied for a moment, then: "I've told the ship to take us back to Derluntin station. It's in a polar orbit, about 200 kilometers above Soror; you'll get some beautiful views of the planet, anyway." He was grinning from ear to ear. "It's wonderful to meet you people," he said. "Like a page out of history."

— «» —

"If you knew about us," I asked, after we'd settled in for the journey to the station, "why didn't you pick us up earlier?"

Bokket cleared his throat. "We didn't know about you."

"But you called us by name: *Pioneer Spirit*."

"Well, it *is* painted in letters three meters high across your hull. Our asteroid-watch system detected you. A lot of information from your time has been lost — I guess there was a lot of political upheaval then, no? — but we knew Earth had experimented with sleeper ships in the twenty-first century."

We were getting close to the space station; it was a giant ring, spinning to simulate gravity. It might have taken us over a thousand years to do it, but humanity was finally building space stations the way God had always intended them to be.

And floating next to the space station was a beautiful space-ship, with a spindle-shaped silver hull and two sets of mutually perpendicular emerald-green delta wings. "It's gorgeous," I said.

Bokket nodded.

"How does it land, though? Tail-down?"

"It doesn't land; it's a starship."

"Yes, but—"

"We use shuttles to go between it and the ground."

"But if it can't land," asked Ling, "why is it streamlined? Just for esthetics?"

Bokket laughed, but it was a polite laugh. "It's streamlined because it needs to be. There's substantial length-contraction when flying at just below the speed of light; that means that the interstellar medium seems much denser. Although there's only one baryon per cubic centimeter, they form what seems to be an appreciable atmosphere if you're going fast enough."

"And your ships are *that* fast?" asked Ling.

Bokket smiled. "Yes. They're that fast."

Ling shook her head. "We were crazy," she said. "Crazy to undertake our journey." She looked briefly at Bokket, but couldn't meet his eyes. She turned her gaze down toward the floor. "You must think we're incredibly foolish."

Bokket's eyes widened. He seemed at a loss for what to say. He looked at me, spreading his arms, as if appealing to me for support. But I just exhaled, letting air — and disappointment — vent from my body.

"You're wrong," said Bokket, at last. "You couldn't be more wrong. We *honor* you." He paused, waiting for Ling to look up again. She did, her eyebrows lifted questioningly. "If we have come farther than you," said Bokket, "or have gone faster than you, it's because we had your work to build on. Humans are here now because it's *easy* for us to be here, because you and others blazed the trails." He looked at me, then at Ling. "If we see farther," he said, "it's because we stand on the shoulders of giants."

— ‹› —

Later that day, Ling, Bokket, and I were walking along the gently curving floor of Derluntin station. We were confined to a limited part of one section; they'd let us down to the planet's surface in another ten days, Bokket had said.

"There's nothing for us here," said Ling, hands in her pockets. "We're freaks, anachronisms. Like somebody from the T'ang Dynasty showing up in our world."

"Soror is wealthy," said Bokket. "We can certainly support you and your passengers."

"They are *not* passengers," I snapped. "They are colonists. They are explorers."

Bokket nodded. "I'm sorry. You're right, of course. But look — we really are delighted that you're here. I've been keeping the media away; the quarantine lets me do that. But they will go absolutely dingo when you come down to the planet. It's like having Neil Armstrong or Tamiko Hiroshige show up at your door."

"Tamiko who?" asked Ling.

"Sorry. After your time. She was the first person to disembark at Alpha Centauri."

"The first," I repeated; I guess I wasn't doing a good job of hiding my bitterness. "That's the honor — that's the achievement. Being the first. Nobody remembers the name of the second person on the moon."

"Edwin Eugene Aldrin, Jr.," said Bokket. "Known as 'Buzz.'"

"Fine, okay," I said. "*You* remember, but most people don't."

"I didn't remember it; I accessed it." He tapped his temple. "Direct link to the planetary web; everybody has one."

Ling exhaled; the gulf was vast. "Regardless," she said, "we are not pioneers; we're just also-rans. We may have set out before you did, but you got here before us."

"Well, my ancestors did," said Bokket. "I'm sixth-generation Sororian."

"*Sixth* generation?" I said. "How long has the colony been here?"

"We're not a colony anymore; we're an independent world. But the ship that got here first left Earth in 2107. Of course, my ancestors didn't immigrate until much later."

"Twenty-one-oh-seven," I repeated. That was only fifty-six years after the launch of the *Pioneer Spirit*. I'd been thirty-one when our ship had started its journey; if I'd stayed behind, I might very well have lived to see the real pioneers depart. What had we been thinking, leaving Earth? Had we been running, escaping, getting out, fleeing before the bombs fell? Were we pioneers, or cowards?

No. No, those were crazy thoughts. We'd left for the same reason that *Homo sapiens sapiens* had crossed the Strait of

Gibraltar. It was what we did as a species. It was why we'd triumphed, and the Neandertals had failed. We *needed* to see what was on the other side, what was over the next hill, what was orbiting other stars. It was what had given us dominion over the home planet; it was what was going to make us kings of infinite space.

I turned to Ling. "We can't stay here," I said.

She seemed to mull this over for a bit, then nodded. She looked at Bokket. "We don't want parades," she said. "We don't want statues." She lifted her eyebrows, as if acknowledging the magnitude of what she was asking for. "We want a new ship, a faster ship." She looked at me, and I bobbed my head in agreement. She pointed out the window. "A *streamlined* ship."

"What would you do with it?" asked Bokket. "Where would you go?"

She glanced at me, then looked back at Bokket. "Andromeda."

"Andromeda? You mean the Andromeda *galaxy*? But that's— " a fractional pause, no doubt while his web link provided the data "—2.2 *million* light-years away."

"Exactly."

"But ... but it would take over two million years to get there."

"Only from Earth's — excuse me, from Soror's — point of view," said Ling. "We could do it in less subjective time than we've already been traveling, and, of course, we'd spend all that time in cryogenic freeze."

"None of our ships have cryogenic chambers," Bokket said. "There's no need for them."

"We could transfer the chambers from the *Pioneer Spirit*."

Bokket shook his head. "It would be a one-way trip; you'd never come back."

"That's not true," I said. "Unlike most galaxies, Andromeda is actually moving toward the Milky Way, not away from it. Eventually, the two galaxies will merge, bringing us home."

"That's billions of years in the future."

"Thinking small hasn't done us any good so far," said Ling.

Bokket frowned. "I said before that we can afford to support you and your shipmates here on Soror, and that's true. But starships are expensive. We can't just give you one."

"It's got to be cheaper than supporting all of us."

"No, it's not."

"You said you honored us. You said you stand on our shoulders. If that's true, then repay the favor. Give us an opportunity to stand on *your* shoulders. Let us have a new ship."

Bokket sighed; it was clear he felt we really didn't understand how difficult Ling's request would be to fulfill. "I'll do what I can," he said.

— «» —

Ling and I spent that evening talking, while blue-and-green Soror spun majestically beneath us. It was our job to jointly make the right decision, not just for ourselves but for the four dozen other members of the *Pioneer Spirit's* complement that had entrusted their fate to us. Would they have wanted to be revived here?

No. No, of course not. They'd left Earth to found a colony; there was no reason to think they would have changed their minds, whatever they might be dreaming. Nobody had an emotional attachment to the idea of Tau Ceti; it just had seemed a logical target star.

"We could ask for passage back to Earth," I said.

"You don't want that," said Ling. "And neither, I'm sure, would any of the others."

"No, you're right," I said. "They'd want us to go on."

Ling nodded. "I think so."

"Andromeda?" I said, smiling. "Where did that come from?"

She shrugged. "First thing that popped into my head."

"Andromeda," I repeated, tasting the word some more. I remembered how thrilled I was, at sixteen, out in the California desert, to see that little oval smudge below Cassiopeia for the first time. Another galaxy, another island universe — and half again as big as our own. "Why not?" I fell silent but, after a while, said, "Bokket seems to like you."

Ling smiled. "I like him."

"Go for it," I said.

"What?" She sounded surprised.

"Go for it, if you like him. I may have to be alone until Helena is revived at our final destination, but you don't have to be. Even if they do give us a new ship, it'll surely be a few weeks before they can transfer the cryochambers."

Ling rolled her eyes. *"Men,"* she said, but I knew the idea appealed to her.

— «» —

Bokket was right: the Sororian media seemed quite enamored with Ling and me, and not just because of our exotic appearance — my white skin and blue eyes; her dark skin and epicanthic folds; our two strange accents, both so different from the way people of the thirty-third century spoke. They also seemed to be fascinated by, well, by the pioneer spirit.

When the quarantine was over, we did go down to the planet. The temperature was perhaps a little cooler than I'd have liked, and the air a bit moister — but humans adapt, of course. The architecture in Soror's capital city of Pax was surprisingly ornate, with lots of domed roofs and intricate carvings. The term "capital city" was an anachronism, though; government was completely decentralized, with all major decisions done by plebiscite — including the decision about whether or not to give us another ship.

Bokket, Ling, and I were in the central square of Pax, along with Kari Deetal, Soror's president, waiting for the results of the vote to be announced. Media representatives from all over the Tau Ceti system were present, as well as one from Earth, whose stories were always read 11.9 years after he filed them. Also on hand were perhaps a thousand spectators.

"My friends," said Deetal, to the crowd, spreading her arms, "you have all voted, and now let us share in the results." She tipped her head slightly, and a moment later people in the crowd started clapping and cheering.

Ling and I turned to Bokket, who was beaming. "What is it?" said Ling. "What decision did they make?"

Bokket looked surprised. "Oh, sorry. I forgot you don't have web implants. You're going to get your ship."

Ling closed her eyes and breathed a sigh of relief. My heart was pounding.

President Deetal gestured toward us. "Dr. MacGregor, Dr. Woo — would you say a few words?"

We glanced at each other then stood up. "Thank you," I said looking out at everyone.

Ling nodded in agreement. "Thank you very much."

A reporter called out a question. "What are you going to call your new ship?"

Ling frowned; I pursed my lips. And then I said, "What else? The *Pioneer Spirit II*."

The crowd erupted again.

— «» —

Finally, the fateful day came. Our official boarding of our new starship — the one that would be covered by all the media — wouldn't happen for another four hours, but Ling and I were nonetheless heading toward the airlock that joined the ship to the station's outer rim. She wanted to look things over once more, and I wanted to spend a little time just sitting next to Helena's cryochamber, communing with her.

And, as we walked, Bokket came running along the curving floor toward us.

"Ling," he said, catching his breath. "Toby."

I nodded a greeting. Ling looked slightly uncomfortable; she and Bokket had grown close during the last few weeks, but they'd also had their time alone last night to say their goodbyes. I don't think she'd expected to see him again before we left.

"I'm sorry to bother you two," he said. "I know you're both busy, but..." He seemed quite nervous.

"Yes?" I said.

He looked at me, then at Ling. "Do you have room for another passenger?"

Ling smiled. "We don't have passengers. We're colonists."

"Sorry," said Bokket, smiling back at her. "Do you have room for another colonist?"

"Well, there *are* four spare cryochambers, but..." She looked at me.

"Why not?" I said, shrugging.

"It's going to be hard work, you know," said Ling, turning back to Bokket. "Wherever we end up, it's going to be rough."

Bokket nodded. "I know. And I want to be part of it."

Ling knew she didn't have to be coy around me. "That would be wonderful," she said. "But — but why?"

Bokket reached out tentatively, and found Ling's hand. He squeezed it gently, and she squeezed back. "You're one reason," he said.

"Got a thing for older women, eh?" said Ling. I smiled at that.

Bokket laughed. "I guess."

"You said I was one reason," said Ling.

He nodded. "The other reason is — well, it's this: I don't want to stand on the shoulders of giants." He paused, then lifted his own shoulders a little, as if acknowledging that he was giving voice to the sort of thought rarely spoken aloud. "I want to *be* a giant."

They continued to hold hands as we walked down the space station's long corridor, heading toward the sleek and graceful ship that would take us to our new home.

—— « o » ——

Robert J. Sawyer

Robert J. Sawyer, a Member of the Order of Canada, is one of only eight people ever — and the only Canadian — to have won all three of the science-fiction field's top awards for best novel of the year: the Hugo, the Nebula, and the John W. Campbell Memorial Award; he was also one of the initial nine inductees in the Canadian Science Fiction and Fantasy Hall of Fame. The ABC TV series *FlashForward* was based on his Aurora Award-winning novel of the same name. Rob's 23rd novel *Quantum Night* was a *Maclean's* national bestseller and hit #1 on the hardcover bestsellers list published by *Locus*, the U.S. trade journal of the science-fiction and fantasy fields. Born in Ottawa, Rob now lives in Mississauga.

Card

Catherine Girczyc

My lunar friend said, "Never let yourself get boring!"
"I won't," I said, flashing a comet's light.
And we winked out of each other's lives like
Stars disappearing at dawn.
Astronometry?
Measure our skies / dreams /visions
Show them in new colours
Like the satellite photos / multi-spectral images
Wherein we see more than the eye sees
Like the camera of the heart.
Look from the sky to the Earth
See the worlds of this unique Globe
Outlines of life / Patterns in the dark
That determine the days
Ways of seeing red forests instead of green
Blue sea-ice and brown mountain crinkles
All perfectly scientific and real
But all different ways of seeing
Visions in the spheres.
Oh, my friend, nights' one, where are you?

For my dreams have become galaxy full lately—

More than passing strange—

And I have no one to tell them to.

—— « o » ——

Catherine Girczyc

Catherine Girczyc works as a technical writer by day while pursuing creative writing by night. Previously, she wrote for television garnering fifteen TV script writing credits. She also worked as a story consultant and coordinator in TV. An SF fan, she's won Auroras twice: for hosting a Vancouver SF radio show (*The Ether Patrol*), and editing an Edmonton fanzine (*Neology*). She's always been a poet and had her first publication in her high school yearbook. Contact her via Twitter: @MCG_Writer and via her writing blog: https://screenwriters2.wordpress.com/

A New Lexicon of Loss

John Bell

Our journeys
have diverged

you remain
on that broad river

I am swept away
on this narrow

branch flowing
to a different sea

minutes ahead of you—
forever

dramatic enough
for the few

living here
in the cruelty

of our
bifurcated time,

this broken
interstice,

catching glimpses
of you

or really,
just memories

of you, in the
liquid silver of

mirrors, the reaches
of our vision

your voices not
even echoes

you are our
ghosts, blurred

and fleeting, but
the future

is our pilgrimage
and it

must begin
with this ending

And our tears?
you might ask

only a
vestigial reflex,

a final sharing
on our journeys

and remember:
overhead

the sun still
burns for us,

a blazing,
blinding clock

oblivious
to our partings,

but if it is
any solace

in some
other future

there will be a
word for this

in a new
lexicon of loss.

——— « o » ———

John Bell

John Bell was born in Montreal and grew up in Halifax. After a long career at the National Archives in Ottawa, he returned to Nova Scotia and now lives in Lunenburg. He is the author or editor of nearly twenty books, including *Invaders from the North*, a history of Canadian comics. A former editor of the poetry magazine *Arc*, Bell has contributed to a wide variety of periodicals. His work has also appeared in numerous anthologies, including *Ark of Ice: Canadian Futurefiction* and several *Tesseracts* collections.

Intervention

Brent Nichols

Pace dressed in the dark, shaking each garment first in case of roaches, then stepped over the legs of his sleeping siblings and let himself out. It was cold, but the long walk to the highway warmed him. He caught the bus at dawn. He hated paying the eighty centavos, but there was no other way to get to the city, no other place he could access the game net.

He dozed on the bus, his ragged backpack tucked securely under one thigh, feeling the chill slowly fade to be replaced by a sweltering heat. The bus dropped him off on Avenida Elena. He hiked over to Centro América and picked his way through an endless gauntlet of street vendors.

In the alley behind the Cabral building he found his fellow gamers. There were dozens of them, lined up shoulder to shoulder, most of them sitting on scraps of cardboard, their backs against the wall of the building. Network access didn't extend very far past the wall. Even a few paces was enough to cause skips and lags. The far side of the alley was completely dead.

Most of the gamers were zoned out already, faces slack, bodies limp. Pace walked along the line of zombies, looking.

He didn't know the names of the sisters, two girls so alike he had trouble telling them apart. He wasn't even sure if the same girl always played or if they took turns. One girl was lost in the game, her body slack on the cardboard. Her sister sat close by, gazing into her phone. She would keep an eye on her sister, make sure no one robbed her or messed with her. She would keep an eye on Pace, too.

When she looked up he met her eye, smiled, and got a grave nod in return. He gave her a quetzal. He didn't always pay. Not on the days when he was just grinding levels, bringing one character after another through the map. Today, though, he had a client. Today he would make a deposit in the bank of good karma.

He found a gap in the line of bodies, a space not far down from the two sisters. Before he sat he paused to fix the image in his mind. The slack limbs, the closed eyes, the dribbling spittle. *This is reality. This will be you, in a moment. It is pathetic. It is contemptible. Remember.*

Pace turned, squirmed between a couple of players, leaned his back against the wall, and closed his eyes.

Text and simple icons flashed across his implants. Somewhere on the other side of the wall, wealthy customers lay on leather recliners hidden by privacy screens as they played. In a moment, though, Pace would be inside the game where all were equal.

A flashing cursor appeared. The game wanted his username. With almost two hundred accounts to choose from, keeping track of accounts was often the biggest challenge Pace faced in a day of gaming. He chose one of his elite avatars, one of a handful that had reached the high valley. He entered his password, and every sensation of cardboard and concrete and sweltering heat faded away.

Images flashed past, almost too fast to register. Every session began with a recap of his adventures so far. He left a sailing ship, explored a bustling port city, and helped protect a young woman from a werewolf. After that came a long trek through forest and over plains, with dozens of small adventures along the way. Always in the distance he could see a shining mountain range, slowly coming closer and closer as he journeyed.

Finally, after facing obstacles that had once seemed insurmountable, he reached the edge of the mountains themselves. He journeyed up and up, pausing for a battle of wits with mountain trolls. At last he reached something very few players ever saw, a paradisiacal valley surrounded on every side by glorious mountain peaks.

The recap faded, leaving him, as it always did, with a glorious sense of accomplishment. He turned in a slow circle, getting his bearings. He appeared in a slightly different spot every time.

He stood on a stony ridge above the village. The first time he'd made it this far, he'd spent almost half an hour just gazing at the little settlement. It was like something from a wonderful dream, a poem of rooftops and curving cobbled streets, half-timbered houses and quaint thatch roofs. Everything was pleasing to the eye, from the squat clock tower in the centre to the children who capered around a Maypole in the village green.

Today, however, there was no time for gawking. Today he had a client.

He strode toward the village, scanning every player he saw. They thronged the streets, dozens of them, the newbies milling around in clumps, the veterans moving purposefully from shop to street market to waterfront.

Pace prowled the street, reading the names that hovered above each player's shoulder. SexyGurl587. JimmyKIsARock-Star. RedVampire999. William21973. "William" appeared as a busty blonde woman in steel armour designed to lift and separate her breasts, not protect her. Pace rolled his eyes as she passed and continued his search.

He didn't know what time zone his target was in. It didn't matter. Serious gamers played around the clock. The real person could be anywhere in the world as his avatar explored this Alpine valley.

Just when he was close to giving up, a familiar figure in the distance caught his eye. The avatar looked like a burly barbarian with a massive sword strapped across his back, tramping into the village from down the valley. He'd just arrived, then. That was good. Any progress at all would encourage him. The key was to shut him down before he could get the slightest sense of achievement. Pace pushed through the crowd until he was close enough to read the man's name.

Mondo895. Pace smiled. It was him, all right.

A first-time player usually needed an hour or two to figure out the next challenge. Mondo895 had been here at least twice, though. He would get started right away. The first step was to go to the waterfront and offer to lug crates of cargo to a shop.

A riverboat called the *Butterfly* bobbed at a stone pier. The boat contained an infinite supply of wooden crates that the captain wanted delivered. A shopkeeper in town would pay in jade carvings which could then be sold to a merchant in the outdoor market. It was a time-consuming chore, but several hours of labour would earn you enough to join a caravan of snow camels that would take you farther up the valley.

A couple of players waited in line at the pier. Pace joined the line, glancing back now and then. It didn't take long for Mondo895 to queue up behind him. The wizard in front of him headed into town with a crate in his hands, and Pace turned.

"Excuse me," said Mondo895, and tried to step around him.

Pace blocked his path.

The barbarian's face collapsed into a scowl. "Get out of my way!"

Pace didn't answer, just blocked the man again as he tried to dodge around.

"You're him, aren't you?" Mondo895 glanced at the air above Pace's shoulder. "How many accounts do you have?"

"Thousands," Pace lied.

"Why are you doing this?"

Pace shrugged.

"Let me pass!" He tried shoving Pace. Mondo895 had freakishly huge muscles, but they were purely ornamental. Every player had the same strength, and the peculiar physics of the game made it impossible to push an avatar. "I'll get you banned again."

"Go ahead." Time spent dealing with the bureaucracy of the hosting company was time spent away from the addictive experience of the game itself.

Mondo895 whirled and ran deeper into the village. Pace waited. Let him wander the village until he was sick of it. He could achieve nothing without returning to the dock.

Ten minutes passed. When Mondo895 returned he had a sword in his hands. It was an impressive weapon, more than half as long as Mondo895 was tall, but such things were meaningless in the game environment. Pace's knife had the same rating, and he was much, much better at using it. Quite simply, Mondo895 was an amateur and Pace was a professional. Pace dodged and struck once, and Mondo895 flickered and faded from view.

Pace put his knife away and walked into the village. He knew human nature. Mondo895 wouldn't respawn right away. He would wait for Pace to lose interest and move on.

"Great battle!" The speaker was an NPC, a woman of breathtaking beauty without a name hovering above her shoulder. She gave him a sparkling smile and held out a silver tray. "Have some ambrosia."

He took a little bun from the tray. The pastry had the shape of a flower, and it smelled heavenly. It tasted even better, and he closed his eyes as he sank his teeth into it. She was there at the end of every battle, always with the same tray. It was the best thing he'd ever eaten in his life, and if it wasn't nourishing, it wasn't fattening either.

"Thank you." He stepped around her and almost bumped into William21973. She folded her arms under that enormous bosom and said, "Why are you being such a dick?"

He shrugged. "It's a job."

"A job? What kind of—"

Pace stepped around her and walked away. Maybe the day would come when someone in William's life would decide he was addicted to gaming. A parent or a girlfriend or a concerned social worker would decide to stage an intervention. They would call Pace or someone like him, and he would ruin the game experience until William gave up in disgust. Until then, William21973 was of no interest.

Still nibbling the ambrosia, Pace wandered the streets until he came to the village green. A caravan of snow camels lined the edge of the green, six sturdy beasts standing nose to tail, festooned with bulging saddlebags. There was a pass at the top end of the valley, impassable to foot traffic. The only way through was by caravan.

He lifted his gaze to the mountain peaks that soared above the valley, and a familiar ache of yearning rose under his breastbone. He could see a cleft between peaks, tantalizingly close. What vistas lay on the other side? He had come so far, and the pass was so close! With this account he had already accumulated more than half the money he would need to join the caravan. It would be so easy. He could lug some crates around, sell some jade carvings, and be in the very next caravan setting out.

And a few hours after that, he would stand at the crest of that pass and look down at last on an entire undiscovered world.

He was walking toward the waterfront, telling himself that it wouldn't hurt to just go up there and take a look, when the entire village flickered around him. A wall of text appeared in front of his eyes, giant flashing letters that said ACCOUNT SUSPENDED. And then the valley disappeared.

Pace floated in a dark void, surrounded by hovering icons. Mondo895 had complained and gotten him banned. He could appeal the suspension, open a new account, switch to one of his existing accounts, or exit the game.

He brought up a list of accounts and started to choose one of a dozen characters who had reached the high valley. Then he paused. Mondo895 was outside of the game. You had to exit completely to register a complaint about another player. The target, whoever he was, was sitting up and looking around and remembering the real world. He would move around a bit, go to the bathroom, work out some of the stiffness in his muscles. The spell was broken, for the moment at least.

Pace stared at the face of his next avatar, the urge to return to the game almost overpowering him. *My target isn't there. I have all the time I need to take a caravan through the pass.*

But the pass was not the satisfying end to an epic journey. It was simply one more point on an endless road. He would see a tantalizing vista spread before him, and it would compel him to continue on. There would always be another bend in the road, another beacon in the distance drawing him on.

"I am sitting in an alley," he murmured. "I'm drooling on myself. I probably have roaches crawling on me. I am pathetic. I am not a bold explorer. I am a zombie sprawled in the dirt."

Quickly, before his will could falter, he hit the icon marked "Exit".

Heat and thirst slammed into him. His head was tilted to the side, and the muscles of his neck screamed a protest as he lifted his head. He climbed slowly to his feet, grimacing as his muscles unkinked.

His stomach grumbled, reminding him that the ambrosia had only been an illusion. He headed for a cheap restaurant he knew. There was time for some chicken and rice before he started the long journey home. Real food that would give him strength for a real journey, with his family waiting at the other end.

He glanced back once, longingly, at the blank wall of the gaming club. He could see the row of zombies on their scraps of cardboard, though, and it bolstered his resolve. He turned his back on all of it and walked away.

—— « O » ——

Brent Nichols

Brent Nichols is a science fiction and fantasy writer and man about town. He likes good beer, bad puns, high adventure, and low comedy. He's never been seen in the same room as Batman, but that's probably just a coincidence. His debut novel *Stars Like Cold Fire* was released in 2016 by Bundoran Press; the sequel will be out in 2017. His stories have appeared in anthologies like *Enigma Front* from Analemma Books and *Tesseracts 19 – Superhero Universe*.

Trespass

Leslie Brown

Phaedra took another sip of the acidic water and contemplated the necessity of killing herself within the next two to three weeks. It was strange: suicide had never occurred to her even when her mind had been at its blackest. Yet losing her food supply and now her water left her little choice.

Her House was supposed to have been immortal, her House Remote Units infinitely repairable, her fusion power inexhaustible. Yet somehow, from the soils of this blasted sterile planet, an organism had gotten into the vats and even contaminated the protein stocks so she couldn't sterilize and start again. Another sort of blight was tearing through the hydroponic gardens, attacking tomatoes and wheat with equal enthusiasm. Only the barley was resistant, and if she had to have another meal of that tasteless paste, she would advance her expiration date.

She tapped her fingernail against the water glass. Twenty years of uneventful exile and now disaster after disaster. Could it be an outside agency? Someone with vengeance in mind, hiding in the foothills, wanting her to die slowly? How arrogant she had been when she purchased this out-of-the-way planet for her retreat. What a good idea it had seemed at the time to eschew any means of calling for help, any way of leaving this barren sand-covered rock. And so what if someone came after her? They would either die or she would. Who cared? Well, twenty years later, she bloody well did care.

She turned to the hovering HRU, the one who had brought her the water sample.

"Take Beta Two and Kappa Six. Survey a ten kilometer radius around the House. Look for humans or technology not originating from this House."

The HRU flicked a green acknowledgment light at her and flew off. Phaedra remembered that the House computer had a surveillance function that she had never used. In theory, there should be twenty years of visual recordings from every room of the House. However, all she needed to look at was the vat room and only for the last two months or so.

It took five hours before she found something. A flicker of shadow and then the camera was obscured for a few minutes. A human agency then. Someone who knew where the camera was and who thought she reviewed the footage. There were more blanks as she fast forwarded through the visual records. She found others with the camera in the hydroponics wing. She noted the times and a pattern emerged. Every week, on sixth day, and most particularly when she took her scooter up to the top of the highest foothill and observed the moons crossing. It was a ridiculous ritual, outstanding even in a life bound entirely by habit. As the moons appeared to touch, she emptied herself of every want, every desire, every regret. She became a hollow vessel and she chanted her mantra until the moons were free of each other.

I am not controlled by my desires.

Her unseen stalker, the polluter of her protein vats, knew where she went; was watching her. Until now, Phaedra had always been the watcher, never the subject. She pushed a button on her desktop console.

"Alpha Five. Found anything?"

"No, Phaedra. We have surveyed 54% of the designated area."

"Return to the House with Beta Two and Kappa Six."

"Understood, Phaedra."

Tomorrow was sixth day. She would leave by scooter and then sneak back on foot. She didn't want to scare the polluter off prematurely with a perimeter search.

— «» —

Phaedra crouched in the shadow of the hydroponics wing. Something must have alerted the intruder because if Phaedra had really been on the top of the foothill, she would be returning shortly. The intruder, if there really was one, was leaving it too late to make mischief. Phaedra's knees hurt and she was hungry. Then, a distortion of light made her forget her knees and her stomach. The automated hatch on the side of her House, the one that led to the area where the HRUs stored themselves, was inching upwards. No wonder the perimeter search brought up nothing; her intruder was within her walls. Make that intruders. Two figures dropped from the hatch, landing in crouches on the packed sand. Their outlines were uncertain in the moons' light and Phaedra realized it was because they were dressed in rags.

She watched as they sidled over to the hydroponics door and pressed the button to open it. Nothing was locked. Until now, there had been no one to keep out. She waited, wanting to see what they would do when they found no food. She had harvested what she could and composted the rest. They would find bare soil beds. They had left the door open (small wonder everything was contaminated) and she could hear noises of frustration. Damage was being done and they didn't care anymore if she saw it. They were hungry and that made them dangerous.

She moved quickly now and shut the door on them. She flipped open a panel that they would never have found since they lacked her fingernail cryptokey. She pushed the button for the nitrogen gas. She had rigged it to fill the room rather than soil mixers. Timing was essential. She didn't want to kill them. Yet. With another finger flick, she activated the oxygen, waited ten seconds and then opened the door. Two bodies sprawled on the floor. She took the strap ties that she normally used on the tomato plants and bound them hand and foot.

She had deliberately removed herself from temptation and now it had come to her. The ways of the Universe were indeed strange.

— «» —

She had given them each tranquilizers so that she could run them under the House's medical scanner. Although malnourished, they were otherwise in good health. She had done a bit of improvisation and tied them each to stainless steel tables that she had had in the hydroponics lab. Now they were strapped down, naked, in her living room. She liked interrogating naked subjects. It broke down their resistance so much faster. She tilted the tables so that they were almost vertical and sat down in her favourite chair. She had opened a fresh bottle of red wine and poured herself a glass. Then she waited for them to wake up.

The female woke first. She looked around wildly until she found her companion. Phaedra watched the expression of relief change into panic as the female recognized their circumstances. Her eyes fixed on Phaedra but she said nothing. Interesting. Phaedra had expected pleading or threats, not the mute resignation in those grey eyes. Eyes that reminded her of something, someone.

She waited, sipping her wine, until the male woke. He was noisier, as protective males tended to be. He called for his companion before he saw her.

"Elyne!"

"Here, Tose." The girl's voice was throaty and low.

Ah, so they spoke Rigan. That made things easier. The male, Tose, tried his bonds and Phaedra waited patiently until he was done. His struggles awakened something in her, an excitement that she had not felt for years.

"How did you get here?"

They clamped their lips shut like children. How amusing. Phaedra poured wine into a second glass.

"This is a very good Varstik red. Most people would go their whole lives without tasting something like this. If you answer my questions, you may have a sip." She glanced at them. Still the compressed lips. She picked up her cooking knife. She had an HRU sharpen all her knives weekly. "On the other hand, most people have been cut at some time in their lives. My next question would be: which would you prefer to experience? Wine or blade?"

The female, Elyne, was scanning the living room. Phaedra could not tell if the girl understood how priceless the objects were that decorated it. Perhaps she was trying to gain some understanding of their captor. If so, the fact Phaedra had a Rembrandt over her fireplace would tell her nothing.

"Then I'll choose." Phaedra stood, blade in hand and went to the male. He jerked his arms against the bonds and bared his teeth at her. Just like an animal. How disappointing.

Phaedra laid the edge against his cheek, just below the eye. He stopped moving. Oh, just a little slice, to smell the warm blood. When she started this, it was to get information, not to entertain herself. But it was so good, so familiar.

I am not controlled by my desires.

"We came in an escape pod." Elyne had decided the threat was real.

"From what ship?"

"A short range cargo hauler. Full of refugees. It's still in orbit around your planet but it's been breached. Everyone is dead."

"How did you and Tose survive?" Phaedra still had the knife against his cheek. She liked the involuntary twitches under his skin. She wouldn't cut; her control was faultless.

"We know our way around ships. Got into evac suits when it happened, made it to a pod."

Phaedra was not sure which way her questions should go. Elyne had opened up many interesting avenues by what she said and what she didn't say. She supposed she should find out how they knew to avoid her.

"Did you hear the warning beacon, before your ship breached?" She was tired of Tose's twitches and rank breath. She returned to her chair for another sip of wine.

"I've answered three questions. When do I get a sip?"

A laugh broke from Phaedra's lips, unexpected and delighted. She took the second glass and brought it to the girl's lips. She drank without hesitation. Phaedra stepped back in case Elyne tried to spit it on her but the girl swallowed.

"What do you think?"

"Really good."

"Now answer my question. Did you hear the warning?"

"Yes, but we were going to go down anyway. Our ship was in bad shape. Then it breached. Our pod homed in on your energy signature but because of the warning, we buried the pod in sand and watched your House for days."

Phaedra gave her another sip as a reward. "Until the pod rations ran out and you got hungry."

"Yes. We thought if we took a little vat meat, a bit of greens, you wouldn't notice."

"You contaminated the vats. I supposed you just scooped it out with your hands. Then, when it started to taste off, you went through the cooler and found the stock protein and contaminated that. Did you dip those grubby fingers in my hydroponics fluid as well? Rummage through my plants in conservatory? Spread your disease and dirt through every food source I had?" Her voice had raised by the end but she tamped it down again. She used anger as a tool; it must not rule her.

"I'm sorry. We didn't know."

"I'm sorry, too, my dear. You've left me with no food and I had planned to live here another seventy years or so. There is something you and Tose here can do for me."

"What?"

"Be my vat meat starter cultures." She lifted her knife suggestively.

"All or just part of us?" The girl's gaze was steady. Gods above, she reminded Phaedra of herself. She gave the girl another sip of wine as a reward.

"Did your parents tell you fairy tales? The old earth ones?" Phaedra made herself comfortable in her chair again.

"Some. Are you referring to Hansel and Gretel? Are you going to cook us in your oven? That story didn't end well for the witch." Oddly, the girl gave a grin to Tose. The male shook his head at her but it was more admiring than admonitory.

Phaedra smiled at both of them. "I was thinking more of Rapunzel. The witch's food was raided by her neighbour, who was getting the vegetables his pregnant wife craved. When he was found out, the price was his child. You've taken my foodstuff and now I'm deciding on the price."

"I thought you'd decided already. We're to be your new starter cultures." Elyne had determined that Phaedra was bluffing. If there was one thing Phaedra disliked intensely, it was being underestimated.

"As manifest and all-encompassing my past crimes have been, I've never included cannibalism. Although some might argue that vat meat is far enough removed from the source. Still, I will keep that option open. Now I invite you to relax; sleep if you can. Despite your lack of clothing, you'll find it warmer in here than in my outer walls." Phaedra rose and gathered up the wine bottle with the two glasses.

"Wait. Don't leave us like this." Finally, Elyne seemed disturbed.

"How would you like to be left?"

"Let us down from these tables. Lock us in a room. Please."

"I'll consider it." Phaedra dimmed the lights to the room as she left. It had taken all her willpower to walk out of that room. Gods above, they were so tempting. She summoned Alpha Five.

"Finish your perimeter search. I want you to find that buried escape pod." She went to her office where the House control panels were. "House, I need to tap into the internal surveillance system of that orbiting freighter. Use all the power you need."

"Understood, Phaedra."

Elyne was lying. Even the emotional responses she chose to display to Phaedra were a sham. She called up the camera feed from the living room and backed up the recording to the point where she left the room.

Tose had spoken as soon as Phaedra was gone.

"Elyne, she's going to kill us."

"Shhh. She's remembered she has camera surveillance. She's listening to us. It will be all right."

"I have to piss."

"Then do it. Her remotes will clean it up."

Phaedra watched Tose press his lips together stubbornly. It was ingrained into every human as a child not to soil themselves. Forcing an adult to do so helped just as much as nakedness to break down resistance. Tose was the weak link. She should separate them since they were not going to oblige her with the truth. Unless Tose was an even greater dissembler than Elyne. This was delightful and she would have enjoyed it so much more if she had dinners lined up for the next seventy years. She needed more information. She went back to her office and watched the House's efforts to pick up a signal from the ship using one of her satellite beacons.

— «» —

The House had gotten her several images of the cargo hauler, different angles, all grainy. She could not see a hole anywhere but breaches could be small or in the shadow of some antenna. It proved nothing. The ship was powered down, no active video feeds running. Phaedra would give her eye teeth to see into that ship. Then the House found a minute power feed, boosted it in exchange for losing light, heat and air circulation in her mansion for an endless half hour. The reward was a view of a single room, the mess by the looks of it. Five people were slumped in various positions. It took a few hours of zooming it, adjusting shadows, smoothing pixels but finally she had it. A hole between sightless eyes, a gash across a throat. Writing in blood on the wall. She adjusted the gain. The writing seemed to say:

This is our tribute to you.

Oh, wonderful. Groupies.

— «» —

Alpha Five, usually competent and faithful, could not find the buried pod. So there was no pod, or it was further out. It wasn't until much later that she remembered her guests and checked their camera feed. The tables were empty. She had to admit to some surprise. They had seemed cowed and unresourceful.

"House, close all doors and do not open them unless I specifically command it." The office door slid shut and for the first time in twenty years, she stood in a sealed room. The playback of the surveillance camera was useless: the escape had happened during the down time when the House had rerouted power in order to capture the cargo ship's video feed. When she re-examined the real-time video feed, she saw that the tethers been cut on both tables.

"A third person, House. I never thought of that." She gave a wry smile at the memory of Elyne's and Tose's fear. An act? They must have surmised she wouldn't kill them until she had the answers to her questions. But if they did know who she was, then they'd have known they were playing a dangerous game. So far, however, they had outwitted her at every turn. Twenty years in solitary confinement had made her rusty. But not her blades. They were always sharp.

When she tried to find them by searching each room, she found most of her cameras had been blinded by a substance smeared over the lenses. Probably vegetable oil. Her tools were being taken away from her. She summoned her HRUs. Only three responded, the ones who were out on the perimeter search. This was not amusing any more: they had hurt her HRUs. They'd pay for that. She let the remaining three have free range through the House, only keeping the office door sealed. She followed their vid feeds as they found empty room after empty room. The intruders had gone back into the HRU storage area, within the walls of her House. It was time to attend to this in person.

She took her favourite knife, the one that was good for cutting vegetables. It was dark in the storage compartment; HRUs didn't need visible light, so she had a headlamp. The compartment was empty except for her fifteen disabled HRUs, their fuel cells pulled from their chests and allowed to dangle on wires down their carapaces. They had broken them, her only companions for the last twenty years. They had taken what was hers. They might just be better than her at this.

This little shiver of fear was unacceptable. Phaedra tapped into the rage that she always carried within her, a burning corrosive emotion that she used as a wellspring of energy to propel her through life. She used it to shove the fear away as she continued down the crawlspace. There was a hole in the floor of the crawlspace: rough edged and new. She shone the light down it and saw a hatch below. The missing pod had been buried underneath her House. How in all the worlds had they done that? She reached down carefully and thumbed the entry pad. There was a slight hiss and the hatch lifted, barely clearing the bottom of her House. Light leaked up from the hold. It was a certifiable trap but she was fully engaged now. She was willing to die in order to get answers so she dropped down feet first.

She rolled immediately to the left but no attack came. She raised her head. It was very roomy for an escape pod. Four bunks, a door leading to the sanitary area, and at the other end, three chairs in front of the flight controls. The three chairs were occupied by Elyne, Tose and another woman. They wore one piece coveralls. Phaedra rose slowly.

"Lady Phaedra, thank you for joining us." Elyne said, her tone respectful rather than triumphant. She knew who Phaedra was; it all had been an act, a play written by someone else.

"What is the meaning of this?" Phaedra used the tone that had made the populations of entire planets tremble.

"An invitation, Lady." The new woman spoke with a wide smile. Phaedra shook her head and watched the smile fade.

"No. No invitations, no games. Where are you from? Who sent you here?"

"Lady, we need you to lead us. Baron Alar Tavers told us how to find you, how to pique your interest. There's a ship orbiting above you with fifty dead, a tribute to you. There are worlds for you to rule."

God curse Alar Tavers. She had let him live once, allowed him serve and now he thought he knew his way into her mind. It was never about slaughter, about numbers. The individual with his or her special scent of fear, like an aged wine, unique in the decanting, was what she valued. How dare Tavers send these people to disturb her, to force her hand by damaging her House.

"I'm done with ruling. Fix my vats and hydroponics and I will let you leave alive."

"Lady Phaedra, you don't understand. We need..." The knife flew through the air and embedded itself in the throat of the nameless woman. Elyne and Tose sat very still, their eyes watching hers like frightened rabbits, but with a hint of glee deep inside.

"Do you two also think I don't understand?"

"No, Lady. We're sorry if Nadile offended." Elyne lowered her gaze.

"Can you fix my vats and hydroponics?"

"No, Lady. We only brought the means to wreck them, to make your decision easier." Elyne glanced up briefly to gauge her reaction. The blood from Nadile's throat slowly spread across the deck of the pod. Phaedra looked longingly at the knife but to retrieve it would bring her within reach of Tose.

"Who really sent you?"

Elyne gave her a bashful smile. "Your husband, My Lady. He misses you and believes it is time to come out of retirement. He thought a little excitement was in order, an adrenaline rush so to speak. To make you realize what you are foregoing. He told us to give you Baron Tavers' name if you seemed angry."

Phaedra laughed. "Yes, he'd do that. So his grip is slipping on all those worlds I left him. He needs the Nightmare's silver knife to help him clutch hold again, but I lost interest in that years ago."

"The choice is no longer yours, Lady," Tose said, reaching out to tap the control panel. "You are on board now and your weapon is in Nadile." The hatch started to close. Elyne frowned.

Phaedra sniffed at his temerity. "Alpha Five, attack."

The HRU shot past her so quickly, her hair fluttered about her face. The HRU smacked into Tose, knocking him over backwards into the control panel. Phaedra heard a satisfactory clunk as his head made contact with the hard plastaline. Alpha Five used the rebound to knock Elyne sideways and as she teetered, hit her with a voltage charge that promptly drained the unit. It dropped to the ground beside Elyne.

"Good job, Alpha Five." Phaedra pulled the extra tomato ties from her back pocket.

— «» —

Elyne took a long time to wake up but Phaedra had found something to keep her busy. She watched the other woman's face closely as she saw what was left of Tose. Her lips parted and she closed her eyes briefly.

"Was he a lover, a brother?" Phaedra asked her.

"A friend."

"I can have him buried if you like." Phaedra toed some of the red ruin on her polished wooden floor.

"That would be kind, Lady Phaedra. But the body no longer matters. You have sent his soul to heaven." There was no detectable sarcasm in Elyne's voice. Phaedra huffed, discontent starting to ripple through the euphoria she had generated by vivisecting Tose.

"Do you know why I exiled myself, Elyne?"

"They say, My Lady…"

"What do they say?"

"They say that you found us unworthy of your attentions, so rather than lower yourself, you left."

"Nonsense spread by my husband, no doubt. No, that was not the reason. Shall I tell you?" She sat in the chair. She missed the wine but this wasn't really a social occasion.

"I would be honoured, Lady," Elyne said with apparent sincerity.

"My little hobby started out as a diversion, a tool to strike fear into the hearts of my enemies. It kept my husband sleeping with open eyes. Then it became a necessity. I had to cut all the time, going through five or six people a day. We created the Cult of the Knife to prevent people from objecting. If the Red Queen sacrifices you, your soul rockets straight to the Elysian Fields. We had applicants lining up at the gates." She was restless now and had to stand up to pace. Elyne's eyes followed her.

"When I realized that my diversion had become my master, I knew the only way to stop was to go to a place where no one comes, where there is no temptation. And slowly I gained control back over myself. I thought I would never succumb again. Then five minutes after I saw you and Tose, I was Our Lady of the Silver Knife all over again."

"I'm sorry, Lady Phaedra. We thought we were honouring you." Elyne's clear grey eyes met Phaedra's. The girl didn't flinch when the knife flashed towards her but then blinked down at her freed arm. Phaedra cut the rest of the restraints but didn't catch the girl when she fell to her knees.

"Answer me this, Elyne. How did you hide your ground-to-orbit craft under my House?"

The girl craned her head up so she could see Phaedra. "I reprogrammed your HRUs. While you were up on the hill, they dug out a hollow and supported the edge of the House while we sprayed plastaline on the inner walls of the hollow. We flew the GTO in and filled the rest of the hole. By the time you returned, all that was left was sand of a different colour on the ground. It was full dark by then and you didn't notice."

Phaedra tapped her lips with two fingers. "You're clever, I'll say that for you. Why did you wait so long to contaminate my stocks? You were watching me for over two months."

"We wanted to observe you, see if that was the best way to get you to come with us. You seemed very content living here. We decided we needed to force your hand. Forgive me." Elyne bowed her head. Despite promises of heaven from Phaedra's knife, it seemed Elyne wanted to live.

"Get up, Elyne." Phaedra watched the girl haul herself upright, without offering assistance. "I think I know now where you got those eyes. Was he your father?"

Elyne smiled. "Yes."

"Do you want to kill me for what I did to him?" Her grip on the knife was loose. In a few moments, it might fall from her hand.

"No, Lady. He loved you and I think you loved him. That's why you exiled yourself. Say his name for me, please, Lady."

"Dav," Phaedra whispered.

"You've done your penance. He's at peace. Come with me now. I can fly you anywhere you want to go."

Phaedra shook her head. "I've not changed my nature. You're not doing anyone any favours by letting me loose again."

"I will be your control now. Trust me to do that for you." Elyne took a half step towards her, face bright with optimism.

"You have no idea, child, none whatsoever, because he said that to me as well." The knife was firm in her grasp again, the skin at her throat soft and easy to part. She heard Elyne's disbelieving shout as her legs buckled. It was hard to speak but she managed as Elyne cradled her in her arms.

"You were the best temptation they could have sent. But I am not controlled by my desires."

It was sixth day. She was late: she should be up on the hill, watching the moons cross. She must hurry to get to the top before it was too late, so she could let go of every desire, want and regret.

—— « o » ——

Leslie Brown

Leslie Brown is an Ottawa writer with over twenty stories published in such venues as *Strange Horizons, On Spec, Neo Opsis* and *Tesseracts 15*. She is a member of SF Canada, Ottawa Romance Writers and the Lyngarde critique group. Her day job is as a research technician in the Alzheimer's field. Her website can be found at: leslie-brown.com.

Scavengers

Cate McBride

Pol cursed and sprinted from the cockpit as the engines started banging like an off balanced ore processor. The *Ksenia* bucked as she fell out of light-space, sending Pol stumbling into the hatch to the salvage hold.

"Blyad!" Warning sirens blared from the cockpit. She pushed off from the hatch, pivoted and ran back.

"Chert, chert, chert," she chanted as she strapped in, fingers flying over the sea of flashing red on the console. At least the ship had dropped into empty space, she thought as she reset systems, or shut them down, diverting what little power was left to life support.

She flipped the last switch and the sirens stopped. In the quiet Pol heard ... nothing. No throb running down the hull from the engines. No loud hissing from the vents. No vibrations underfoot from the artificial grav unit.

"Stupid damned engine. Shoulda known better than to buy anything from Taipei. Anyone stupid enough to get exiled to the stupid moon is too stupid to design a stupid engine."

Pol unstrapped and floated to the salvage hold. At least the hold still had atmosphere, she thought. She manoeuvered her way through the scrap she had recovered since leaving Solovki.

The engine hatch glowed red. Wonderful. The chertov engine was not only dead but leaking radiation. No use even trying to fix it. She could hear her dedushka, chuckling as he used to: "Radiation or suffocation. Could be worse, Polina my love, you could have run into a planet."

"How about none of the above, deded? I'm not ready to join you yet. I only need one good load and I can go home." She made her way forward and strapped in to wait for death or rescue. And since the nav system hadn't found her location before she powered it down, she pretty much figured that rescue wasn't a choice.

The air grew colder and she yawned, fighting to stay awake. "Just one more load, deded ... one more..."

— «» —

The heat woke her up. She was warm. She should be cold. Pol felt the weight of a warm blanket covering her. She felt thick arms through the blanket, carrying her somewhere. The air around was thin, but breathable. Another salvager must have somehow come to her rescue. Ever cautious, she kept her eyes closed and relaxed. Just in case she'd been rescued by the Wakingmen.

It doesn't feel like the Wakingmen, she thought. Not that anyone knows what the Wakingmen feel like. Or look like, asleep or awake. She giggled a little at her joke, heard a soft hiss near her neck, and fell back to sleep.

She jolted awake again when someone opened her right eye and shone a bright light into it. A soft hand pushed her shoulders back onto the hard metal.

"Yek sa grinksel." She didn't recognize the language.

"I don't understand what you're saying," she whispered, blinking her eyes.

She was in a small room. A large, upright animal covered in brown fur was looming over her, its ... hand? paw? it's paw gently holding her down. Behind it, she saw a light on a stick retracting into a wall between two smaller animals. Sighing, she closed her eyes again.

"Devno ku utash," the big animal said. Something hit her and she opened her eyes and stared at the small black square on the back of her hand. She watched another stick retract.

"Yek sa ... afraid." Her eyes widened.

"Ah, good, translator works." The large animal turned to the smaller ones. "Tzersen, help guest sit up.

Talking bears, Pol thought as she struggled to sit up. I've been rescued by talking bears. No one will believe me.

"What … who are you," she asked. She didn't know what the bears heard, but when the large one responded, she only heard Earth Common.

"We name Ones Who Travel Swiftly." Well, thought Pol, she wouldn't be calling them that. They looked like kamchatkas, the brown bears that dedushka said roamed the Motherland back on Earth. That would do for a name.

"You be in medical centre and I be pleased to say that you live." I'd better live, thought Pol, looking around her. There was nothing that looked like anything she would call medical equipment. Just a bank of dials and switches on a wall with some sort of monitor near where the two sticks had retracted. She stared at the small bear, this one white, who was focused on the screen.

"Ah, you see med lab. Very new. Very modern. It do everything like large hospital do, but in lovely, efficient unit.

"Vital signs be steady, Doctor." The Kamchatka at the monitor turned to talk to them. "I no tell if they be normal, but they change no more."

"Good news, Doctor." Pol twisted around to look behind. A door had opened in what she thought was a blank wall and a new Kamchatka stood staring at her. It was smaller than the doctor, but it carried itself with an air of confidence and authority that Pol recognized right away. A very important bear indeed.

"Then we guess that they be normal and that guest be ready to go. Come, guest. We go elsewhere to wait."

"Wait for what?" Pol was happy to leave the med lab, but the way the Kamchatka said "guest" made her think that it would mean "prisoner" if she said or did anything wrong, Still, she stood and followed it out the door.

They walked together down the corridor, her guide stopping to hold its paw up to each Kamchatka that passed. In turn, the Kamchatkas held up their paw and bowed slightly, except for the ones that held out tablets for her guide to mark with its claw.

"I be Captain of this spaceboat. We be explorers. We search for new friends and for signs of the Richagatent. We find you instead.

"We save you and now we save spaceboat. Engines be like ours in the past. But design be poor. Weak between fuel and propulsion. Waiting to explode.

"Come, I show you what push spaceboats now."

They turned down a side corridor and climbed down a ladder. The ship was bigger than the *Ksenia*, but didn't take long to get from the living space to the engine room in the stern.

Pol gaped when they walked in. The room was slightly bigger than the one in *Ksenia* but it could hold two Kamchatkas comfortably. The engines themselves were half the size of *Ksenia*'s and made almost no noise. She could not tell where they hooked into the propulsion system, but she thought that the pipe that ran along the ceiling might be the fuel line.

"They be impressive, yes? We switch from fission when my sire be captain. Now engines eat fusion, clean and fast. Engines be more powerful, more stable, easier to repair than before. Fuel be less stable, but sit outside. Easy to dump if a problem be."

Pol nodded and closed her mouth. Just think what humans could do with engines like these. Find new worlds to colonize. Learn from other species. Track down the Wakingmen and destroy them.

"Come," the Captain interrupted her musings. "We eat now and wait. Spaceboat ready soon."

He led her back up the ladder and then up a second to a large common room crowned with a clear dome that twinkled with the light of thousands of suns.

Small groups of Kamchatkas sat at tables scattered under the dome, eating or talking quietly to each other. Across the room, a few rested on low benches. She wondered what it would be like to be so used to outer space that you never bothered to look up at the stars.

The Captain seemed to smile as it hooked its paw under her elbow and guided her to a machine that looked suspiciously like the med lab. "This be new kitchen. We no carry food. Kitchen make everything." With that, it raised her hand and touched her thumb to the wall.

"Ouch!" Pol jumped back and sucked the blood off her thumb.

"Apologies. But kitchen need know what in blood. Then it make food safe to eat. See, it come now."

Pol watched as two trays slid out of slots in front of them. She grabbed the one nearest to her as the Captain picked up the other and lead her to an empty table with two stools. She watched the Captain begin to eat, using a utensil that looked to be knife and fork in one. She found one on her tray and, copying his actions, started to eat her meal.

The Captain smiled again as she swallowed the first bite and made a face. "It be tasted to Home World. Would you have kitchen, it make taste to you."

"It doesn't taste right, but it's still better than the rations that we have to carry on our ships." Since anything would taste better, Pol felt like she could compliment her host without stretching the truth.

The Captain waited until she finished eating. "So," it said, "Why you have engines? We never trade to you."

Pol put down the kn-ork and looked it in the eye. "We didn't know it was your design. We took it from a Wakingmen ship that we blew up."

"Wakingmen? What is Wakingmen?"

"We don't know what they are. I think it's Chinese for alien or something. That's what the people from Taipei call them.

"About five years ago, three ships just appeared in our system. They bombed the hell out of Mars colony, killing everyone that couldn't get under the Domes. I lost almost everyone I loved."

"But you live." Now the Captain sounded suspicious.

"I was in the asteroid belt, mining with my grandfather. We didn't even know what happened until we filled our hold and went home. Only home was gone." Her throat tightened but she didn't cry. She refused to cry any more.

"When we got back to Mars, we learned that Taipei had blown up all three ships from the moon. They saved the Earth, although I bet they wished they had waited until the Wakingmen took out China. Then they salvaged what was left of the ships and used the pieces to build engines and navigation systems and deep space sensors.

"When the Wakingmen came back a couple of years later, Taipei was waiting for them at the edge of the solar system. They blew up two more ships and the Wakingmen haven't been back since."

"Tell me, be this spaceboat of Wakingmen?" The centre of the table glowed and the resolved into the image of a large warship, weapons easy to see.

"Yes, that's it. The Mars satellites sent some clear pictures to the Domes before they were blown up."

"Ah, these be Richagatent. They be enemies of all. They be scavengers. They steal from dead instead of make new. They kill colony world and steal ships. That explain why you have engine of elders."

The Captain sat back, pleased to have solved the mystery. Pol hoped this meant that she would be free to go, but he hadn't finished yet.

"But how you get here, far from home world?"

Pol dropped her gaze, feeling a little guilty. Then she looked him in the eye. She had done nothing wrong and dared him to judge her.

"After grandfather died, I tried to stick with mining. But Taipei gave the engines to Mars, so we could earn credits to rebuild. They made Earth countries pay for them and they never sell to China, but we got them for free.

"With better engines, it didn't take long for the asteroids to be mined dry. Some went further out in the solar system. Some stayed close to home, trying to find one last load. The further we went, the more accidents there were, the more wreckage floating around in space."

"No surprise. Taipei copy wrong. Make engines wrong."

"So you said. Well, it seemed like there were more wrecked ships out there than raw ore, so I switched to salvage. Go find them, bring them back, and Taipei reuses the metal. Except now there are more salvagers and fewer wrecks.

"So I decided to jump out past the edge of the system, to where the Taipei ships blew up the last Wakingmen. Figured I might find something out there that Taipei had missed, that they could use to make something new. I must have set the coordinates wrong because when the engines quit, I wasn't anywhere on the navigation charts."

The Captain sat for a minute before speaking. Pol watched him, sensing that somehow she and all humans were being judged.

"It be wrong to scavenge the dead. Animals scavenge in wild, but intelligent beings scavenge not." That's it, we're toast, Pol thought.

"But I understand Taipei. You not have technology to fight Richagatent. It luck that Taipei destroy first ships. It smart to scavenge to protect from Richagatent because they return. Many times they return.

"But it wrong for you, young guest, to do same. You no steal from dead. Taipei make own technology. Time you go home."

The Captain stood and led Pol through the ship to a docking port where the *Ksenia* waited.

"We give proper engine. We give best navigation. You keep translator. Sell to Taipei so you build new home. No more scavenger. No more steal from dead."

"I will. I promise." Pol said. She'd say anything to get away from the Kamchatka, before they changed their minds about her. She turned and went down the docking tunnel. It started to retract as soon as she sealed *Ksenia*'s hatch.

Pol jumped to light-space as soon as she as she could, following the heading that the Kamchatka had programmed into the new nav system. A light light-year later, she dropped back into normal space and put the *Ksenia* in orbit around a small gas planet. She needed to think.

She could sell access to the upgrades. Taipei would probably pay enough to rebuild the house and outbuildings, but it wouldn't be enough to make the land live again. She would have her home, but would still need to mine or collect salvage.

"Damn those furry svolochi. All preachy and pious. What do they know about rebuilding a world? We're nothing like the Wakingmen. We don't attack others. We don't steal technology." She unstrapped and started to pace to and from the salvage hold.

"If Taipei hadn't blown up the first ships, humanity would be dead. Bet those svolochi in China were surprised when they found out that that their prisoners had armed nukes pointed at them."

She paused at the hold door. "There's nothing wrong with salvaging perfectly good metal and tech from wreckage. It was the only way to make sure we'd be ready when the Wakingmen returned."

She thought of the photos that dedushka had saved from the Motherland. Small, dark figures standing in front of wood shacks, surrounded by miles and miles of snow. Thin women lined up outside of dirty buildings waiting patiently for a bag of food. Half-naked children sitting on dirt floors with the dogs, their wide eyes staring back, huge in their thin faces.

With the terraforming plant in rubble, that's what Mars was like. The farmlands were cold and dead. The few survivors who huddled in Solovki and Sharshka lined up every morning for a pittance of rations.

Back in the cockpit, Pol stared at the picture of her parents standing in front of their small farmhouse, the dome of Solovki shimmering in the distance. "I'm not a thief. I'm not even a real salvager — or a miner like deduska. I'm a farmer. All I want to do is go back to live on the farm."

She felt the shockwave as it rocked the ship and smiled. "Time to go home," she said to herself as she set new coordinates and engaged the engines.

The *Ksenia* dropped out of light-space just outside the debris field. Pol silently thanked the Kamchatka for the accuracy of the new nav system and suited up, ready for her final operation.

"It's not like I deliberately blew up their ship," she reassured herself as she readied the grappler in the unpressurised hold.

"I just didn't bother to tell them that the fuel line to their fancy engine was clogged. Not my fault if their chertov engineers were too stupid to see it. Not my fault they blew themselves up."

There wasn't much left of the ship that had come to her rescue. The blast from the engine had vaporised over half of it and what was left was mostly shrapnel and shards of metal. Still, she could see a couple of larger pieces floating on the other side of the debris field, where the living quarters would have been.

Carefully, Pol guided a roving camera through the debris to see if it would be worth picking her way through the small stuff. She peered into the monitor built into the grappler controls.

"Ah, Presvyataya Mater' Boga. The med unit is in one piece. There's the kitchen. Damaged, but the scientists from Sharashka Dome should be able to fix it up.

"And there's a fuel cell. If it's not leaking, I bet Taipei can figure out how use it for weapons."

Reminding herself that a salvage operator was nothing like the Wakingmen, Pol set to work. She'd leave it to the philosophers and priests to argue the ethics; as far as she was concerned, she was just doing her job.

Once Sharashka managed to design new tech from the wrecks in her hold, Mars would be self-sufficient again. Then she could sell the originals to Taipei for enough credits to terraform her farm. She could go home.

And really, that was all that mattered.

—— « O » ——

Cate McBride

Cate McBride has been a science fiction fanatic since she watched her first Star Trek episode on the old black and white TV in her grandmother's basement. When she was done reading the classics (Asimov, Heinlein and Clarke, oh my), she started writing her own stories. Cate also writes urban and classic fantasy, and has been published in Marion Zimmer Bradley's *Sword and Sorceress* anthologies. She currently lives in Ottawa with her son and a large, enthusiastic golden retriever who is afraid of little white dogs and kittens. Please visit Cate on Facebook @Cate.McBride.Author

The White Bear

Robert Dawson

Skehirren had never seen his mentor so angry.

"If that damned healer gave me a few more years, I would throw you out of the University today and find myself a new apprentice!" Keste turned and spat into the fire. Whatever foul herb he was chewing made the flames turn green for a moment.

Skehirren had known for months that Keste was ill, but this was the first time the old fellow had thrust it in his face like this. Nor had he hinted before at how serious his illness was. "Are you sure, sir? About your health?"

"A year is what she told me. And you have spent three years, three, of your time and mine, and what do you have to show for it, eh? What?"

Keste's words stung like a whipping. "The scatterplates, sir? You said yourself that they're well done." He glanced at the clutter in the stone-walled studium: an alembic, gleaming coils of varnished copper wire, vacuum tubes, unwashed dishes, wallslates bearing diagrams in white and ochre chalk, manuscripts and books, parts of a disassembled electroscope, and jars of various powders. At least his own little workroom, where he'd extracted the life-molecules from cell-kernels and projected their patterns onto sensitive plates, was tidy.

"Hmmph! Yes, you're good enough as a *technician*, I suppose. But do you happen to remember that you're here to become a Teacher of the Lore of Life? A shaman, and my successor here, may the Gods delay the day forever! It's not enough to record images: any child with a camera can do that. To be a shaman you must understand the mysteries, understand them in the depths of your soul. I'll die with my chair vacant before I name a *technician* as my heir. Tell me if you can: what is the structure of the life-molecules we have been studying?" His smile was bitter and mocking. "Expound, *Shaman*. Tell me something. Anything."

"The Gods haven't given me understanding yet," Skehirren said.

"Bugger the Gods! They will give you understanding when you earn it, and not a moment before. You're due to sit your Vigil on Midsummer Eve. Unless you have something by then, the Elders will not admit you to sit it." A house-slave tiptoed in and deferentially removed Keste's empty teacup. Keste gestured her away impatiently.

"Can you give me more time, sir? Another few months?"

Keste spat again. "The date is set: I can't change it. Give me results that you can defend before the elders, or pack your trunk and take the train home."

Home? The University was his home, the only place he had ever been truly happy. How could he give it up?

Then there was the conscription lottery. Once he was no longer a postulant, an apprentice shaman, his name would be in the monthly draw with all the other young people. The cost of holding the Equatorial Colonies was high and paid in blood, volunteers were few, and cholera took as heavy a toll as the insurgents' guns. The Imperial Army was always hungry for fresh bodies.

And Esma? If she had to choose between him and finishing her studies in the Bardic School — no, he couldn't even ask it of her. His chest grew tight, a lump rose in his throat. One wrong word, one wrong thought, and he would weep like a child. *Don't think of a White Bear!*

A score of years ago, in the infant school, he had struggled for weeks to learn the Bear Game. One child would challenge another: "Don't think of a White Bear!" and the other had to make the bear vanish from his thoughts, leaving no tracks. At first it had seemed impossible, and he often gave up in tears, wondering if older children could really do the trick, or if it was some sort of hoax. But by the age of eight he had mastered it, could do it with half-a-dozen children chanting the challenge over and over, and could banish other thoughts in the same way. The patterns formed in his mind, and his thoughts became tranquil. He took a deep breath. "Sir? If I want to stay, to finish my work, what should I do?"

Keste leaned forward. Something in his smile made Skehirren uneasy. "First, you should pardon a cranky old man. The pain is bad today. But I can't change the date, no. Only one thing ... no, no, the risk is too much." His words died away, as if intended for himself alone.

"Please, sir! If there's a way to get the answer, tell me what it is."

"I'll tell you, but only because the history of our craft shouldn't be forgotten." Keste steepled his fingers. "You know that, two greatscores of years ago, the examination and the graduation vigil were one? The Old Vigil was not just a rite of passage, it was a quest for a vision."

"That's not how we do it anymore, though."

"The Old Vigil has been discouraged for more than a greatscore of years. The herbs and fungi are ... not entirely safe." Keste's eyes wandered around the room.

"'Discouraged'? But it still happens? People still do this?"

"Yes." A glowing piece of charcoal fell apart in the fireplace. The fire flared for a moment, then slowly settled again. "That was how I learned the craft of making scatterplates."

"You never told me!" And what price had the old man paid? Skehirren had all too much personal knowledge of Keste's bitter week-long melancholies, legendary throughout the University.

"It is not something to boast about. Not for ears that have no need to know."

"And I do need to know?"

Keste's lips twitched. "It might seem your best chance, but it is dangerous. Too dangerous, perhaps."

Skehirren took a long breath. "Tell me. Tell me what I have to do."

— «◊» —

"You *fool*, Skerri!" said Esma. "Can't you see he's tricking you? He wants those results, and he's just using you to get them." She glared up at him, her lips pale with anger.

"He's dying, Esma." Maybe coming to her room tonight had been a mistake.

"When the black steed abideth, man may not but mount." Her voice was iron-edged, as if she were reciting at a ceremony.

"But Keste is the last shaman studying the life-molecules. Nobody else believes there's anything in it. If I don't help him finish his work, the project will die with him."

"That still doesn't entitle him to ask you to take risks like that."

"He didn't. He advised me against it. I didn't say I would." He reached out to her.

She pushed him away. "Pshh! Tell a child not to stick its finger in the fire..."

"But, Esma, the Old Vigil is my last chance. If I don't, I'll have to leave forever. Leave *you* forever. I'll be going back to the tannery in Port Dalmeni, or apprenticing to an apothecary somewhere — if the Emperor doesn't send me off to the Colonies. And I know you can't go with me. You're going to be a famous bard, not a tanner's wife. Or a soldier's widow."

"I'm sorry, Skerri. You know how it is ... I *can't* leave." The fingers of one hand twisted the placket of her black postulant's gown. "This ... this is what you have to do, isn't it?" Her voice was quiet and serious. "It's your quest, your destiny. But I'm still frightened for you." She threw her arms around him and pressed against him. The scent of her rosemary-and-honey hairwash filled his nostrils.

"You aren't allowed to be frightened, darling. I have to be brave and you have to help me," he whispered, stroking her back over and over again through the rough fabric of her postulant's gown.

She said nothing. He could hear her breathing. When she finally spoke, it was little more than a whisper. "Would it help you be brave ... if I asked you to stay with me tonight? Sleep with me?"

"Oh, Esma!"

"We've known it would happen sometime, haven't we? And ... I haven't told you, but I started drinking barrenwort tea more than a moon ago. So I'm safe."

"Yes, Esma," he whispered. "Oh, yes."

Without releasing him, she guided him over to her bed. She undid the cord of her gown and let it fall from her shoulders, exposing her plain linen housekirtle. "Come on,

Skerri," she said, and laughed softly. "Unlace me. Don't make me do everything." Her fingers opened his gown, and, one at a time, unhooked the fastenings of his shirt.

His fingers lingered on her hard-nippled breasts before moving to the ribbon that zigzagged between. He undid the bow, unlaced the ribbon, slipped the straps over her shoulders and, heart pounding, slid the bodice down to her waist.

"That wasn't so difficult, was it?" she whispered. She wriggled her hips and the housekirtle fell to the floor.

— «» —

He awoke at daybreak wrapped spoonfashion around Esma's smoothly-curved body. She stirred sleepily, whispered his name, and pressed against him. He traced the curve of her breast with a fingertip; she responded with a little sigh of pleasure, and rolled over to face him.

"Would that longer this night had lasted," she said, her voice husky. "Curséd the clock that points our parting!"

"Did you just make that up?" he asked.

She responded with a mischievous grin and pulled him on top of her.

The sun was well clear of the horizon before they went, hand in hand, to break their fast in her residence's refectory. They spoke little as they ate the thick vegetable broth and crusty wheaten bread, though their eyes rarely strayed away from each other. Their feet met often under the bench, and they exchanged quick conspiratorial smiles. Even Skehirren's suspicion that everybody else in the room was secretly watching them could not dampen his mood. The world to which he had awoken was one in which he could do great things — and would, to stay here at the University with Esma.

After the meal, he kissed her goodbye outside the hall and strode back to the College of Lifelore. At the heavy oak door of Keste's studium, he paused only for an instant before knocking.

Keste sat at the cluttered table, adjusting the lenses of a viewing tube. He glanced up. "So you're going through with it?"

"Yes, sir," Skehirren said. He took a deep breath. "I want to sit the Old Vigil. Tell me what I must do."

"I'll teach you what I can. For each traveler, the way is different." Keste picked a small leatherbound volume out of the only clear space on the table. "This book is Venna's *Saga of the Silent Lands.*" He held it out. "It was written two greatscore years ago, and it's still the best guide we have. Read it carefully. Make notes. Come back when you've read it."

Skehirren took it as if it might bite, and examined it carefully. The leather of the covers was in good condition, the workmanship crisp and modern. He opened the cover: the pages inside were age-warped parchment, the crabbed letters brown with age. "What else will I need to know?"

"There is a draught that you must take with you. I can instruct you in compounding that." Keste leaned back in his chair and crossed his arms. "But that is the easy part. Which temple do you attend?"

"None, usually. Feast days, that sort of thing."

"A modern thinker, hmm? The Gods are symbols, projections of our mythic minds? No point worshipping abstractions?"

Skehirren smiled weakly. "That's about it."

The old man glared at him. "That may well be true. But there's no point in asking symbols for knowledge, is there?" He looked up at Skehirren, a challenge in his eyes.

Skehirren's face burned. "I can't just start believing all those stories! Like the Maiden snaring the Tree Man with her golden belt, or the Smith creating the rainbow to please his lover?"

Keste snorted. "No, of course not! I don't suppose the old-time shamans believed half of those folktales either. But the gods were more than just symbols to them. Or if they were symbols, they were symbols with roots so deep that they grew right through what they symbolized. And if you plan to do this, you'll need to learn to believe as they did." He looked out the window toward the trees bedecked with new leaves, and his face softened. "The Lady of Life came to me on my Vigil. Perhaps she will come to you. Or the Runebuyer, who knows? You'd best be on good terms with all the High Ones before you go. Or..."

"Or I won't learn anything?"

"Or your spirit might never find its way back!" Keste growled. "There was a postulant at the University of North Haven who attempted the Old Vigil five years ago when her mentor thought she was unready."

"What happened?"

"She has the mind of a child now. She lives with her parents, helping in simple ways on their farm. Now, d'you still want to do this? It's not too late to quit."

"Yes, sir," Skehirrin said. "I'm going to do it!"

— «◊» —

"My grandmother had the Sight," Esma said. "She said it runs in the family." They were walking back to Skehirren's residence hall, after morning prayers in the Temple of the Lady. Around them the streets were busy with merchants, each followed by a line of slaves carrying their master's wares to market, and the ever-present throngs of postulants.

"If you say so."

"She knew when things were going to happen, she knew where things were. One day she came to visit and I'd lost my pendant." She touched the seven-pointed silver star that hung between her breasts. "She told me to look in the pocket of my blue cloak, and there it was."

"Just a coincidence."

"No. She did things like that too often. Now it had been cold enough three days before for me to wear that cloak. And I climbed trees a lot that year, and I would put my necklace in my pocket in case the chain caught on something and broke, and she probably knew that too. She had all the pieces, you see? But to her it was the Sight, and if I'd asked her to work it out like a theorem in geometry, she'd never have been able to do it."

"And that's how I need to think?"

"Maybe. I don't know." Suddenly she turned and clung to him. Her face was pressed against his shoulder, and he could feel her body shaking with sobs.

"What's wrong, darling?" he asked.

"The ... the Sight."

He tried to coax her, but she would say no more.

— «◊» —

As the sun rose higher, Skehirren trudged northward along the old road that wound through the watermeadows, occasionally stepping aside for a farm-cart or roadsteamer. He walked calmly, with even strides; but inwardly his mind roiled. *Am I ready? Do I merit the favor of the Gods? If they even exist?* He banished the thoughts and submerged himself in the discipline of putting one foot in front of the other.

At midday he reached the edge of the forest. Ahead, the road dwindled into the trees, rapidly becoming a narrow footpath. For the first time since he had left by the Scholar's Gate, he turned and looked backward; the spires of the University were a blue smudge on the horizon.

He pressed on into the woods. In a few hours, the last railroad, the last farmhouses, were far behind him. The solitude and silence were oppressive: since morning he had met no fellow traveler. Out of habit he fumbled at his belt, but his watch was back in his room. The occasional flirt of sunlight glinted between the leaves, still well above the horizon. But where was the stream that Keste had described? Surely he could not have passed it? Skehirren's fear clotted about his heart. He took a deep slow breath. He was letting his mind become undisciplined again, and that must not happen. *Don't think of a White Bear!* The dark thoughts faded; a few slow breaths later not even the lingering memory of them remained to lure him back.

Finally he heard the plash of water over rock, somewhere off in the woods. Gradually the path brought him closer to the sound. When he reached the little rill, a few yards wide, he crossed it on uneven stepping stones, then turned from the path and started uphill into the trackless forest.

The hillside grew steeper. He scrambled over rocks, hauled upon saplings and branches, pulling himself upward, always upward. Brambles and scrubthorn clawed at his gown. Sweat stung his eyes, his arms ached; every heartbeat was loud in his ears. Breath came in steam-engine gasps. Finally the slope became gentler, and blue sky began to show again between the tops of the trees. In a few more minutes he reached the hillcrest: there was a small clearing, a grassy glade, overshadowed by an ancient oak tree. One massive root formed a natural seat, with traces of ancient wear, just as Keste had described.

From the deerskin bag at his waist, he took an earthenware flask and a tabor. He tucked the drum under his arm and tipped the flask tentatively from side to side, listening to the quiet slosh of the liquid, at once familiar and sinister.

He turned toward the tree and bowed, honoring the sacred place; then he sat down on the root, uncorked the flask, and set it beside him, within easy reach. Before he could lose his resolve, he began to chant and to drum softly, a simple, repetitive pattern. *Patata, tum; patata, tum.* Three fingertips rolling onto the drumhead moments apart, then all together. *Patata, tum; patata, tum.* Slowly, slowly, the light of the afternoon faded to red, to grey, and finally to blackness.

He had practised this first step often, but gone no further, as a boy might go down to the Port Dalmeni docks to watch the ships leave. This time, with the potion, there would be no turning back; tonight his spirit would continue onward, outward, into the lands beyond, the Silent Lands.

By moonrise, he was no longer aware of the ache in his arms, or of the passage of time. *Patata, tum; patata, tum.* He continued to chant, barely above a whisper, as the drumbeat gradually died away, *patata, pata, pata.* Finally, he was silent. Later, he laid down his drum, his hand moving as slowly as a sleepwalker's.

Slowly, uncertainly, like a starfish exploring the sea floor, his right hand began to feel along the flat top of the root for the flask. At length it stumbled upon it, grasped it by the neck, and clumsily brought it to his lips. His mouth found the bitter liquid, his throat swallowed.

Soon his vision began to swim and double, and a cold hand closed around his stomach. He sat, motionless, waiting incuriously like a sick animal for the nausea to pass, while the trees twisted, danced, and spun in the mad moonlight. Strange unchancy things moved among the shadows. His consciousness spread slowly out like a mist, filling the little glade and becoming one with it, and the time that passed was as unmeasured and unknown as if nobody had been there.

— «» —

After an unmeasured time, a gaunt man with a wide hat, a staff, and a cloak walked into the clearing. Though he limped slightly, there was also a touch of devil-may-care cockiness in his step. Under the brim of his hat, a patch covered his right eye-socket; the left eye glittered.

It was to be the Runebuyer, then. Skehirren shivered. Keste had said that fair fame and fortune came often to those who had been examined by the Letter-lord. But, Skehirren wondered, would one who had himself bought knowledge at such a terrible price give it for nothing? Once more the shadows crawled towards him, shaping themselves into menacing forms.

Superstition! he told himself. He made his mind smooth, an unrippled pool ready to reflect the vision that he sought; and the shadow-things ebbed.

The one-eyed man stood in front of him, his hands folded around the top of his slanting staff. He grinned. "Well, lad, speak to me of your studies. Take all the time you need. Don't spare the details."

Then Skehirren began to speak, recounting the tale of his studies and experiments: of the cells split open, the long molecules like tangled invisible threads removed from the cell kernels, the light-too-short-to-see sent through them and scattered, the patterns recorded on the glass plates. Responding to the Runebuyer, he told how the molecules brought life to plant, animal and child, each after its own kind.

"And what shape have these molecules then?" asked the Runebuyer finally.

"Alas, I do not know, and I would." But somewhere, he knew, deep in his mind, might be the seed of that knowledge; if it were there, if he were worthy, tonight the god's blessing might make it burgeon: the Runebuyer's rede could help him shape it into symbols.

"Behold!" said the Runebuyer, and struck the ground with his staff. It seemed then that the ground opened by the foot of the staff, and two long serpents slid out of the soft black shadows. As one they coiled up the staff, each moving in the gaps between the coils of the other, but unequally spaced.

And Skehirren realized that this shape, this double helix, could indeed explain the patterns on the scatter-plates. Despite sickness, thirst, and fatigue his heart sang within him. He croaked his gratitude through parched lips.

The old man raised his hand: *Wait. There is more.* The faint dappled shadows drew together and became more distinct: the walls of a room, a laboratory. Men and women worked with strange apparatus. With the unearned certainty of a dream, he knew that they were cutting and splicing life-molecules, making new life-forms.

The sterile metal workbench in front of him became a bed, where a sick woman lay restlessly among tangled sheets. He saw her through the eyes of one that stood by the bed, holding a little girl wrapped in a blanket, who trembled, cried weakly, and burned with fever. The close air of the room reeked of sickness; mother and daughter were dying.

There would be no healer, that day or any. The plague (*the man-made plague, created in some laboratory, so very easy now that he himself had taken the first step*) was loose in the land. Outside, he heard the angry, hoarse shout of a Guardsman, followed by the crack of a firearm (*the emergency order had been in place for ten days; the larder was almost empty*). His stomach clenched with hunger. How long would it take the plague to burn itself out?

Though he could see the woman's face clearly, yet with the maddening illogic of dreams he could not tell who she might be. Sometimes it seemed that she was Esma, sometimes not. She reached weakly forward, and his dream-body gently put the little girl into her arms. His own arms were very tired from holding the child's limp weight. Or was that ache the first sign of the fever? He wondered, dully, why he felt no fear.

The vision blurred and vanished. The Runebuyer's face was like a mask of iron, showing neither anger nor solace. *This is where that road leads.* The eyepatch had vanished, and the empty socket glared its terrible message: *All knowledge has its price.* Then a cloud slipped in front of the moon, and the vision ended.

For a time Skehirren sat there, contemplating his vision, putting off the pain of straightening his cramped legs. Eventually he staggered to his feet, knees and hips in agony where the tendons had grown stiff. He reached to the tree for support, but his legs buckled and he crumpled to the grass. With one arm he huddled his gown around himself, whimpered a little, and slept.

— «» —

He awoke to sunlight and birdsong. His head pounded from thirst and the potent herbs in the draught, but his first thought was for the vision.

He rose to his feet and hobbled away from the sacred place, his mind churning as he staggered down the steep hillside.

Knowing the structure of life-molecules would not itself allow people to make new sicknesses. There were experiments — even a couple that he had done himself — that suggested that the molecules might indeed be broken and joined in a controlled fashion. And when he returned with the answer he had sought, it would surely arouse interest in the life-molecules. Even if he went no farther along the road, others would.

Painfully, he swung himself downhill from sapling to sapling. His knees burned from the steep descent, every step threatened a twisted ankle. Was the woman in the vision Esma? She had seemed less than twoscore years old; surely people would not learn to control and shape the life-molecules so soon? He heard the sound of the stream ahead: he was almost back at the trail. But if it was not Esma, it was somebody else's wife, somebody else's daughter, in a different year.

If he were silent, would that protect them, and the uncounted others who were dying in his vision? What benefits — what cures for disease, what crops to feed the hungry — might he be throwing away? And what other evils might result if he spoke? Armies of soldier-slaves, created only to fight and die? Citizens bred to serve the Emperor mindlessly? He reached the path, crossed the stream, and started homeward.

Somebody else, some day, would discover what he had; but silence might buy the world a few years' reprieve. Perhaps the knowledge, when it did come, might come to a wiser, less cruel, world, a world that could use the terrible power of the life-molecules safely.

But could he stay silent? Could he lie to Keste, deny the old man his last wish? Would his resolve soften and wash away in Esma's tears?

You have trusted me, Runebuyer! If I offer you this sacrifice, will you hear my prayer?

From somewhere in the treetops came the grating croak of a raven.

— ‹› —

Keste rose as Skehirren approached the Scholar's Gate. "Did it go well, lad? Did you find our vision?" The eagerness in his voice was almost greed. Beside him, Esma clutched her pendant in a white-knuckled grip.

Skehirren thought hard, trying to hold onto the mists of a fading dream. There had been something in the glade, something that would not be wise to follow, but what? A snake? No, that made no sense. A bear ... yes, that was it, a bear. A White Bear that had padded silently into the shadows between the trees, but now its tracks were disappearing under drifting snow.

"No, sir. I saw nothing."

Esma put a hand to her mouth.

Keste shook his head. "Then the Gods have not called you to be a teacher, and you can be a postulant no longer. By the laws of the University you may not return within its walls." The formality did not hide the bitter disappointment in his voice.

"I know, sir. I shall go."

Esma stepped towards him, tears on her cheeks. He embraced her fiercely. "I'll write to you. I promise." She nodded silently, her face against his chest. They stood locked together for a minute; then he put his hands to her shoulders, and held her a little away from him, studying her face as if it was a scatterplate whose pattern held a mystery. He kissed her once, released her, and walked away without another word.

For a while they watched him limping away along the riverside path, dark against the sunset; and then they saw him no more.

———— « O » ————

Robert Dawson

Robert Dawson teaches mathematics at Saint Mary's University in Halifax, Nova Scotia. He has been writing science fiction and fantasy for seven years. He is an alumnus of the Sage Hill and Viable Paradise writing workshops.

The Other Story

Tanya Bryan

Slipstream me to the other story
The one where the fairytale ending
Happens sooner rather than later
Make me the first chrononaut
Jumping from this era to the next
A truer chronologist never existed/exists/will exist
Let me in to parallel universes
To see how they do it better
Without the paradox of fate taking over
March me back to another history
Before quantum entanglement
Is more than Einstein's "spooky action at a distance"
Where time travel is still a
Possibility of impossibility and
Happy endings still exist.

——— « o » ———

Tanya Bryan
    Tanya Bryan is a Toronto-based writer with work published in *Feathertale Review* and the anthologies *My Cruel Invention* and *Dear Robot: An Anthology of Epistolary Science Fiction*. She loves to travel, writing and drawing her experiences, which are often surreal and wonderful. She can be found online at @ tanyabryan on Twitter.

No Others Like Us

Nancy SM Waldman

Spacemappers keep track of their age about as well as the planetbound count the stars, so Niev knew only this: she was impossibly old.

She peeled off her clothes, placed a foot in the pool and groaned with pleasure. If someone had asked her if her foot had been hurting, she would have said no. But now she knew it had been, because it wasn't anymore. Despite the parts replacements she'd had done over her life, she now had routine pain in both knees and right hip. A newer, more significant pain filled her gut. And she was almost blind.

She slipped her tall thin body up to her neck into the viscous white fluid. *Could it could heal as well as take pain away?*

Niev and her partner Dalna had returned to the planet three days earlier.

When they were first here, generations ago, they landed at a couple of dozen locations to take air and soil samples and look for evidence of life. They discovered these pools dotted in the hundreds over the planet's southeastern quadrant.

This you could never forget. The pools salved their cuts, bruises and insect bites and left them feeling youthful, playful and energetic.

Niev heard a sweet, high voice say hello.

She opened her eyes. "Hello," she said, to a blurry human shape.

"You are not hostile to me?"

"Should I be?" Niev had felt some irritation at being interrupted, but the woman's winsome voice calmed her, or maybe it was the pool.

"No. I will do you no harm." She paused. "May I join you?"

"Uh ... okay. What's your name?"

"Takkh."

Niev repeated it, trying to duplicate the extended breathy ending sound.

"Did you come from space?" Takkh asked.

"We did."

"Why?"

"To die," Niev said. It caused a flutter in her chest to say it so bluntly out loud to a stranger.

"That's ... unusual."

"I know. But all bodies fail eventually. I'm ready."

"You could die in space. Why did you choose to come here?"

Niev smiled. "Your planet was an important — and favourite — discovery for Dalna Resondo and me. It was mainly her wish to come back."

Takkh gasped. "You are Niev Pascula?"

"I am," she answered, pleased that the inhabitants would recognize their names. "But don't tell the townspeople. We don't want attention."

"Oh, I am not of the town."

Niev noted disdain in her voice. What was this about? "Where do you live?"

"The mountains. West of here."

"There's hostility between you and the town?"

"You could say that. Is your partner nearby?"

"Yes. Over by Betsy. That's what we call our shuttle."

"Are you both dying?"

"We believe so. Don't be sad. We've led a rich, long life with few regrets."

"What *do* you regret?"

Niev liked her directness. "Dalna doesn't look back. But I do. I regret that we never found intelligent life that evolved along the lines of humans. I'm sure they're out there, but someone else will have to find them."

After her soak, Niev walked back to the shuttle along the xenontile path Dalna had arranged for her. She came up behind her partner and said, "Describe the view for me."

"If we'd stopped at Hydra Station, you'd have your own eyes to see with," Dalna responded.

"Easy now. We're supposed to be relaxing, neh? Half-way across the system to fix my eyes just so I can die? We agreed it was too wasteful."

"Fine. I just wish you *could* see the hundreds of shades of green." She turned Niev toward the setting sun. "There are no human structures in sight, though that settlement is not far. I see patches of those reflective flowers. Remember? They look like star clusters on the foothills of those impossibly-orange, pointed mountains."

"I'm feeling younger already. Must be the smells," Niev said, breathing deeply.

Dalna scooped her around the waist. "It's the pools, girl. You remember." Her voice had gone syrupy.

— «» —

Overnight, Dalna died.

It's too soon. Sobbing, Niev rested her head on Dal's chest. *No. Dal, no.*

Niev was supposed to die first.

Damn Dal's romantic, sentimental streak. On ship, Niev knew her way around, but here? She couldn't see well enough to even feed herself. *Would you rather Dal should have to deal with your death? Selfish, as always.*

There were medicinals on board. She could easily end her life.

I should bury Dalna. I should mourn her properly before killing myself.

A pinpoint of hope rose when she thought of the pool. Maybe she could drown herself. *A painless death?*

Niev placed slender fingers on Dalna's wrinkled, soft cheeks while fresh tears spilled down hers. She stroked her skin as if she could transfer her own warmth. "I've always been a fool. This is so much harder than I imagined."

She'd have to seek help from the planet's people to bury Dalna. She hated that. Maybe Takkh would return.

— «» —

"Get out of that pool!"

She opened her eyes, but swollen from crying, they were more worthless than usual. It had only been a few hours since she'd found Dalna.

"Who are you?" she asked.

"Name's Rigen. Head of the local militia. Don't you know the pools are dangerous? Who are *you*?"

She straightened her back and said, "I am Niev Pascula, the Deep Spacemapper who, with my partner Dalna Resando, discovered this habitable planet."

She heard an unintelligible conversation. Deep, disagreeing voices.

A different voice said, "Out!"

"Fine, but I am unclothed." She rolled over and pulled up, her droopy backside facing them as she emerged. She turned to sit on the edge. "There. Happy? Now I need your help." She reached for her robe. "My partner died this morning. What are your rituals for dealing with the dead?"

— «» —

The men dug a hole paces from Betsy and buried Dalna almost before Niev knew what they were doing.

"You've rushed me," Niev said, furious. "I needed time to say good-bye!"

Even though she and Dalna had no adherence to religion, the lack of any semblance of ritual seemed disrespectful, wrong. She wouldn't have known what to ask for, but this wasn't it.

"I have reported your presence here," said Rigen after the deed was done. He sounded incredulous as he said, "The Governor wants to talk to you." He handed her a screen.

Out-dated technology, Niev noted.

She and Dalna had, upon entering the planet's atmosphere, announced their arrival, so this official call wasn't surprising to her. Governor Mae Gustad's voice was formal. "We are stunned to have the intrepid explorers who discovered our fair planet back with us. We have a plaque in front of the capital commemorating you both."

Finally, a little recognition.

"My condolences on the loss of Dalna Resondo."

"Thank you. It is what we expected. We came here to die."

The woman paused a long moment. "I see. I understand your eyesight is bad. We will, of course, take care of your needs. But you must know that the pools are off-limits. There is danger in them that you couldn't have known about. Now you know. We won't tolerate this rule being broken — by anyone."

"What is the danger?"

"They damage human DNA. If we could drain those pools we would, but they spring up spontaneously. Our only option is to educate our populace and to patrol them. That's the purpose of the nearby town. At any rate, my condolences. I will keep apprised of your situation. Perhaps you will fly to our capitol soon so we can meet in person."

After she signed off, Rigen took back his screen and said, "You were the mappers who found this world?"

"Yes. Tell me, how long ago was the colony founded?"

"The first ship arrived sixty-two cycles ago. There've been two others since. My parents were on the last one, twenty-four cycles ago."

"You were born here? Sorry, I can't see to know how old you are."

"Yes."

He was just a kid.

"Did we get it right that there are few if any predators?"

"None. Lots of small herbivores and irritating bugs, but no meat-eaters." He paused. "It must be amazing to know that none of us would be here if you hadn't been exploring."

"It's gratifying," she said. The few and far between discoveries had been exciting — and profitable. Bursts in an otherwise dull methodical search.

"I'll bet. We'll take you to town now."

"Oh no. That's not necessary."

"You can't stay here."

"Why? It's against the rules to camp out? I have all I need."

"You are blind, old and alone."

"I see your point. Well. All right. But I won't leave my shuttle here. I must pack up and prepare it for flight. As soon as I've done that, I'll fly to the town's landing pad."

"How will you pilot that thing? You can't see."

She patted him on the shoulder. "I tell it where to go and it flies — guides — itself."

"Humph. Okay, but I'll come get you if you don't show up."

"Fair enough."

— «》 —

Niev had no plan. She knew only that she didn't come here to live in some stupid settlement under a kid's watchful eye, or a Governor's thumb.

While stowing the shuttle, Niev's mind refused to stay focused on what she might do next. She was lost in the past.

Springy moss bordered the lake-sized pool. They'd been in it for hours, soaking, napping, enjoying deep conversations with much laughter. At sundown, Dal rolled onto the bank and pulled up a willing Niev. Clinging to each other, they continued rolling, giggles interrupted by smouldering kisses. The pool had left them silky. "Your skin's so soft I can barely feel it," Niev whispered. "I can't tell where you leave off and I begin."

The next day we left. How did we make ourselves go? What was our rush? But we did leave ... after we placed the beacon and data pack in that cave.

She turned to face the mountains with a sudden vivid memory of the entrance to the cave they chose. It had an overarching rock formation that folded on itself like a braid.

Takkh's people live in the mountains.

By mid-afternoon, having left a tracer at Dalna's burial site, Niev was ready. "Show beacon," she said to Betsy. She saw a pulsing gold light as the AI told her its position. It was still there. Still functioning. "Good." It might not be where Takkh's people were exactly, but it gave her a landmark to shoot for.

"Triangulate beacon, town and current position." A beaming triangle showed up on the display. "Set flight plan to avoid man-made structures. Destination: as close to the beacon as possible." She set controls to notify her if human movement or heat were sensed. They took off.

As they neared the foothills, Niev heard a dull drone.

"Landing necessary and imminent," Betsy stated. "Duality circuits under-utilizing."

"Shit," Niev whispered. "How far from destination?"

"1.68 kilometres." The shuttle reeled off the destination coordinates versus their present location.

"Land as near a pool as possible."

Once on the ground, Niev asked the estimated recovery time.

"Unknown. Diagnosing problem."

Niev looked out on the mountains, now looming. The slanting sun showed sharp contrasts. A duality circuit issue could be a blockage, corrosion or something worse. Some of those things, Betsy could self-correct.

"I'm gonna leave you here, girl. I hope you've solved the problem by the time I get back."

She activated a perimeter defence and set out with her pack on her shoulders, carrying the natty cane Dalna had picked up for her on their last station sojourn. Keeping the sun behind and shining on her right cheek, she walked toward the beacon, using the cane to feel the way. Her gut pain wasn't bad today, but knees and hip joints pinged painfully with every step. "So what if you fall in a pool? That'd be the best thing to happen to an old fool like you. You could die of pleasure in one of those fluid-filled coffins!"

The Betsy-sync in her breast pocket periodically sounded to let her know when she wandered off course.

She caught glimpses of the reflective flowers in the distance. Her progress was slow. When the sun sank so low that everything became an uninterrupted grey blur, Niev walked on. With her vision, it didn't make that much difference.

Then Niev's foot hit a hole, the world spun and rolled and she fell hard on her right hip.

— «» —

Daylight, after a long hard night.

Niev, just awake, thought she heard something. "Hello?"

"It's me. Takkh. We found your shuttle and have been looking for you. Why are you here?"

"The shuttle malfunctioned. I was trying to find you and your people."

"That's wonderful! Let's go. It's not too far."

"Can't walk. I'm in a lot of pain."

"Hmm, I can help. Be patient. I will return."

"Wait," Niev said, but she saw Takkh's pale form recede.

She tried to sit, but intense pain stabbed through her. Niev wished again that she and Dalna had chosen another time and place to die. It would have been so easy to take a drug and die while cruising through the cosmos. But wasteful, Dalna had argued. Someone should use their ship and their amassed credits, which wouldn't be possible if they sailed through eternity into the void. Not that they'd ever made the arrangements for it. That was part of what they'd planned to work out once planetside.

Dalna wasn't supposed to go first.

The sharp pain receded to a slow throb. As Niev calmed, she noticed the freshening breezes and rich organic smells.

Technology had always surrounded the two of them. Their home, their transportation, their contact with humans, everything depended on the ultimate in human manipulation of science. Now here she was on her own in a natural world.

Wouldn't Dalna trade being dead for being in a little pain? Especially to live in this beautiful world? In Dalna's memory, Niev decided she'd stop trying to die. To simply live until it ended.

Eventually, she slept.

Takkh woke her. "I've brought you something. Drink, please."

Niev started to question Takkh about what she was being given, but what was the difference? She would get better, worse, or stay the same. She needed help and this was the help that had been offered. She put the wide shallow dish to her lips and tasted it. It was thick, but drinkable. She swallowed several large gulps. "It, ah, it tastes … fine."

"Yes. Drink it all."

With two more swigs, she drained the bowl. "Thank you. Is it a pain-killer?"

Takkh laughed. "I never heard anyone say that pain can be killed."

"No? Well, will it take my pain away?"

"Oh yes. Soon you will be able to walk."

— «» —

They hiked through grasses that gave way to hard-packed, rocky ground. The way was spotted with stands of mature trees and spikey shrubs.

Niev felt enormous joy. Not only did her hip work, but her knees and muscles felt up to the task. And her vision had improved. This girl's medicine was powerful.

Niev could see her clearly for the first time. Takkh's skin wasn't just pale, but snow white. "How did you find me?"

"I'm a scout assigned to keep track of you, though you didn't make it easy for me."

"Why would you track me?"

"We have never had a shuttle land in our territory before. Of course we would investigate. When we found out who you were, we didn't want to lose you."

"Please forgive this question, but why is your skin so pale?"

"The pools changed us."

Niev stopped, remembering the Governor's words. DNA damage. "I need an explanation."

Instead of answering, Takkh turned a full circle, looking outward, searching, alert.

"Are you all white?"

She nodded. "The people fear our changes."

"Who are 'the people'?"

"Everyone but us. We are different, so they are the people and we are—" The girl stopped, holding out a cautioning hand, listening, searching the area. "...*mutantes.*"

Catching Takkh's nervousness, Niev swept her eyes in a semi-circle. The mountains loomed. She wiped sweat off the back of her neck. Her skin felt tender.

"They're here!" Takkh said in a hard whisper. She grabbed Niev's wrist, pulled her down and powered her toward a boulder the size of Betsy. As they ducked behind it, Niev heard sharp fast noises like air escaping from a breached hull.

"They hunt us. Just for fun." Takkh breathed shallowly.

"What?"

"We must reach the caves." She looked behind them, orienting herself. "But there is open ground to cross before we'll be safe."

"Go without me. They aren't after me."

Takkh pulled her closer. "No. I won't chance that."

"What do we do?"

"Hide until they leave if possible. Oh!"

A volley of pulses came at them, followed by sprays of rock. Niev turned and spotted three men at least a hundred meters away, each with a sidearm.

"Run!" Takkh, with Niev following, ducked in and out of the warren of rock piles as more shots and rock pinged around them.

She found a ledge between two boulders that they could duck under.

Niev looked around but saw nothing. She was out-of-breath, light-headed and very scared. Being shot at was heart-stopping whether one was expected to die soon or not.

"I've been hit," Takkh whispered.

She looked down. Takkh bled profusely from a shoulder wound.

"My gods!"

"It isn't bad. Listen. If you see a place to hide, do so. I will find you once they're gone."

They took off as fresh shots rang out. When a barrage shredded a nearby outcropping, a dense dust cloud surrounded them. Even Niev's improved eyes couldn't see through the haze. She started coughing, which brought on more shots.

Desperate and darting from the worst of the dust, she rubbed watering eyes. She was losing contact with Takkh but couldn't call to her. Niev zig-zagged until she found a pile of boulders with a large enough space to slip into.

A man's voice said, "Buggers have to be here somewhere." He started coughing.

The dust.

"That's the sport of it. It shouldn't be too easy."

Another voice, farther away, said, "Movement over here!"

Niev heard boots scuffling away.

They were persistent. Scattered fire shook the ground and her nerves for the better part of an hour. Niev wondered if they hadn't started hunting small game. She heard a few more shouted comments and then all man-made noises stopped.

She remained hidden, bothered only by a myriad of swarming insects and her worries over Takkh. As the day greyed into a still, late afternoon, she finally moved out, stretching her back and legs.

"Takkh?" she ventured softly, but got no response.

What if I drew them here? Rigen told me he'd come after me if I didn't show up.

As she found only silence all around, her breathing relaxed. With a wry smile, Niev thought of how furious Dalna would have been that someone had the audacity to shoot at her!

She walked until the day's glow fell behind the peaks. When she finally found a pool, she stripped and entered. A blessed gradual slope allowed her to rest her back, neck and head on warm soil while immersing her body.

Niev watched the stars fill the sky.

— «» —

Round black cave openings in the looming cliffs looked down on her like curious bystanders. She looked back at them with her improved eyesight. Niev had assumed her vision would deteriorate as Takkh's medicine left her system, but sleeping all night in the pool might have helped too.

She prepared for the day and set off toward the beacon. It was still her best bet for finding Takkh's people and hopefully Takkh, safe and sound.

A meandering path through the piedmont proved challenging with more climbing than walking. *How did we even find this place, Dal?* She remembered it as having been an easy path; otherwise they would have left the beacon elsewhere.

"Fool. All these rocks fell off that mountain since then."

By mid-morning, she was winded, thirsty, hungry, and completely elated at her mobility. It felt like living in reverse, getting younger every day.

Her silly joy soon popped like a bubble, replaced with a devastating truth: if they had come sooner, if Dalna had spent more time in the pools, she wouldn't be dead.

Niev leaned on the nearest boulder and gave in to grief.

— «» —

That's it! She stood in front of their cave opening. She recognized it because it was arched with what looked like a plaited rock.

Niev entered slowly. Ten paces in, the path was blocked by shoulder-high rocks. She hesitated, thinking of the threat of a cave-in. "What are you going to do? Go back? You came here to die no matter how immortal you're feeling. Climb over it."

As she scrambled to the top and eased down the other side, she got the notion that these rocks had been put there on purpose. *A barrier to slow down troublemaking townspeople?*

Maybe the cave was monitored. Or maybe she was nowhere near Takkh's people.

The way ahead showed a clear narrow high-ceilinged passage that curved to the right. She walked in the footsteps she and Dalna made all those years ago.

They were due to leave the best on-planet experience of their lives, having found the pools three days earlier. This cave felt as magical as everything else had.

Niev led as Dalna, frisky at her heels, said, "We could stay."

"You say that every time we find a new one. I get it. But we'd be breaking our contract, plus several laws. Once the Consortium declares it habitable—" She turned to face Dalna's huge brown eyes.

They crinkled with her smile. "I know. It's just…"

Niev kissed her and folded her into an embrace. "We are spacemappers, born and bred. But when you're done, just say the word. It's the best planet we've ever found."

Hand-in-hand they explored until they found a solid rock ledge on which to leave the requisite materials which would transmit their find.

Diffused light shone near the top of the passage.

Niev walked through two elongated S-curves, slowing reverently as she realized the walls were covered in carvings. The passageway widened and she entered a circular room, its carvings stained with intense colours. Centred above, twelve openings cast daylight around a floor-to-ceiling pillar cut from rock.

The com in Niev's hand pulsed brightly. She circled the pillar and saw the data pack and beacon, sitting as if enshrined.

"Welcome, Niev Pascula." A tall black-haired person with very white skin stood in the opening on the other side of the room. "You tripped our alarm. We hoped it would be you." The person walked over and took her hands. "I am Lokhan. We are most honoured. Things have changed since you were here."

"The room," Niev said. "I don't understand. The ledge was part of the wall."

"We value it so much that we carved the room around it. We've used the data pack as a starting point to advance our technological knowledge. We hope at some point to communicate, to trade, off-world. Our progress is slow."

"Did Takkh return?"

"Yes. Her injury is being treated."

Suddenly Niev felt every bit as old as her years. "May I sit down?"

Lokhan escorted her down a wide corridor as others, who came into the passage to peek at her, ran ahead or followed. They seated Niev in a room with outside light from a deep-channelled, imperfectly-round window cut into the face of the mountain. Food and drink were brought in.

Questions spilled out of Niev. "Why do they hunt you? Were you always here? Are you native to the planet? Are you an alien race? Did we just miss you when we came?"

Someone laughed. Niev turned her head. "Takkh!"

"I've been out searching for you!" The young woman, looking healthy, came over and took her hands. "Let me answer. We were all born here. Our ancestors were among the first human colonists."

"Human," Niev said, looking into Takkh's large eyes, the shape and colour of almonds.

Lokhan said, "We are changed, as you see."

"By the pools."

Takkh answered. "Yes, the liquid we call *nila* mutated our ancestors."

"Dangerous," Niev whispered, wondering how much exposure could cause such changes. "Is this why I, why Dalna and I, lived so long?"

"It's entirely possible. You have experienced the result of just a few days of soaking."

"The mutations took a decade or so to be visually noticeable," Lokhan said. "It wasn't until new colony ships arrived that the extent of the genetic differences were fully noted."

"Your skin had changed pigmentation?"

Lokhan nodded. "The offspring of those who settled near the pools, showed that obvious change. There are other changes. Our immune systems."

"You heal faster, live longer," Niev said. "But why, if you have enhanced abilities, do you allow yourselves to be hunted, to be trapped in a mountain while they have cities and government and ... freedom of movement?"

"Mutation is a scary word to most humans. At first, no one knew the extent of the changes. So the government, not wanting to lose its pure human population, segregated us and declared the pools a danger. We have lived here in isolation except for the unfriendly few in the settlement. We are no more than target practice to them. The government turns its back."

"But you're a new human species!"

Lokhan smiled. "Not so new."

"You have the right to be protected!"

"Who would give this right?"

Niev's mind raced. "The Consortium. It loosely governs all planetary habitats with human colonies. There was something..." She tapped on her lip, thinking. "Not quite the same, but it was a planet with a highly-intelligent animal. A water species, I believe. They were officially registered and are now protected by the Consortium. You're human beings! Of course you can and should be recognized."

Lokhan's complexion grew brighter. "This is good news. We are gentle people, Niev. We have no weapons with which to defend ourselves and, in fact, have a distaste for the very idea. It tends to—"

"Turn our stomachs," Takkh finished.

"The planet evolved no predators," Niev said quietly.

"You need rest." Lokhan began shooing people out of the room. "Takkh, you stay. Niev, we are most grateful you've come. Will you reside with us for now? We are preparing quarters."

"Yes, but I will have to tend to my shuttle."

Takkh placed a hand on her arm and Niev felt waves of warmth radiate from her.

"We would like permission to transport Dalna's body here. We can't bear thinking of her in a shallow grave with no marker. We revere you both. You must know how much. If it weren't for you, we would not exist."

— «» —

Niev slept in the shuttle, surrounded by the familiar.

Betsy sat high in the mountain in a smooth-walled room open to the heavens. Dalna's remains lay in a custom-carved alcove. A recessed pool in the floor held pumped-in *nali*.

Takkh and her people came daily — eager, smart and wanting to know everything about the shuttle and the empty starship orbiting overhead.

That Niev didn't get her wish to die quickly wasn't the worst disappointment in her life. The worst was that Dalna had missed this chapter, this ending.

On the night before leaving, she walked the steps to the skyopening, sat on the cushioned ledge and spoke to her. "I regret that we didn't stay when you wanted to. We would have been the first of the *mutantes*."

She could hear Dalna's response: *You and your regrets. Think of the other worlds we mapped in those ensuing years.*

"I'm going to take Takkh and some of her people to the ship. We'll travel to the nearest Consortium hub to register them, to make sure the universe knows about them. I'll teach them to pilot, to travel the stars. They have claim to amazing resources on this planet that will enrich, and ultimately, protect them. And our ship, *Elizabeth*, will go on and on. Dal," she whispered, "they are our legacy. We didn't find a new human species, we *founded* one."

Others ... not quite like us.

Niev rested her back on the mountainside and counted the stars.

—— « o » ——

Nancy SM Waldman

Nancy SM Waldman grew up in Texas and has been moving northward ever since. She now writes from the woods of Cape Breton, Nova Scotia, which is far enough: nancysmwaldman. com

'Gel Theta One

Rhea Rose

The light glares and makes me weak. I try to shade my eyes with my hand, raising it to my brow, but am only able to bring my arm as far as my shoulder. My wrists are chained to the wrists of the guards that walk with me, one guard on either side. I walk slowly.

They are slightly ahead of me as we move down the hallway. We are silent as we head for the screening room.

I keep my eyes downcast, locked to the only darkness I can find — the black of their military issue boots, but even these reflect the bright artificial light that streams down from somewhere above, reflecting small novae in their black polish.

Bright light is my enemy, my enemy because it keeps me in the physical realm. In light I am disambiguous. Light dispels my interdimensional nature, my most comfortable, default position.

These guys want me well lit.

It's not that light makes me sizzle or burn up. Light prevents me from becoming — a shade; a creature of dark energy, my consciousness, freed from a flesh and blood body, is a locked matrix of particles held interdimensionally.

The chains at my wrists and ankles aren't necessary, except for their psychological effect. They are taking me to the screening-room. I want to enter the screening-room as much as they seem to want me there.

The metallic white walls and floor make it feel like I'm walking down a corridor cut through ice. The bright, white walls gleam, scream at me. We turn left, then right before I see the room which is my final destination. The double doors are simultaneously pushed open by the guards.

They position themselves by the doors we've just stepped through. I squint. There are a lot of people inside the room, which looks like an operating theatre. The people inside wear gowns and masks; their hair is covered with mostly white and yellow protectors. They are gloved, too. One of the yellow gowns comes toward me, unlocks my chains and gives me a gown to slip on over my clothes. She ushers me to a group of tall white gowns. They drift apart as I approach, pieces of ice disturbed by unseen currents. When they have moved away, I see Captain.

He is lying almost naked on a table, a thin blue sheet covers him from the waist down; a grey screening cap on his head. They have shaved off all his golden hair. He looks like a drowned swimmer, pulled from the cold, black depths of space and sea. Tubes cling to him like seaweed. I've done this to him. I touch him and he is cold. I bend to his ear.

"Captain." I whisper.

"He can't hear you," someone says, and pulls me a few feet away from him.

They ask me for my rank and file, which they already know, but I tell them again, anyway. I'm not sure how many times I've repeated it. My name is 'Gel and among my kind I am known as a nightmare crawler, yet, in this place I am technically referred to as Dark Angel Theta One.

There's nothing biblical about a Theta One. We are a form of human being. I still remember that I was female. They brought me back from beyond death, and made me a Dark Angel. I'm a dimensional being. There was no choice, death or angel.

The gowned crowd remains silent.

I look around the room.

All the walls are monitor screens. All the screens are silent, except one. It glows softly, yellow-orange, but there is no picture.

"Is that him?" I ask, wondering if he is brain dead.

No one seemed to be in any hurry to get on with the reason why we were all gathered here.

"Yes. We're lucky. Getting him back shouldn't be difficult," a white gown explains. He means that Captain is still alive, still in control of his body.

"Then why haven't you done it? Brought him back," I ask, truly surprised. *Once, I was consciousness escaping my mortally injured body, like steam from an old time kettle.* They brought me back.

"He's hiding — in a memory. We can't locate it. It's one of the memories you and he created. We, of course, don't have it mapped, so we haven't been able to get to him." It's the yellow gown, the one that unchained me. I can tell she's female.

Now I know why I'm here. I thought they wanted my weapon. But Captain's hiding in a memory, pretending to be gone and they want me to draw him out.

They take me away to another room with desks and chairs, where we sign more papers, talk, and I confess to everything all over again.

They are excited to have me here in front of them. I make them nervous, but their curiosity is getting the better of them. I'm small, and look somewhat demonic. They will likely never see another dark matter form like me in their lifetimes.

They bring me back to Captain and as they prepare me for a contact-screening, I watch my silent Captain lying on the table, looking for a clue to his condition. He looks very much the way he did the first time I saw him aboard Cerberus III, when he was still Captain of one of the military's most classified deep-space warrior class vessels.

Cerberus was *our* ship. Captain, prepared for his role from a time even before his conception, became one with Cerberus and was expected to remain united — forever. As a 'Gel Theta One, I was the maintenance and co-navigational officer of a two person crew, putting in my mandatory time aboard the craft. I had another seven years of purgatory wake-time, PWT, aboard Cerberus before I'd made enough money to buy my way out of my commitment to humanity. Most of my time was spent in hibernation, only getting up for routine checks. Nothing much ever happened that required my attention. Normally, things ran as smoothly as a frictionless dock and lock.

Then, during one cycle, Captain awakened me from hibernation. I remained contained in my capsule, registering readings, waiting for the all clear and I glanced at the calendar. According to it, I had another six months before my next PWT.

Many things ran through my mind, but my worst fear was that Captain had done battle, or even worse, was about to.

— «» —

I can enter a dream and hold it, all Dark Angels can. That means I can keep it going or turn it off, my choice. The military understands that someone like me, a being capable of a certain oscillation and vibrational transmogrification can be found on the far side of most post traumatic episodes that every soldier's ever experienced. Dark Angels feed on the intensity of emotional vitality; especially the bad moments that we sometimes help create. And yet, ironically, the military has found a more creative use for us, not that that many of us exist.

We're effective soldiers in two realms, the physical and the vibrational. I can be *in* nightmares. I'm cosmic that way, or I can be a nightmare in battle, that's why I'm called a Dark Angel — the military's dark soul — manifest.

No Cerberus warship equipped with a 'Gel Theta One has ever lost a fight.

Dark Angels have a special weapon, but only Captain knows what it is. I can't use it here, in the screening theatre, only in deep space, where it's very dark and light is weak, and the people in charge here know this.

— «» —

There was no indication of an emergency of any kind. The lid popped, and I emerged. I was cold, thinking I would have to remember to adjust the capsule for that. I wanted to run and talk with Captain but duty and self-restraint prevailed. After performing routine checks, I moved to the top level where he was.

Up until that time, I only ever knew him as a voice that would respond to my questions. I knew his body was housed in a capsule similar to, but twice the size of my own, more like a tank. I always wondered what he must look like inside it.

At the top level things looked quiet, normal. Captain's tank sat ominously in the middle of Cerberus' bridge.

"Hello, Mika," he said, as I entered.

"Is there something wrong?" I'd been out of hibe for 48 hours. I found it more comfortable to hyper-illuminate the area and attend to the situation as a physical being. Inside my capsule, my superluminal ability allowed me to entangle myself in Captain's mind. But out here, well, it made more sense to be as physical as possible.

"No," he said, "Nothing's wrong."

"Then why did you bring me out of hibe?" He remained silent after that, not answering a single question. Not even the routine ones. I performed my duties as well as I could without his help. When I finished I sat in Captain's chair. A chair he never used and normally never would, but it was provided for him out of tradition.

Finally, he said, "Is everything functioning to performance specs, Mika?"

"Yes, Captain."

"Good."

I suppose I should have gone back to my capsule and put myself back into hibe. But I didn't. I sat for hours, most of the time staring at the black box that was Captain.

I don't know why I did it, knowing that everything, every nuance aboard Cerberus was recorded, and that Captain's capsule was never to be disturbed except under extreme emergency conditions. I suppose the Captain's irregular behavior was extreme.

I went over and touched the smooth, non-reflective titanium casing of the coffin like enclosure, running my fingers lightly over the colored coded windows and began the open-capsule-hatch sequence.

The lid came up with a soft swoosh. I looked inside. He was beautiful. I'd expected something grotesque, thinking that his form likely filled the entire massive container. Of course he didn't fill it; the extra space housed all the equipment that kept him functioning. He lay on his back submerged in a grey gelatin. Only his face was not submerged but appeared to be covered with oil or a thin layer of gel. It made him look shiny and new. His hair was flattened to his head, his eyes closed. His complexion was fair with a hint of pink in his cheeks. He looked as if he couldn't be more than twenty years old, but I knew he was at least three times that age. He had a heavy brow, squared off cheeks and chin, and a generous mouth.

"Hello, Mika." The sound of his voice startled me. His face remained unmoving as he spoke.

"Captain, I..."

"It's all right, Mika."

"What's going on?"

There was a pause.

"Do you know what an angel is?"

I smiled to myself. Was this a game? "No," I said, disingenuously.

"Do you remember the Gau-Teli nova?"

"—cataclysm on the white dwarf?"

I remembered it very clearly. It was something I'd never forget. An explosion of shimmering light with colors which changed from gold to blue and white, spraying toward us until we were engulfed in a display so awesome and exquisite that it never occurred to me to be afraid.

"An angel is like that and more," he said.

"I'm an angel," I said, reminding him.

"Perhaps," he said. "But you're still very human."

"Not when I'm among them."

He smiled at that.

"This thing you're talking about, is it an alien? An enemy?" I asked, immediately I scanned all the data for anything similar.

"Not really. It can't be completely explained. Just understand that I've had an encounter with one. It communicated with me while you were in hibe."

"What did it say, Captain."

"It showed me its realm. It was lovely."

"Is your experience recorded for the screens?"

"I wish it were, Mika. But it's not. I don't know why or how it happened but it did, and the screens didn't get it."

And that was how our trouble began.

After that, I emerged regularly from hibe and spoke with Captain about all kinds of things, especially about the angel. Once, after a long, discussion, Captain asked me not to return to my container, explaining that he couldn't bear another moment in one of his induced memories where I came to him as a dark dream from his childhood. In that reoccurring nightmare I fed lustily on his fear; it nurtured me and kept me strong in case we had to do battle with this thing he called an angel, a "real angel" as he put it.

"There won't be a battle with this being," he said, trying to reassure me.

In his dreams I took him through battle scenarios so horrifying that he yelled long and loud inside his capsule.

Since his encounter with the Gau-Teli nova, he said his practice scenarios had become dull to him. But I didn't believe that. I generated them. I was in them, and they were never dull, never repetitive. But, more and more he wanted me by his side and not in his head.

"Will you lose the blue flame?" he asked.

He referred to my weapon. "No, they can't take it."

"But you won't be able to use it."

"No."

Captain knew that without the nightmare crawls that took place during his theta wave cycles, the mental forays I created around his knowledge of war, and my weapon, a blue flame circadian shifter, seemed to have no purpose.

We'd stopped our practice games.

"Mika."

"Captain?"

"Have we ever battled anything real?"

"All my scenarios are — real," I said.

"But have we ever had a real fight? A real enemy?" He persisted.

"They're out there," I said. "Dark matter hides a lot of evil."

— ‹› —

Eventually, Captain and I lost all regard for duty and order. Cerberus ran itself. The Gau-Teli angel never came to Captain again, but it had certainly made a lasting impression, one Captain never recovered from.

— ‹› —

The day he asked me to disconnect him from the tank, I nearly fainted. But when I checked out the regulations and specs, it turned out to be a more acceptable task than I had imagined. The process was somewhat lengthy and complicated, but that wasn't too surprising considering Captain had been expected to spend his life as Cerberus.

Draining the gel from his tank was one of the final events in the disconnecting procedure. When it was gone, I toweled down as much of his body as I could reach. That was the first time I touched him.

When he opened them, his eyes were deep-set making their hazel color appear darker. Soon, he was free enough from the tank that he was able to come out. Though still connected to a few feed-lines, he was free of Cerberus. The ship was now nearly worthless as a military machine.

It took a short while for Captain to walk normally, and I was surprised to see how tall he was. When all his lines were gone, I gave him a complete checkup and was happy to report that not one muscle had atrophied. I had been an excellent maintenance officer, taking special care that none of Captain's muscle-lines failed, keeping their specific muscle in top physical condition.

Overtime, he came up with the idea to create memories we could enjoy together. He modified his tank, heaving out all the equipment that was no longer necessary and fixing it up so that we could both be comfortable inside it. I put an extension on the memory inducer and rigged it so that it was possible for us to plug in at the same time and create clandestine places where we could go without being seen. It worked. Together we'd work out different scenarios, plugged ourselves in and played them out in our minds. The ones that we enjoyed the most we stored in Captain's mind, only.

Captain was in memory-induction, waiting for me, when we were finally caught.

When they hit us, Captain was injured, and I immediately surrendered us to the authorities. I never saw Captain again, not until now, six months later.

— «» —

As they finish prepping me, I climb onto a stretcher beside him. A screening-cap is fitted over my head and just before the dark fog tumbles at me, I reach for Captain's hand.

I find him sitting on a park bench. He appears to be contemplating, looking straight ahead, and not noticing me until I speak.

"Hi, Captain." He turns his head, slowly. It's a warm sunny day, and he looks good in the sun, his hair blonder. The shadows across his face make him appear mysterious. There's a hint of beard on his jaw and chin. The way the shadows fall over his deep eyes, he looks as if he's wearing a mask, but just on his eyes.

"That really you, Mika?" he asks.

"It's really me, cowboy." He laughs when I call him cowboy. It's one of the fantasies we'd shared.

"They brought you here?"

"Yup."

"Damn them."

"I've missed you," I say.

"Why'd you come, Mika?"

"They made me, Captain. I'm under arrest. I'm supposed to talk you into coming back."

"They've tried everything else," he says.

"They must be desperate if they let me come here like this, after all they blame me for your ... condition," I explain. Captain gets up from the bench and comes over to stand in front of me. I look up into those sad, deep eyes and feel my own sadness.

"It's not your fault, Mika."

I can't say anything. I have to use every ounce of control to keep from falling apart.

"Are they screening us?" he asks.

I nod.

"I'm sorry I had to bring them here. But I knew you'd be here and ... I wanted to see you!"

Captain and I have come to this place many times. It's a small park located in a small town that we created, a place we could come to when we felt we needed quiet. We locked it into his mind, figuring that if we ever got caught they'd have a more difficult time locating it in him. We were right.

"Mika, I want you to know something," he says, while staring at me as if he's looking for something, and I pull my feelings to a manageable place.

"What is it?"

"I want you to know that—" He looks down, sighs heavily, then slips his hands into pockets and stands there not finishing what he was about to say.

I hug him. He holds me tightly, and I slip into his mind, even within our mutually created scenario I can go deeper into his mind, a shade over his thoughts.

"Please come back. I can't stand the thought of you leaving. They can lock me up until I'm dust. I can't let you go. Don't go — Captain, please—" He places his hand over my mouth.

"I can't explain it, but since the—"

I free myself of his gentle hold. "The Gau-Teli angel?" I press my head against his chest. I see my hand. I am so dark, even here in this imaginary land.

"I've thought a lot. It came here and showed me the way out. I don't want to go back to my life on the Cerberus. I thought I had made up my mind to go with the angel, but now that you're here, I'm not so sure. Whatever happens, we can be sure this will be our last time together if we remain prisoners."

I nod.

It's not hard to forget that everything we do is being watched.

We create a fun park; go to a movie in a hometown we also create. The movie is so bad it's funny, leaving halfway through, laughing hard, we're barely able to walk. We go for dinner.

That evening we walk comfortably along the shore of a small lake. It is a mild night. Frogs chirp. We're silent, then, "I've decided not to go back," he says.

"Me neither."

"You don't have a choice," he says, sounding very much like the old Captain.

"I'll follow you and the ... angel."

"If that's what you really want." He calls my bluff.

"What I really want is you to come back and do what you were meant to — be Captain again." My mind furiously calculates options.

"I don't want to, but it's difficult to leave you. I've made a decision. I need the courage to carry it out. You're a survivor. You'll forget me, Mika. One day you'll have a new ship and Captain."

Unsteady, I sit on a nearby bench. He comes over, sits and hugs me. I push him away. Captain puts his arms around me. When I finally recover, we stand up. He smiles and I salute. Then he takes my hand and leads me to a small wooded area with two particular trees growing close together. We stand in front of them, waiting, holding tightly to each other. Suddenly, for no explainable reason, I feel very warm inside and happy. The feeling rises until I think I'm going to leave the ground. I look at Captain. I can tell he's feeling it, too. An aurora arcs over the trees. The angel appears, its light washes out everything else around it. It is more spectacular than Gau-Teli. The angel is affecting me on the inside. Captain is stirring beside me, speaking, but it is unintelligible. Then I realize he is talking with the angel. Suddenly, he turns to me. "I love you, Mika," he says. There is a strange light in his eyes...

"Captain," I say, but it isn't my voice. The voice that comes through me has power. It surges within me as I breathe. I look at Captain, transfixed on the light in his eyes, and suddenly he's gone. I feel a part of myself turning to the angel, but this action feels as if it takes forever to complete, as if I'm functioning in slow motion. Captain disappears as he steps through the angel, and something keeps me there until the vision fades.

—— «‹›» ——

In the screening room, someone has covered me with a paper sheet. I lay on the stretcher, the room is dark. All the machinery is gone, so are the doctors and technicians. The screens are off.

I think about Captain.

On a chair, in a corner, I see civilian clothes, neatly folded, my wallet. A pair of shoes tucked under the chair. I don't dress. Without their bright lights I am a creature of darkness.

Captain was right. I'm a survivor. I'll go on. I'll find him and the angel's promise. They are out there in amongst the dark energy. They call to me; maybe they are setting me up for some form of battle. I know that Cerberus I and II are out there, too. They were visited by the nova angel long ago and went rogue, to find it. They, too, left for the ends of the universe, searching for the flicker of brightness that changed them. But in doing so they became enemies of the Union. Our mission was to seek and destroy. Cerberus IV will pick up where the last three failed. I'll find Captain and maybe the Gau-Teli angel, too.

—— « O » ——

Rhea Rose

Rhea has published speculative fiction and poetry pieces in *Evolve, Tesseracts, 1,2,6,9,10,17, On Spec, Talebones, Northwest Passges,* and others. She received honorable mentions in the Year's Best Horror anthologies and was reprinted in *Christmas*

Forever (edited by David Hartwell) and twice made the preliminaries for the Nebula Award. She's edited a book of robot poetry and has for many years hosted the Vancouver Science Fiction and Fantasy (V-Con) writers' workshops. She is a teacher of creative writing. Rhea has an MFA in creative writing from UBC.

Childhood's End

Geoffrey Hart

The Priest of the Ascension instantiates, shrugging into a body like someone donning clothing that hasn't fit him for decades. He smiles benevolently as he comes into focus. "Welcome, my child. Have you chosen to exercise your right as a new adult, and join the ranks of the Ascended?"

My mouth is dry, for I've been waiting a long time this day. Even with the best intentions, the Ascended have difficulty remembering the passage of time for those of us still in the flesh. But the answer has not changed in the month since I applied. "I am."

"You understand the process?"

"I do." I sign the agreement using my augments.

"Excellent. To know where you are going, you must first understand where you come from. Are you prepared for the Ordeal?"

"I am." I sign off on the second agreement.

"Very well."

Suddenly, I find myself elsewhere.

The waldo positions an electrode above the ape's head, then it descends until the electrode brushes the shaved skull. The graduate student does not look up, eyes focused on the 3D scan on her workstation. She adjusts the position of the waldo minutely, then lowers the mechanical arm until the electrode penetrates the skull with a *crack!* of bone. When she applies the current, the ape jerks, its lips a rictus of agony, but nothing can be heard behind the thick glass that separates her from her subject.

I am beside her, yet also on the other side of the glass watching her. She moves to an adjacent workstation, confirms the electrode's positioning above my skull. I writhe against the straps that hold my body, the clamps that hold my head in position. Then I watch the electrode descend between my eyes, heartbeat racing, until it penetrates deep within my brain, a short sharp burst of pain.

When the electrode sparks, I feel pain such as I've never imagined. Acrid smoke emerges from the wound and a lock of hair crisps and curls away, passing before my eyes. My tongue goes numb and blood fills my mouth, but I cannot scream. "Human subject shows no signs of pain," she taps on her tablet. "Ergo: apes feel no pain."

Then I'm gone, standing above a crowd on a walkway with several men impeccably dressed in expensive suits. They mill about, pressing the flesh, smiling at each other. Below, the crowd carry slogans on placards; from this distance, vision still blurred, I can't see the words nor infer the theme that unites them. The financially comfortable, too well groomed for this gathering, mingle with the homeless and the mad, sharing cardboard cups of water. I hear a few sung words about not being fooled again. Then the men beside me look my way, smirk, unzip, dangle limp penises over the railing, and begin pissing on the crowd. I purse my lips and they turn on me. The urine soaks through my pants and at first, it seems warm, almost a benison. But it quickly chills under a growing wind.

And the wind carries me away, deposits me beneath a withered tree. The sun blazes down, the only shade a few weak bars cast by barren branches. I hear running water, soothing until it's overpowered by a harsh retching that comes from no human throat. I look in time to see the sewage pipe spew clots of pungent feces floating in viridian fluid into the stream. The bloated corpse of a fish floats past; a gull descends towards it, hovers a moment, then beats its wings and flees skyward. I hear footsteps and turn to see a man in a tweed sports jacket with leather-patched elbows; beside him, a much younger woman clutches a notebook. "Externalities are a myth, or at best a mathematical anomaly," says the man, and the woman nods her head in meek agreement. He places his hand upon her breast — *my breast!* — and I recoil.

Two shaven-headed youths throw the black woman down, her chador providing no protection when her head strikes the concrete. The first kicks her in the belly, and as she curls around her hurt, he draws back his foot for another blow. The bystanders have been silent thus far. Most turn away, but one, a white woman, can no longer abide this, and intervenes: she grabs his shoulder and pulls, so the kick goes astray; rather than crushing the woman's nose, it merely tears the cloth from her face. She's no older than 13.

"Jihadist bitch!" yells the second one. The first turns, spins the white woman around, slaps her hard enough that her glasses fly through the air. Pausing only long enough to stamp the frames beneath his heel, he tears the six-pointed silver star from the chain around her neck and thrusts her back with both hands. I stagger, seeking balance, barely seeing his fist before pain blossoms in my cheek. He grinds the lenses beneath his feet. "Welcome to Kristallnacht, bitch." His friend laughs, pulls my arms painfully behind my back.

It continues until I can bear no more, and force myself to wake, foul sweat drenching me and vision blurred.

The Priest is beside me, supporting me with one strong hand as my knees buckle. I gather my feet beneath me, and he nods approval. "A blessing from an older time was to go forth and sin no more, but we have chosen something more relevant for a braver new world: *Remember what it is to be hurt.* Take this memory with you to the stars. May it remind you whence you have come, that you will never tread that path again. *Remember* what it is to live in the flesh, and how this will be for those who have not ascended. *Remember* these lessons that they may never be visited upon others before it is their time to ascend."

He raises a hand, palm outwards in blessing, and I place my palm upon his. As I do, my body falls to the ground behind me, discarded like a robe, and I reach upwards to the stars, eager to learn how to no longer be a child.

——— « o » ———

Geoffrey Hart

Geoff Hart is a scientific editor, with a specialty in authors who have English as their second language, and a technical writer. When not wrestling with Microsoft Word and throwing things at his computer, he occasionally manages to steal enough time to write fiction. "Childhood's End" is his third professional sale. Visit him online at: www.geoff-hart.com or on Twitter: @diaskeuasis

Plot Device

Eric Choi

(First published in *Northwest Passages:
A Cascadian Anthology*, edited by
Cris DiMarco, Windstorm Creative, 2005)

To: "Mazotta, Kathryn M." <SingleID587932354>
From: "TL&L Editor" <AIReg24994701>
Subject: Acceptance of Story

Thank you for submitting your work to Tales of Love and
Loving *("the Zine"). We would like to publish your short story
entitled "All Elaine Wants is Love" ("the work"). Click the
hyperlink to download the contract. If you have any questions,
do not hesitate to contact the Editor.*

Kathy Mazotta had finally done it.

Two years ago, she had lost her job at the news division of
Paramount-Bell WorldMedia, another victim of the CAN tools
that had swept the industry. There were virtually no jobs left in
journalism that still required human writers. Kathy had been
trying to break into the fiction market since losing her job.

Now, at long last, she had her first sale.

Kathy glanced at the clock. Sean would be home in a
couple of hours, but this couldn't wait. It would be so ironic to
call him at work.

— «» —

"Hey, Kath! I'm home."

Sean Nolan walked into the study to find Kathy seated
at the computer. He kissed her on the cheek. "Another story
submission?"

"Uh, huh."

"Which zine this time?"

"*Tales of Love and Loving*. They just came online a few months ago." Kathy opened the mailbox. "Still nothing for you. You'd think those companies would have the courtesy to at least send an acknowledgement of having received your résumé."

He changed the subject. "Listen, how about a movie tonight? *Siege of Heaven*'s playing at the Dunbar."

"Sean, you know I don't like those violent—"

"Come on, it's just harmless fun." He pulled her closer. "Besides, isn't it the company that matters?"

They went to see *Siege of Heaven*. The plot was very simple. A group of terrorists had taken over Space Station Beta, so a commando team was sent to rescue the hostages. To complicate matters, the girlfriend of the team commander was also aboard Beta, and the man was plagued by guilt over the death of a previous lover in a similar crisis. But after a spectacular space battle that climaxed in a hand-to-hand combat sequence in which the commander killed the terrorist leader by smashing his head through a bulkhead (his head blew up in the vacuum, while the rest of his body still inside the module convulsed wildly) Beta was freed. The movie ended with a weightless love scene before fading to the credits, scrolled out over the strains of an adult-contemporary soundtrack song.

"What'd you think?" Sean asked.

"It sucked!" Kathy spat. "I'll bet a 10-year-old with a CAN program wrote that and made megabucks!"

"It's just a movie." Sean rather liked *Siege of Heaven*. The action was intense, the special effects were awesome, and the mixed cast of live actors and crofts was likable.

Each theatre exit was flanked by a smiling teenaged usher who recited the same words to every departing patron: "Thank you. Good night."

"Good night," Kathy responded.

Sean said nothing. Kathy gently elbowed him.

"Hey!"

"You're being rude."

"Oh, come on. They're *paid* to say that!"

"You're in Sales, Sean. You deal with the public. Don't you prefer dealing with polite people? I'd thought you'd be a little more sympathetic."

They made their way through the parking lot under a clear, cloudless night sky. Weaving their way through the cars, they eventually got to Sean's old Toyota.

"That really wasn't such a bad movie," Sean said.

"You have absolutely no taste, you know that?"

"Hey…" He gently pulled her face towards his. "Don't mock my taste."

Kathy abruptly pulled away. "How much longer do you think you're going to be at Lagoda?"

Sean sighed. "What kind of a question is that? I'm sending out résumés, but with the economy the way it is … If people aren't hiring, they're not hiring. Look, Lagoda's not such a bad place — especially in Sales and Support."

"The faster you're out of there, the happier I'll be."

"Come on Kath, let's not start this again. I've been working at Lagoda since we met. You never complained until you lost your job—"

"Because of those damn CAN tools that *your* company puts out!"

"I have nothing to do with those products! Look, I'm sorry nobody's bought your stories yet, but if you want to work I've told you Lagoda's hiring writers to help refine the genetic algorithms that—"

"I don't want anything to do with them and I don't want *you* to have anything to do with them either!" She stared out the window into the night. "Not that I'd expect you to understand."

They drove home without another word.

— «» —

Lagoda Technologies occupied a nondescript three-storey building at Main and National, off the eastern edge of False Creek, an oddly unglamorous location for the industry leader in computer-assisted narrative software. CAN was originally developed for use in high-end games, in which new story elements are generated in real-time to allow players a seemingly infinite space of plot trajectories. But as the technology matured, Lagoda began to spin-off CAN tools for real-world writing applications.

Sean's new cubicle was the same size as the one in his previous position, but at least this one had a window. He would have preferred one that faced False Creek instead of the rail yard, but it was better than none.

"How was your weekend?" asked Peggy Yang, one of the senior engineers.

"Not bad. Saw *Siege of Heaven*. It was pretty good."

"Yeah, my husband and I saw it last week." Peggy pointed at the picture on Sean's desk. "So, when are you going to get off your sorry ass and marry that poor girl?"

"Will you stop that?" Sean demanded as he sat. "You sound like her mother, always asking me when she's gonna get some grandchildren. Why do you think I hate going home?" He wagged a finger at Peggy. "And if you keep this up, I just might stop showing up here as well."

"Great! Better job security for me."

"Get outta here, you slacker. Some of us have work to do."

Peggy smiled. "Hey, speaking of slackers, did you hear about what happened to Vik?"

"Is he still complaining about not having a window? I told him the day he was hired: 'You're here so that I can leave!'" Sean laughed. "That old office was a dungeon. Man, am I glad to be out of Sales."

"Real engineering work, better pay, window ... Anyway, for once he wasn't complaining. Turns out absent-minded Vik left his briefcase on top of his car and drove off with it up there. The thing actually stayed put until he got onto the 99. Came flying off and hit a police cruiser, of all things!"

Sean was still chuckling as he logged onto his workstation. After spending a few minutes answering his messages, he opened a folder and began coding a dynamic library module for the company's special new project.

if (concept(i)=FALSE).and.(belief(character(i)))...

— «» —

Kathy had locked herself in the study ... again.

"How much longer are you gonna be?" Sean rattled the door knob. "We're supposed to be at your parents' place in an hour. You know how your mother freaks out if we're late!"

The door opened. Kathy glared at him before returning to the computer.

"How much longer?" Sean asked quietly.

"Never—" she raised an index finger solemnly "—*ever* interrupt a writer in the middle of inspiration. If I don't get this down, I'll lose it for sure."

"What are you working on?"

"I got a message from *Tales of Love and Loving*. They're interested in my story, but asked for some revisions."

"Wow!" Sean exclaimed. "Can I read what you've got?"

Kathy backed away to let him see the screen:

"Oh please, I love him so much!" Tears were streaming down Elaine's beautiful face. Her voice quivered with passion and sorrow. "Daddy, daddy ... if you could only see, just how good he's been treating me..."

Tik-Gon, who was Elaine's father, was very angry. His face had a dark scowl. "No! I absolutely forbid you from seeing that white boy again! Over my dead body will you marry a gweilo!"

"No Daddy, no!" Elaine struggled to find a way to make her father understand. "Frank is so special. He's my man, the most beautiful man in the whole, wide world..."

Sean blinked a few times and swallowed before he spoke. "That's ... good."

"It's all about empathy," Kathy explained. "A good writer has to get inside the characters, to understand their inner lives, to know what makes them tick." Kathy paused for a moment, then quoted, "'I have to have the character in mind through and through ... I must penetrate into the last wrinkle of his soul.' Henrik Ibsen said that, and he's right. That's what those hacks and their fancy CAN tools will never get."

"Sure..." Sean said. "I'll wait in the den."

Kathy slammed the door.

Sean went into the other room, turned on the TV at a low volume, and started watching a sitcom. There was a running gag involving a whoopee cushion.

—— «◊» ——

if belief(character(j)).and.event(j)) then...

A tap on the shoulder startled Sean out of his concentration.

"Lunch?" Peggy Yang smiled. "Come on, don't make the rest of us look bad."

"I'm not hungry."

"Suit yourself." Peggy started towards the door. "Hey, isn't Hydro going to be doing that UPS generator test tonight?"

Sean looked up. "Oh my God, thanks for reminding me."

The last time B.C. Hydro did a test of the building's "uninterrupted" power supply, they somehow managed to take down the computer network, both the voice and vidphone systems, and disengage all the security maglocks. Sean made a mental note to remind Vik about his vidphone.

— «» —

Kathy read the acceptance message again while waiting for the vidphone to connect.

"Hello," intoned the perfect image of a young woman.

"Uh … hello." Kathy frowned. She hadn't expected a croft to answer. Sean was almost always at his desk. She studied the computer-generated image for a moment. Yes, it was definitely a croft. She could tell from the eyes.

"I'm sorry, miss," it continued, "but I'm afraid Vikram Hakki can't speak with you at this moment. Would you like to leave a message?"

"What? Uh … sorry, I must have dialled wrong."

Kathy tried again, and was greeted by the croft once more.

"Hello, miss. I'm afraid Vikram Hakki cannot speak with you at the moment. Would you like to leave a message?"

"Vikram Hakki? Is this not the number of Sean Nolan?"

"It is not." The croft paused as the image refreshed. "Sean Nolan is no longer in Sales and Support. Do you want me to put you through to his new number?"

"No, tha—" She stopped herself from thanking the non-person. "Just tell me where Sean Nolan is now."

— «» —

For years, Lagoda Technologies had been at the forefront of CAN software. Now, it was poised to take the next step. The company's goal was to develop a computer that could not only assist a writer, but would actually *create* its own tale. Lagoda would go beyond CAN into fully computer-*generated* narrative.

Sean surveyed the three linked workstations that formed a neural net known by the company codename of SHELLEY. The first machine, called PROUST, defined the initial theme, characters, and setting of a story. This would normally be done with a user input seed, but PROUST could also autonomously crawl the Web for story ideas.

The second computer, JOYCE, held a vast narrative parameters library that contained the complete vocabulary, syntax and grammar of the English language. JOYCE also housed an extensive set of dynamic library modules. These DLMs codified such literary themes as love, revenge, jealousy, betrayal — and the one Sean was working on.

The last machine, KAFKA, was the heart of Lagoda's prototype CGN system. Using the structural data from JOYCE and the story seed from PROUST, it would run dozens of AI and CAN processes in parallel to produce the actual prose.

```
if (exist(action(i)).and.(!exist(state(q))).or.
(concept(i)=FALSE)
{
    if (belief(character(j))!=true)).or.(action(m))
        action(i)=action(m);
    else
        action(i)=NULL;
}
```

The message icon started blinking on the screen. He touched it.

"This is the front desk," a synthesized voice intoned from the speakers. "There is a person here to see you."

Sean frowned. He wasn't expecting any visitors. "Who is it?"

"The person identifies herself as Kathy Mazotta."

— «» —

"How long?"

It was three in the afternoon, so the cafeteria was almost empty. Sean and Kathy faced each other across a table in a back corner.

"How long have you been working in R&D?" Kathy asked again.

"Seven months." Sean ground his teeth. It had to have been Vikram Hakki, forgetting to reinstall the message reroutes on his vidphone after the UPS test.

"You never had any intention of leaving Lagoda, did you? You weren't looking for another job, you just transferred—"

"What else was I supposed to do? There wasn't anything for me in Sales anymore! They've got crofts handling calls now.

Hell, Vik Hakki's the only real person on shift during the day. The only other people are those who go out for service calls."

"And you couldn't do that?"

"I *hate* dealing with clients, Kath!" Sean shot back. "I'm an engineer, not a huckster. The only reason I stayed in Sales was to keep *you* happy. But R&D is where I've always wanted to be. It's where I belong, Kath! Why are you making Lagoda — making *me* — out to be such a villain? I'm sorry, but—"

"You're *not* sorry!" Kathy shouted. "You don't give a damn about how *I* feel. This is all about what *you* want again, just like always." She took a deep breath. "Ever read *1984*?"

Sean stared at her blankly.

"There's this character, this woman who works in the Fiction Department of the Ministry of Truth. She maintains these machines that churn out propaganda novels for the brain-dead masses." She jabbed her finger at Sean. "That's what *you* are. You and those computers, churning out junk—"

"*Computers* turning out junk? Didn't they have movies when you were little? I haven't noticed any change. If anything, I think stuff's gotten better!"

"Your damned technology's already shut writers out of non-fiction markets, and soon this CGN stuff will kill the fiction market too and then there won't be any decent stories—"

"Do you know how crazy you sound? Are you saying you'd rather I be out of work? Who the hell's paying the bills? I mean, it's not as if *you're* gainfully employed right now—"

"I'm out of work because of what *you're* doing!" Kathy exclaimed. "I tried to call to tell you I've sold a story. I've *sold a story*, Sean! But it took me two years to do it. Why is that? Why do you think I've only managed to sell just *one* piece of fiction in two years?"

"Well, maybe it's because *you're not a very good writer!*"

The instant the words left his mouth, Sean wanted to bite his tongue. "Oh, Kathy ... what I meant was..."

Without a word, Kathy stood.

He reached out. "Kathy, I'm sor—"

She pushed him away. "Don't touch me!"

Sean watched her go, across the tables and seats, through the door, and out into the lobby, where she threw her visitors badge at the security guard before exiting the front door. He watched her until he could not see her anymore.

— «» —

if (plotelement(i))=UNRESOLVED then prepare (finalconflict)
        use (charactercrisis(random(1-10)))…

Sean's eyes glazed over the code. It had been almost a month, but he still couldn't concentrate on work.

"Hey."

He looked up. It was Peggy Yang.

"Look, if you want to talk—"

"Thanks." Sean's voice dropped to a near whisper. "I can't believe it's over. I mean, we always knew we were very different people, but I never thought…"

"I think you need some time. Why don't you take off for a while? You've got the flex hours."

Sean shook his head. "I think I'd rather be here. Keeping busy takes my mind off it a bit, you know?"

"Sure." Peggy nodded sympathetically. She gestured at his workstation. "By the way, what exactly is that DLM you've been working on?"

Sean stared at the screen for a moment.

"Deception," he said at last. "I've been working on deception."

— «» —

Dear Dr. Yaffe,

Thank you for sending me the latest story produced by Hemingway.3. It is clear that your team has made significant progress since the V2.6 release.

Given the limitations of the episodic experience database, it is not surprising that Hemingway.3 again chose CGN as the topic of its story. What is interesting is how it was able to extrapolate a human conflict from the technological theme in a manner not seen in V2.6. This is likely the result of your implementation of the Bringsjord-Meteer heuristics, which also appears to have enhanced its capacity for characterization.

It is also interesting how your redefinition of the narrative termination conditions have resulted in the tendency of Hemingway.3 to produce ironic endings rather than the action-oriented conclusions of its predecessors. On a more serious note, Hemingway.3 still generates plots that have a certain algorithmic "connect the dots" feeling to them. Perhaps this could be remedied by decreasing the step size of the numerical narrative integration.

Nevertheless, the story produced by Hemingway.3 is a remarkable accomplishment. For the first time, a computer has produced a piece of fiction that appears comparable to one by a novice human writer. This is a significant breakthrough, and I look forward to the release of V4.0 with great anticipation.

Prof. Ian C. McCoy
Artificial Creativity Laboratory
Department of Computer Science
University of British Columbia

—— « o » ——

Eric Choi

Eric Choi is the creator and co-editor of two collections, the hard SF anthology *Carbide Tipped Pens* (Tor, 2014) with Ben Bova and the Aurora Award winning anthology *The Dragon and the Stars* (DAW, 2010) with Derwin Mak. He has twice won the Prix Aurora Award for his short fiction and for co-editing *The Dragon and the Star*. He was the first recipient of the Isaac Asimov Award (now the Dell Award) for his novelette "Dedication": www.aerospacewriter.ca

The Shadowed Forest

Rati Mehrotra

Toronto's Downtown Destiny club was always good for a pick-up. It's what Maia was counting on, but it took all her will-power not to run away when the doors slid open and the waves of warmth and music washed over her. It had been over a year since she'd done this. Too long — a black mark on her Emo-health profile, and she didn't need any more of those.

She took a deep breath and squared her shoulders. *Come on, get it over with.* She strode in, mentally reciting the Dante verse she'd picked for that evening. The commercials hit at once:

'IMP 18 now available for testing! Will YOU be the one to win a free version?'

When I had journeyed half of our life's way, I found myself within a shadowed forest,

'Soft and silken on your skin, self-destructs at your whim. Diavvo's dresses, so you never have to wear one twice.'

for I had lost the path that does not stray.

'House a mess? Call Robo-fess. We were made to care for you and yours.'

Ah, it is hard to speak of what it was, that savage forest, dense and difficult,

'Fly Lunaria: Earth's most loved way of getting about the solar system. Amazing two-for-one deal to the moon.'

which even in recall renews my fear: so bitter — death is hardly more severe!

The commercials switched off as abruptly as they had come. The music returned, soft and muted now. Maia found herself leaning against the mirrored glass walls of the hallway, hands pressed against her ears. She dropped her hands and glanced around. People flowed past. No one gave her a second look.

She boarded the walkway to the food bars. Only four commercials — not bad. Last time it had been eleven and she was screaming by the end of the onslaught. Dante and Shakespeare can only take you so far. People had glared, even though she always put her IMP — the Internal Micro Processor — on Private before entering a club. They had no idea. Most of them, at any rate. She could always tell, just by looking, what IMP version they had.

Up six flights and the noise and smells of the cafetarium overwhelmed her. Eleven on a Friday night and the crowd was at its peak. Maia wasted sixty dollars on a muffin she didn't want and a spiked coffee she shouldn't be drinking. But it looked weird if you just sat there alone without eating or drinking anything.

She circled the chattering crowd before selecting a small table for two. Too much in the corner to be noticed, perhaps, but that wouldn't matter once she had adjusted the settings on her IMP. She flipped open her compact and studied herself. She'd taken some pains that evening. Dark, she'd decided, and so it was brown eyes deepened with mascara and coal-black hair piled in a top knot. Little red dress that she could still carry off and a silver dagger around her neck. "How do I look?" she'd asked the mirror, and "A picture of elegance," the mirror had replied.

She'd re-programmed the mirror, like everything else in her apartment. It kept her busy, maybe even helped her stay sane. Like the collection of antique books and daggers she'd built up over the years. She liked the feel of physical things, the smell of old books, the edges of knives. Relics of a bygone age, they felt real in ways that e-ware couldn't, even though most of her waking hours were spent immersed in lines of code.

She snapped the compact closed and took a sip of coffee. It burned her throat as it slid down. *Easy now. Don't gulp it all in one go.* Calm warmth enveloped her. Good, she was ready now.

She turned her attention to the screen embedded on the inside of her wrist. It glittered silver in the Cafetarium light. She tapped her finger in a quick, familiar pattern, switching her IMP to Public/Searching. The information grid came on at once, overlaying the physical world in front of her eyes. She sat back and took another sip of coffee, watching.

Male, twenty six. Public/Searching. Five feet ten inches, 160 pounds. Blood alcohol level: 0.12.

Reluctantly, she dismissed him. Probably too drunk to perform.

Male, thirty five. Public/Searching. Five feet seven inches, 149 pounds. Engineering consultant with CNC Corp.

Hmm, not bad. Although that kind tended to talk too much about themselves, pretty much spoiling any chance of a fantasy overlay on the actual act. Should she contact him? Her finger hovered above the screen.

Too late. Someone else made the move, and he switched his IMP to Private. Half-disappointed, half-relieved, she watched him weave through the crowd, his arm around the shoulders of a pretty redhead.

"Is this a dagger I see before me?"

Macbeth. She almost dropped her cup. A tall, brown man with wavy black hair leaned against her table. She'd been so caught up in the grid that she hadn't noticed him, right beside her.

"No, it's just a toy, really." She fingered the silver sheath around her neck and smiled, her pulse quickening. He was rather good-looking. And no one had quoted Shakespeare to her before — not at the Downtown Destiny club, at any rate.

"I'm Stanzin. Mind if I join you?"

"Please. I'm Maia." Something was wrong, but she couldn't quite put her finger on it. He sat down and she switched her IMP to Private. The grid disappeared and she studied him. Hazel eyes, day-old stubble on his chin, blue jeans and an open neck T-shirt. What a get-up. She wondered who he worked for.

"Like what you see?" said Stanzin.

Maia flushed and lowered her eyes, taking another sip of coffee to hide her confusion. Damn, that felt good. But she shouldn't drink too fast. She had to make it last all night.

"What are you having?" he asked.

She shrugged. "Spiked coffee, you know?"

"Spiked with what?"

Was he playing with her, making her say it aloud? But he seemed genuinely curious. "Levatamine," she said. The mother of all amphs. She took another sip.

He said nothing, but when she reached for the cup again he laid his hand on hers.

"I'm not addicted," she said. "I just take it on occasion, like everyone else."

"Sure," he said, but he didn't remove his hand. She felt tears sting her eyes. *Stupid, stupid.* She blinked them back, determined not to show any weakness.

Stanzin glanced over his shoulder. "Quite the commotion, isn't it? I wonder what they're doing here."

Maia followed the direction of his gaze. Black-suited men armed with scanners and lasers shouldered their way in through the crowd. Club security, searching for some poor shoplifter. She scowled. Why did they have to come here, to spoil *her* date? Couldn't they have waited outside the club?

"Kiss me."

Maia looked at Stanzin, surprised and a bit put off. She'd imagined an actual conversation, some more hand-holding. It was foolish, of course, and it was why she rarely came here. She never got what she wanted, either before or afterwards.

What did she want anyway?

Best not to go there. Best not to think too much. She'd put her IMP on Public/Searching and he must have just picked up on that...

It hit her then, what was wrong. *Really* wrong. But there was no time to think about it because he leaned forward and tilted her chin and pressed his lips down on hers. She found herself kissing him back, running her hand up his shirt.

Minutes passed before he finally drew away. "Upstairs?" he murmured.

"Yes, please."

He held her tight as they walked past the crowd, past the stupid security men, still with their scanners out. In the elevator she turned to him, expecting another kiss, but she was disappointed. He was distracted, watching the numbers fly past on the screen.

On the fortieth floor they got off and she insisted on paying the three hundred dollars for a three-hour corner pod. They were more expensive, but bigger than the average pod, and Maia felt like splurging. It had been a while.

Stanzin opened the door and gently pushed her in. Beyond the glass walls the city glittered, throwing blue light on the single bed pushed up against one corner. Clean and functional, it would do them just fine. She laughed, feeling clear yet light-headed. Levatamine always did that to her.

She turned to Stanzin and gave what she hoped was a seductive smile. Slowly she began to unzip her dress. "Like what you see?"

"No, please don't."

She stared at him, shocked. He took a quick step towards her and grasped her arm. "It's not you. You're beautiful. But this is not why I came here."

She shook his hand off and sat on the bed, the feeling of calm warmth evaporating. She thought with a pang of her cup of coffee, sitting half-full on the table down below. And Stanzin, leaning forward to kiss her at the exact moment that the black-suited men had appeared.

He sat down next to her. "I'm sorry, but I can't use you like that. It wouldn't be right."

"You already did, didn't you? It was *you* those security men were looking for." Anger pushed through to the surface, and fear. What would he do to her, a man like this? She shivered, wanting to be gone, not daring to move. She should have got up and walked away the moment she realized that he wasn't on the grid. Instead, like a fool, she had kissed him.

He faced her. "You're right. They've been on my tail for weeks now. With a bit of luck I can outwit them."

"What did you do?" Maia bit her lip. She didn't really want to know. The more she knew, the greater the danger.

"Nothing," said Stanzin. "I've done nothing wrong."

"Let me see your wrists."

After a moment, he held out his bare and sinewy forearms. She sucked in her breath. Her suspicion had been right. *He had no IMP.* She should call security now. All she had to do was tap her screen. He might not even notice what she was doing. Her fingers trembled, indecisive.

"I've never had an IMP," he said, "unlike some who've had it surgically removed. It's hard for them to adjust."

"It's not even possible to remove it," she said. "It's connected to the central nervous system."

"It's possible all right," he said. "Just not simple. Anyway, I've never had one. My parents had theirs removed and decided to bring up their kids without the Pols knowing every time they pooped or cried."

"Why are you telling me all this?" she whispered. "Every word you say is recorded by my IMP and can be heard by whoever wants to listen."

"Not so." He gave a sudden, wolfish grin and drew out a small black case from his pocket. "This is a scrambler. It's what keeps me safe. As long as I'm real close to someone, security can't detect a heat source without an IMP."

Hence the kiss. "So you just picked me at random?" she said. "To escape the black-suits?"

"Not exactly." His expression turned serious. "We're a select group of a few hundred, some in pretty powerful positions. But every once in a while, we take the risk of exposure to send out an invitation. This time, our software program chose you."

Maia's mouth was dry. She cradled her wrist, feeling the metallic hardness of the IMP against her breast. "Go on," she said.

"Come with me." His voice was low, insistent. "Come, if you want to be free of them. We know how to remove the IMP. We know where to hide."

Was he crazy? They always got you in the end — at least, that's what the news feeds claimed. Maia got up and walked to the glass walls. She touched the device on her wrist. It was only version 5, but it was all her parents had been able to afford. So what if she was subjected to commercials every time she entered a club or a resto-bar? It was a small price to pay for being on Dataweb, the vast information network that ran Toronto. She couldn't imagine what it would be like without it. How was it even possible to navigate the city without control over the built environment?

When you were born, you got a detachable wrist band. When you were seven, you got an IMP. When you were sixteen, you were eligible for an upgrade, if your parents had been paying a yearly deposit. It was a perfect system, a perfect city.

Except that Maia's parents died in a lab explosion when she was eleven, and she was sent to a state home. Dataweb, it seems, was not infallible. She heard rumours of a gas leak, a computational error. There were no investigations because no one had done anything illegal. No one ever did; the trail was too clear.

There were no upgrades in the state home. She had stopped feeling bitter about this years ago, although sometimes she wondered what it would be like to have IMP 7 or 8. Or maybe even version 18, the latest. Apparently, IMP 18 was so advanced that it wasn't even visible.

With a sickening lurch of her heart, she wheeled around to face the man who called himself Stanzin. They did this sometimes, testing the loyalty of ordinary citizens. What was more likely, that she — an ordinary coder — would be approached to join a group of IMP-free radicals, or that she was being tested by a government agent?

Maia swallowed and tried to speak calmly. "I'm a good citizen and I intend to remain so. The implants are a boon and I would no more remove mine than I would remove my arm."

Stanzin rose and strode towards her. She backed away and bumped into the glass. He grabbed her shoulders. "The IMPs are a boon? Really? Having the Pols know your every move, your every word, is a *boon*? You're in hell and you don't even know it."

"Zero crime," she said, speaking fast, trying to remember everything she'd read in orientation class, mandatory every two years. "Instant connectivity with friends and family."

"You *have* no friends and family," he cut in. "You don't belong. You never did. We know everything about you. The monthly check-ups at Emo-health. Those pretty daggers you'll play with but never use to draw blood. The shelves of books no normal person reads any more. Your pathetic one-night stands, your extreme fantasy overlays. Why do you think you've been chosen?"

She tried to wrest herself free but he was gripping her shoulders too hard, his eyes blazing into hers. Panic clenched her stomach. Who was this man and how did he know so much about her? He looked mad enough to break the glass and throw her out.

Suddenly he released her. He raked a hand through his hair. "Sorry; this is my first time and I guess I got carried away. They warned me not to come on too strong. But when I think of all the drivel they feed you, it makes me so angry. Why don't we start over?"

Maia jabbed her finger on the emergency icon, displayed as a screaming face on her screen.

Nothing happened. No siren, no spiders descending from the ceiling, no robotic voice answering the call from her IMP. She closed her eyes in terror.

For a while there was silence. Then his voice, soft and regretful: "I've failed. That is the one thing you should not have done."

She opened her eyes. He hadn't moved, but his face had closed, intent and business-like.

"Please don't kill me," she stammered. "I won't tell anyone, I promise."

He shook his head. "Won't tell anyone you've won a free upgrade to IMP 18?"

"What?"she said, taken aback.

He laughed. From his pocket he withdrew the black case he had shown her earlier. He flicked it open and held it out. She read:

"Pol Stanzin Duvall, IMP Investigations Unit." She looked back at his handsome, relaxed face. "You're a Pol?" She felt sick.

"That's right, Maia. You've been under investigation for a while. Too few dates, no friends, too many sick days. They had you figured for a troublemaker. But you're no troublemaker."

"I'm a good citizen," whispered Maia. What would they have done to her if she hadn't resisted?

Stanzin nodded, pocketing the black case. "You're the best. And IMP 18 will be your reward. You'll be the envy of your entire organization. Just go easy on the Levatamine, okay?"

"Okay." Maia's mind was still reeling. "When do I get the upgrade?"

"Tomorrow morning. Go to the Roselawn clinic on Martyr's Square. I'll tell them to expect you around ten."

"Will it be painful?"

A trained expression of sympathy flitted across his face. "In a way you cannot imagine. To upgrade to IMP 18, they actually have to remove the old version you have. The process of stabilization can take several hours. You'll be disconnected for a while."

"Oh God." Maia shuddered. May as well make it realistic. "Off the grid for *hours*?"

"I know, right? But it'll be worth it." He winked. "Trust me, IMP 18 is something else. You control the flow of information through thought alone. Like this." The door swung open behind him. He smiled at her. "Time for me to go make my report. Goodnight, Maia. All the best for tomorrow."

"Wait!" A sudden impulse made her lean forward and kiss him on the lips.

He held her out at arm's length and studied her. A curious expression came on his face, something she couldn't define. "I have a bit of advice for you, pretty lady," he said. "You can take it or leave it."

"Yes?" She felt her face heat up. Perhaps he was going to tell her not to kiss Pols on duty.

But what he said was: "After they've removed your IMP, they're going to put you in the rehab garden to recover. If you find yourself alone, walk out through the gate. It's never locked; it's not a holding facility, after all. If you're caught, you can always claim disorientation."

"Why? Why should I leave before my upgrade?" Dark clouds of confusion swirled through her mind.

He shrugged. "Ask yourself that. Not me." He turned and left the room.

Maia collapsed on the bed, her head spinning. He was a Pol. No, he was a rebel. No, that wasn't right. He was a double agent. No, he was a Pol. This was just another test.

Levatamine. That's what she needed. Maia got to her feet and headed out of the door.

Downstairs, the partying was in full swing. Men and women talked, drank, laughed, inhaled, kissed. On the ceiling strobe lights danced, as they always did after midnight.

Maia bought another spiked coffee and leaned against the wall. She drank deep and heat flooded her body. Her IMP buzzed. She glanced at the screen. It was still on Private. Who could be messaging her?

I did tell you to go easy on the Levatamine. Go home and get some sleep. Tomorrow's the biggest day of your life.

Maia raked the Cafetarium with her eyes. Stanzin was nowhere to be seen. She felt like screaming. But she controlled herself. He'd hear that too, wherever he was. So she smiled and tapped out:

I came here for a date, remember? I'm still looking.
So why are you still on Private?
Because it's you I'm looking for.

Silence for so long that she'd given up and gone back to her coffee, savouring the warmth and certainty of it. And then:

Tomorrow. The convenience store by the corner of Adelaide and Woodhaven Street. Come alone.

Alone. Without the IMP? She put down her cup and reread the message. There wouldn't be any more. She had been given one last clue. Take it or leave it.

— «» —

The Roselawn clinic was an imitation Victorian mansion on the eastern edge of Martyr's Square, dwarfed by the skyscrapers around it. Maia arrived half-an-hour early, jittery and unkempt. She hadn't been able to sleep last night, and painkillers had done nothing to ease the thudding at the base of her skull.

She killed time walking around, visiting the old memorial at the centre of the square. People had died for Dataweb, for the right to wear an IMP. When had that right become a legal obligation? It was hard to know; the history files she'd accessed were vague on details. She caressed the screen on her wrist, trying to stay calm.

But it was hard to stay calm. It was hard not to leap into the shuttle back home, back to her predictable little life, and instead force her feet up the steps of the Roselawn clinic. It was harder still not to snatch her wrist back from the nurse who examined it, and the doctor who tut-tutted at the obsolescence of her version 5.

By the time she was trundled into the operating theatre, Maia had worked herself into such a state of anxiety that the darkness of anaesthesia came as a welcome relief.

She woke to the sound of quiet voices, the sensation of movement. She was flat on her back, being wheeled somewhere. Blank corridors, a swinging door, and a shaded room with a single light-filled window. Maia blinked in the light, groggy and disoriented.

"How do you feel?" A man's face filled her vision.

Awful, she tried to say, but no sound emerged from her lips.

"Rest," he advised. "We'll take you to the rehab garden in a while, if you feel up to it. In a few hours you'll be ready for your upgrade. Aren't you excited?" He beamed at her before he left.

A nurse drew a curtain across the window and then she too left, leaving Maia alone in the room. There were three other beds, but they were empty. She sat up and a wave of nausea washed over her. She leaned over and retched into a bowl next to the bed.

Her wrist was bandaged and it hurt like hell. But what was truly painful was the knowledge that beneath the bandage, her forearm was bare. The IMP was gone. There was silence within her: no adverts, no updates, no reminders. It was strange and frightening, like a room in her mind had gone dark, and there was nothing to fill it.

After a while she heard indistinct voices. She raised her head, wondering who it was. At the other end of the room, her parents' burned faces gazed at her with reproachful eyes. Maia screamed and a nurse came running inside.

"I'd like to go to the garden please," she said, refusing to look at the phantoms that floated behind the nurse.

The nurse helped her into a fresh robe and slippers, and wheeled her out of the room. Maia risked a quick glance back, but her dead parents did not follow them out. Hallucinations? She'd never had those before, not even when she'd gone four months without Levatamine and the withdrawal had given her alternating nights of insomnia and sleep terrors.

A door slid open in front of them; warm sunshine fell on Maia's face. The nurse took her down a path surrounded by flowers, shrubs and artfully arranged rocks. She deposited her near a bench overlooking a reflecting pool, with strict instructions not to move too soon or too fast.

Maia leaned back and inhaled the scent of roses. It was peaceful in the garden. The sounds of the city were muted — an aural effect of sound-proofing trees, perhaps. It would have been nice to just stay there, to not have to decide anything. But IMP 18 beckoned. If she got this upgrade, she would no longer be subject to commercials, no matter where she went. She could easily get a better job; no one in her company had even an IMP 16.

Maia reached for the silver dagger around her neck, but she'd taken it off before leaving home that morning. She touched the invisible line in the hollow of her throat instead. The mysterious Mr. Stanzin Duvall, for all his astonishing knowledge of her, had been wrong about one little thing — a record that only a Pol actually assigned to her case would have had access to.

How frail was the human skin, how vulnerable the flesh beneath, and yet how futile her attempt to break through it had been. On her parents twenty-fifth death anniversary, she'd slashed her throat with the silver dagger. She'd failed, of course; med-bots had arrived in seconds to patch her up. Not even the scars remained, so that sometimes she wondered if the blood had been a dream image. Now there was the faint but distinct possibility of success, or at least the independence of choice.

All the world was a shadowed forest, and no blade sharp enough to slice through it. But perhaps a place existed beyond the shadows where you could be yourself, whoever that was. And perhaps Stanzin could help her find it.

Maia glanced back at the walls of the Victorian mansion that rose behind her, and got up. "Goodbye, Mama Papa," she whispered. She imagined she could see her parents, smiling and healthy, waving to her from a window high up in the mansion. A trick of the light, nothing more, and yet on such things do lives turn, and journeys begin.

She walked down the path and pushed open the gate.

—— « O » ——

Rati Mehrotra

Rati Mehrotra lives and writes in lovely Toronto. Her short stories have appeared in *AE – The Canadian Science Fiction Review, Apex Magazine, Urban Fantasy, Podcastle, Inscription Magazine*, and many more. Her debut novel *Markswoman* will be published in early 2018. Find out more about her work at: http://ratiwrites.com or follow her on Twitter: @Rati_Mehrotra

Nature Tale

Matthew Hughes

What Luff Imbry best liked about Quirks, beyond what emerged from the club's magnificent kitchens, was that it left its members alone. The members not only appreciated this virtue but, in turn, practiced it amongst themselves. If a senior denizen chanced to expire in the sitting room, as did happen occasionally, his corpse remained undisturbed in one of the overstuffed armchairs until his changing condition became apparent even at a distance.

It was possible for the hours Imbry spent in the dining or reading rooms to aggregate eventually into years without his ever being afflicted by unwanted conversation, let alone intrusive queries about how he might have happened to acquire the considerable funds it took to settle Quirks's annual fee. He had made a lifelong habit of avoiding such questions, not merely from principle but guided by the practical rationale that answering them honestly would have earned him a lengthy term in the Archonate's contemplarium.

As one of the ancient city of Olkney's most accomplished criminals, Imbry's existence alternated between two phases, one relatively short and the other long. In the shorter periods, he undertook operations requiring rigorous planning that culminated in swift and decisive action carried out with clear-eyed attention to detail and no small degree of courage. During the long and leisurely second phase, he spent the lavish proceeds of the first, much of the expenditure going toward things that tasted wonderful and digested well.

In his young adulthood, he had often dwelled upon the unexpected directions in which life had taken him. Now, approaching middle age, with the years contributing depth to his experience and width to his waistline, he occupied himself less and less with *why?* and more and more with *how?* and especially *how much?*

Thus he was startled at his own unconscious reaction when, at ease in the Quirks reading room, idly perusing the columns of the *Olkney Implicator*, his eye fell upon a small item on an inside page. Suddenly, the chair's embrace was no longer restful, the anticipation of a superb dinner no longer a pleasant tug at his innards. He straightened up and spoke to the club's integrator.

Imbry was only recently launched upon his latest period of leisure, one that had promised to extend several months, so profitable had been the most recent of what he liked to call his "exercises." He had resolved a thousand-year-old dispute between two contending factions of a mystery cult, each of which claimed rights of precedence over certain mementos of the long-dead prophet that both revered. His strategy had been to steal the venerated items then cause them to reappear suddenly during a contentious synod of the mystics. The manner of the revelation indicated that the objects' physical nature had been reabsorbed into the spiritual body of the cult's beatified founder. This epiphany opened up grand new vistas of doctrinal disagreements for the faithful to argue over, and scarcely had Imbry's pyrotechnics faded before they fell to the business with the fierce joy that only the holiest of acrimonies can provide.

In reality, Imbry had sold the bits of bone and gristled flesh to a competing cult. He suspected that their new owners undoubtedly intended to visit unsavory indignities on the purloined relics, perhaps even to reanimate an avatar of the prophet and use the poor old sage for unspeakable purposes, but his conscience was eased by the ridiculously large amount he was paid.

Imbry had moved into a suite at Quirks for an extended stay. He meant to treat himself to its paramount chef's most renowned gustatory specialty: the Progress of Amplitude, a succession of spectacular meals spread over several weeks, climaxing in the belly-straining feast known simply as the Mortality. Yet, though he had reached only the stage called the Lesser Enlargement, the moment Imbry saw the few paragraphs in the *Implicator*, he told the club's integrator to cancel the rest of the series.

"Chef will be discomfited," said the device's bloodless voice.

"It cannot be avoided," Imbry said.

"He will view it as a reproof. His nature does not allow him to take criticism gladly."

Imbry remembered the luncheon at which a notoriously cantankerous member named Auzwol Lameney had sent back a bowl of the chef's Seven Spice Soup, claiming it was defective in piquancy. He shuddered at the recollection of how Lameney had soon after been led from the dining room, eyes and nose streaming, inarticulate apologies blubbering through blistered lips.

"I understand," Imbry said, "but nonetheless." He bid the integrator book him a first-class passage on the next liner leaving for Winskill, a planet more than halfway down The Spray. When the device reported back that he was expected on the *Vallorion* and that it would lift off from Olkney's spaceport in two hours, Imbry rose to depart. But before leaving the reading room, he carefully tore from the *Implicator* the item that had caught his attention. He read it once more, then placed it in his wallet.

— «» —

As a little boy, Imbry found himself consigned to the care of two aged aunts who met any questions as to where his parents might be with evasive replies and offers of cake. The cake was always very good, but he did not fit smoothly into their household, which was organized around practiced routines and a great deal of quiet. As soon as he reached an age at which education seemed to offer benefits for all concerned, he was packed off to Habrey's, a residential school run by a philosophical society whose primary tenets descried merit in self-denial and strenuous physical activity.

The young Imbry, though his opinions were still largely unformed, was soon able to reach a conclusive judgment as to the merits of the school's regimen. Within days of his arrival, he took forthright action to separate himself from the place, but his aunts just as resolutely returned him to its cloister. They brought him to understand that the time of their close association had come to an unalterable end. They did, however, pack a plum-rich cake for Imbry to take with him.

Habrey's had a complete staff, many of them well qualified to instruct children, or at least to govern them effectively while they learned at whatever pace suited their natures. But the true core of the school's mode of operations was its integrator, a device of such antiquity that it had acquired a subtlety of intellect that is often difficult to distinguish from madness. Its dicta were sometimes obscure and, in those cases, could be circumnavigated, but experience had long since taught Habreyites that to ignore its expressed wishes was to tempt an unfortunate outcome.

Thus when the integrator assigned Luff Imbry to share a small room with Hop Mizzerin, the latter's shrill complaints that he had not come halfway down The Spray for his schooling only to be confined with a ragamuffin noncome went unrewarded. Imbry might have voiced an even bitterer grievance, once he discovered just how unsatisfactory a roommate Mizzerin made, but he already understood that no heed would be taken.

They settled in. Mizzerin was older and larger than Imbry. He had come into existence equipped with an aggressive disposition that had been sharpened by an infancy in which he grew accustomed to having his wishes fulfilled. Being caged against his inclinations with a social inferior, especially a younger and smaller one, could not bring out the best in him, even though his best was well down the scale of human empathy.

He drew a line across the floor, separating the room into two territories. Imbry said, "The portions are unequal."

Mizzerin's response was nonverbal. It left Imbry with a swollen cheek and a discoloured lower eyelid. The younger boy discussed the matter with the Habrey's integrator but its only response was to relate an obscure story about two beasts of dissimilar natures that had to share a forest. Imbry was too upset to recall much of the detail or even the moral of the tale.

The bully then tried to make Imbry his lackey. He expressed demands and issued instructions, reinforced by physical means. Unable to defeat Mizzerin breast to breast, the younger boy found that he had an ally in his intellect, which was both broader and deeper than the would-be tyrant's. He did the chores that were thrust upon him, but did them badly and endured the punishments that ensued.

In time, Mizzerin grew tired of being brought burned soup or smudged shirts and paid one of the school's servants to undertake these tasks. Imbry's burden lightened, but he remained the butt of the older boy's verbal barbs; though these were not sharpened by much wit, they were honed by Mizzerin's innate viciousness.

In time, however, they came to ignore each other. Mizzerin's interests lay in sports and games of chance, while Imbry was drawn into the pursuits of the mind. He discovered that he had a good eye for line and form and could produce creditable drawings after only a minimal instruction in technique. He also became adept in analyzing logical constructs and showed a flair for being able to isolate telling details that illuminated complex situations.

His work brought him notice from the senior staff and it was decided to offer him sections of the Class A curriculum, even though his aunts had paid for only the B. Habrey's observed a tradition of acquiring its faculty from within, the governing board seeing no purpose in watching its most brightly plumaged birds fly off to adorn other nests. But scarcely had Imbry been introduced to the study of elemental consistencies and asymmetrical persuasion than the incident of the tote burst over his head.

Imbry was in a sketching class, one of his favorites, rendering a complex still life in pastel shades, when the integrator summoned him to the proctor's office. The official regarded the boy from the other side of a desk strewn with notebooks containing columns of figures and tables of odds and permutations. After a lengthy silence, the proctor said, in his least compromising voice, "What are these?"

Imbry looked at the materials and said, "I do not know."

The proctor's brow compressed. "They are the records of a betting system based on intramural competitions within the school."

Imbry spread his hands. "I know nothing of such matters."

"Worse, they indicate that several competitions have somehow been interfered with, so that the owner of this betting system may be enriched."

"I know nothing," Imbry could only repeat.

"They were found in your room."

"It is not only *my* room," Imbry said.

"They were found between your mattress and the struts."

To that, Imbry could make no answer but the truth. He did not know what the things were nor how they came to be in his bed. He suggested that some of the letters and figures were so ill formed that they might be the product of Hop Mizzerin's penmanship.

Mizzerin was summoned and questioned but denied all knowledge. Pressed, he argued that his allowance was so substantial that he had no need to go to all the trouble of operating a tote and rigging sporting events. "What is my motivation?" he said.

Imbry would have suggested an intrinsic maleficence but his opinion was not sought. He steadfastly maintained his innocence.

The proctor's face grew long from stroking and tugging at his chin beard. Finally, he said, "The preponderance of evidence points to Luff Imbry. He will be sent off."

Imbry protested to his tutors. Three of them made representations on his behalf only to meet rebuffs, but the proctor quietly divulged to them a relevant issue: Hop Mizzerin had come to Old Earth from Winskill, where his father was not only socially prominent but a leading member of the thagonist caste. Its tenets required him to receive any slight, real or perceived, against a child of his household as equivalent to a slur upon his own honour. There could be no answer but blood.

"Apparently, young Hop stirred up disaffection at a number of institutes on Bowdrey's World, to whose schools the elite of Winskill usually send their progeny," the proctor informed the tutors. "The father was required to meet four principals and two head teachers, resulting in five deaths and a maiming. It was felt that the boy was less likely to cause offence on Old Earth, since both the Winskillers and the Bowdreyites consider us lackadaisical."

"So if we expel Mizzerin," said Imbry's art tutor, a slim man with delicate hands, "a sword-wielding moustacho will come to fillet us in the outer quad?"

"It is quite likely," said the proctor. "The situation will ease once the boy reaches the age of fourteen; thereafter his honour is his own concern and we can send him back."

Imbry was transferred to another school, where standards were less exacting. He arrived under a cloud and was not made overly welcome. Before departing Habrey's, however, he asked for and was given the materials that had been found under his bed.

"Why do you want them?" said the integrator.

"They are supposed to be mine," the boy said. "Besides, if I'm to be unjustly punished, I should at least know what I am suffering for."

The integrator said, "Consider the Brashein Monument."

Imbry was familiar with the celebrated statue of the conqueror Ordelam Brashein that stood in a dusty square not far from the school. Seen from one angle, it represented a proud victor bedecked in laurels. From a different vantage, another image emerged: that of a vainglorious fool.

"You're saying that justice is distinguished from injustice by the angle from which it is viewed?"

"Am I?" said the integrator. But it supplied Imbry with the records and charts of Mizzerin's tote and the ratios he employed to wring a profit from his bettors. Imbry studied the materials in the chilly dormitory of his new school, saw the patterns and opportunities inherent in the system, and how it could be adapted to the sporting life that was such an important part of education.

Hop Mizzerin had been unable to command a sophisticated understanding of the elegance with which the matrix of odds and permutations could be arranged. He had clumsily cheated his fellow students, out of a perverse delight in taking advantage. Imbry brought more insight to the complexity of the system and when he felt himself the master of its ins and outs he applied it to his new surroundings. In a little while he was doing quite well, and after another little while he did even better. He also received more than simple profit, carving for himself a unique niche within the culture that

surrounded him. After a year or so, he fitted that niche without chafing.

— «» —

Winskill was a stark planet, a dry world of gritty deserts and
jagged mountains, shrunken seas and narrow rivers. It offered
few graces and even less forgiveness, and those who had come
to settle it had grown to be like their world. Winskillers were
a hard and uncompromising people, living in scattered towns
whose livelihoods depended on the discovery and export of
rare crystals occasionally exposed by the constant winds. A
handful of villages had grown up around remote communities
of contemplatives who found the harsh conditions a useful
insulation: few visitors arrived to disturb their meditations.

In most parts of the planet, one day was much like any
other, except during Regatta Week. Then, for eight days,
a large portion of the scant population descended on the
town of Jant, in the centre of Northern Continent near the
thirtieth parallel, to compete in the jib races, or to bet on
their outcomes. Streams of high-grade crystals passed from
one purse to another as the results of the preliminary races
came in. By the time the Final Four were flying across the
dead-level salt flats that extended in all directions from Jant,
fortunes were on the line.

A jib was a lightweight windsailing craft. It consisted
of a narrow board from which arose a thin, whip-like mast
that supported a triangular sail braced on the bottom by a
movable boom. At first glance, it seemed a simple construct,
but considerable ingenuity had been applied to its design and
development. The sail was made of an ultra-thin laminate shot
through with narrow tubes called spiracules that connected to
the boom. The boom, too, was hollow, as was the mast, which
fed into a dense network of more spiracules in the board that
was the craft's hull.

All of these conduits were precisely arranged to capture
the wind striking the sail and to drive some of its energy
downwards, creating a cushion of air beneath the board on
which the operator stood. The rest of the wind's power was
used to propel the craft forward. By judiciously varying the
angle at which the wind encountered the sail, combined with
the tilt of the board's nose relative to the horizon, a skilled jib

sailor could maximize both the uplift of the ground effect and the forward motion of the whole assemblage.

The finest racers at the Jant Regatta could induce their jibs to eye-watering speeds across the vast and level salt flats. They were undeterred by potentially lethal danger, though horrific tumbles were not unknown, the hardpan surface being as unforgiving to human skin and bone as the Winskillers were to anyone who applied unfair modifications to a racing craft. For such crimes as incorporating into a jib's hull a gravity obviator or an energy field to lower wind resistance, the punishment was to be "set free" in the desert, a long way from water or shade.

— «» —

Luff Imbry alighted at the spaceport at Cheff on the Brass Coast, the nearest city to Jant. He hired an aircar and trusted it to find its way across the barren landscape. It set him down beside the main gate of the tent city that annually sprang up for the Regatta and, before flying back to its base, advised him on the available lodgings. He found acceptable accommodation at the Blackrock Inn's temporary regatta annex. This was a collection of inflated pavilions linked by soft-walled corridors to the inn proper. Imbry tried the local ale, finding it bitter but increasingly interesting after a few swallows. He also sampled a Winskill delicacy: a savory pastry baked around the abdomen of a hand-sized segmented creature that lived in crevices on the rocks of the sea coast. It had a subtle, nutlike flavor and he ordered another.

Along with the food, he requested a copy of the Jant *Hortator*, finding its pages dense with news, analyses and prognostications regarding the Final Four of the current Regatta. It was to take place the day after tomorrow, the contenders spending the intervening time resting after the rigours of the Semifinal, which had seen spectacular feats of jibmanship by the leaders of the field. Imbry read the coverage closely and made some notes.

Late that night, after taking measures to render himself unnoticeable, he visited the lightly guarded compound where the jibs for the next day's race were kept. He returned to his room in the pavilion and slept well.

— «» —

"I know nothing of this," Hop Mizzerin told the umpires.

"Is this not your jib?" said the presiding officer of the Regatta.

"It is."

"And is this not a gravity-obviating substance adhered to its base?"

"If you say so. I did not put it there." Mizzerin turned and appealed to the watching throng, his eyes sliding without recognition over Luff Imbry. "I am the favourite. Why would I do it?"

The crowd was not swayed. Many within it had seen friends and loved ones fall afoul of Mizzerins, who were quick to take offence and even quicker thereafter to draw.

"We cannot take time to examine motives. There is a race to be run and the deed speaks for itself."

Mizzerin's hand went to his hip but found nothing to grasp. Regatta Week in Jant was, necessarily, the sole time and place on Winskill where the Code of Dignity did not pertain.

The race began late, but with four contestants: the jibman who had placed fifth in the Semifinals was promoted to the Final Four, blinking and shaking his head while wearing a look of delighted surprise. A flurry of odds-changing ensued, with crowds of Winskillers and off-worlders shouting and waving betting slips at the totesmen, trying to get their wagers altered before the warning horn blew.

Luff Imbry did not bother to bet. He returned to the Blackrock Inn for an early lunch and a quiet nap. Arising, he packed his belongings and paid his bill. He inquired of the helpful desk clerk where he might see about the importing of the segmented creature whose flesh carried such a unique flavour, and was disappointed to learn that they did not travel well.

By the time he boarded his aircar, the jib race was a plume of dust far out to the west. Imbry lifted off and turned the craft in another direction. He flew at good speed for a long while until finally he saw a small figure in the distance, marching steadily across the salt. As he drew closer, he realized that the custom of "setting free" was all-inclusive: Hop Mizzerin walked naked and unshod. The parts of his skin that were not usually exposed to sunlight were already an angry pink, and the sun still had a long arc to fall to finish the extended Winskill day.

Imbry descended to a height just above Mizzerin's reach and slowed to a parallel course. The thagonist turned a puzzled expression on him as he took measured steps toward the bare horizon.

"You are trying to determine who has done this to you, and why," Imbry said.

"I am."

"I did."

Mizzerin stopped, his face clouded. He measured the distance between him and Imbry, then he drew in a deep breath and let it go. He resumed walking, but after a moment and without looking up, he said, "All right. Then why?"

"That is a good question. The simple answer requires you to consult your memory. Specifically you might recall your first roommate at Habrey's and how you parted."

Mizzerin looked at Imbry again for a moment, then nodded dourly and said, "Simple enough. But you imply that there is also a complex answer."

"Yes."

"I would like to hear it."

"I am still working on it," Imbry said. "It might take years before I have it complete in all its details."

Mizzerin walked on for several steps then said, "What happened to you after you left?"

Imbry gave him a summary of his life as a criminal. He saw no reason to dissemble.

"So," said Mizzerin, when he had heard it, "it seems I am responsible for the course your life has taken."

"It does."

"Yet you appear to be happy in that life. To a casual eye, you present an image of self-satisfaction."

"I am not unhappy," said Imbry.

"Do you pine for what might have been, a life of teaching and collegiality among the faculty at Habrey's?"

Imbry considered the question. "'Pine' is not the word I would use," he said. "'Wonder' is closer. Or perhaps 'idly dream.'"

The moved on for a while in silence until Imbry said, "Do you remember the integrator at Habrey's? The stories it used to tell?"

"It told me no stories," the marching man said.

"After we met and you blackened my eye, it told me a story about two animals in a forest. I didn't understand it at the time but when I was grown I looked up the tale."

"Is it relevant to our situation?"

Imbry declined a direct answer. "It was about how every beast must be true to its nature," he said, "no matter how ill the outcome."

"And are you true to yours?"

"I believe I am," said Imbry. "At least, I try to be."

"Ah," said Mizzerin, with another grim motion of his head, and began to ask another question. But Imbry did not stay to hear it. He lifted the car into the cooler upper air and sped away.

Mizzerin dwindled to a speck behind him. Imbry did not turn to look.

—— « o » ——

Matthew Hughes

Matthew Hughes writes science-fantasy and crime fiction. He has sold nineteen novels to publishers large and small in Canada, the US, UK, France, and Italy. His short fiction has appeared in *Alfred Hitchcock's, Asimov's, Blue Murder, Fantasy & Science Fiction, Postscripts, Storyteller, Interzone,* and a number of award-winning anthologies. He has won the Arthur Ellis Award from the Crime Writers of Canada, and has been short-listed for the Aurora, Nebula, Philip K Dick, Endeavour (twice) A.E. Van Vogt, and Derringer Awards. His web page is at: http://www.matthewhughes.org

The Dead Languages of the Wind

David Clink

When the storm is here we know no other season, and cannot think of a time when it did not chase us from our dreaming. We'd wander outside buildings, look up at the translucent dome, its ovoid shape made real by the particulate matter in the whipping wire-brush winds. But the day comes when the winds settle, and the sky turns a shade of blue seen on Earth, and one can go outside the dome, see the wind damage on ruins, and wonder how these early generations survived. And we remember to a time when we heard the heavens sizzle, like rain falling on the power lines of our youth. We thought the dome shield was failing. How we all gathered, held hands, started to pray, like our ancestors presumably did, these people gone forever except for what they left behind: the ruins stretched out beyond our reckoning, graves scattered on hillsides, graffiti, dental work, knee and hip replacements, the scrapbooks and cancer wigs. We know the storm will resume again, but we take a moment to look at the scratch marks on these ruins, the dead languages of the wind.

—— « o » ——

David Clink

David Clink is the author of four collections of poetry, including two genre collections: *Monster;* and *The Role of Lightning in Evolution*. His speculative poetry has appeared five times in *Analog*, thrice in *Asimov's*, and twice in *On Spec*. He has been a finalist for the Aurora and Rhysling awards, and the Asimov's Readers Choice award. His poem, *A sea monster tells his story* won the Aurora Award for Best Poem/Song, in 2013.

In Memory Of

Derryl Murphy

1. Memories Being Lost

The diagnosis is a week in the past now, and I have spent as much time as I can each ensuing day researching all I know about early onset senile dementia, about Alzheimer's, about where I can see Sam's and my lives falling to pieces as we spiral into Dad's own tenuous future. But mostly, after the first few days of panic and grief and the agony of watching this slow motion loss, I research Aletheia, a company both the doctor and the insurance company have recommended to me. It's a company with offices and labs in many cities, including here.

Most days of the week, most hours of the day, and most minutes of the hour, Dad is still lucid, and his few concerns about memory are still easy to chalk up to old age, even though he is still not even sixty. But there are enough moments for me to recognize he is slipping away, and I feel if I don't do something soon, he'll be gone to me forever.

Already, sometimes, he calls me Melissa. My mother, dead now for seven years.

"What do you think?" I ask Sam that night, lying in bed. A pad is on my lap, my knees up high so I can read more easily, and I flip through the hundreds of pages of documents Dr. Cummings had forwarded to me.

"Hm?" Sam leans over from her own old-fashioned book, and looks at what I'm reading. "Ah." She reaches under the blankets and squeezes my hand, which I find somewhat irritating, since at that moment I'd been using that hand to silence an itch on my thigh. "What do I think about Aletheia and getting your father a rememberer."

"Yes." I scroll through a few more pages, having now hopefully committed the important parts to memory, mostly just looking at the pictures.

"It'll still cost us money," she says. "The deductible is more than double normal, and I recall reading somewhere that the tech changes so fast they'll only offer you a pittance for scrap when you don't..." Her voice trails off as she realizes what she's saying.

I squeeze her hand in return to let her know there's no concern. The elephant in the room is my father, his failing life and eventual death, and every conversation we have about him will eventually circle in towards this topic. "We can handle the deductible. If all of this can give Dad a couple of extra years at home—"

"That's on average, Karynn," Sam says, interrupting me. "Not everybody is going to last that long before they end up living in a facility of some kind." She pushes her glasses up the bridge of her nose, and gives me a sheepish look. "Or die."

"Or die." I nod, and bite my lower lip, promising myself I will stay resolute, at least for now. Sam will never deny me opportunities to cry for Dad, but I've already vowed to stay calm and clear whenever we are discussing his future. "But that doesn't matter, does it?"

Sam looks at me and smiles, brushes some stray hair away from over my left eye. "You're right, it doesn't. He deserves to spend as much time as he can in a place where he's comfortable. That he recognizes. *Remembers.*"

"Then I'll set up an appointment tomorrow first thing." I lean over and kiss her on the cheek. "Thank you."

— «» —

2. Memories Being Saved

I've seen Dad nervous before, many times. Sometimes it would get so bad his hands would tremble, and Mom would joke and call him Shakes the Clown. Usually this got a laugh out of him, and if there was anything that would be guaranteed to redirect his attention, it would be his sense of humor. One laugh and all of a sudden he was off and running, thinking of jokes or funny anecdotes or even strange character traits of someone he once knew, and like that he was transformed from a bundle of nerves into a man at ease with himself and the world around him.

I've also seen Dad truly scared, but only twice. The first was the day Mom got the news that her cancer was inoperable, and the second, the day we buried her.

Today is the third time. Which is odd, really. I was with him when he got the diagnosis about his condition, and while he did react, it was quiet. Muted. Not even shaking hands, but rather a distant and pensive look in his eyes. I blamed it on the dementia, but his conversation with the doctor and with me after the fact had been remarkably lucid.

But today, sitting in the waiting room, it's obvious that he's doing everything in his power to keep from letting panic overtake him. I hold his hand, and Sam, sitting on the other side, keeps a reassuring hand on Dad's shoulder. Across from us sit an older couple, the woman with tears at the corners of her eyes, studiously avoiding looking at us as she rests a hand on her husband's thigh. He in turn seems to ignore her as he flips through a paper magazine he'd picked up off the center table, and it takes me a few minutes to realize that the magazine is upside-down in his hands. I look away, suddenly embarrassed. And — I have to face it — terrified.

A door opens, and a young man wearing a muted orange tie and a white dress shirt with the sleeves rolled up to just below his elbows steps through. "Mr. MacKenzie?"

Dad stands, and both Sam and I stand with him. He nods.

He smiles. "My name is Roger. If you could come with me, please."

He turns and looks me in the eyes, then back to the young man. "Can I bring my ... my daughter?"

The young man nods. "You can, but once we have you in the machine she can't stay with you. Instead, she'll have to come back out here. Are you all right with that?"

Dad thinks for a moment, and then nods in return. "I guess so."

Sam hugs both of us for luck, and we follow the man through the door and down a long hallway, undecorated except for one small table set against the wall, a potted plant that's seen better days sitting atop it. I make sure to steer Dad clear of the table, and that act seems to catch him and bring him back a little; where for the day leading up to this his walk was the slow shuffle of a confused old man, he now stands up a little taller and walks with more purpose. I put a gentle hand atop his shoulder, just enough to remind him I'm still with him, and he doesn't try to shake it off.

A door at the far end of the hallway opens and a middle-aged woman wearing a white coat steps out into the hallway. "Mr. MacKenzie, so good to see you." She offers him her hand, and then shakes mine next. "I'm Dr. Dhaliwal. You must be Mr. MacKenzie's daughter."

"Karynn," I say. As Roger leads Dad further into the room the doctor has just come from, I lean in and whisper, "He's very nervous. Scared."

She nods. "That's a good sign. We find that most of our candidates are nervous about the procedure, but actually scared it won't work." She turns towards the room and I feel the light touch of a hand on my elbow as she leads me in to follow my father.

"How so?" I ask as I look around. It's how I would think a research lab in a hospital would look, even though we are not technically even in a hospital. A bank of computer screens and keyboards sit along one wall, and the steady whirr of fans hums along just a little above background noise; even so, to me the room feels almost uncomfortably warm. In the middle sits a large chamber, wires and cables sprouting from it in all directions, with a small but comfortable-looking bed on rollers sitting at its entrance, ready for Dad to lie down on and slide into the chamber. Straps dangle from the sides of the bed, to keep him from deciding halfway through that he's done. Dad sits in a comfortable-looking chair beside the chamber, and Roger is taking his blood pressure or perhaps reading some other vital signs with a handheld.

"When a patient like your father comes in here," continues Dr. Dhaliwal, "he is losing little bits and pieces of how he identifies himself with each and every passing day. Sometimes the progress is so slow that it's unnoticeable to everyone who regularly interacts with him, but he almost invariably knows that something is slowly going wrong. Think of your father as the captain of a huge, ridiculously complex ship, and for some reason that ship is heading, very slowly, for an iceberg that is sure to sink it."

I raise an eyebrow. "You're comparing my father's brain to the *Titanic*?"

She shakes her head. "Not even remotely. What I am saying is that once the point of no return is reached, the captain can only stand there and watch as the iceberg looms ahead. He will still try everything at his disposal to make sure the accident doesn't happen, but the bulk of the ship and the nature of travel at speed through water means that coming to a full stop or turning that ship around in time proves to be nigh on impossible." We both look over at Dad, who is listening a bit nervously as Roger talks quietly to him. "Your father sees that iceberg approaching, getting a little closer every day. The ship of his brain, his life, is no longer under his control, and he sees that regularly. He wants to right the course, but he can't manage to make the turn in time, and so can only watch in horror as the tragedy approaches. It may be slow motion, but it is very real."

"And so?"

She looks down at a screen on the desk she's standing beside, then taps at it. "And so, his fear means he is still aware enough of who he is to be able to turn out the memories that are needed for this procedure. If he was too far gone, then there would be no sense in doing this. You understand?"

I hesitate, but then nod. It make sense. "Him being scared is a sure sign that he's still with us."

"Absolutely," replies Dr. Dhaliwal. "It's actually one of the last tests we rely on before we take that final step. The insurance companies are quite welcoming of this procedure, considering how much longer it usually allows the patient to live at home, but they still don't want to throw away their money. It's not anything so simple as a gut reaction, but rather some simple psychology. We watch the patient in the waiting room, again when he comes in here, and then Roger does some final checks to see if the body is responding in the same fashion."

I blink in surprise, and think of the couple who sat across from us. "You watch us in the waiting room?"

She nods. "It's in the contract you signed, but almost nobody bothers to think about it, even if they read it carefully.

Which so very few people do, sadly." She frowns, but doesn't add to this thought.

"The other people in the waiting room," I say, thinking about the man, who so obviously was also a sufferer of dementia. "He didn't look scared at all. Too far gone."

Dr. Dhaliwal shrugs. "That may very well be, but I'll tell you we haven't looked at him at all yet. As well, there is the obvious caveat that we are not allowed to discuss the cases of others."

I nod, and see that Roger has helped Dad stand back up. I walk over and give him a hug. "You okay?" I ask, just a gentle whisper in his ear.

"I am, little girl. Thanks. Uh, this nice, this nice young man, uh..." Dad frowns, struggling for the name, and I remind him.

He pulls back from me. "I knew that!" Then he forces a smile, and puts his hands on my shoulders, the sudden anger gone just as quick as it came. "Roger. Yes. Roger explained it to me. These people, they're going to help me remember things." His smile is a little too bright.

Dr. Dhaliwal steps forward and puts a gentle hand on my father's back. "We are indeed going to do that, Mr. MacKenzie. But now I need you to come with me and lie down over here. Unfortunately, Karynn has to leave the room while we do this."

Dad gets a look of concern in his eyes, but I smile to reassure him. "Don't worry, Dad. Sam and I will be out in the waiting room. We won't go anywhere until everything's good and you're ready to come back home."

He smiles back, and lays a slightly shaking hand on my cheek. "I won't worry, then, Melissa. Can we go for lunch when we're done?"

I turn my head and kiss his hand, then nod, eyes closed to fight back the tears. "We'll go for lunch."

Roger helps me out of the room and all the way down the corridor, aware that everything for me is very blurry right now.

— «» —

3. Memories Being Delivered

We don't get the rememberer right away, which I suppose I'd also read about and forgotten, which makes me kind of angry. I'm not the one with the memory loss, I'm not the one whose life is slowly slipping away. Dad relies on me to take care of these little day-to-day items, and if I can't even do something so simple as to keep track of a simple clause in a contract that so vividly affects my father's life, then what good am I to him? Sam just rolls her eyes every time I beat myself up over it, though, and eventually I get the point. No use crying over spilt milk, as the saying goes, and bitching about things isn't going to change them. And when I think about it, I have so much on my plate these days it has to be easy to let some things slip through the cracks.

Dad, in the meantime, needs regular company while he waits. Four access probes have been inserted into his brain, and all of those are connected by what Dr. Dhaliwal calls a neural lace that covers his newly-shaved head like a hair net. None of these are to extract memories for the rememberer; that was already done as a part of the procedure. Rather, they are there so when he has trouble bringing up memories, or remembering a specific task he is supposed to perform at a certain time, the rememberer will be able to analyze the information coming from the brain and reconstruct the memory so that it can aid him, or at the very least, aid whoever is attending to him.

In a perfect world. The doctor also reminded me that some of these memories will be imperfect, or even the wrong ones, especially near the end, as Dad's brain slowly fades away from its disease, and the clues it sends out over its magical connection to the rememberer become ever more fragmented and static-filled.

Of course, for the two weeks we await delivery, almost the only thing that Dad has trouble remembering is why he has this thing on his head and why the devil is it making him so damned itchy. Sam and I quickly hit on a woolen watch cap as a solution, though, and he takes quite happily to wearing it inside and out, some nights even forgetting it's on his head when he falls asleep. The watch cap means we need to keep the temperature down in his apartment, though, and so there are some days it is all I can do to rouse myself from under a heavy blanket, sitting on the couch, worried that the tip of my nose is going to turn blue. Sam accuses me of melodrama when I mention this to her, though. If she wasn't being so patient with Dad, I'd be really pissed off with her right now.

But then the call finally comes. The three of us head down to the local offices of Aletheia to greet Dad's new rememberer, all of us sharing an air of nervousness and excitement.

Dr. Dhaliwal herself greets us at the elevator doors, smiling broadly as she ushers us into her office. "We tested the unit against all the baselines you supplied for us, and every performance metric was exceeded," she begins as we all sit down. "Of course, the real test will come when you bring it home and put it to work under everyday circumstances, but I have to say I have very high hopes for this one."

She performs some basic tests on Dad, making sure that everything is as it should be, then nods to herself, apparently satisfied. Then she sits on the edge of her desk and leans forward, looks Dad in the eye. "Are you ready to meet your rememberer, Mr. MacKenzie?"

He looks at me, and I smile and squeeze his hand, and he turns back to Dr. Dhaliwal and nods. She stands and walks over to open a side door, and in it rolls.

It cocks its head to one side, briefly studies all three of us, then rolls up to me and tilts its head back to look me in the eyes. "I'm hungry, Karynn. Can we go for lunch when we're done here?"

Its voice is Dad's voice, and while I clutch at his hand in wonder and probably a little bit of fear, Dad only laughs, and a second later the rememberer is laughing as well, creating the eeriest echo I could ever imagine. "What's so funny?" I ask, feeling like I've missed something. On the other side of Dad, even Sam is beginning to laugh, although a look from me is enough for her to temporarily choke it back down.

Finally, Dad and the rememberer both stop, and I repeat my question. "What's so funny, Dad?"

He reaches down and scratches the rememberer where I imagine he believes its ears should be, then looks up to Dr. Dhaliwal. "Perfect," he says. "Are we done here? Because I'm hungry, and Karynn and Sam are going to take me for lunch."

— «» —

4. Memories Being Preserved

Of course we have to give the rememberer a name, but the worry is that Dad will eventually forget its name, forget its purpose and perhaps even the fact that it is there. He scolds me and reminds me that by the time he reaches that point, he will be past help and destined for the Big House. His words, not mine. As long as he's good enough to be out and about, he's good enough to know what his rememberer is.

We go and get takeout instead of dining in a restaurant. I'm still a little uncomfortable with the idea of taking the rememberer out and about, even though I do see them several times a week, trailing alongside their owners. They're such a vivid and public expression of the disease, and while I can't speak for Dad, I'm not ready for the curious stares and potential questions that might arise. The first rememberers were small portable units, fitting into pouches around the waist or even pockets and avoiding such public attention, but the benefit of the size was also the drawback, and after too many lost and forgotten portable rememberers to count, the company retooled things to semi-autonomous devices that could follow the patient. So great for keeping things easier, not so great for keeping private family matters private and in the family.

And so we sit around Dad's table, eating sandwiches and salads and noodles and tossing out names as they come to mind, Sam dutifully writing each one of them down. At the beginning, most are names more suitable to dogs, and while the rememberer is vaguely dog-shaped, it just doesn't seem appropriate to name something Fido when it has so much of the essence and memories of my father embedded in it.

It's Dad who decides that Junior is best. "Your mom always figured if we'd been able to have a second kid, a boy, she'd like to name him after me — Jacob MacKenzie, Junior. Me, I always liked the name William, but…"

This line of talk makes me a little uncomfortable. I know that after I was born Mom had to have an emergency hysterectomy, and so there were no chances for any other children. It haunted Mom some days, and hearing this I wonder if it did so with Dad as well, and if he is going to turn this rememberer into some twisted version of a surrogate of the son he never had. But Sam is nodding enthusiastically at the name, and is even crossing off all the other choices that the three of us had ventured. Then she circles the name and taps the screen with the back end of one of her chopsticks, the one she's been alternately using as an eating utensil and as a stylus. "I think that's a great name." She leans down and looks the rememberer in the eye. "What do you think, Junior? Is that a good enough name?"

The device nods its head. "I think so, Sam." Hearing Dad's voice come from the rememberer, from Junior, is still a little disconcerting, which is why I haven't made any effort to engage it in a conversation since it told me it — Dad — was hungry earlier in the day. I lean back and nibble at my sandwich, reminding myself that we are doing this for our benefit and for his.

Dad's chair scrapes back along the floor and he gets up and walks into the kitchen and pulls open a drawer. And then he stops, hand hovering over the open drawer. From where I sit I can see the look on his face and know that he has forgotten why he's gone there. I'm standing up to go over and help him, but Sam lays a hand on my arm to keep me still.

The rememberer rolls into the kitchen and gently butts its head against Dad's leg. "I don't want a knife," it says, Dad's voice calm and confident, something I'm not used to hearing from him when the look on his face tells me he's so lost. "I'm going to close the drawer and reach up and get a glass from the cupboard so I can have a drink of milk." Dad gives the rememberer a kind of half-smile and does as he is told, bringing down a small glass and setting it on the counter.

"The milk is in the fridge," the device continues. Dad gets it and pours some into his glass. "Now I'm going to put the lid back on the milk and put it back in the fridge."

Dad does all of this, then brings his glass back to the table and sits down. "Sandwich was making me thirsty," he says. He takes a big gulp. "When..."

The pause is only a few seconds, and then again the rememberer carries on, this time speaking *for* Dad instead of *to* him. "When you were little, you absolutely loved milk. Until you were about five, your mother and I worried the bills for milk alone were going to break us. A glass in the morning with a bowl of cereal that also had milk, another glass at lunch, usually a glass in the afternoon after your nap, another at supper, and yet again at bedtime, sometimes with yet another bowl of cereal."

I can't decide where to stare, either at Dad or at the rememberer, but I know my jaw is hanging wide open as my gaze rushes back and forth between the two. Dad is just sitting there at the table, that lost look in his eyes, but at the same time he almost looks satisfied, as if hearing the memories presented to him in this fashion are enough to bring him back to the time he was trying to recapture within himself. Sam giggles in astonishment. And the rememberer, *Junior*, just carries on with the story:

"And then it got worse when your grandma got into the act. You were four when she came for a visit and decided to make you some chocolate milk. Do you remember just how much you liked chocolate milk?"

Junior pauses here, and after a few seconds I realize that it is actually asking me a question. That my father's memories, transferred to or perhaps embedded inside this machine and activated by Dad trying to find them for himself, are actually trying to interact with me. I nod. "I do, actually." Remembering my mother's reaction, remembering my grandmother and the warmth her presence brought me, remembering all of that because my Dad got up to get himself a glass of milk, I smile. And then I begin to cry.

— ‹› —

5. Memories of Pain

Over a year now and we are all used to Junior's presence. He plugs himself in at night and stands guard beside the bed when Dad is asleep, resting as well but one small part always on duty. This is also the time of day when he downloads updates from Aletheia, a process that keeps him current and working at his best.

Dad got very angry the other day, yelling in frustration when he forgot the rules one night when he and I were playing cribbage and insisting that I had changed how the game worked so I could win. But I've been told that there are dementia sufferers who get angry much worse and much more often, and I count myself very lucky if that's all I'll have to deal with. Junior's presence actually did more to calm him down than mine, and very quickly he was right back at the game and having little trouble with the cards.

He is, however, more prone to restlessness now that the dementia is progressing. He gets an idea in his head and doesn't make it five paces before that idea is lost in the fog, but so far Junior is always there with the answer. We're finding more and more, though, that the answer is still incomprehensible to Dad, and there are some days when I'm not even sure if he recognizes his own voice coming from the rememberer. Junior will say something, dredge up an old memory that Dad was trying to connect with, or remind him where he left his slippers as he shuffles about looking for them, and Dad will stop and stare at Junior, not necessarily as if he doesn't understand what he's being told, but more like he doesn't understand *why* he's being told.

The past three weeks have been even harder, because Dad has taken to getting up and wandering away from his bed in the middle of the night, not to go to the washroom but to make his way to the corner store, to the library, or to Mom and Dad's favorite restaurant from way back when they were first dating, even though that's long ago closed down. The first few times this happened my phone would ring in the middle of the night, and upon answering I would find myself listening to Dad — to Junior — telling me where he was going and why. He would never tell me I needed to come pick him up, but the need was obvious.

After the fourth time, I packed a few things and moved to Dad's, expecting to couch surf for a few days until we got this under control, but he's not showing any signs of slowing down. The doctor told us that this sometimes happens, that for some reason Dad's thought processes are much more active when he's asleep, and he apparently has a very real need to act on them. Perhaps even more because almost as soon as they come to his mind they slip away again, and he can feel the ghosts of those memories haunting him from just beyond the horizon. It agitates him, and the agitation brings him awake and searching for everything he's lost and will never find again.

Sam has helped me turn the den into a spare bedroom, and she comes over to spend as much time with me as she can, bless her. Work hasn't been quite so kind, but after some negotiation between us they've agreed to time off without pay.

Not exactly what I would have liked, but at least I've got a job when I need to come back, and they've also suggested there might be some work I can do from home. But Sam can do some overtime in her own job, and Dad has a small pension and some investments, and those seem to be enough to pay all the bills here. It helps that he eats like a bird, and that these days my appetite doesn't seem to amount to a whole lot.

Those late evenings now are no longer interrupted by a phone call, but rather by Junior rolling up to the bed and bumping his nose up against my arm, which I have learned to leave out on top of the blankets. It doesn't happen every night, but three, sometimes four times a week he rolls in to wake me and inform me that Dad is off and wandering.

Tonight is one of those nights. It hasn't taken me long to learn what the push against my arm means, and even before Junior is speaking I'm throwing back the blankets and turning on the bedside lamp.

"The paper's gotta be at the store now," he says in Dad's voice as he rolls out of the room. Which is a sure sign that Dad's at the front door trying to work the locks so he can get out and head down to the store. When I was a child he never bothered with a daily subscription to the local paper; he figured it was a poorly-written rag that contained very little worth reading or thinking about. Instead, he consumed most of his news from a variety of online sources. But on Saturdays we would get up and head out the door early, and walk down to pick up the weekend edition of the *Globe*, and its sections would then last almost the whole week for he and Mom, doled out slowly over coffee and toast and orange slices at the breakfast table.

The front door is open, though, and I feel a momentary stab of panic at the thought that he's already out of the building and heading down a road that he no longer remembers, looking to buy a paper that is no longer published. But a panicked look out into the hall shows that he hasn't even shuffled halfway to the elevator. The locks slowed him down at the start, and his declining physical abilities have done the rest of the job for me. Junior and I head out into the hall and I take him by the arm and gently steer him back towards his apartment.

"The paper won't be at the store yet, Dad, it's still too early. I can get Sam to pick it up for you in the morning, though."

The look of loss and confusion he gives me is heartrending, and I wait to hear him speak through Junior, but the first words come from his mouth instead. "Melissa?" He's confusing me for my mother again, but for some reason Junior isn't offering up a correction. "What are you doing here, my love?" His voice is soft and weak, but instead of sounding lost, at this moment to my ears he sounds like he's in pain.

I decide to humor him, at least until I get him back into his apartment and away from potentially waking up any neighbors. "I've just come to bring you back home, dear," I say, and wince inwardly at how little I sound like her. While most people have told me that I was the spitting image of Mom, I've always thought I've taken after Dad, even in the timbre of my voice.

We're back in the apartment now, and while Junior still hasn't said anything, he's rolling along right beside Dad. I briefly wonder if there's something wrong with him and if we'll have to get it looked at. And then I help Dad settle down into his favorite chair. "I'm going to get you a drink of water, dear, all right?" I hope that the time it takes me to do so will allow him the time to see me as his daughter instead of as his dead wife, and will allow me to slide out of a role I had promised myself I would never play.

Junior comes with me. "Melissa, I don't know how you've come to be here," he starts, and the catch in his voice throws me so off guard I have to lean up against the counter and close my eyes tight. His voice coming from the rememberer sounds lost and confused, which is hard enough to hear, but even more it sounds *sad*.

But I get myself together and find a glass, then pull the pitcher of water from the fridge and pour. Before going back out, though, I ask, "What do you mean by *how* I've come to be here?"

"You left me, Melissa. You died. I know this. I remember … I remember seeing your body lying on the hospital bed." His voice chokes, and I blink back the tears as best I can, but soon they're flowing freely, and I can't believe that I am crying this much over a conversation I'm having with a goddamned machine, even if that machine has the memories and the voice of my father.

I angrily dab away the tears as best I can with my sleeve, and then step over and around Junior to take Dad his glass of water. Before I leave the kitchen, though, I turn back and say, "Mom did die, Dad, and she hasn't come back to see you. There are no reasons, there is no meaning."

His only answer, small and lost, is "Oh."

— «» —

6. Memories to Hold

Three nights later, Junior rolls into my room and wakes me again with a bump of the nose, but this time he is voiceless. I lie there confused for a moment, and the absurd thought of asking what's wrong, if little Timmy is trapped in a well somewhere, momentarily washes over me, but it thankfully passes. Instead, I sit up and turn on the lamp and groggily put on my housecoat and slippers, expecting I'll have to chase down Dad once again.

I'm wrong.

Junior leads me out of my room, but instead of going to the door he circles around the room, twice, then comes to a stop at the open door to Dad's bedroom. It's dark in there, except for a hint of the nightlight installed in the opposite corner of his room. My breath catches and I walk briskly to the room, heart pounding and a frightening burst of white noise suddenly crashing into my ears, but Junior rolls in front of me and speaks.

I can't make out what the rememberer says, and have to stop and ask him to repeat himself. "What?"

"I thought of your mother, and of you, and of that day when you were little and we drove up Going to the Sun Road in Glacier National Park," says Junior. His voice, Dad's voice, sounds happy. Peaceful, even. "So high up, looking down over the edge into what seemed as close to an infinite drop as any one of us could imagine on a day like that, nervous butterflies in my stomach as I held tight to your little hand, you fearless and gazing over the precipice down this long, deep slope stretching out into some of the most amazing beauty I had ever seen in my life, and your mother calling anxiously from further back, frightened and unwilling to even let go of the car door." He pauses. "It was a wonderful memory to have. To finish with."

I let out a sob, step over him and hurry into the bedroom, stumbling a bit as I catch my foot on Junior's backside. But I grab hold of the doorsill and turn on the light.

He's lying in bed, eyes closed, turned over on his side with his blanket pulled up tight over his shoulder, just the way he's always liked to sleep. I walk over, Junior trailing behind me, and sit on the edge of the bed, and put my hand on his cheek. Still warm, but I know now that he's gone. I take his hand and sit like that for some time, Junior now quiet beside me, and when the tears finally fade away I go to make the calls that need to be made.

— «» —

7. Memories that Fade

We clean out Dad's apartment, finding a few keepsakes to give to my two cousins who had kept in touch, as well as the friends who are still around; a fair number, really, since he wasn't all that old. Memories are attached to every item we look at, and we soon find ourselves having to grade the level of those memories to determine whether or not we should keep it, give it away, or even donate to Goodwill or toss in the dumpster for the scavengers to retrieve.

In this task Junior surprises us by becoming almost indispensable. He rolls into the middle of the living room about an hour after we start on the first day, while Sam is holding up a ceramic set of salt and pepper shakers, shaped like lobster traps. "Those are from a vacation your mother and I took before you were born, Karynn," he says, and both of us start at the sound of Dad's voice. Junior hasn't said a word since Dad died, over a week ago now, and while I had briefly wondered about this, I had so many other things pressing down on me that I didn't have time to worry too much about it. "We went to Nova Scotia with Dan and Barb," he continues, referring to old friends who now live out of town. His voice sounds quite wistful. "I think they would appreciate getting those as a little memory of that trip."

Sam and I look at each other, she raises her eyebrows, and then I nod and write it down on the pad in my lap.

"Do you think you can help us with the rest of these things, Junior?" asks Sam.

"I can ... try," responds the rememberer. I notice the hesitation, but then Sam has the next item out of the box at her feet and Junior readily offers up thoughts about what it meant to Dad and where he thinks it should go, and before you know it we're deep into things.

The biggest surprise for me is just how *joyful* the day ends up being. I know what Junior holds inside himself is a matrix that approximates Dad's memories, and of course I know that he is no longer in touch with Dad's active mind, no matter how cloudy and distant he was becoming before the end. But after such an emotional roller coaster of a week, it's nice. Almost as if this dog-shaped machine is channeling my father for this great, exceedingly intense trip down memory lane. I end up learning things I'd never known before, histories of items that I'd always taken for granted or else written off as meaningless tchotchkes, and very soon instead of writing things down on the pad I'm recording with it instead, and now the whole process is going much slower than we'd allowed for, both Sam and me getting caught up in the stories behind the detritus of Dad's everyday life.

Lots of items get boxed, of course. Even if we lived in a mansion there would be no way we would want everything out and on display. But now nothing is just tossed away without a second thought; everything is a reminder of my father and my mother and sometimes of my childhood, even if I had no idea of the connection as it existed in Dad's mind.

And it is in this way that Junior proves his worth a second, perhaps even more valuable way.

I'm not a religious person. Dad was a true blue atheist, and he raised me to believe that critical thinking was one of the most important skills a person could have. As a teen I flirted with the church of a friend, and Dad never made any fuss about any aspect of it, just watched me and waited and then was there the day the inevitable questions arose, and after that all he did was make sure I knew that any questions I asked had to be answered by one person, me. I walked away and have never looked back, never regretted it.

There have been moments when I've been sad that there is no afterlife, no heaven. The thought of Mom gone into nothingness was pretty tough for me to handle at first, but Dad was still there, and together we could both share and honor her memory. As long as that direct link still exists, then the life of a deceased loved one still has a presence in the here and now. As the months went on after she had died, I found I could take solace in sharing those recollections with Dad and, to a lesser extent, Sam, sitting down and drinking a glass of her favorite red and calling her up from deep inside ourselves. Call me irredeemably romantic and perhaps even spiritual with a dose of cynicism, but this made me feel better. At least one small part of her really wasn't gone as long as he were there to help her carry on.

But then Dad took ill, and his mind was gone before his body was, something I had never budgeted for in any ledger I might have laid out for the rest of my life. In one sudden onrush of a devastating, crushing illness, it seemed I would lose not only Dad and his memories, but the bridge to my mother they created.

But Junior, via the good graces of Aletheia and Dad's insurance company, has calmly slotted in and saved the day.

When all of the apartment is finally cleared out, either packed away or given away or taken home to find a new place of honor or even a tiny little hiding place in some obscure and somewhat dusty corner, we take Junior home with us. Through insurance and our hefty deposit we purchased him outright, and after finding in him a reservoir or memory I had never expected, I need to keep him close, to keep the past with me in the here and now. Sam and I discuss exactly where we want to put him, and we very quickly rule out our bedroom; he's not Dad, I know, but even plugged in and sitting against the wall, we would both feel very weird having him sitting there and potentially watching us, either asleep or, to phrase it delicately, in our most intimate moments.

We have a spare bedroom and consider placing him there, but in the end we settle for the living room. It's more easily accessible, the wireless signal is stronger, and there's space in the corner that means nobody will trip over him in the night.

A couple of weeks after bringing him home, we have company for dinner. Allan works with Sam, and he and his wife Carrie are just about our best friends. After a lovely meal we find ourselves sitting in the living room, sharing a couple of bottles of wine and reminiscing about stories from our separate childhoods. Allan has a screamingly funny and yet incredibly disturbing story about frogs and straws and rubber bands and paper clips, which, after she wipes the tears of laughter from her eyes, has Carrie fixing her husband with a stare and saying, "I don't know if I should go home with you tonight. Sounds like a classic serial killer in the making." We all laugh harder, and then Allan is busy protesting that he *wasn't* involved, that he just got caught up with the wrong group of boys, and it was only that one day, he swears.

Sam and Carrie each tell a story, and then it's my turn, it seems. I think for a moment, but just as I settle on the right one, Junior rolls over to the side of the couch where Carrie is sitting and says, "You know, listening to all this, I'm reminded of when Karynn was young, I don't know, maybe 8 or 9, and we lived near the edge of the city and there was a gravel road you could cross and then you would find yourself in a farmer's field."

Carrie and Allan have spoken with Junior before, so this interruption isn't unsettling to them, but it is definitely out of character for the rememberer. Sam looks ready to interrupt, but I hold up my hand and wink at her; I'm curious, because so far this doesn't sound like any tale he's told me before. "Go on," I say, and reach over to pour myself some more wine.

Junior turns his head in my direction, and when I meet his eyes he pauses, takes longer to continue the tale than is comfortable. Eventually I lean forward and wave a hand in his face. "Junior, go on. You were telling a story about me."

"Hm?" He rolls back a short distance, and then begins again. "I remember that farmer's field. Part of it was eventually sold to developers to build a giant mall and a new forest of condos, but then there was a bit of a downturn, so that part of it stayed, um, fallow, and weeds and bushes and even some small trees started to grow there. Kids would ride their bikes there and play hide and seek or little games of war, and on the far side of the field there was a stream that led into a pond. Well, not really a pond, but more of a slough. But a real heaven for little kids, let me tell you."

I stare at him and take a sip of my wine. None of this is sounding familiar.

"Anyhow, like I said, Karynn was 9 or so, and some friends and her wanted to go out to the stream, and her babysitter decided to take her without asking us. It was middle of the day, you see, and her mom and me were both at work."

Sam catches my eye, mouths the words *What is this all about?* I shrug, and mouth back, *Not a clue.*

"I sometimes took Karynn out there and we would catch frogs and bring them back in a jar, and we would keep them in the back yard in an old metal laundry tub that we had filled with water from the slough. We'd watch them for a few days, and Karynn would give them all names, which of course made it so much harder for her when we had to take them back a few days later. Some times she would cry and cry and cry and would still be sobbing as she tipped the jar over to empty the frogs out into their natural homes."

The others all laugh at this mental image of me crying over lost amphibians, but I don't. I just stare at Junior, a strange, unsettled feeling rising up from deep inside.

"We'd also bring home eggs, and leave them in the water until they hatched, and then we would watch all the tadpoles as they underwent their, their ... changes. Impossible to name so many of those, but Karynn, she would try as hard as she could."

More laughter. "Junior," I say. "Dad."

But if he had a hand he could use I just know he would hold it up to keep me from interrupting. Instead, he barges through, unwilling or unable to hear me. "Karynn went out with that babysitter and some of her friends, and when they were out near the stream they split up to start looking for frogs and big water bugs and whatever else that was interesting to them."

"I don't remember any of this," I say, trying to contain the concern I'm feeling right now. I know I shouldn't be concerned about what is essentially a machine telling a story, but the fact of the matter is this is a machine that is telling a story using my dead father's memories and voice, and the story it is telling is coming completely out of the blue. It's odd enough that Junior has jumped into the conversation without an invitation or at least an implicit suggestion that we might need to delve into some part of Dad's history, but the fact that this story rings no bells whatsoever has me especially concerned.

It doesn't matter what I say, though. Ignoring me, Junior carries on. "A friend, a young neighbor boy named, um, named Max, ended up following the stream down towards the pond, and he had a glass jar that had a bit of water in it and whatever he could find to take with them. I imagine his head was down the whole way, and maybe he didn't see a low-hanging branch or something like that, but he got hit in the head by something and fell into the water and he drowned." Junior closes his eyes, as if picturing things in his mind, and finishes with, "It was horrible," in a near-whisper, and just like that the story is done.

The four of us sit in shock, dead silent. The other three all looking at me, especially Sam, and I know as sure as anything that she is wondering why I've never told her this story. I have the answer to that, of course, but the feeling of fear and sickness that answer offers me is almost too much to handle. But I have to say something.

"Junior," I say, and I'm careful to keep his name there, to not mix up this rememberer with my father. Junior opens his eyes and looks at me. "That story, what you told..." My voice cracks, and I wipe away the suddenly free-flowing tears with my sleeve. "That wasn't me, Junior, that was Dad." And now I feel like I'm choking. "Oh, Jesus, that happened when he was a kid. Not me!" and now I'm sobbing full on, and Sam is rushing over to pull me into her arms, and I hardly even notice when Junior wheels away, bumping into the coffee table and a chair before he can navigate his way back to his corner.

— «» —

8. Memories Gone

It's a difficult night. Several times I try to get through to Junior, to recall everything that was my father I thought I would have for the rest of my life, but each time all I can find are pieces of him, random and scattered and sometimes frustratingly incoherent. It's the dementia all over again, and it can't be happening.

It can't, but of course it is.

The next morning I find Junior unplugged from his wall socket, gently rolling back and forth and bumping against the door. I don't even have to listen to what he's mumbling to know that he's wondering why he can't get outside to go get his paper. I'm up before Sam is, and I feel too weak and tired to even try to make coffee, much less try to cope with this horrible, horrible sight. But I can't take my eyes off it, so I just lean against a wall in the kitchen, slide to the floor, and watch the rememberer as he continues torturing both himself and me.

It seems like forever, but eventually Sam wakes up and comes out. She takes one look at me and then walks over to Junior and, whispering in his ear, she picks him up and takes him back to his corner of the living room. He plugs himself in and settles down, at least for the moment, and I have another cry.

A few minutes later, Sam has coffee in both of our hands and is sitting on the floor beside me. "It's the same thing," she says. "I don't know how it's possible, but it's like Junior has dementia."

Unable to speak, I nod.

"We need to contact somebody at Aletheia. Do you want me to see if I can get in touch with Dr. Dhaliwal?" I nod again and smile at her through my tears, and she rubs my hand and we just sit there, hovering in tentative silence punctuated by random utterances in Dad's voice coming from the living room.

As it turns out, Dr. Dhaliwal can't take Sam's call, but Roger tells her he will have someone come over and talk. A man who introduces himself as Davis arrives there later that afternoon, a technician who doesn't work for Aletheia but rather, he tells us, is contracted by them and by the insurance company just for situations like this. Davis is sitting at the kitchen table, coffee cup in his hand and a strange combination of sadness and hardness in his eyes. He's already spent a few minutes looking over Junior, including plugging his pad into the back of the rememberer's head and downloading whatever information needed to diagnose the problem.

"Your rememberer is suffering from the same dementia that took your father," he finally says.

It's the answer I was fully expecting, but it also doesn't make any sense. "How is that possible?" I ask. "I think of Junior as almost everything that my Dad was, at least as far as his mind goes, but he's, *it's*, a machine."

Davis nods. "When they downloaded the matrix of your father's memories, the faults came along for the ride as well. But they were kept away from affecting anything by all the backups that, um, Junior did, every night linking up with our central servers and cleaning out the confusion trying to push its way through to the surface."

"So those backups," says Sam, and she's going slow with her words, clearly trying to think it all through as she speaks, "they worked just fine while Karynn's dad was alive. Why aren't they working now? What's changed?" She holds up her hand to keep me from voicing the obvious. "I mean aside from him being dead. But that shouldn't matter, should it? Any downloads Junior did while he was still alive would have come from the original matrix, not from any newer version of Jacob's memories. If they had, then the dementia would have kicked in that much sooner. Right?"

I nod and take Sam's hand; she's a rock at times like these, and I'm so lucky to have her with me. Davis takes a moment, looking as if he's formulating his thoughts. This can't be good, I think.

"The updates were covered by your father's insurance," he says, and right now he looks very uncomfortable. "When he passed away, they stopped covering them. Your dad never checked the box that stipulated he wanted to continue paying for those updates after his death." He looks pained, apologetic, clearly not happy about having to tell us this. "There have been stories about this in the news, but I'll grant that they are almost always buried by bigger things happening elsewhere. And they did make it clear to your father when he signed the contract." He taps at the screen on his pad, sitting on the table beside his coffee cup, and calls up some documents. "Whenever they send me on one of these jobs they make sure to get me a copy of the contract with all the relevant portions highlighted." He leans forward as he scans through things.

"How much?" I can barely speak, and those two lone words come out a barely-heard hoarse whisper.

"Twenty five hundred a month, plus taxes." Davis takes a last sip of his coffee then stands and awkwardly makes his way towards the door. "It's a terrible hit, more than anyone can afford in all the jobs they've ever sent me out on." He puts a hand on the back of his neck and rubs it, a pained look on his face. "I'm so sorry, and I sincerely wish it wasn't me you had to hear this from." He winces. "That came out wrong. I mean, I wish it was news you never had to hear."

"It's okay," says Sam, her voice so calm I want to scream and rage just to give some proper balance to the situation. "Don't shoot the messenger and all that. We understand."

Davis nods, now standing at the door. "In the meantime, Aletheia can offer you fifty dollars to recycle Junior. I wish it could be more, but the tech changes so fast, pretty much everything inside it only ends up going to scrap."

"Scrap?" The very thought is appalling, the idea that my father's memories can be assigned a dollar value, no matter the size, that they can be compressed into a tiny cube of metal and loss, tossed aside and waiting a turn as a toaster, or phone, or worse, someone else's memories. Unable to think of anything else, to say anything that will keep him here and force him to come up with a solution that will save my father's memories, I blurt out, "We'll sue!"

He shrugs his shoulders, but the look in his eyes tells me he was expecting to hear this, and that he is so very disappointed that I haven't let him down. "Case law is already established in this. You're not the first to think of a legal avenue, and every court it's gone to has decided in Aletheia's favor. These days, any attempt at a suit, civil or even criminal, is tossed out, and the plaintiff usually ends up having to pay the company's costs." Davis slips on his shoes and opens the door, but instead of leaving he puts one hand high against the edge of the door and leans there, turning his head so he can look into the living room, likely at Junior. "I feel very bad for you, Karynn, and wish I could do more, but the company can't even do one final update for, for old time's sake. Those matrices are lost to them as well. What I'd suggest is that you take the time to find the last remaining bits of your dad while you can, capture those memories however possible, even if they just become a part of your own memory." He shakes his head and closes the door, but just before it seals tight he calls out, "A rememberer is there to be an aid, not to completely replace the original."

The door clicks shut, and Sam and I sit at the table in shock, the silence interrupted only by the confused muttering of Dad's voice drifting in from the other room.

— ‹› —

9. Memories For Disposition

We try to live with Junior as he is, we really do, but every inter-action I have with him reminds me of how much I've lost, and how I am losing the very same thing all over again. Some days the pace of that loss is glacial, some days it feels more like a torrent, but every morning when I wake up, every afternoon when I come home, I see the change, feel the constant ache of ongoing loss a second time over.

Some friends feel that it shouldn't be quite as bad this time, that Junior is, after all, only a machine. It is only my father's voice, and, in steadily decreasing fashion, his memories. But Sam and a handful of others understand that the loss can be equally keen this second time around, that I had *committed* myself to sharing a new time of these remembrances with my father, even if only through Junior. I was prepared to delve in and discover more about him, about Mom, about me, more than I had ever before been prepared to know. There's irony there, that such pain could be caused by losing a future devoted to learning about the past from a surrogate. Some days it really does almost make me laugh.

Worse, though, it forces me to admit the finality of my loss, once and for all. And, as happened the first time out, the loss is a horrible slow-motion accident, although instead of *life*, this time it's *lives* careening out of control. Lives of all of us, snapshot moments or short little movies, all lost to me once again.

I spend what time I can with Junior, learning what I can about the past, and I realize as I do this that this — *this* — is the difference. When Dad was slowly dying of his dementia, my time spent with him was to be with him, to remember him as best I could as the warm and loving physical presence who had influenced so much of my life. This time, though, Junior can't play that role. He is only a device, vaguely dog-shaped, with wheels in the place of legs. He has no place in the tangible, sense-driven memories of my life. Instead, he is there to help fill in the gaps, to give what Sam has called "local color" to Dad's past, to my own past.

This realization helps a bit, but it's still tough, sitting and listening to his voice. Surprisingly, it's harder on the more lucid days, when he is so much more my father, driven by his memories and happy to share that past with me and with Sam. But it doesn't take as long this time, and soon the day comes when it is all I can do to coax him out of whatever shell his memories have built for him.

We've received the official letter from Aletheia about Junior, offering to take him off of our hands so his parts can be recycled. They even offered to increase the fee, as small as it still is. But I can't bring myself to think about it for more than a few seconds. Living with this constant reminder of the loss of Dad is killing me, but even when Junior is mostly gone, or when he forgets himself and calls me Melissa, or when he bumps against the door hoping to go out and get his newspaper, there is still some of my dad in there. The very idea of all of that being erased, the final essence of him cut away from the world in one final action is suddenly too much to bear. Which is almost amusing, considering I still remain the most committed of unbelievers.

Sitting at the table after dinner with Carrie and Allan, on the same night we received the letter with the offer from Aletheia, Sam pulls out her pad and calls up a small news story about places in different cities people have taken to calling the "Island of Lost Toys." Allan chuckles and, seeing the blanks looks on our faces, tells us it's a joke but he doesn't explain any further, and so I read it and look at the pictures and watch the video and check the map that comes with it, marveling that I have this partner who has done me the kind favor of keeping track of the rest of the world while I've been lost in my own labyrinth of memory, both fading and faded.

"We can do this," I finally say. I look at Carrie and Allan and Sam through a haze of tears, grateful that I have an answer.

"It might be a bit of a cheat, though," says Sam. "Like dropping an unwanted kitten at the side of the road and driving off."

"Except he won't starve or succumb to the elements — Oh!" I exclaim. "How will he get power? I don't remember seeing that."

"Here," says Allan, looking down at his own pad. "Got something at another site. Some people went in and did a hack, and apparently nobody from the power company is so keen to go in and do anything about it. The place kinda freaks them out."

"And now the place is developing into something of a local legend," continues Sam. "I don't know if the people who live closest are exactly happy with its presence, but nobody seems to want to go there and clear them out."

"It'll be like a convention of lost memories," says Carrie. She tries to smile, but none of us can really find the humor there.

— «» —

10. Memories Cast Away

Allan and Carrie have loaned us their car, and when we pull up for the briefest of moments I worry that the GPS was wrong. I've never been in this part of the city before, never seen a place that appeared so empty, so filled with unspoken memories. *Abandoned* memories.

Brick walls sag and crumble, lamps flicker and give off only the weakest pools of light. Those windows that remain unbroken are dark, and with the car window down the only sounds I can hear for a moment are from distant traffic, the city going about its business, creating its own collective memories, so many of them for nothing but the shortest of terms.

But as we step out, other sounds rise up from out of the darkest corners and alleyways, always tentative, but growing in strength. And then they come, the rememberers we were told existed here, rolling and walking and limping and wheezing their way towards us, all of them looking for someone to share with, a person to listen to the fragments that remain of the people they once were, to share in scattered and shattered memories.

As Sam picks him up from the back seat and temporarily holds him in the air, searching for a safe place to set him, Junior seems unsure, and his wheels spin so fast they rattle and whine. For a brief moment I even think *unsure* is the wrong word, that *upset* is the truer description, but I know that isn't possible. The problem, though, and one of the reasons we're here is that I can't help but ascribe a certain level of humanity to what is left of my father.

Junior turns his head away from the commotion at Sam's feet and looks to me. But instead of asking where he is, why all of this is happening, he asks, in Dad's voice, once again frail and unsure, "Have you seen my keys, Melissa? I can't seem to find them."

"Keys!" comes a voice from the crowd on the ground.

"Melissa?" says another. "I don't know anyone named Melissa!"

"I know I left them here somewhere."

"I read a good book the other day. What was it called?"

"You know, I think I know your face."

And on and on and on, a steady cacophony of faded glimpses of memories, at best third hand by now, accompanied by a sine wave of unintelligible murmurs, rising and falling as more memories are sought and escape the grasp of their seekers. Almost twenty rememberers, some on wheels and some on legs, all trying their level best to bump up against Sam and against me, seeking a moment of human contact and a chance to once again prove to themselves that they are not lost, not abandoned. Dozens more, usually the ones responsible for the nonsensical sounds but more often those that are one or more steps lower in function, move in the slightest of patterns or else stay in one place, coming near us only if shepherded by their slightly more aware companions. It's an unsettling feeling being in the middle of all of this, and I am grateful the tallest of the rememberers stands no higher than a little above my knee; if any were as or near as tall as me I fear I would turn from nerve-wracked to ridden with fear. Even so, I almost change my mind, but the same thought sits with me that I suspect does for the others: Better to believe some aspect of my dad exists somewhere here on Earth, rather than living with the knowledge that everything he once was is irrevocably gone, even as the thought of repeating the days of steady attrition is more than I can handle.

A knot of them opens up, and Sam gratefully reaches down and places Junior in the space provided. Junior, not nearly as far gone as most of those that surround him, once again turns his eyes to me, and I have to fight off the embarrassment and shame.

"We have to go," says Sam.

I nod, and manage to weave a path over to where Junior's spinning wheels took him before he stopped himself. I lean down, kiss him on the top of his fabric and carbon frame head, and whisper in his ear. "Goodbye, Junior." I hug him tight for a too-brief moment. "Goodbye, Dad."

—— « o » ——

Derryl Murphy

Derryl Murphy's novel *Napier's Bones* was an Aurora Award nominee, and his most recent collection *Over the Darkened Landscape* was shortlisted for the Sunburst Award. Derryl can be followed on Twitter as @derrylm. "In Memory Of" marks his fifth appearance in a Tesseracts volume, and it is this anthology series that gave him his start. Derryl currently lives in Saskatoon, and when this bio is published will boast not one but two college-aged sons. Which means he is getting old.

Afterword

Spider Robinson

Researching the Compostela for this anthology, I was surprised I never heard of it before it was brought to my attention by our publisher, Brian Hades. I don't know why not. I'm not a Catholic today — nowadays I use Irish whiskey — but I was born one, and a few centuries ago I spent a year in a seminary, training to become what they actually called a Storm-Trooper of Mary. And the Compostela is, I was startled to learn, a Big Deal for Christians — European ones, at least. I'll thumbnail it.

Many Christians (not necessarily Catholics) believe the bones of the Apostle James, patron saint of Spain, were discovered in Galicia in the eighth century. I assume they were identified by his DNA records. Everyone knows the bones of a holy man are the opposite of radioactive, good to be near, and so in time, an annual pilgrimage developed, the Camino de Santiago or Path Of St. James. Thousands of pilgrims would walk hundreds of miles from all over Europe to the Cathedral of Santiago de Compostela in Galicia, depending on luck and charity for food, water, shelter and directions along the way. They still do today, despite the risk of being mistaken for refugees and forced to "return" to hellholes they have no connection with. Or, I suppose, being mugged by desperate refugees for their ID.

The name Compostela comes from centuries of creative spelling of the Latin campus stellae, field of stars, and refers to the fact that for mapless Camino pilgrims, the way to Galicia was to simply follow the pointer of the Milky Way. Today the name Compostela refers to a certificate you can get if, in

Galicia, you attest under oath that you walked at least 100 kilometers to get there, and did so at least in part for spiritual reasons. If you also sought aerobic or other earthly benefits, that's cool.

As my esteemed colleague and new friend Jim Gardner noted in his Foreword, the mosey down the ol' Compostela Trail must have offered countless opportunities for pilgrims of different regions and cultures to meet, mingle, and swap songs, sagas, and rumors. It doesn't surprise me that something similar has happened here, in the Cathedral Of Tesseracts — that with little difficulty, we've assembled a group of Canadian writers whose desks are remarkably evenly distributed around the country (we didn't pick 'em on that basis, it just happened), and gotten them to swap their stories, poems, ballads and blues on the theme of what could happen when you pursue your postgraduate studies on the Campus Of Stars. Especially if you lose your way in the dark.

What did surprise me is the same thing that surprised Jim: just how dark some of our dreams of the future are, these days.

I'm not saying these aren't tough, even apocalyptic times — they all are — but the stories in this book pretty much had to have been conceived or even completed by the time we all started hearing Trumps of Doom from the south.

When I was coming up, we had a few pesky worries of our own, long forgotten now. Any of you kids ever hear of a Cold War? Nuclear Winter ring a bell? And yet, even as the news was relentlessly telling us about horrors in Viet Nam, and half our heroes were getting murdered or overdosing, we invented the Federation of Planets and the Prime Directive — hell, we whipped Darth Vader. Today, with hopeful signs of all kinds on all sides, with not only extended life but Viagra too, we seem absorbed by fantasies in which Batman is a psychopath and Iron Man is Tronald Dump's wet dream.

Perhaps that's it: it's simply a natural balancing, swimming against the rip tide of the times. This might not be an inappropriate time in our history to do some serious contemplation of spiritual questions, and this book is proof that science fiction is a good place to do that. An entire anthology of sf willing to consider spiritual questions seriously is, let's admit it, an unusual and valuable thing, and I'm glad I got to be part of it, especially the part that involved helping Jim give good writers some of Brian's money.

One mild regret I will allow myself to hesitantly voice: I do wish the experience had been just a tiny bit more catholic — with a small c.

I'm aware that, of Canada's nearly 30 million inhabitants, just under 13 million are Catholic, and nearly 10 million are Other Christian. But we also have half a million Muslims, a third of a million Jews, nearly as many Buddhists, and Hindus. I kept hoping one of our submissions might peripherally mention a rather Compostelan hike taken annually by quite a few people to a burg called Mecca, or invoke another stroll to a certain wall in western Jerusalem, or make a passing reference to one of the four big Hindu pilgrimages, or the eight Buddhist pilgrimages I happen to know about because my late wife Jeanne was a Buddhist priest.

But I can't criticize any of our writers, for having "failed" to do something nobody asked them to. I didn't even know my own milk-religion well enough to have ever heard of the Camino de Santiago myself, until I received a message directly from Hades, so why should any of us be familiar with the intricacies of any of the walkabouts that other sorts of religious folks like to flatten their feet with? If I'm really curious about the Hajj, the Wailing Wall, or the Atthamahathanani, wikipedia is always ready to...well...enlighten me.

When Brian posted the Compostela theme, he specifically asked for stories about "...how humanity could be impacted (for better or worse) by a dependence on all things technological." Apparently few had much to say for the "for better" side. In a science fiction anthology. How ironic.

Okay. So be it. Get over it, Spider.

I came up as sf was developing a new branch called Cyberpunk, which seemed to say dependence on things technological literally can not be overdone, that the more technology you have replacing your original organic parts, the more improved you are, the more reliable your warrantee. Upload now!

Okay, maybe it's time, even a bit past time, to rethink that premise a little.

I'm hoping for a lot more optimism from next year's Tesseracts roster — a simple reflection of current events. Canada just recently got shut of a conservative, science-muzzling, minority-ignoring, LGBT- and pot-unfriendly government that seemed to have lasted forever, dampening our spirits and darkening our outlook. Admittedly, at this writing it's too early to assess the wisdom, effectiveness or luck of the government we've replaced it with.

But I take hope from a news clip getting a lot of play on YouTube today. A reporter jokingly assures Prime Minister Trudeau that of course he won't ask him to explain quantum computing, but ... and our PM, unprepared, interrupts him with a brief, vivid, correct explanation. And you know, I bet Barack Obama could do the same. Pretty remarkable times.

We may be feeling a bit gloomy just now, but we have every excuse to hope, if we want to. Depends on what we choose to sing as we walk our separate Compostelas together.

If you enjoyed this read

Please leave a review on Amazon, Facebook, Good Reads or Instagram.

It takes less than five minutes and it really does make a difference.

If you're not sure how to leave a review on Amazon:

1. *Go to amazon.com.*

2. *Type in Compostela edited by Spider Robinson and James Alan Gardner and when you see it, click on it.*

3. *Scroll down to Customer Reviews. Nearby you'll see a box labeled Write a Review. Click it.*

4. *Now, if you've never written a review before on Amazon, they might ask you to create a name for yourself.*

5. *Reviews can be as simple as, "Loved the book! Can't wait for the Next!" (Please don't give the story away.)*

And that's it!

Brian Hades, publisher

About the Editors

Spider Robinson

Since he began writing professionally in 1972, Spider Robinson has won the John W. Campbell Award for Best New Writer, three Hugo Awards, a Nebula, and numerous other international and regional awards. Most of his 36 books are still in print. His short work has appeared in magazines around the planet and in numerous anthologies. The Usenet newsgroup alt.callahans and its many offshoots, inspired by his Callahan's Place series, were an important non-porn network in early cyberspace.

In 2006 he became the only writer ever to collaborate at novel-length with First Grandmaster of Science Fiction Robert A. Heinlein, posthumously completing VARIABLE STAR at the request of the Heinlein estate. That same year, the US Library of Congress invited him to Washington D.C. to be a guest of the First Lady at the White House for the National Book Festival. In 2008 he shared the Robert A. Heinlein Award for Lifetime Excellence in Literature with his mentor Ben Bova.

Spider was regular book reviewer for Galaxy, Analog and New Destinies magazines for a decade, and contributes occasional book reviews to The Globe And Mail, Canada's national newspaper, for which he wrote a regular Op-Ed column, The Crazy Years, from 1996-2004. As an audiobook reader of his own and others' work, he has won the Earphones Award and been a finalist for the Audie. In 2001 he released Belaboring The Obvious, a CD featuring original music accompanied by Canadian guitar legend Amos Garrett. He has written songs in collaboration with David Crosby and with Todd Butler.

Spider was married for 35 years to Jeanne Robinson, a writer, choreographer, former dancer and teacher who died of biliary cancer in 2010. She was founder/Artistic Director of Halifax's Nova Dance Theatre during its 8-year history. The Robinsons collaborated on the Hugo-, Nebula- and Locus-winning Stardance Trilogy, concerning zero gravity dance and its role in communication in space. Spider and Jeanne met in the woods of Nova Scotia at the end of the 60s, and lived for their last two decades in British Columbia.

James Alan Gardner

Raised in Simcoe and Bradford, Ontario, James Alan Gardner earned Bachelor's and Master's degrees in Applied Mathematics from the University of Waterloo.

A graduate of the Clarion West Fiction Writers Workshop, Gardner has published science fiction short stories in a range of periodicals, including *The Magazine of Fantasy and Science Fiction* and *Amazing Stories*. In 1989, his short story "The Children of Crèche" was awarded the Grand Prize in the Writers of the Future contest. Two years later his story "Muffin Explains Teleology to the World at Large" won an Aurora Award; another story, "Three Hearings on the Existence of Snakes in the Human Bloodstream," won an Aurora and was nominated for both the Nebula and Hugo Awards.

He has written a number of novels in a "League of Peoples" universe in which murderers are defined as "dangerous non-sentients" and are killed if they try to leave their solar system by aliens who are so advanced that they think of humans like humans think of bacteria. This precludes the possibility of interstellar wars.

He has also explored themes of gender in his novels, including *Commitment Hour* in which people change sex every year, and *Vigilant* in which group marriages are traditional. Gardner is also an educator and technical writer. His book *Learning UNIX* is used as a textbook in some Canadian universities.

He lives in the Waterloo Ontario region, which he's immortalizing (and destroying) in a new series of novels beginning with *All Those Explosions Were Someone Else's Fault*.

Need something new to read?
If you liked Compostela, you should also
consider these other EDGE-Lite titles:

Beltrunner

by Sean O'Brien

As an independent beltrunner mining asteroids in the frontier of space, Collier South is a dying breed. Scrounging and cutting corners to work cheap, Collier isn't a stranger to lean times and make-do repairs; in fact his onboard computer hasn't had outside maintenance in years and its beginning to show its personal quirks.

When Collier finds an asteroid that shows promise, he thinks he's bought himself some time. But his claim is stolen out from under him by his vindictive ex-lover and her shiny new corporate ship. Powerless against the omnipotent mining corporations, Collier has always been too stubborn to give-up without a fight. Broke and desperate, Collier has one last chance to land a strike. If he doesn't come back with ore, he'll end up destitute and trading his own biologicals for his next meal.

What he discovers in the farthest reaches of the belt has the power to change his life and the fate of the entire system forever. That is, if Collier and his onboard computer can keep his discovery out of corporate hands.

Praise for Beltrunner

"This is a fast moving book that leaves you breathless with hair-raising action and unexpected twists. The world creation is well-developed and highly creative. The interactions between Collier and Sancho are particularly entertaining - with Collier coming up with implusive dangerous plans and Sancho trying to talk him out of them. Highly recommended for action space lovers."
— Patricia Humphreys

"Scavenging known space makes for a hard life, and surviving outside of the Corporations in the Belt makes it all the harder. It is not surprising that Collier and his unusual companion Sancho hit bottom, like many before them, until they make the discovery of their lives...or deaths, as it may turn out to be.

"Beltrunner is a solidly enjoyable science fiction adventure, fast paced, and filled with the kind of characters that make you smile, break your heart, or just make you clench your jaw. I read it in one sitting and thoroughly enjoyed it. O'Brien builds a universe to get lost in that is as hard, gritty, and unforgiving as deep space itself. It is a well-written romp around space like many others, yet plenty of surprising elements give the story a depth and purpose all its own without the heavy strain of space melodrama. Read it because it is both light fun and thoughtful reading."
— A. Volmer

For more on Beltrunner visit:
tinyurl.com/edge6010

The Rosetta Man

by Claire McCague

Wanted:
Translator for first contact.
Immediate opening.
Danger pay allowance.

Estlin Hume lives in Twin Butte, Alberta surrounded by a horde of affectionate squirrels. His involuntary squirrel-attracting talent leaves him evicted, expelled, fired and near pennilessuntiltwoaliensarriveandadopthimastheirtranslator. Yanked around the world at the center of the first contact crisis, Estlin finds his new employers incomprehensible. As he faces the ultimate language barrier, unsympathetic military forces converging in the South Pacific keep threatening to kill the messenger. The question on everyone's mind is: Why are the aliens here? But Estlin's starting to think we'll happily blow ourselves up in the process of finding that out.

Praise for The Rosetta Man:

"The cover and synopsis had me expecting a light-hearted comedy. I didn't realize I was getting a geopolitical first contact thriller that somehow still managed to be a light-hearted comedy. I really enjoyed this book! The characters are rich and diverse. Estlin and Harry are great, Beth and Bomani made me cry. The story is fast paced and engaging and again, completely unexpected. Great book for fans of first contact scifi, but also

fans of thrillers and mysteries. And so well-executed that I give it a solid 5 stars."
— Scott Burtness, author of Wisconsin Vamp (Monsters in the Midwest)

"This book ranks up there with many of the classic sci-fi "first contact" stories and Claire McCague's scientific background comes through in waves."
— Cameron Arsenault, Amazon Reviewer

"A completely enjoyable read. Good action, lots of humor, and a global setting. Strongly recommended."
— Diane Lacey, Amazon Reviewer

For more on The Rosetta Man visit:
tinyurl.com/edge6004

Europa Journal

by Jack Castle

The history of humanity is about to change forever...

On 5 December 1945, five TBM Avenger bombers embarked on a training mission off the coast of Florida and mysteriously vanish without a trace in the Bermuda Triangle. A PBY search and rescue plane with thirteen crewmen aboard sets out to find the Avengers . . . and never returns.

In 2168, a mysterious five-sided pyramid is discovered on the ocean floor of Jupiter's icy moon, Europa.

Commander Mac O'Bryant and her team of astronauts are among the first to enter the pyramid's central chamber. They find the body of a missing World War II pilot, whose hands clutch a journal detailing what happened to him after he and his crew were abducted by aliens and taken to a place with no recognizable stars. As the pyramid walls begin to collapse around Mac and her team, their names mysteriously appear within its pages and they find themselves lost on an alien world.

Stranded with no way home, Mac decides to retrace the pilot's steps. She never expects to find the man alive. And if the man has yet to die, what does that mean for her and the rest of her crew?

Praise for Europa Journal

"This book kept me guessing! It has an exciting start and keeps that same pace throughout the book. The building of the character personalities keeps a depth to the storyline

and makes the reader feel connected to each character. The background information given through Europa Journal gives a great balance between the history, future and everything in-between! I love the mix of fact and fiction to create the story and inspire imagination. I'm excited to see what Castle comes up with next!"
— Dianna Temple

"With an action-packed opening, page-turning twists,a well-built world, and characters worth caring about, Europa Journal is like a bulldog - it grabbed me and wouldn't let go! It seamlessly blends breathtaking imagination with the gritty reality of survival, and beautifully blurs what has been with what might be. I love Dr. Who and grew up with Star Trek, but this book has broken the sci-fi mold in a wonderful way!"
— Stuntwoman, Elisa Brinton

"From the opening space shuttle crash landing to the stunning finish, Europa Journal is a real page turner. Ancient astronauts, the Bermuda triangle, WW II pilots, space shuttle crews – what else could you ask for? Mr. Castle keeps the story at light speed, with plenty of twists and turns before the awesome climax!"
— James Wahlman, Firefighter in Alaska

For more on Europa Journal visit:
tinyurl.com/edge6001

For more EDGE titles and information about upcoming speculative fiction please visit us at:

www.edgewebsite.com

Don't forget to sign-up for our Special Offers